Among the Mad

Also by Jacqueline Winspear

Maisie Dobbs
Birds of a Feather
Pardonable Lies
Messenger of Truth
An Incomplete Revenge

Among the Mad

A Maisie Dobbs Mystery

JACQUELINE WINSPEAR

JOHN MURRAY

First published in Great Britain in 2009 by John Murray (Publishers)
An Hachette UK Company

I

© Jacqueline Winspear 2009

A CIP catalogue record for this title is available from the British Library

ISBN 978-0-7195-6981-4

Typeset in 11.25/13.5 Monotype Bembo by Servis Filmsetting Ltd, Stockport, Cheshire

Printed and bound by Clays Ltd, St Ives plc

John Murray policy is to use papers that are natural, renewable and recyclable products
and made from wood grown in sustainable forests. The logging and manufacturing
processes are expected to conform to the environmental regulations of the country
of origin.

John Murray (Publishers)
338 Euston Road
London NW1 3BH

www.johnmurray.co.uk

Dedicated to my wonderful godchildren:

Charlotte Sweet McEwan
Charlotte Pye
Greg Belpomme
Alexandra Jones

'Keep true to the dreams of thy youth'
Friedrich von Schiller
1759–1805

'But I don't want to go among mad people,' Alice remarked.
'Oh, you can't help that,' said the Cat. 'We're all mad here.
I'm mad. You're mad.'
'How do you know I'm mad?' said Alice.
'You must be,' said the Cat, 'or you wouldn't have come here.'
                          —Lewis Carroll, *Alice's Adventures in Wonderland*

A short time ago death was the cruel stranger, the visitor with
the flannel footsteps . . . today it is the mad dog in the house.
One eats, one drinks beside the dead, one sleeps in the midst of
the dying, one laughs and sings in the company of corpses.
                          —Georges Duhamel, French doctor serving at
                                      Verdun in the Great War

I

Maisie Dobbs, Psychologist and Investigator, picked up her fountain pen to sign her name at the end of a final report that she and her assistant, Billy Beale, had worked late to complete the night before. Though the case was straightforward – a young man fraudulently using his uncle's honourable name to acquire all manner of goods and services, and an uncle keen to bring his nephew back on the straight and narrow without the police being notified – Maisie felt it was time for Billy to become more involved in the completion of a significant document and to take more of an active part in the final interview with a client. She knew how much Billy wanted to emigrate to Canada, to take his wife and family away from London's dark depression and the cloud of grief that still hung over them following the death of their daughter, Lizzie, almost a year earlier. To gain a decent job in a new country he would need to build more confidence in his work and himself, and seeing as she had already made enquiries on his behalf – without his knowledge – she knew greater dexterity with the written and spoken word would be an important factor in his success. Now the report was ready to be delivered before the Christmas holiday began.

'Eleven o'clock, Billy – just in time, eh?' Maisie placed the cap on her fountain pen and passed the report to her assistant, who slid it into an envelope and secured it with string. 'As soon as this appointment is over, you should be on your way, so that you can spend the rest of the day with Doreen and the boys – it'll be nice to have Christmas Eve at home.'

'That's good of you, Miss.' Billy smiled, then went to the door where he took Maisie's coat and his own from the hook.

Maisie packed her document case before reaching under the desk to bring out a wooden orange-crate. 'You'll have to come back to the office first, though.'

'What's all this, Miss?' Billy's face was flushed as he approached her desk.

'A Christmas box for each of the boys, and one for you and Doreen.' She opened her desk drawer and drew out an envelope. 'And this is for you. We had a bit of a rocky summer, but things picked up and we've done quite well – plus we'll be busy in the new year – so this is your bonus. It's all well earned, I must say.'

Billy reddened. 'Oh, that's very good of you, Miss. I'm much obliged. This'll cheer up Doreen.'

Maisie smiled in return. She did not need to enquire about Billy's wife, knowing the depth of the woman's melancholy. There had been a time, at the end of the summer, when a few weeks spent hop-picking in Kent had put a bloom on the woman's cheeks, and she seemed to have filled out a little, looking less gaunt. But, in London again, the routine of caring for her boys and keeping up with the dressmaking and alterations she took in had not lifted her spirits in any way. She ached for the milky softness of her daughter's small body in her arms.

Maisie looked at the clock on the mantelpiece. 'We'd better be off.'

They donned coats and hats and wrapped up against the chill wind that whistled around corners and blew across Fitzroy Square as they made their way towards Charlotte Street. Dodging behind a horse and cart, they ran to the other side of the road as a motor car came along in the opposite direction. The street was busy, with people rushing this way and that, heads down against the wind, some with parcels under their arms, others simply hoping to get home early. In the distance, Maisie noticed a man – she could not tell whether he was young or old – sitting on the pavement, leaning up against the exterior wall of a shop. Even with some yards between them, she could see the greyness that enveloped him, the malaise, the drooping shoulders, one leg outstretched so passers-by had to skirt around him. His damp hair was slicked against his head and cheeks, his clothes were old, crumpled, and he watched people go by with a deep red-rimmed sadness in his eyes. One of them stopped to speak to a policeman, and turned back to point at the man. Though unsettled by his dark aura, Maisie reached into her bag for some change as they drew closer.

'Poor bloke – out in this, and at Christmas.' Billy shook his head, and delved down into his coat pocket for a few coins.

'He looks too drained to find his way to a soup kitchen, or a shelter. Perhaps this will help.' Maisie held her offering ready to give to the man.

They walked just a few steps and Maisie gasped, for it was as if she was at once moving in slow motion, as if she were in a dream where people spoke but she could not hear their words. She saw the man move, put his hand into the inside pocket of his threadbare greatcoat, and though she wanted to reach out to him, she was caught in a vacuum of muffled sound and constrained movement. She could see Billy frowning, his mouth moving, but could not make him understand what she had seen. Then the sensation, which had lasted but a second or two, lifted. Maisie looked at the man some twenty or so paces ahead of them, then at Billy again.

'Billy, go back, turn around and go back along the street, go back . . .'

'Miss, what's wrong? You all right? What do you mean, Miss?'

Pushing against his shoulder to move him away, Maisie felt as if she were negotiating her way through a mire. 'Go back, Billy, go back . . .'

And because she was his employer, and because he had learned never to doubt her, Billy turned to retrace his steps in the direction of Fitzroy Square. Frowning, he looked back in time to see Maisie holding out her hand as she walked towards the man, in the way that a gentle person might try to bring calm to an enraged dog. Barely four minutes had passed since they walked past the horse and cart, and now here she was . . .

The explosion pushed up and outward into the Christmas Eve flurry, and in the seconds following there was silence. Just a crack in the wall of normal, everyday sound, then nothing. Billy, a soldier in the Great War, knew that sound, that hiatus. It was as if the earth itself had had the stuffing knocked out of it, had been throttled into a different day, a day when a bit of rain, a gust of wind and a few stray leaves had turned into a blood-soaked hell.

'Miss, Miss . . .' Billy picked himself up from the hard flag-stones and staggered back to where he had last seen Maisie. The silence became a screaming chasm where police whistles screeched, smoke and dust filled the air, and blood was sprayed up against the crumbling brick and shards of glass that were once the front of a shop where a man begged for a few coins outside.

'Maisie Dobbs! Maisie . . . Miss . . .' Billy sobbed as he stumbled forwards. 'Miss!' he screamed again.

'Over 'ere, mate. Is this the one you're looking for?'

In the middle of the road a costermonger was kneeling over Maisie, cradling her head in one hand and brushing blood away from her face with the kerchief he'd taken from his neck. Billy ran to her side.

'Miss . . . Miss . . .'

'I'm no doctor, but I reckon she's a lucky one – lifted off her feet and brought down 'ere. Probably got a nasty crack on the back of 'er noddle though.'

Maisie coughed, spitting dust-filled saliva from her mouth. 'Oh, Billy . . . I thought I could stop him. I thought I would be in time. If only we'd been here earlier, if only—'

'Don't you worry, Miss. Let's make sure you're all right before we do anything else.'

Maisie shook her head, began to sit up, and brushed her hair from her eyes and face. 'I think I'm all right – I was just pulled right off the ground.' She squinted and looked around at the melee. 'Billy, we've got to help. I can help these people . . .' She tried to stand but fell backwards again.

The costermonger and Billy assisted Maisie to her feet. 'Steady, love, steady,' said the man, who looked at Billy, frowning. 'What's she mean? Tried to stop 'im? Did you know there was a nutter there about to top 'imself – and try to take the rest of us with 'im?'

Billy shook his head. 'No, we didn't know. This is my employer. We were just walking to see a customer. Only . . .'

'Only what, mate? Only what? Look around you – it's bleedin' chaos, people've been 'urt, look at 'em. Did she know this was going to 'appen? Because if she did, then I'm going over to that copper there and—'

Billy put his arm around Maisie and began to negotiate his way around the rubble, away from the screams of those wounded when a man took his own life in a most terrible way. He looked back into his interrogator's eyes. 'She didn't know until she saw the bloke. It was when she saw him that she knew.' Maisie allowed herself to be led by Billy, who turned around to the costermonger one last time. 'She just knows, you see. She *knows*.' He fought back tears. 'And thanks for helping her, mate.' His voice cracked. 'Thanks . . . for helping her.'

❦

'Come on in here, bring her in and she can sit down.' The woman called from a shop just a few yards away.

'Thank you, thank you very much.' Billy led Maisie into the shop and to a chair, then turned to the woman. 'I'd better get back there, see if there's any more I can do.'

The woman nodded. 'Tell people they can come in here. I've got the kettle on. Dreadful, dreadful, what this world's come to.'

Soon the shop had filled with people while ambulances took

the more seriously wounded to hospital. And as she sat clutching a cup of tea in her hands, feeling the soothing heat grow cooler in her grasp, Maisie replayed the scene time and again in her mind. She and Billy crossed the road behind the horse and cart, then ran to the kerb as a motor came along the street. They were talking, noticing people going by or dashing in and out of shops before early closing. Then she saw him, the man, his leg stretched out, as if he were lame. As she had many times before, she reached into her bag to offer money to someone who had so little. She felt the cold coins brush against her fingers, saw the policeman set off across the street, and looked up at the man again – the man whose black aura seemed to grow until it touched her, until she could no longer hear, could not move with her usual speed.

She sipped her now lukewarm tea. That was the point at which she knew. She knew that the man would take his life. But she thought he had a pistol, or even poison. She saw her own hand in front of her, reaching out as if to gentle his wounded mind, then there was nothing. Nothing except a sharp pain at the back of her head and a voice in the distance. *Maisie Dobbs . . . Miss.* A voice screaming in panic, a voice coming closer.

'Miss Dobbs?'

Maisie started and almost dropped her cup.

'I'm sorry – I didn't mean to make you jump – your assistant said you were here.' Detective Inspector Richard Stratton looked down at Maisie, then around the room. The proprietress had brought out as many chairs as she could, and all were taken. Stratton knelt down. 'I was on duty at the Yard when it happened, so I was summoned straight away. By chance I saw Mr Beale and he said you witnessed the man take his life.' He paused, as if to judge her state of mind. 'Are you up to answering some questions?' Stratton spoke with a softness not usually employed when in conversation with Maisie. Their interactions had at times been incendiary, to say the least.

6

Maisie nodded, aware that she had hardly said a word since the explosion. She cleared her throat. 'Yes, of course, Inspector. I'm just a little unsettled – I came down with a bit of a wallop, knocked out for a few moments, I think.'

'Oh, good, you found her, then.' Stratton and Maisie looked towards the door as Billy Beale came back into the shop. 'I've found your document case, Miss. All the papers are inside.'

Maisie nodded. 'Thank you, Billy.' She looked up and saw concern etched on Billy's face, along with a certain resolve. Though it was more than thirteen years past, the war still fingered Billy's soul, and even though the pain from his wounds had eased, it had not left him in peace. Today's events would unsettle him, would be like pulling a dressing from a dried cut, rendering his memories fresh and raw.

'Look, my motor car's outside – let me take you both back to your office. We can talk there.' Stratton stood up to allow Maisie to link her arm through his, and began to lead her to the door. 'I know this is not the best time for you, but it's the best time for us – I'd like to talk to you as soon as we get to your premises, before you forget.'

Maisie stopped and looked up at Stratton. 'Forgetting has never been of concern to me, Inspector. It's the remembering that gives me pause.'

A police cordon now secured the site of the explosion, and though there were no more searing screams ricocheting around her, onlookers had gathered and police moved in and out of shops, taking names, helping those caught in a disaster while out on Christmas Eve. Maisie did not want to look at the street again, but as she saw people on the edge of the tragedy talking, she imagined them going home to their families and saying, 'You will never guess what I saw today,' or 'You've heard about that nutter with the bomb over on Charlotte Street, well . . .' And she wondered if she would ever walk down the street again and not feel her feet leave the ground.

⸻

Detective Inspector Richard Stratton and his assistant, Caldwell, pulled up chairs and were seated on the visiting side of Maisie's desk. Billy had just poured three cups of tea and filled one large enamelled tin mug, into which he stirred extra sugar before setting it in front of his employer.

'All right, Miss?'

Maisie nodded, then clasped the tea as she had in the shop earlier, as if to wring every last drop of warmth from the mug.

'Better watch it, Miss, that's hot. Don't want to burn yourself.'

'Yes, of course.' Maisie placed the mug on a manila folder in front of her, and as she released her grip, Billy saw red welts on her hands where heat from the mug had scalded her and she had felt nothing.

'How does your head feel now?' Richard Stratton's brows furrowed as he leaned forward to place his cup and saucer on the desk, while keeping his eyes on Maisie. The two had met almost three years earlier, when Stratton was called in at the end of a case she had been working on. The policeman, a widower with a young son, had at one point entertained a romantic notion of the investigator, but his approach had been nipped in the bud by Maisie, who was not as adept in her personal life as she was in her professional domain. Now their relationship encompassed only work, though, as an observer, it was clear to Billy that Richard Stratton had a particular regard for his employer, despite it being evident that she had brought him to the edge of exasperation at times – not least because her instincts were more finely honed than his own. Regardless, Stratton's respect for Maisie was reciprocated, and she trusted him.

Maisie reached with her hand to touch the back of her head, a couple of inches above her occipital bone. 'There's a fair-sized bump . . .' She ran her fingers down to an indentation in her scalp, sustained while she was working as a nurse during the war.

The scar was a constant reminder of the shelling that had not only wounded her but eventually taken the life of Simon Lynch, the doctor she had loved. 'At least it didn't open my war wounds.' She shook her head, realizing the irony of her words.

'Are you sure you're up for this?' Stratton enquired, his voice softer.

Caldwell rolled his eyes. 'I think we need to get on with it, sir.'

Stratton was about to speak, when Maisie stood up. 'Yes, of course, Mr Caldwell's right, we should get on.'

Billy looked down at his notebook, the hint of a grin at the edges of his mouth. He knew there was no love lost between Maisie and Caldwell, and her use of 'Mr' instead of 'Detective Sergeant' demonstrated that she might have been knocked out, but she was not down.

'I'll start at the beginning . . .' Maisie began to pace back and forth, her eyes closed as she recounted the events of the morning, from the time she had placed the cap on her pen, to the point at which the explosion ripped the man's body apart, and wounded several passers-by.

'Then the bomb—'

'Mills Bomb,' Billy corrected her, absently interrupting as he gazed at the floor watching her feet walk to the window and back again, the deliberate repetitive rhythm of her steps pushing recollections on to centre stage in her mind's eye.

'Mills Bomb?' Stratton looked at Billy. Maisie stopped walking.

'What?' Billy looked up at each of them in turn.

'You said Mills Bomb. Are you sure it was a Mills Bomb?' Caldwell licked his pencil's sharp lead, ready to continue recording every word spoken.

'Look, mate, I was a sapper in the war – what do you mean, "Are you sure?" If you go and fire off a round from half a dozen different rifles, I'll tell you which one's which. Of course I know a Mills Bomb – dodgy bloody things, saw a few mates pull out the pin and end up blowing themselves up with one of them. Mills Bomb – your basic hand grenade.'

Stratton lifted his hand. 'Caldwell, I think we can trust Mr Beale here.' He turned to Billy. 'And it's not as if it would be difficult for a civilian to obtain such ordnance, I would imagine.'

'You're right. There's your souvenir seekers going over to France and coming back with them – a quick walk across any of them French fields and you can fill a basket, I shouldn't wonder. And people who want something bad enough always find a way, don't they?'

'And he hadn't always been a civilian.' Maisie took her seat again. 'Unless he'd had an accident in a factory, this man had been a soldier. I was close enough to judge his age – about thirty-five, thirty-six – and his left leg was in a brace, which is why people had to walk around him, because he couldn't fold it inward. And the right leg might have been amputated.'

'If it wasn't then, it is now.' Caldwell seemed to smirk as he noted Maisie's comment.

'If that's all, Inspector, I think I need to go home. I'm driving down to Kent this evening, and I think I should rest before I get behind the wheel.'

Stratton stood up, followed by Caldwell, who looked at Maisie and was met with an icy gaze. 'Of course, Miss Dobbs,' said Stratton. 'Look, I would like to discuss this further with you, get more impressions of the man. And of course we'll be conducting enquiries with other witnesses, though it seems that even though you were not the closest, you remember more about him.'

'I will never forget, Inspector. The man was filled with despair and I would venture to say that he had nothing and no one to live for, and this is the time of year when people yearn for that belonging most.'

Stratton cleared his throat. 'Of course.' He shook hands with both Maisie and Billy, wishing them the compliments of the season. Maisie extended her hand to Caldwell in turn, smiling as she said, 'And a Merry Christmas to *you*, Mr Caldwell.'

Maisie and Billy stood by the window and watched the two men step into the Invicta. The driver closed the passenger door behind them, then took his place and manoeuvred the vehicle in the direction of Charlotte Street, whereupon the bell began to ring and the motor picked up speed towards the site of the explosion. Barely two hours had elapsed since Maisie saw a man activate a hand grenade inside his tattered and stained khaki greatcoat.

Turning to her assistant, she saw the old man inside the young. What age was he now? Probably just a little older than herself, say in his mid-thirties, perhaps thirty-seven? There were times when the Billy who worked for her was still a boy, a Cockney lad with reddish-blond hair half tamed, his smile ready to win the day. Then at other times, the weight of the world on his shoulders, his skin became grey, his hair lifeless, and his lameness – the legacy of a wartime wound – was rendered less manageable. Those were the times when she knew he walked the streets at night, when memories of the war flooded back, and when the suffering endured by his family bore down upon him. The events of today had opened his wounds, just as her own had been rekindled. And instead of the warmth and succour of his family, Billy would encounter only more reason to be concerned for his wife, for their children, and their future. And there was only so much Maisie could do to help them.

'Why don't you go home now, Billy?' She reached into her purse and pulled out a note. 'Buy Doreen some flowers on the way, and some sweets for the boys – it's Christmas Eve, and you have to look after one another.'

'You don't need to do that, Miss – look at the bonus, that's more than enough.'

'Call it danger money, then. Come on, take it and be on your way.'

'And you'll be all right?'

'I'm much better now, so don't you worry about me. I'll be even better when I get on the road to Chelstone. My father will have a roaring fire in the grate, and we'll have a hearty stew for supper – that's the best doctoring I know.'

'Right you are, Miss.' Billy pulled on his overcoat, placed his flat cap on his head, and left with a wave and a 'Merry Christmas!'

As soon as Maisie heard the front door slam shut when Billy walked out into the wintry afternoon, she made her way along the corridor to the lavatory, her hand held against the wall for support. She clutched her stomach as sickness rose up within her and knew that it was not only the pounding headache and seeing a man kill himself that haunted her, but the sensation that she had been watched. It was as if someone had touched her between her shoulder blades, had applied a cold pressure to her skin. And she could feel it still, as she walked back to the office, as if those icy fingertips were with her even as she moved.

Sitting down at her desk, she picked up the black telephone receiver and placed a telephone call to her father's house. She hoped he would answer, for Frankie Dobbs remained suspicious of the telephone she'd had installed in his cottage over two years ago. He would approach the telephone, look at it, and cock his head to one side as if unsure of the consequences of answering the call. Then he would lift the receiver after a few seconds had elapsed, hold it a good two inches from his ear and say, with as much authority as he could muster, 'Chelstone three five double two – is that you, Maisie?' And of course it was always Maisie, for no one else ever telephoned Frankie Dobbs.

'That you, Maisie?'

'Of course it is, Dad.'

'Soon be on your way, I should imagine. I've a nice stew simmering, and the tree's up, ready for us to decorate.'

'Dad, I'm sorry, I won't be driving down until tomorrow morning. I'll leave early and be with you for breakfast.'

'What's the matter? Are you all right, love?'

She cleared her throat. 'Bit of a sore throat. I reckon it's nothing, but it's given me a headache and there's a lot of sickness going round. I'm sure I'll be all right tomorrow.'

'I'll miss you.' No matter what he said, when it was into the telephone receiver, Frankie shouted, as if his words needed to reach London with only the amplification his voice could provide. Instead of a soft endearment, it sounded as if he had just given a brusque command.

'You too, Dad. See you tomorrow then.'

Maisie rested for a while longer, having dragged her chair in front of the gas fire and turned up the jets to quell her shivering. She placed another telephone call, to the client with whom she and Billy were due to meet this morning, then rested again, hoping the dizziness would subside so that she felt enough confidence in her balance to walk along to Tottenham Court Road and hail a taxi-cab. As she reached for her coat and hat, the bell above the door rang, indicating that a caller had come to the front entrance. She gathered her belongings, and was about to turn off the lights, when she realized that, in the aftermath of today's events, Billy had forgotten the box of gifts for his family. She turned off the fire, settled her document case on top of the gifts and switched off the lights. Then, balancing the box against her hip, she locked her office and walked with care down the stairs leading to the front door, which she pulled open.

'I thought you might still be here.' Richard Stratton removed his hat as Maisie opened the door.

She turned to go back up to the office. 'Oh, more questions so soon?'

He reached forward to take the box, and shook his head. 'Oh, no, that's not it . . . well, I do have more questions, but that's not why I'm here. I thought you looked very unwell. You must be concussed – and you should never underestimate a concussion. I left Caldwell in Charlotte Street and came back. Come on, my driver will take you home. However, we're making a detour via the hospital on the way – to get that head of yours looked at.'

Maisie nodded. 'I think you've been trying to get my head looked at for some time, Inspector.'

He held open the door of the Invicta for her to step inside the motor car. 'At least you weren't too knocked out to quip, Miss Dobbs.'

As they drove away, Maisie looked through the window behind her, her eyes scanning back and forth across the square, until her headache escalated and she turned to lean back in her seat.

'Forgotten something?'

'No, nothing. It's nothing.'

Nothing except the feeling between her shoulder blades that had been with her since this morning. It was a sense that someone had seen her reach out to the doomed man, had seen their eyes meet just before he pulled the pin that would ignite the grenade. Now she felt as if that same someone was watching her still.

— ⌒ —

Stupid, stupid, stupid, foolish man. I should have known, should have sensed he was on the precipice. I never thought the idiot would take his own life. Fool. He should have waited. Had I not told him that we must bide our time? Had I not said, time and again, that we should temper our passion until we were heard, until what I knew gave us currency? Now the only one who knows is the sparrow. An ordinary grey little thing who comes each day for a crumb or two. He knows. He listens to me, waits for me to tell him my plans. And, oh, what plans I have. Then they will all listen. Then they'll know. I've called him Croucher. Little sparrow Croucher, always there, sing-song Croucher, never without a smile. I have a lot to tell him today.

The man closed his diary and set down his pencil. He always used pencil — sharpened with a keen blade each morning and evening, for the sound of a worn lead against paper, the surrounding wood touching the vellum, scraping back and forth for want of sharpening, set his teeth on edge, made him shudder. Sounds were like that. Sounds made their way into your body, crawled along inside your skin. Horses' hooves on wet cobble-stones, cart wheels whining for want of oil, the crackle and snap as the newspaper boy folded the *Daily Sketch*. Thus he always wrote using a pencil with a long, sharp but soft lead, so he couldn't hear his words as they formed on the page.

2

Faced with advice to go home and rest, and knowing that it would be foolish to embark upon a long drive following a diagnosis of concussion, Maisie revised her plans and decided to travel on the train to Kent that very evening, given that trains would not run to Chelstone on Christmas Day. It would be a surprise for her father, who now did not expect her until Christmas morning. First, though, she wanted to ensure that Billy's boys received their gifts, so upon arrival back at her flat, she loaded the box into the MG and drove with care across London to Shoreditch. The city was wet, with an unyielding quality of grey light that made the words *Merry Christmas* seem hardly worth saying. In poorer parts of London, the soup kitchens had been busy, and rations had been distributed to those for whom the festive season was another reminder of what it was to want. Yet in some windows red candles burned a white-gold flame, as the occupants attempted to uplift spirits and reflect the season.

She pulled up outside Billy's house and was not surprised to see a Christmas tree lit with candles, and paper chains framing the window. Silhouettes in the parlour suggested the family was gathered there to decorate the tree. As she walked to the door with the box of gifts, she heard a raised voice coming from the parlour, and wondered if she should not have come.

'Don't you touch those presents. They're for Lizzie. I bought them 'specially for a little girl, so don't you dare touch your sister's things.'

A child began to cry. Maisie thought it was probably Bobby,

the younger son. She was about to turn away, when she heard Billy, the elder boy, shout out to his father.

'Miss Dobbs' motor car's outside. Quick, let's have a look at it, Bobby!'

And before she could leave the box of gifts on the step and turn back to the MG, the front door opened.

'Aw, Miss, you shouldn't've gone to all that trouble, what with you not feeling well and all.' Billy stood on the doorstep without a jacket, his shirt collar and tie removed and his sleeves rolled up.

'Is them for us?' Young Billy's eyes lit up when he saw the packages wrapped in Christmas paper.

'Yes, they're for you, Billy – and for your brother too! Merry Christmas!'

'Come on in, Miss, and have a cuppa with us before you go.'

'Oh, no, you're all busy and—'

'Doreen and me won't hear of it, not after you bringing all this for the boys.' Billy stood back to allow Maisie to come into the passageway, and then opened the door to the parlour. 'Doreen, it's Miss Dobbs.'

Maisie tried to hide her dismay when she saw Doreen Beale standing close to the Christmas tree, clutching a child's threadbare toy lamb to her heart. Her hair was drawn back, which accentuated sallow skin that had sunk into her face, and cheekbones that seemed to jut out from under her eyes. The cardigan she was wearing was soiled at the cuffs and her dress had some dried food on the front. Though Billy and his wife were working hard to put money by for passage to Canada, and what they hoped would be a new life, they were proud people, and Doreen was especially meticulous when it came to keeping the family's clothing clean and pressed, no matter how old it might be, or how many owners it might have had before.

'It's lovely to see you, Doreen.' Maisie approached her and placed her hand on the woman's arm. 'How are you keeping?'

She looked at Maisie's hand as if she could not quite fathom who this visitor might be, and how her arm had become thus burdened.

Then, her eyes filling with tears, she beamed a smile filled with hope. 'Have you brought a present for my little girl? She loves her dolls, you know, and her lamb. Did you bring her something?'

Maisie looked around at Billy, who set the box of gifts under the tree, and came to his wife, placed his arm around her and began to lead her to the kitchen.

'Let's go and put the kettle on for Miss Dobbs, eh, Doreen? Let's have a nice cup of tea, then we can all sit down and look at the tree.'

'All right, Billy. I'll be better when I've had a cup of tea.'

Billy returned to the parlour. Now that he was not wearing his jacket, as he did at all times in the office, Maisie realized that he too had lost weight.

'Sorry, Miss, she's having a bit of a turn. All the excitement of putting up the tree, I suppose. And – as you know – it's coming up to a year ago that we lost our little Lizzie. Apparently, it does this sort of thing, an anniversary.'

Maisie wanted to ask questions, wanted to know how she might be able to help, but this was Christmas, and she knew Billy would want to settle his children and his wife, so the family might have a calm day tomorrow.

'I'd better be off, Billy. I've got to get down to Kent, and I'm taking the train – don't want to drive down, not with this bump on the back of my head.'

'Oh, Miss, and you drove over here for us.' He turned to his boys, who were silent and watching, and as Maisie could see, were fully aware of their mother's plight. 'What do you say to Miss Dobbs?'

They echoed thanks, and Maisie said they could each sit in the driver's seat of the MG for a minute or two, then she had to leave. And as she drove away, Maisie looked back and saw Billy standing on the doorstep, one boy held to him, the other clutching his hand. The children waved and then the three turned and went inside the house.

Christmas Day had passed with a mellow quietness, as Maisie and her father spent time by the fire, sometimes talking, sometimes reading, with her father's dog, a lurcher known as Jook, temporarily changing allegiance to sit at her feet. They shared a hearty festive meal of roast capon and all the trimmings, and enjoyed a short walk across fields whitened by ground frost, the length of the stroll dictated by Frankie's years and her lingering concussion, which, though subsiding, still caused some dizziness if she remained on her feet too long.

Maisie had planned a return to London early on the morning of 27th December, taking Boxing Day off to further recuperate and enjoy her father's company. She had arrived at Chelstone railway station late on Christmas Eve, and was collected at the station by the estate's chauffeur, who had been released to do so by her father's employer, Lady Rowan Compton, who was delighted to know that Maisie would be returning for the holiday. Lady Rowan held a special affection for Maisie and had played a part in her rise from a lowly position on the household staff to the professional woman she was today. For his part, Frankie Dobbs had been relieved to have his daughter home on Christmas Eve, and felt all was well as they dressed the Christmas tree together and placed their gifts underneath, as they had done when Maisie was a child.

Now, waking on Boxing Day morning, Maisie reached for the small clock next to her bed. It was six o'clock. Her father was already downstairs pottering in his kitchen and talking to Jook as he prepared breakfast. For once, Maisie did not scramble out of bed to go to the kitchen, though she loved to share in the cozy warmth while sitting at the table in front of the black cast-iron stove that seemed to push out enough heat to drive a train. She had always enjoyed this time in the morning with her father, when the tea was strong in the pot, the hearth welcoming and the sizzle of bacon and eggs tempting her senses. But today she wanted only to listen to the morning sounds – a solitary bird outside singing despite winter's onslaught and the wind against the glass panes. She closed her eyes and must have fallen asleep again, for it was the shrill ring of the telephone that woke her. She heard her father complain, heard his steps along the red flagstones that led from the kitchen to the sitting room, and heard the telephone continue to ring while he considered who it might be.

Picking up the receiver and without first reciting his telephone number, Frankie shouted, 'What do you want?' and then was quiet. Maisie sat up in bed, waiting.

'Well, she's not well, Inspector. Caught a bit of a throat and hasn't been feeling her usual self, you know.' Silence again. 'All right, all right, you wait here and I'll get her for you.'

Maisie leaped from her bed and reached for her woollen dressing gown hanging on a hook behind the door. 'I'm coming, Dad.'

She ran downstairs and straight into the sitting room, where she smiled at her father as she took the receiver from his hand. 'Yes, this is Maisie Dobbs.'

'Miss Dobbs. Richard Stratton here. Sorry to bother you at home.'

'How did you find me?' She paused. 'Stupid question, Inspector. How can I help you – and on Boxing Day?'

'We have a situation of some urgency and importance on our hands. I would like you to come to the Yard as soon as you can.'

'Well, I was planning to come back to London tomorrow on the train – I decided not to drive after all.' She looked around to see whether her father was in earshot, then turned her back on the kitchen. 'And thank you for not saying anything to my father about the incident on Christmas Eve. I can't have him worrying.'

'Of course, I understood the situation. Now then, can you return today? I can have a motor car at your door by eight.'

'That's certainly urgent.'

'I wouldn't ask if it were not critical. We need to draw upon all resources, Miss Dobbs, and in this case, I believe you are a most valuable resource.'

'I'll be ready at eight.'

'Thank you. I will brief you on your return to London.'

'Until then.' Maisie frowned when she realized that Stratton would himself be coming to collect her. She set down the receiver and walked into her father's kitchen. Jook rose from her place alongside the stove and came to Maisie, nudging her hand with a welcoming wet nose.

'Dad, I'm sorry about this, but I've got to go back to London.'

'I thought as much. You don't get these Scotland Yard blokes making telephone calls early on a Boxing Day morning for nothing.' He paused, taking a frying pan from the stove and slipping two eggs and a rasher of bacon on a plate. 'I've had mine, but you can't be shooting off up there without a good breakfast inside you, so get stuck into that. We can at least sit together for a while until you've to leave.'

Maisie sat at the table and, as she began to eat, her father filled two mugs with tea, set one in front of her and seated himself opposite his daughter.

'You know, I don't hanker after the Smoke at all.' Frankie shook his head and shrugged. 'I thought I would when I first came down to Chelstone, in the war. But aside from sometimes missing the market, you know, a bit of banter, the companionship of it all, I don't miss London. Not one bit. Last time I went up there to see you, it'd changed too much for my liking. I couldn't believe the racket. I mean, when I was boy, you had your noise, but not like now, not with all them motors and lorries and the horses and carts vying for a bit of road. And when you go into a shop, there's tills with bells, and them adding and typewriting machines in the background when you're at the bank. Can't hear yourself think. And now it's full of people out of work. Then, of course, there's them who've got too much – mind you, that's always been the way. But it seems, oh, I dunno – a desperate sort of place to me.'

Maisie stopped eating for a moment and regarded her father. It was at times like this that he surprised her most. He often began such proclamations with the words, 'I'm an ordinary bloke, but . . .' And on such occasions Maisie found him far from ordinary.

'Yes, it's a desperate place for a lot of people, Dad. And the irony of it is that it means, in many cases, someone like me stays in business.'

Frankie nodded. 'That's what worries me. And Detective Inspectors who know where to find you and ring early on a Boxing Day morning. Desperate, I would say.'

Maisie changed the subject, though she knew Frankie was more than aware of her conversational manoeuvre. He would take her lead and speak of this and that, of minor goings-on at Chelstone Manor, anything except the fact that soon his beloved daughter would be collected by a senior Scotland Yard detective because something untoward had happened in what he considered to be a desperate sort of place.

───～───

'Here's the situation.' Stratton turned to Maisie as the driver negotiated the narrow country lanes that led from Chelstone to Tonbridge and then on to the main London road. 'A threat has been received by the Home Secretary and is now in the hands of Scotland Yard. I am one of three senior officers designated to deal with the situation. Seeing as the threat pertains to what amounts to murder, I was called in immediately.'

'What sort of threat is it?'

'That's just it, it hasn't been spelled out, just the consequence. A letter was received at Westminster – you'll see it later – plain vellum, no postmark, no prints, no distinguishing marks at all, the handwriting could have come from anyone, though we have an expert looking at it, obviously.'

'But there are demands.'

'Yes. The man – or woman – is asking the government to act immediately to alleviate the suffering of all unemployed, starting with measures to assist those who have served their country in wartime. There's a bit of a rant about what they did for their country and now look at them, and there's a threat to the effect that, if no action is forthcoming within forty-eight hours – which will be up tomorrow morning – then he will demonstrate his power. We have to entertain the possibility that such a threat may be to the life of the Home Secretary, the Prime Minister or another important person.'

'And what about the possibility of a hoax, or some disenfranchised individual letting off steam?'

'As you know, Miss Dobbs, some of those disenfranchised people can be dangerous – take the Irish situation, the Fascists, the unions. There are a lot of holes in which this particular rodent might be concealing himself.'

'Yes, of course.' Maisie paused, looking out of the window as she considered Stratton's synopsis of the situation. She turned back to Stratton. 'Look, I must ask you this, especially as I am now travelling back to London when I could have spent the day with my father – but what has this got to do with me? You have senior detectives working on the case – how can I help?'

'I can think of several different ways in which you can help, Miss Dobbs, and the talents that might render you a valuable member of the group. Certainly you are known at the Yard, and your contribution to the training of our women detectives has not gone unnoticed. But the fact is that your presence has been' – he slowed his speech, as if choosing his words with care – '*requested*, because whoever is behind the threats has mentioned you by name. "If you doubt my sincerity, ask Maisie Dobbs." That's what he said. So, whether you like it or not, you are part of this case. And, unfortunately, the first thing you will have to do is submit to questioning.'

Maisie shook her head. 'So that's why you're accompanying me to Scotland Yard, to bring me in for questioning. I'm a suspect. I wish you had been honest at the outset.'

'It's not quite like that, Miss Dobbs.' Stratton took a deep breath. 'On the one hand, we know who you are, we know your reputation. But at the same time we need to ensure that you are on our side before we go any further, especially as there's a suspicion that you may be implicated in some way.' He paused. 'And there's one more thing: Special Branch is taking care of this one.'

'I should have guessed. And how are you connected to Special Branch?'

Stratton turned to look at Maisie directly. 'Let's just say I'm moving in that direction. Detective Chief Superintendent Robert MacFarlane is leading the enquiry. And it's on the cards that I'll be reporting to him by Easter – leaving the Murder Squad and joining Special Branch – and that information is a bit hush-hush.'

'Congratulations, Inspector Stratton.' She wiped a hand across condensation inside the window and looked out at the frost-covered landscape for a moment. 'Tell me more about MacFarlane – "Big Robbie" has a reputation that goes before him. Maurice Blanche has worked with him, and he came to talk to us when I was studying at the Department of Legal Medicine in Edinburgh.' Maisie smiled and shrugged. 'To tell you the truth, I liked him. I had a sense that you knew where you stood with MacFarlane – though I'll be honest, I thought he was a bit of a one with the ladies.'

Stratton gave a half laugh. 'Oh yes, and probably more so since his wife left him a couple of years ago. But there's no doubt, you know where you are with Robbie, all right. He's fair, speaks his mind, and gives his people the leeway they need to get the job done. Mind you, at the same time, he expects every ounce of you on the case.'

'Well, I look forward to meeting him again. I wonder if he remembers me.'

'Yes, he remembers you, Miss Dobbs. That's another reason why you were summoned at an unearthly hour on Boxing Day morning.'

Maisie's first visit to New Scotland Yard, on the Embankment, had taken place when she was working with Maurice Blanche as his assistant. She found the grand red-brick building intimidating, with its ornate chimneys, projecting gables and turrets at each corner. In the intervening years, she had come to take visits to 'the Yard' in her stride. Today, though, she was escorted to the area of Scotland Yard occupied by Special Branch, and led into a sparsely decorated room, where she waited while Stratton left to inform others involved in the investigation that they had arrived. Soon she heard a voice booming down the corridor, but when Robert MacFarlane walked into the room with Stratton, the timbre was lower, with a soft Scottish burr belying his position, and the situation. Maisie rose from her chair and extended her hand in greeting.

'Miss Dobbs, thank you for coming.' The Detective Chief Superintendent shook her hand, then nodded towards the chair. 'Sit down, lass, sit down. I trust your father was not too upset by your sudden departure from the family hearth.'

'He understands the nature of my work.'

'Good, I'm glad one of us does.' Taking his seat behind a wooden desk that seemed too small to accommodate his height – MacFarlane was well over six feet tall and, thought Maisie, had the frame of a docker. He was about fifty-five years of age, light of foot and precise in his movements. A track of baldness revealed a scar where a stray bullet had nicked him in the war – the fact that he had simply wiped blood away and sworn at the enemy for putting a hole in his tam o'shanter was the stuff of legend – and the cropped hair that flanked his shining pate was gunmetal grey and controlled with a whisper of oil.

'Stratton, bring in Darby, if you wouldn't mind.' .

Soon the four were seated: Maisie, MacFarlane, Stratton and Colm Darby, a man who had worked alongside MacFarlane before the war and, when the policeman returned from France, had joined him once more. Darby was probably a good five years older than his superior. Maisie knew him to be an expert in the analysis of personal markers left behind by the perpetrator of a crime. The nature of one's handwriting was an area in which he was said to have great insight. He had been with MacFarlane since the days when the main roles of the department encompassed intelligence and security to protect the country from extremist activity known as the 'Irish problem'. Now Special Branch had a broader role, and it seemed as if Colm Darby might never retire. MacFarlane introduced Maisie, then leaned forward so that his forearms rested on the desk.

'Miss Dobbs, I am dispensing with protocol here – because I can, and because I believe we have no time to lose.' He sighed, looking directly into Maisie's eyes. 'I know Maurice Blanche, I've worked with him in the past, and I remember you from Edinburgh – Blanche sent you there, I understand.'

'Yes, that's correct, in preparation for my work with him, when I was his assistant.'

MacFarlane looked down at an open manila folder, flipped over a page of notes, then closed the folder before resuming eye contact with Maisie. 'Now, first of all, in your own words, describe the events of Christmas Eve.'

Maisie drew breath and, as she had for Stratton before, described approaching the man on Charlotte Street, and witnessing him take his life with a Mills Bomb.

'Not a pretty sight, I'm sure.'

'I've seen some ugly sights in my time, Chief Superintendent.'

'I bet you have, Miss Dobbs. And we don't, any of us, want to be seeing any more, though I imagine that might be a wee bit of a faint hope.' MacFarlane cleared his throat. 'Can you explain how a man who has made veiled threats that amount to a risk to our country's security might know the name of a little wee lassie like yourself?'

Maisie bristled, but checked herself, aware that the goading was deliberate, though she knew that, in the circumstances, she might have employed the same tactic herself. She leaned forward, mirroring MacFarlane's position. Darby looked at Stratton, and raised an eyebrow.

'Chief Superintendent, to be perfectly honest with you, at this juncture I have no idea why I was mentioned in such a letter. However, your line of questioning regarding the tragedy I witnessed on Christmas Eve would indicate that you see a relationship between the two events, and I am inclined to veer in that initial direction myself.' She turned to face Stratton and Darby, bringing them into the conversation. 'I was the closest person to the victim to walk away without significant physical injury – and yes, I see him as a victim. So if – *if* – there was an associate of the dead man nearby, I would have been seen. If the two cases are linked, the person who wrote the letter could be that same individual, perhaps using my name as leverage to give some kind of weight to his endeavour. It might also be a means of subverting your attention, of course.'

MacFarlane leaned back in his chair, as did Maisie in hers. The policeman smiled. 'Just like bloody Blanche! I move, you move. I do this, you do the same thing. It's like being followed.' He shook his head. 'Look, Miss Dobbs, I know – *know*, mind – that you haven't anything to do with this tyke, but you might have had some brief contact with him, you might have seen him, or he might have an interest in you.' He brushed his hand across his forehead. 'I know this could be the work of a bit of a joker, but my nose tells me this boy is serious, that he means what he says. Now then, we can play a waiting game, see what happens next, or we can start looking. I favour action, which is why I've asked you here. You're involved in this whether you like it or not, Miss Dobbs, and I would rather have you under my nose working for me than anywhere else.'

'I'm used to working alone, Chief Superintendent.'

'Well, for now you can get un-used to it. First of all, let me apprise you of the work of Special Branch. Even though I am sure you have some familiarity, if you are going to be reporting to me, then I want to start us off on the right foot. So, a little lesson, and I'll make it snappy. The Special Branch is, technically, part of the Criminal Investigation Department, but as you may have heard we like to go about our business in our own fashion. Suffice it to say that we only answer questions when the person asking has a lot of silver on the epaulettes, or around the peak of his cap. Our normal work is in connection with the protection of royalty, ministers and ex-ministers of the Crown, and foreign dignitaries. We also control aliens entering our country. We are responsible for investigation into acts of terrorism and anarchy, and to that end have a lot of people to keep an eye on. Before I go on, I should add – mainly because I can see a bit of a problem looming here – that on occasion we cross paths with Military Intelligence, Section Five, for obvious reasons. We try to get along, and they need us, mainly because we have powers of arrest. There, now I can take off my professoring hat and get down to business. Do you have any questions?'

'No, sir.'

'Good. Back to the case in hand. Let's look at what we've brought together here in the way of information – facts. I want action and I want the man behind the letter brought in as a matter of urgency. And Miss Dobbs – whatever you're doing, I want you to report to Inspector Stratton here every single day.'

Maisie nodded. 'If that's the case, Chief Superintendent, before I see the letter, perhaps we can discuss my terms. The financial terms, that is.'

'Not exactly music to the ears of a Scot, you know.' The edges of MacFarlane's mouth twitched into a grin.

'That's why I didn't want to leave it any longer, Chief Superintendent.'

'Inspector Darby, what do you think about the downstroke of the pencil, here, where the letter-writer makes his demands? It seems so thick, almost laboured.' Without touching the paper, Maisie used her forefinger to indicate her observation.

'Yes, I noticed that myself. Very deliberate, isn't it?'

'Like a child's hand – not in presentation, but in the execution,

28

as if the person writing the letter were moving his hand slowly, so as not to lose control.' She closed her eyes, her hand moving back and forth on the wooden desk to describe holding a pen. The three men looked at one another.

MacFarlane made an effort to control his voice, keeping it low while Maisie was thinking. 'Stratton, I know you're not a tea-boy, but poke your head around that door and tell them that this isn't the desert and throats are parched in here.' He turned back to Maisie, who opened her eyes and spoke again.

'I think he or she has trouble with dexterity and concentration. Don't you think so?' She turned to Darby.

Colm Darby nodded agreement. 'I do – but what do you make of this?' He handed her a magnifying glass, then pointed to two places on the vellum. Stratton entered the room again and sat at the table alongside Maisie.

'It's been moistened – by saliva, I would say.' She looked up, then down at the paper again. 'Yes, that's saliva. The person who wrote this letter was so intent on the words that his mouth was open and spittle drooled on to the paper.'

'So what does that tell us? That we have a dribbling person out there with perfect spelling?' MacFarlane was growing impatient.

The door opened again and a younger man in civilian clothes entered with four cups of tea on a wooden tray. He set the tray down on the table and left the room.

'It tells us that the person has trouble with muscular control, and that concentration is difficult. It tells us that the person is compromised in some way.'

'That's if you're right.'

'Yes, that's if Inspector Darby and I are right.'

There was silence in the room. Stratton reached for two cups of tea, placing one in front of Maisie, who was beginning to feel the stirrings of a headache. She thanked Stratton and touched the bump on the back of her head.

'All right?'

'Yes, it's just reminding me, that's all.'

MacFarlane reached for a cup of tea, as did Darby. 'Well, that's bloody marvellous,' said the Scotsman. 'Thousands of – what did you say? – *compromised* people in London and we've got to find one of them. Needle in a bloody haystack.' He scraped back his chair and began to pace the room.

'Do we have an identification on the dead man yet?' asked Maisie.

Stratton shook his head. 'Proving very difficult, as you can imagine.'

Maisie looked at each man in turn, then up at the clock above the door. MacFarlane followed her gaze. 'Yes, it's time we got on with it. Miss Dobbs, a motor car will collect you from your office this afternoon at four, and we'll reconvene here to discuss progress – or, heaven forbid, lack thereof. In the meantime, I'll allow you to work in the way that you've said is best – alone. But be ready at four, otherwise you'll have someone from the Branch at your heels from dawn until dusk until we've closed this case. The forty-eight hours' grace our letter-writer has allowed us will be up by six o'clock tomorrow morning or thereabouts. If we haven't got him, we'll soon find out if we have a practical joker on our hands. And with a bit of luck, by then we'll have an identification on the other nutcase in Charlotte Street.' He held out his hand. 'We'll see you later, Miss Dobbs.'

'Indeed, later.'

'And don't forget – in all the work you do on this case, you're under the jurisdiction of Special Branch.'

'I understand, Chief Superintendent.'

MacFarlane nodded and took up the letter once more.

━━━◦━━━

Stratton walked Maisie to a waiting Invicta police motor car.

'He may be a bit of a maverick, but he's very good.'

'Yes, I know. Maurice has spoken about him in the past. And I expect the reason I am here is not only because my name was mentioned in that letter, but because he requested Maurice's help first.'

'Blanche said to contact you, that you were his successor in every way. He told Big Robbie to trust your instincts.'

'And does he?'

'He trusts Blanche, so yes, consider yourself trusted.'

'I must be – his questioning was mild, to say the least.'

As they reached the motor car, Maisie turned to Stratton and held out her hand. 'I look forward to working with you again, Inspector.'

'Ditto, Miss Dobbs. But we have to work fast.'

'I know – I'm working already.' She stepped into the Invicta. 'I'll see you at four.'

———

Hickory, dickory, dock. Tick tock, tick tock. Clocks and watches, clocks and watches, time in, time out. Here comes a chopper to chop off your head!

The pencil began to scrape, so the man shuffled to the kitchen, took a knife from a drawer and whittled a point to the lead, the chips of wood hitting a brown stain where the single cold tap dripped water day and night. He winced at the noise, tested the sharpness with the tip of his finger as if he were about to tune a stringed instrument, then shuffled back to the table again and proceeded to write.

They do not know, do not know which end is up, and that's always been the trouble with the brass. I remember, see. Oh, it was all very well, sending out those watches, so we all had the same time, down to the second, so that we all, thousands of us, went over the top at the same time, and . . .

Holding the pencil above the page, the man gasped as memories pushed forward to become fast-moving pictures in his mind – the twisted grin of death on a uniformed corpse, the silent scream of a man he'd laughed with just moments past – and the relentless noise of battle reverberating from inside his skull into the solitude of his room, enveloping him in the fury of war. He dropped the pencil and pressed his hands to his eyes, hard, so that as his fingers touched the soft roundness he imagined that he could pluck the pictures from his head if he could stand the pain. And if he thought he would be left in peace.

In time the ghosts drew back to the place in his mind where they were quiet, spent, so he read back over his own words, picked up his pencil and began again.

So what's the point of getting the time right, if it's all you can get right? Time and consequence, time and consequence. Croucher knew about time and consequence. Poor Croucher. Very poor Croucher.

The man set down his pencil between the pages of the leather-bound book, then tied a string around the cover so the pencil would not be mislaid or clatter to the floor. He stood up and, taking small steps towards a cupboard, pulled out a large box containing a collection of empty demijohns, tubes and rubber piping. Another box held a series of bottles filled with liquids and tins of various sizes, each one labelled with care, in pencil. If Darby had brought his magnifying glass to the labels, he might have seen the paper discoloured in spots here and there, where it had become soiled by saliva from the man's open mouth.

Setting the two boxes on the table, he began to attach tubing to a demijohn. Had an onlooker been observing the man, he might have been reminded of the tale of Dr Jekyll and Mr Hyde, and might have felt concern at the recollection. Having completed construction of what was to be something of an experiment, the man pulled at the string around his diary, opened the leather-bound book again and took up his pencil.

I was good at something, once. I was good at something, one thing, that could be of service. But they don't want to know now. I'll just have to show them. Toil and trouble, toil and trouble.

3

Maisie slotted her key into the lock and opened the outside door to the mansion in Fitzroy Square that housed her one-room office on the first floor. She closed the door behind her and walked upstairs with a certain weariness, but stopped to listen when she heard voices coming from the office. At first she was concerned, but then a child's squealing laughter echoed across the room, and a young voice said, 'Chase us, Dad, chase me and Bobby.' She wondered why Billy was at work – not only was Boxing Day a holiday, but they often only worked a half day on a Saturday, unless a significant assignment demanded their round-the-clock attention. And he had his children with him.

'Hello, Billy – and young Billy, and Bobby.' Maisie smiled as she entered the office, taking off her hat and scarf, but keeping her coat on. 'It's cold in here, Billy – why didn't you put on the gas fire? You don't want the boys catching cold.'

Billy had been on the floor playing with his sons, but stood up, blushing, when Maisie came in. 'You two play with your toys while I'm talking to Miss Dobbs – and what do you say, again, for the presents she bought you?'

The two boys stood up side by side and in unison said, 'Thank you, Miss Dobbs,' with young Billy adding, 'I really liked my fire engine!'

Maisie tousled the wheaten-hued hair of each boy in turn and told them they should play with their toys where the carpet gave way to wood. 'Your fire engine will go faster there.' She turned to Billy. 'Come on, let's have a cup of tea and you can tell me what's going on – if you want to.'

Over tea Billy explained that Doreen had become more withdrawn as the festive season approached, and though they had never been able to afford a big Christmas Day, as a rule they would try to put by enough money for a roast chicken, and a gift each for the boys. This year she had taken almost no interest at all, except for placing a small collection of toys for Lizzie under the tree, toys that Billy tried to remove so as not to upset the boys.

'She's just a shadow at times, Miss, a shadow. I thought over the summer she'd picked up a bit, that we were getting through it. I mean, I miss my little Lizzie too, but we've got two cracking boys here and they need their mum. I tell you, Miss, I come home of an evening and sometimes she's just sitting there, staring. The stove's gone down, she's got some dressmaking half done and I have to sort of get her going again, you know, help her to her feet, show her how to do this or that. There's days when you'd think she was right as rain, then it comes again. She's not eating much either, and I've always made sure there was food on the table. We might not live in clover – there's folk round our way making do in terrible conditions, rats from the river up and everywhere – but we always kept the house nice, kept the boys clean and going to school. Now it's like trying to stop someone falling down a big black hole.'

'Oh, Billy, I am so sorry.'

'So, I didn't think you'd be here until Monday, and we'd nowhere else to go, because I wanted to give Doreen a bit of a rest in peace and quiet, and – to tell you the truth – I wanted to get the boys out of the house, away from it all for a bit. The museums on Exhibition Road are closed today – and I wanted to take them to the Science Museum, you know, to that new children's gallery they've opened, with all the little machines for the kids to see how a steam train works and what happens down a mine, that sort of thing. But the office was here, so after we'd

34

been for a walk to look in the shop windows, I brought them back for a bit of a play before we went home to Shoreditch.'

'That's all right, Billy. You and the boys can stay here as long as you like today.' Maisie paused. 'Has Doreen seen a doctor? Or the nurse?'

'Well, she went when we first lost Lizzie, but it's hard to get her to go anywhere.'

'But she might need a tonic, something to give her a bit of a lift. And she needs to be eating properly.'

'I bought a tonic for her, and as for food, as I said, she's eating like a sparrow, and it's not as if Doreen ever carried weight.' He put his hand to his forehead and rubbed it from side to side. 'I tell you, Miss, it scares me sometimes, reminds me of me when I came back from the war – reminds me of men I saw in the hospital, you know, the ones you weren't supposed to see before they were sent off to another special hospital in the plain black ambulance. There's times she's got that look in her eyes, as if she was staring across an ocean.' He paused again. 'And every time she's like that now, I think about the bloke on Christmas Eve. That was just how he looked, out into the distance, as if there was no one else there.'

'I think she needs to see the doctor again, Billy. She's suffering and she should see someone.'

'I've got the bonus money. I thought I'd put it away for Canada, you know, to save for the passage, but I'll put it towards Doreen getting better.'

'Do it soon, Billy.'

'I will, Miss.' Billy looked across the room to his boys, who were making motor noises as they pushed their toys back and forth. Then he brought his attention back to Maisie. 'I didn't think you'd be here today, Miss – weren't you going to stay with your dad until tomorrow?'

'Yes, I was, but I was brought back by D.I. Stratton – and this is confidential, mind: Special Branch is involved.'

Billy exhaled with a low whistle.

'I know – if they're on the job, it's serious. A threat has been received by the Home Secretary and my name is mentioned in the letter. In addition, it is likely that the threat has some connection to the man with the Mills Bomb who committed the crime of suicide on Christmas Eve.'

'Can't get that out of my mind, Miss. At first I was a bit scared, I'll be honest with you. For a minute I thought I was back over there. But there's Doreen and the boys to think of, so I can't be letting myself slip now, can I?'

'No, you can't.' Maisie paused, thinking of the time, two years before, when Billy's own slide into the abyss was caused by the lingering pain from his war wounds. 'I've been seconded to work on the case with Special Branch,' she went on, 'so I'm going to have to depend upon you to keep our present customers happy. I'm to meet with Stratton each day, though you and I can start here in the mornings to go through work in hand.'

'Right you are, Miss.'

'But about the man in the street – we both believe he'd been a soldier, wounded in the legs, and it's likely he'd been shell-shocked to some degree.'

'I would say so.'

'So, who was he? The police don't seem able to get to the bottom of it, and I would like to have a name as soon as possible. If we know who he is, we can find out who he knows, then with luck we can find our way to the man who sent the threat.'

'What will he do, the man?'

'I don't know – he wasn't specific. But he said he would wait forty-eight hours for his requests to be met, which means we now have only a very limited time to find a very angry or unhappy person in London who could be mentally ill.'

'That doesn't narrow the field down much.'

'I know. I sometimes wonder who's sane.'

Their conversation was interrupted as a squabble broke out between the boys.

'Now then, now then, what's all this about?' Billy moved

toward his sons and held each of them gently but firmly by the arm. 'You're brothers, you're not supposed to fight – that's how wars start, with people fighting over the little things.'

Blaming started as one boy pointed at the other, and vice versa, but Billy soon calmed the situation and the brothers made up, shaking hands like little men.

'We'd better be going, Miss. They'll be hungry by the time we get home.'

Maisie helped Billy put the boys' coats on, winding scarves around their necks and slipping mittens on to little hands that would only too readily feel the cold. As she pulled a woollen hat down on young Billy's head, she saw his father take out a hand-kerchief and wipe Bobby's mouth.

Billy saw her watching him and shrugged. 'I hope he gets over this soon. He's going on five now, you know, and this dribbling business started when we came home after the hop-picking. I reckon it's to do with his mum. She used to give them cuddles a lot, but now she don't. I've seen him run to her, but she just pushes him away. Same with young Bill here.' Billy spoke softly while the children claimed their toys. 'I try to give him a cuddle, when I see it happen, but I'm not there when they come in from school. He sits there with his fingers in his mouth and before you know where you are, the front of his cardigan is all wet and matted.'

Maisie was thoughtful. 'The best thing for now is not to draw attention to it. Just keep him dry so that he doesn't get chapped in this weather. You're doing the right thing in trying to step in when Doreen can't, but it just points to the fact that she needs to see someone, as soon as possible.'

Billy sighed. 'We'll be off now. See you on Monday morning, Miss.'

Maisie bid farewell to Billy and the boys, and walked to the window to watch them make their way across the square, each boy holding on to his father's hand as they skipped alongside him. Although she had been aware of time passing, and the letter-writer's deadline looming ever closer, she understood that Billy needed to talk about his wife and the threat her state of mind represented to the well-being of their family. Now Maisie knew she needed to think. She turned back into the room and pulled the armchair closer to the gas fire.

Sitting down, she gazed into the flaming jets, reflecting upon Bobby Beale and his distress as his mother receded into herself. She wanted to support the family as much as she could, but knew her efforts must be balanced with an employer–employee relationship with Billy, and must not compromise his pride. But she kept going back to the child and his physical response to emotional disappointment. Of course, one couldn't draw too many conclusions from a single serendipitous event, but she could not help but reflect upon the days following recuperation from her own war wounds. Once well enough, she had felt drawn to return to nursing, and because of the wounds suffered by her sweetheart in the same incident, she decided to work in a secure hospital caring for men whose minds were ravaged by war.

Now, still staring into the rasping white-hot gas jets, she saw once more the twisted bodies, muscular responses not to physical injury but to mental anguish. She saw the eyes rolled back or staring into the distance, the constant weeping, the uncontrolled reflexes. There were men who cried, those who could not eat, those who would cause themselves injury, as if to feel, physically, the wounds that lay in their souls. And there were those who would sit alongside a wall, banging their heads against the hard surface again and again and again while saliva streamed from their open mouths, as if to mirror the cavernous hell they looked into from the time consciousness claimed them in the morning, until nightfall, when a sedative would send them into oblivion.

Maisie came to her feet and walked across the room to a chest of small drawers that resembled something one might find in a pharmacy. She opened a drawer and flicked through the cards until she found the one she wanted. Tapping it against her hand, she walked back to the desk, picked up the telephone receiver and dialled one of two numbers listed on the card. She continued looking at the card until her call was answered. Only some-one close to her would have heard her whispering, *Please be there, please be there, please be there . . .*

Maisie started when the telephone was answered. 'Yes, is Dr Anthony Lawrence on duty today, by any slight chance? Oh, good. May I speak to him, please?'

Maisie waited while the doctor was summoned, running the telephone cord through her fingers as the seconds ticked by.

'Lawrence here.'

'Oh, Dr Lawrence, I'm glad I've caught you, especially on Boxing Day. I don't know if you remember me, my name is Maisie Dobbs — I was a staff nurse on Oak ward at the Clifton Hospital in 1918, then sister on Ash, and—'

'You're the one who left to go back to Cambridge. Sustained a nasty head wound in France, if I remember correctly.'

'Yes, that's right.'

'What can I do for you, Miss Dobbs?'

'It's rather difficult to explain on the telephone, but it is urgent, and confidential — would you spare me about twenty minutes this afternoon, say about half past one?'

'I have to leave to keep an appointment at approximately two o'clock, so . . . well, all right, yes, but perhaps you could come along to my office a bit earlier — one o'clock?'

'Yes, thank you, Dr Lawrence. I look forward to seeing you at one.'

'And you, Miss Dobbs.'

Maisie smiled as she replaced the telephone receiver in its cradle. There was something that Anthony Lawrence and Robert MacFarlane had in common — they were both honest, no-nonsense men dedicated to their respective professions. But with Lawrence, now considered an expert in the treatment of psycho-logical trauma, she had observed his compassion when they had both worked at Clifton, had seen him square up against pension authorities who tried to label mind-wounded men as malinger-ers, and had seen him spend hours with one man simply to try to get him to speak his own name out loud. She didn't hold out hope for a breakthrough in the meeting, but if a conversation with Lawrence helped to crack into the frozen lock on this case, it would be more than worth the time.

Arriving at the Princess Victoria Hospital by half past twelve, Maisie went first to the porters' office, whereupon her name was verified and a porter picked up a hefty bunch of keys attached to a bracelet-sized brass ring and instructed Maisie to follow him. The hospital where Lawrence now worked was much like other institutional buildings constructed in the heyday of Victoria's reign, with a certain flourish to the red-brick design signifying the industrial and commercial wealth of her Empire and a legacy for the people. The wooden banister was buffed to a shine, as was every brass fixture and fitting, and as they made their way towards the doctors' offices, a lavender fragrance wafted from just-polished floorboards. Maisie wondered if Sheila Kennedy, the hospital's almost legendary matron, was still in charge – certainly the level of order suggested that she remained at the helm. It was an order that belied the name accorded the hospital by the locals, who referred to it as 'the Bin'. First built as an asylum, it had been turned over to military cases of neurasthenia and other neuroses during the war, as had the Clifton Hospital. Although many of those wartime patients had been discharged over the years, some after just a few weeks of care, the hospital remained more or less full, with an increasing number of patients starting to be admitted in recent years whose mental anguish was rooted in an inability to deal with the ordinary and extraordinary in everyday life, rather than battles on foreign soil.

Where there might have been double doors that flapped open in hospitals for the physically infirm, the porter at the Princess Victoria Hospital unlocked each door and took care to secure it again as they passed through. Soon they reached the upward-spiralling back staircase flanked by cream-painted walls with maroon and cream tiles at the base. The staircase opened on to a corridor with offices on both sides, each with a heavy oak door. In this part of the hospital there was not the same level of security, though the porter remained with Maisie at all times. He stopped at the door to Dr Lawrence's office and knocked, only opening the door when a voice boomed, 'Come!'

'A Miss Dobbs to see you, sir.'

'Ah, yes, of course – oh, and I'll see Miss Dobbs out again later when I leave.'

'Right you are, sir – but she will have to sign out.'

'Not to worry, I'll ensure she stops at the office.'

The porter stepped aside to allow Maisie into the room, then touched his forehead as if in salute and backed out into the corridor while closing the door as he went.

Maisie shook hands with Dr Lawrence. His hair was combed to either side from the same centre parting he favoured as a younger man, though it was now grey, and not the coal black Maisie remembered when they both worked at the Clifton Hospital. His moustache seemed longer than it had once been, and Maisie noticed the ends were waxed, giving him something of a haughty appearance, though she could not recall such a character flaw. He wore round wire spectacles, and his skin bore the lines and folds of one who worked instead of slept over many nights, suggesting that worry and concern were elements he could never escape. His collar was tight around the neck, his tie pulled almost to his Adam's apple, and he was still wearing his white coat, which indicated that he had just finished his rounds.

'Please, take a seat, Miss Dobbs.' He held out his hand towards a plain wooden chair.

'It was good of you to see me, Dr Lawrence, especially at such short notice.'

'Think nothing of it, glad to assist, if I can. You were a fine nurse, Miss Dobbs. I always thought you might enter medical school yourself – women seem to be turning their hands to everything nowadays, don't they? I suppose it's a case of "needs must", what with so many remaining spinsters, eh? Certainly we don't have so many nurses leaving to get married, because there's not enough men to go around!' He smiled briefly as he took his seat on the other side of the desk. Maisie noticed that his chair had two flat and worn cushions on the seat, probably brought from home in an attempt at creating more comfort. 'And what have you been doing with yourself since you returned to Cambridge?'

As Maisie began to describe her life over the past twelve years, she took account of her surroundings. Lawrence's office was neat and tidy, with books shelved according to subject matter and a general sense of order. It was something that Maisie had liked about the doctor, that sense of order. He always counted instruments before and after procedures, always made legible notes immediately following each patient consultation, while thoughts were still fresh in his mind. But that was ten years ago. Now, as she spoke, she noticed he absently corrected the pile of papers and files on his desk, making sure that each was only so far from the edge, and never more than two inches apart. He reached forward and lined up his pens and pencils, then took a clean handkerchief from his pocket and wiped it back and forth across the wood.

' . . . so, when Dr Blanche retired, I took over the business and set up on my own. I now have an office in Fitzroy Square.'

'Hmm, impressive, Miss Dobbs, impressive.' He looked up and returned the handkerchief to his pocket, pulled out a fob-watch from his waistcoat and checked the time before replacing the watch once more. 'Mind you, we always hate to lose a good nurse.' He cleared his throat. 'So, what can I do for you – you said it was urgent.'

'Yes, indeed – and confidential.'

'Of course. As you know, we're used to keeping a confidence here, so do bear that in mind.'

Maisie sighed. 'The fact is, I do not have very specific questions, but I am anxious to make a dent in a very serious investigation. Suffice it to say that I am working on secondment to Scotland Yard on a sensitive case.'

'Go on . . .'

'Did you read about the man who committed suicide in Charlotte Street on Christmas Eve?'

'Yes, of course – nasty, nasty business. It's a miracle he didn't take anyone with him, though according to the press, there were wounded.'

'Thankfully, nothing too serious – though, as we both know, to witness such a thing scars the mind for ever.'

Lawrence ran his fingers along the sides of a pile of folders as he nodded. 'Indeed. I take it the suicide is connected with your current work?'

'It is a distinct, but not confirmed possibility. I believe the man had been a soldier in the war. I was walking along Charlotte Street at the time, and was close enough to him to see that one leg was crippled in some way, perhaps an inability to bend at the knee, while the other leg was either amputated at the knee or bent backward. I would say there had been an amputation. His remains would support such a conclusion. And though I was not able to speak to him – had I been any closer, I might not be here today – I observed movement of the head and hands that might suggest a shell-shock case.'

'How can I help?'

'Dr Lawrence, there are a considerable number of men who have remained locked away in institutions since the war and who are still suffering from war neurosis. And many more have been discharged in recent years, possibly to relatives, or to live in a hostel. Our man may have been one of them.'

Lawrence sighed, rubbing his chin. 'Miss Dobbs, the truth regarding this country's treatment of its shell-shocked soldiers is harrowing, and to someone like yourself – trying to discover the dead man's identity, for I imagine that must be of prime importance – it presents an obstacle of considerable proportions.' He sighed again, picked up a pen and put it down, ensuring that

43

the writing instruments remained parallel to one another. 'There were approximately, say, seventy-five to eighty thousand men diagnosed with shell-shock during and immediately after the war. These were the cases that could be easily identified, corroborated and signed off to return to England or to receive treatment.' He looked at Maisie with eyes the colour of slate that reminded her of the sky on a bitterly cold day. 'In my estimation – and I could be taken to task by the authorities for such comments, so please reflect upon this conversation with care – the numbers of shell-shocked men ran into the hundreds of thousands. And, arguably, there is no man' – he held Maisie's eyes with his own – 'or woman, who returned from Flanders unscathed in the mind.'

'I know.'

'Yes, you do. However, I wonder if you know what pressures were brought to bear on doctors during and after the war?' He did not wait for an answer before continuing. 'Not only were we pressed to declare a man fit for duty as soon as any physical wounds were healed, but in all but the most obvious cases – and here's my personal experience – our instructions, perhaps to send a man to a secure institution for additional care, were overruled by senior military staff who would label a man as a lazy item, or with low moral fibre. And off they would be sent, back on to the battlefield with their minds half destroyed.' He shrugged. 'Of course, there was another reason – pensions. If a man is physically wounded in battle, there is a small pension allowance. With increasing numbers of men suffering mentally from the effects of war, the government was becoming queasier and queasier about having to pay pensions it would never be able to afford – so those men were discharged at the earliest possible opportunity, because for many, there was no bleeding, no physical wound or scarring. Miss Dobbs, if you haven't realized it already, you must be aware that you are looking for a needle in a haystack. You could go through every record of every patient suffering from neurasthenia, war neurosis, melancholia and hysteria, and you would have touched only the tip of the iceberg.'

'You are very frank, Dr Lawrence.'

'For every man on our wards who will never see the outside of an institution, there are five, six, seven out there' – he pointed at the window – 'who are in a cell in their mind. They are trying to find work, trying to live from one day to the next. Some might have families or children, but they are ticking away inside, so that one day, when the baby wails in a certain way, the man will end up cowering in the corner or, worse, inflicting harm. And some take a deep breath every day, working, living, eating, breathing, holding all the components of life together in a vice-like grip so that no one will ever know they are broken as much as if their bodies had been crushed.'

'I'm sorry if—'

Lawrence held up one hand. 'Please, don't. You came to ask a question or two and you got more than you bargained for.' He reached for a folder, taking care to pull it towards him without disturbing the rest of the pile. He tapped the top of the folder. 'This is a collection of letters from the powers-that-be instructing me to decrease numbers of soldiers from the war still held here. They are to be sent out into the raw reality of London in the midst of winter, and with no prospects of work or any sort of support. Where will they go? Who will care for them? This is the sort of battle I have on my hands – now everyone wants to forget the war.'

Maisie nodded. 'Dr Lawrence, you have been most kind to spare me so much of your time. However, I wonder if I can just ask one or two questions. Are there any behaviours common among men who are discharged? Do they remain close to the hospital? Do they go further afield?' She breathed deeply. 'You see – and it's my turn to remind you of my need for confidentiality now – to give you more of an idea of the situation, there has been a threat received by a high-ranking government official. While others are working to see if the demands of the person who issued the threat could be met in some way that might placate him and give us time, my task is to try to find him. I have said the words *needle in a haystack* myself – I know from my war experience and my work at the Clifton how difficult that task might be. But I must continue, and in a short time follow any lead that presents itself to me. So, clutching at straws – if I take a gamble and assume the man who took his life on Christmas Eve was released from a secure institution at some point in the past couple of years, how might I find him?'

Lawrence replaced the folder and ran his fingers along the sides once more to align the pile. 'You could start with the pensions people, but I can tell you now, that door is indubitably locked shut. I will try to gain permission for you to view the records held here of former patients. And I can give you an introduction to other secure hospitals. When people leave an institution – be it a hospital or prison – there is sometimes a need to retain a sort of relationship with that place. They might find digs with a view of the hospital chimneys; they might need to come back for out-patient examinations or medication. They might just want to know that the nest, even if it was the most dreadful place they had ever known, is still close. But that's just my opinion. My peers might suggest otherwise.'

Maisie gathered up her gloves and scarf. 'Thank you, Dr Lawrence.' She looked at the clock on the wall. 'I had better be off now.' She took a card from her black document case and put it on the desk in front of Lawrence, who had pushed back his chair. 'Please send word as soon as you have permission for me to view the records. I hate to say this, but to gain informal access to the files would be so much better than having a warrant issued. I am sure Matron would walk on hot coals rather than have that sort of thing going on in her hospital.'

Lawrence laughed. 'I will be in touch. Now then, I'd better escort you to the porters' office.'

As they made their way down the staircase, Lawrence and Maisie spoke of times past, of improvements to the Clifton Hospital since she relinquished her nursing position, and of the doctor's children, who were now grown. He unlocked doors and locked them again as they passed through the lower corridors, and soon they had reached the entrance.

'Here we are.' Lawrence stopped alongside the porters' office and knocked on the door. 'Please let me know if I can be of any further assistance to you, Miss Dobbs.'

Maisie shook his proffered hand, and turned to the porter who had just opened the door.

'Will you be back today, Dr Lawrence?' the porter enquired, while holding the ledger for Maisie to sign out.

'Yes I will,' replied the doctor. 'See that Miss Dobbs doesn't have to wait too long for a taxi-cab, there's a good chap, Croucher.'

'Right you are, Dr Lawrence. I'll make sure she gets on her way.' He turned to Maisie and smiled.

4

The man opened his eyes and waited for a moment or two while sleep ebbed from his mind, in the way that the sea recedes from the shore, going back a little, then returning, going back, then returning. It was in the first few seconds of waking that he sometimes panicked and was paralysed by fear, for there were times when he took to his bed not because it was night and therefore time to rest, but because being awake – even in daytime – was more than he could bear. His body was always chilled, and though the room was dry enough, his clothes felt damp, and his toes were bitten with cold. He pulled the blanket up over his coat-clad body and closed his eyes, smacking his lips as if to soothe his jaw so that sleep would come again and he could be delivered from his waking nightmares, which always seemed worse than those inflicted upon him in slumber. There were times when he woke and held his breath, for he couldn't remember why he was steeped in melancholy, why his heart ached and his body hurt. Then the pictures began to play in his mind's eye again, and the sounds tormented him so that he would clutch his head as if to rip it from his shoulders. Those were the times when he would have welcomed death, if only to be cast free.

Once more he came to, rubbing his hand across his stubbled chin, and pressing his fingers to his tired, sunken eyes. He rolled over to bring the clock on the mantelpiece into focus. It was nearly time. The man sat up and, when he'd garnered strength enough, swung his legs over the side of the narrow, iron-framed bed, and stood, reaching for his stick. He wavered for a moment, as if he might fall back, then shuffled towards a wireless set on the table. He switched it on. First the pips, signifying the hour, then the news.

He listened, his head to one side, close to the wireless. Nothing. Nothing for him. There was no news indicating that he had been heard. No surprise announcements telling of handouts coming from Westminster, no word of special festive-season meetings to discuss the plight of those who had given all for their country, no acknowledgement of the suffering of those who had nothing. His throat was dry in the way that thirst came after day-time sleep, so he limped towards the stove, lifted the kettle to see if there was sufficient water, and put it down on the gas-ring, which he ignited with a match. *It was to be expected,* he thought, as he stood back, considering, again, the substances he'd employed earlier, endeavouring to be as dexterous as he had been in the past, lest he make a mistake. Of course, he had cleaned his laboratory, such as it was, but you never could be too careful. There was a right way to do things, and in his work, he did things as they should be done. He stuck to the rules.

He waited for the kettle to come to the boil, then poured the scalding liquid into the mush of soggy leaves left in the pot from the morning's tea. With the weak but hot brew in hand, he sat at the table and pulled his diary towards him. He sipped the tea, put the chipped cup to one side and opened the book to a clean page.

I am not heard. I am not taken seriously. I thought the Dobbs woman might believe me, if she were summoned. I saw the police go to her premises, so I know they have the letter.

He paused, then began writing again.

There was concern in her eyes when she walked towards Ian. Not pity, not disgust, and she did not cross to the other side of the road to escape the futility of him. She showed

49

He tapped the pencil on the table, then flinched at the sound.

She showed care. That is all I have asked for, these many years, that people are concerned, and that in their actions they demonstrate care. It occurred to me that the woman did not wait for someone else to approach Ian. She did not ignore him. She walked towards him without looking in another direction. I noticed that. I have come to notice that people do not look at the Ians of this world, but instead turn their heads here and there.

The man paused and rubbed his hand across his chest, then took several breaths. Not deep breaths, because the air would scald his lungs with its coldness, which in turn would cause him to cough. And if he coughed, he might not stop and then the blood would come. He tempered the urge to gag, calmed his body, then began writing once more.

Oh, stupid boy. He should have listened to me, he would not have had to wait long, not now, not now when I have them almost where I want them. 'Cry havoc and let slip the dogs of war.' Yes, let them slip, poor unwanted beasts.

Maisie paid the taxi-cab driver and dashed across the square just as Stratton's Invicta pulled up outside her office.

'Blast!' She had wanted to be alone for a while to consider the meeting with Dr Lawrence before having to go back to Scotland Yard and another encounter with MacFarlane.

'Ready?' said Stratton, as she approached the vehicle.

'Yes – and no. I would have liked more time before being called to report on my activities today.'

'I agree, but let's face it, at least we know which side you're on.'

Maisie rolled her eyes and shook her head. 'I am really growing tired of this innuendo due to the fact that my name was mentioned in the letter. MacFarlane has questioned me and indicated his trust in me. I have told you all that I believe the threats should be taken seriously, so I would be obliged if you — and Colm Darby or anyone else who chooses to — would just cease baiting me. You know which side I'm on.'

Stratton was taken aback by the strength of Maisie's response. 'I apologize if I offended you, Miss Dobbs. My comment was meant to be taken lightly, given that we find ourselves in a troubling situation — I don't know about you, but I hardly made any headway today.'

'I have had better days,' Maisie conceded, sighing. 'So I'm sorry if I was quick on the defensive. Mind you, I've chipped away at one avenue that might be promising — the possibility that the suicide was a soldier suffering from some level of traumatic neurosis.'

Stratton shook his head. 'I can't believe we've been unable to give a name to the dead man, unable to identify him. We've talked to the shopkeepers, residents — no one knows him, and he's not a regular.'

'Known unto God.' Maisie spoke the words softly, as she saw the man in her mind's eye again.

'I beg your pardon?'

'Oh, I'm sorry, Inspector. I said, "Known unto God". That's what it says on the new gravestones for unidentified soldiers buried in France, "A Soldier of the Great War, Known unto God".'

'Well, we'd better know something soon, or MacFarlane will be in high dudgeon.'

'I can imagine.'

'Oh, for pity's sake! Anyone would think we'd all just come in off the beat. Two days and we still don't know that poor bugger's name.' MacFarlane made no concessions to the fact that there was a woman in the room, and gave weight to his voice with a thump on the table with his right hand.

Maisie did not flinch, though Stratton moved on his chair in a way that revealed his discomfort. *He'd better get used to this if he wants to work with MacFarlane by spring,* thought Maisie.

'Miss Dobbs, perhaps you could enlighten me as to your activities this afternoon?'

'Of course, Detective Chief Superintendent MacFarlane.'

MacFarlane raised an eyebrow as she came to her feet and pulled out a roll of wallpaper and several tacks from her document case. She unfurled the paper, held it to the wall and proceeded to pin the paper in place.

'If I'd wanted a decorator, I might have called one in, Miss Dobbs.'

'Bear with me, please.' She reached into her case and removed several thick wax crayons, keeping one and placing the others on the table, then turned her attention to the men. 'My assistant and I use this as one of several means to follow developments in a case. It provides a map, if you will, of our progress, and no thought, idea or speculative hunch is ever considered too foolhardy or insignificant to record. We add to it as we proceed and it has proved useful in helping us to identify links, clues and opportunities that might not otherwise have been visible with the usual linear note-taking.'

'We tend to prefer facts.'

'This may sound contradictory,' said Maisie, 'but I do not think we have the time to entertain only firm facts – we have to broaden our canvas, in the short term at least.'

MacFarlane acquiesced. 'Continue broadening the canvas, Miss Dobbs.'

Maisie paused, looking at each man in turn. If she was to work as part of a crew rather than alone, she would ensure that she was not only listened to, but heard. And she did not care to be under surveillance.

'Given our speculation that the Charlotte Street suicide was a soldier with rather serious wounds, I—'

'Serious?' queried MacFarlane. 'He obviously walked to the place where he died. Can that be called serious?'

'Sir, as we believe, the man had an amputation and was also probably lame in his other leg, plus he might well have suffered exposure to chlorine or mustard gas. To say nothing of war trauma. I would say those wounds constitute "serious". I would add, further, that in becoming used to seeing those who have suffered in the war, we have also become somewhat immune to their plight. As we now know, contrary to the belief of military superiors, it takes more than fresh air and a week in the country to cure a man before we pack him off again into battle or, in this case, the skirmish of everyday society.'

'Point taken. Go on, Miss Dobbs.'

'Thank you.' Maisie began writing on the strip of wallpaper. 'So, I called on Dr Anthony Lawrence, one of the country's leading experts in the care of those who remain sufficiently unstable as to warrant remaining in hospital care.'

'Is that a nice way of saying "locked up"?'

'Having been a nurse in a secure hospital and caring for men with shell–shock, I try to retain a level of respect, Detective Chief Superintendent. But yes, they are locked up. They require a degree of supervision that is not to be found in the home – if, of course, there is a home to go to. Now then, back to my meeting with Dr Lawrence – I wanted to discover more about the habits of those who have been released. In short, I wanted to know if there was something about either the man in Charlotte Street or the letter-writer that would indicate they had been released from a hospital recently, and were perhaps feeling abandoned, at sea, so to speak. I confess, it was a stab in the dark, but I had to start somewhere.'

'We're all stabbing in the dark.' MacFarlane reached for a red wax crayon from the jar on the table and began to twirl it around in his fingers, as if it were a baton. 'And your stab was as good as any. Did you come away with anything?'

Maisie shook her head. 'Precious little, to tell you the truth. Dr Lawrence made the point that the number of men so afflicted is far beyond official tallies. In addition, regression following release from hospital could happen at any time – one month, one year, five years.'

'So what's your next move?'

'I'm not sure. However, I would appreciate it if I could report back to you in a less regimented fashion. Coming back here has deprived me of valuable time. My schedule is not prescriptive. Might I instead telephone Detective Inspector Stratton at a given time each day?'

MacFarlane looked at the other men. 'Richard? Colm?'

Both nodded their accord.

'Right you are, Miss Dobbs.'

Maisie thanked the men and returned to her seat. She had at least skirted the question of her next move, though she realized that MacFarlane might address the question again. In the meantime, she would do all she could to keep her next moves to herself. She might be one of a team, but she also knew she made greater headway when left to her own devices and following her own direction along the way.

Stratton was next. Taking up a wide black crayon he turned to the wallpaper. 'I feel like a teacher at the blackboard.'

'Don't tempt me.' MacFarlane grinned, then waved his hand for Stratton to continue.

'Very straightforward – continued questioning of shop-keepers along Charlotte Street, working back to Oxford Street, though we were hampered by the shops not being open today, so we had to locate proprietors and so forth. We're hoping to retrace the dead man's movements. Of course, we have to entertain the possibility that these two events have no relationship one to the other, in which case, all we will find, eventually, is the deceased's name.'

'Anything else?'

'We've located a woman who works at Bourne and Hollingsworth, who says she saw a man bearing the deceased's description alighting from the number thirty-six bus. She travels in from Camberwell and says she always sits in the same place close to the door and cannot remember him getting on the bus, so he must have got on anywhere from, say, Lewisham to Camberwell. We'll have men at bus stops along the number thirty-six route on Monday, at a time coinciding with the commuting habits of the woman. We'll question people along the way to see if anyone recalls seeing the man on Christmas Eve.'

Maisie cleared her throat, then spoke directly to MacFarlane. 'The man who made the threat is expecting a response first thing tomorrow morning. We seem to have forgotten that the threat stands. Will there be some announcement from the Home Office, perhaps on the wireless, by way of placating this person? Or are we waiting to see whether he is serious?'

'I'm sorry to say that, given our lack of headway, Miss Dobbs, we are presently in a wait-and-see situation.'

'I don't think we'll be waiting long.'

'Aye, I think you're right, as much as I hope you're wrong.' He sighed, then motioned to Stratton. 'See that Miss Dobbs is escorted home, Stratton. And settle upon a time to speak to each other tomorrow. I know it's a Sunday, but I can't see the PM making any offers as a result of the letter, so we'll still be on the case, come what may. The PM, by the way, has cut short the festive season with his family, and returned from Chequers.' He turned to Maisie. 'Do not rule out the possibility that we may have to convene here as a matter of urgency at any time over the next couple of days. In the meantime, you are on your own, but you are on our clock.'

Maisie held out her hand to MacFarlane. 'I'll be in touch, Detective Chief Superintendent.'

— ❦ —

Stratton escorted Maisie home in the Invicta. When the vehicle pulled up yards from the main entrance to the block of flats in Pimlico, Maisie turned to Stratton.

'I can walk from here, Inspector.'

'Are you sure?'

'The main door is just along this path, so if you wish, you can sit here to ensure I go in without being accosted.'

'I'll do that.' Stratton opened the door and stepped from the vehicle, then held out his hand to assist Maisie. 'And let's not forget your luggage,' he added, reaching back into the motor car.

'Thank you, Inspector.' Maisie took the brown leather suitcase. 'May I suggest I telephone your office at Scotland Yard tomorrow — certainly it will not be before six o'clock in the evening.'

'And at what time should I send out the cavalry, if I do not have word from you?'

'You'll hear by eight, Inspector — how does that sound?'

'Perfectly acceptable. May I ask what your next move will be?'

Maisie began to turn towards the modern building with glass doors leading to the flats within. 'To be perfectly honest with you, I'm not sure yet. But I know it will involve as much speculation as detection.'

'I'll be out with my men knocking on doors between Lewisham and Camberwell tomorrow — and I'll be in touch if there's news.'

Maisie bid goodbye, waving from inside the small foyer before entering her flat. The radiators had been left on low, yet she could still see her breath condense in the air before her. She was tired and wanted nothing more than to go to bed, so without removing her coat, she took her suitcase into the bedroom and then went into the kitchen to put on the kettle for a hot water bottle.

Once settled under the covers, sleep did not come as she had hoped, and instead Maisie lay awake listening to the sounds of the night. Foghorns up and down the river, a motor car in the distance. It was a quiet night, a Boxing Day night. Soon the year would be done, soon it would be 1932. And as she edged her way into sleep, Maisie wondered if there would be any developments in the case, come morning. Another letter, perhaps? Or would the threat be revealed as a hoax, with no more said and her involvement with MacFarlane and Special Branch at an end? But as she shivered, despite the soothing hot water bottle held close, she had a distinct feeling that there would be more news on the morrow, and it would not be good.

27th December 1931

Billy was at his desk when Maisie arrived at the office the following morning. She was surprised to see him, and could not help but notice that he seemed even more drained than he had the day before.

'Billy, what are you doing here on a Sunday? You don't have to give up your Sunday just because I'm working on an urgent case.'

'Well, I thought you might need a hand, and what with one thing and another . . .' He placed some papers in a folder, and shrugged.

Maisie thought it best not to press the point, and suspected that the situation at home might have deteriorated even more. She began talking about the case while removing her coat, hat and gloves.

'Billy, do you remember the coster who came to my aid in Charlotte Street on Christmas Eve?'

'I could recognize him in a crowd, if that's what you mean. Don't know the man's name – I was too worried about you, Miss, to tell you the truth. Mind you, I reckon I could find him, if that's what you want.'

'Yes, that's exactly what I want. He may have seen the dead man before, know who he is, or at least have some nugget of information for us.'

'Come to think of it, when I went back to find your document case, I don't recall seeing him again. Mind you, the police were moving people on, and he did say something about getting his horse out of there, that she was good and solid, but he didn't want to push it because even though she'd not bolted when the bomb went off, she was on her toes and a bit skittish.'

'Do you think there will be anyone down at the market this

57

morning? I know it's a Sunday, but there's sometimes someone around, a caretaker or watchman, someone who might know the man we're looking for.' She sat down behind her desk.

'Tell you what, I'll nip down and have a look around. As you say, there might be a caretaker or someone like that. Could even be a copper on the beat who can put a name to the face, if you know what I mean.'

Billy turned to gather his overcoat from the hook behind the door, continuing the conversation as he went. 'I reckon I'll be back by twelve, then get on with that Barker case. Will you be here, Miss?'

'Probably not. I have a distinct feeling that I'll be talking to MacFarlane today – he's the Special Branch chappie I told you about. But in the meantime, I think I'm going to have to engage in speculation simply to get some names in the hat of people who might have sent the threatening letter.'

'How will you do that?'

'By coming up with a template of the kind of person who would do such a thing – if they are serious. And we've assumed some link to the Charlotte Street suicide, as you know.'

'Why is that, Miss? Why do you think they're connected?'

'That's a good question, Billy – and it comes down to me. The letter mentioned me by name, and the fact that it came hot on the heels of my being seen to approach a man who then killed himself in a very visible manner, as if to make some sort of point, has drawn the two together.'

'Makes sense,' Billy continued as he wound a scarf around his neck. 'So what kind of person do you think he is?'

'That he has made a threat at all indicates a level of disengagement with everyday life. He's also drawn attention to the plight of old soldiers and wants to see something done about their situation. We know there are so many still suffering with their war wounds at a time when a job is hard to find for those sound in mind and body, but not everyone will be pressed to make a threat in such a way.'

'You see that on the streets, Miss, men limping from one line to another waiting for work, but I reckon most people just moan to their mates or their missus, or they join one of them associations, you know, to try to get something changed.'

'But this suffering has been going on for some years, yet this person has only just made his move. Of course, he could have been simmering for a long while, but at the same time I am going to stick my neck out and assume – at this stage, in any case – that the person we are seeking is a man who has either lost the support of a family or was released from an institution in the past two years. Frankly, if it's the former, it makes the job nigh on impossible, but if it's the latter, I might at least be able to get hold of some names.'

'Still looking at a lot of people, though.'

'I'll narrow it down to London – Dr Lawrence gave me enough information to suggest that there is cause for a man to linger in the region of the hospital, unless he has a home to go to in another area.' Maisie paused, slipping the cap of her fountain pen on and off as she considered her plan for the day. 'The truth is, Billy, that if the man does carry out his threat, if there is an "or else", it might give us more information to work with. And I have avoided coming back to the fact that he mentioned me by name. Why? How does he know me?'

'Do you think he might be a danger to you, because if that's the case—'

Maisie looked at Billy, who stood in front of her desk as if wavering between leaving her alone and remaining with her. She leaned back in her chair.

'I didn't want to say anything, but on the day of the suicide, as we were leaving Charlotte Street with Detective Inspector Stratton, I had a distinct feeling that I was being watched.'

Billy leaned forward. 'And I didn't want to say anything either, Miss, but I kept looking back, something was making me shudder. I put it down to the noise, you know, reminding me of being back there, in the war, but it felt right strange, make no mistake.'

'I have to entertain the possibility that we were followed back to the square, and that I may have been followed since. And there's something else.'

'What's that, Miss?'

'People in this situation, people who make threats, or carry them out, have also been known to harbour a desire to be seen, to be apprehended. They want to be caught so that they can be heard. There's something about that attention.'

'Not another one hiding in plain sight, Miss. We seem to get our share of those, don't we?'

'I don't know if he's in plain sight, but he may be closer than we think. In the meantime, I am going to prepare my template and then see if I can fill it with a few names.'

'And I'll be off down to the market.'

'Keep your eyes and ears sharp, won't you?'

Maisie worked on after Billy left. She had deliberately not asked about Doreen. If she enquired each day, it might give the impression that she was interfering in the family's domestic affairs. Even though she had come to know the Beales well and bore a great affection for them, on this occasion Billy's pride made it difficult to reach out a helping hand. It seemed to her that, in his manner, Billy seemed to think she had done enough for them already. Nonetheless, she worried about them, and particularly about Doreen's melancholia, which she realized was having an untoward effect on the children. Maisie knew only too well that the path of grief could not be scripted and was one taken alone, even if one grieved with family.

At half past eleven the telephone rang, and before Maisie could give the number, Billy began speaking.

'Miss, I don't know if this is important, I mean, I don't think the police know about this, but it seemed a bit funny to me.'

'What's that, Billy?'

'I was having a bit of a chat with this bloke I know who

works down here at the market. Talk about having a stroke of luck – turns out he had a bit of a row with the wife and came over to the market for some peace and quiet, that's how I came to get talking to him. Anyway, his son works down at Battersea Dogs and Cats Home, a bit of a job on the side. Turns out that when he goes in to feed them this morning, in this one section six of the dogs were dead. He said he'd never seen anything like it – this stuff like beaten egg whites coming from their mouths, and their eyes popping out of their heads. They'd died gasping for air and choking on their own blood. Terrible sight it was for the poor young fella.'

'What's happened since, do you know?'

'Apparently, they've got the vet in there today looking at the bodies, just in case it's a disease that spreads. But when he told me about it, you know what it put me in mind of?'

Maisie felt her body shudder with cold. 'I know what you're going to say, Billy – chlorine gas.'

'I knew you'd know. You'd've seen it, eh? Chlorine gas.'

'Stay right where you are – I'll pick you up at Covent Garden Tube in twenty minutes. We'll go straight to Battersea and see if we can talk to anyone there. I want to find out how someone might get in after they're closed – and if they were open on Boxing Day. They might have been – there always seem to be more strays on the street at this time of year.'

'If it is what we think it is, that'd be terrible, wouldn't it? I mean, not just for the dogs, but because it means that someone can do this sort of thing. It could be people next, couldn't it?'

'I know.'

'Oh, and Miss—'

'Yes?'

'The coster – name of Bert Shorter. Got the name of the pub where he drinks, down the Old Kent Road.'

'Good work. Now then – I'm on my way. See you at the Tube, on the Long Acre side.'

5

'Miss Dobbs and Mr Beale?' The smell of disinfectant and bleach wafted out of the room where surgical procedures were performed, as the veterinary surgeon closed the door behind him, still clutching a towel with which he continued to wipe his hands.

'Yes, thank you for seeing us, Mr Hodges,' said Maisie.

'I can't think why you might be interested in our six deceased dogs.' He threw the towel into a basket at the side of the door.

Maisie stepped forward. 'We heard that there were untoward symptoms prior to death, and – in confidence – given the nature of my work, I was interested, from a purely professional standpoint, you understand, as I explained to the administration clerk. The symptoms seem to mimic a condition I've seen before, so I was curious—'

'That's interesting, because they mimic something I've seen before. I was in the Royal Veterinary Corps during the war and one of the most terrible things I ever encountered was the effect of poisonous gas on both man and beast. In terms of canine sickness, I just can't imagine what disease or virus would mimic those markers for chlorine gas.'

'Then that's what you're looking at – swollen lungs, fluid, the albumen-like saliva and severe blistering?'

'That's it.'

'May I see a specimen, Mr Hodges?'

'Well, it's not regular, but . . .' he faltered, rubbing his chin. 'Oh, all right. I understand you've just made a nice contribution to our establishment here, so I should say it would be in order for you to come in.'

'I'll stay here, Miss, if you don't mind.'

'That's all right, Billy.' Maisie turned to the veterinary surgeon. 'Shall we?'

The spaniel-like mongrel of a dog lay on the cold metal operating table, its chest open to reveal the viscera. The head lay to one side and, crusted around blistered lips, a foamy substance had dribbled from the carcass to the table. The veterinary surgeon drew Maisie's attention to the lungs, pointing with a scalpel.

'I don't know how familiar you are with the physiology of the average canine, but the lungs here are swollen to about four times the normal size, an expansion due to the intense pressure of fluid building up as a response to inflammation and blistering. The dog was doing its damnedest to suck in air and stay alive. Now, see here' – he indicated where the incision extended to the base of the throat – 'the blistering is closing off the windpipe.'

'Just as it did with soldiers in the war.' She looked up at Hodges. 'I was a nurse in France, so I've seen my fair share of gas cases.'

'Yes, of course, you would have.' He set down the scalpel, pulled on a pair of rubber gloves, lifted the animal's head with one hand, and pulled out the tongue with the other. 'And here's the blistering again – froth and pus-filled.' With gentle respect he rested the head on the table once more, stroked an ear, then walked to a sink to remove the gloves and wash his hands, leaning forward and lathering the soap to cleanse every crevice in his skin. 'I just wish I knew what had caused it. Never seen anything like it, not the usual sort of thing we come across here – and we have some poorly animals in this establishment. No, this is not your usual kettle of fish.'

'I realize this question might elicit some concern, which is why I have taken care to ensure your confidentiality. Can you test to confirm exposure to gas?'

'To tell you the truth, in some ways, I don't need to – at the moment I'm trying to find some evidence to indicate it wasn't, because my first thought was, "Bloody hell, they've been gassed!" Then I pulled myself together and began searching for another cause, because I can think of no good reason why anyone would want to gas a poor innocent creature, and how would they gain access?' Hodges sighed. 'But the truth is that I *know* this has been caused by chlorine gas and, yes, though I can test to corroborate my suspicions, I am confident of the outcome.'

Maisie nodded. 'But you're right, you must confirm before you reach a conclusion.'

'And who would do this? Who would take leave of his senses and punish an animal in this way – especially with a weapon of war – and a particularly nasty one at that. This is a place where abandoned dogs and cats are supposed to find shelter and, we hope, a good home, eventually.' Hodges seemed thoughtful for a moment as he looked at the dog splayed out on the table. 'The sad thing is that so many of our dogs are enlisted for military purposes. A good many served in the last war, you know, carrying messages, first-aid packs, patrolling, and generally keeping up morale. I'd love to get my hands on whoever's responsible.'

Maisie looked up at the veterinary surgeon, the pained expression revealed in the lines around his eyes, and touched him on the sleeve. 'Don't worry, I'll do that for you. I'll find out who did this. It's best to do all you can not to let news of these deaths travel too far, and in the meantime continue with your tests. I hope you don't mind me asking if, just for now, you wouldn't mind making up an ailment that would result in similar symptoms.'

'Of course, I can see your point. I should probably tell the police,' said Hodges as he pulled a sheet across the spaniel's carcass.

'I'll inform them, Mr Hodges. Although I generally work independently, I am currently seconded to Scotland Yard for a period of time.' She reached into her pocket and pulled out a card. 'Here's my card. You can reach me at this telephone number if you have any more observations you think might interest me, and if I am not there, you can send a postcard or telegram to my address. And please, remember that this must be held in tightest confidence.'

Hodges regarded Maisie once more, tapping the card on the edge of the table. 'If a man could do this to a dog, he might do this to a human being, mightn't he? Is that at the heart of your interest?'

'I should hope it doesn't come to that. Scotland Yard has some of its best detectives on this case, and no doubt you will be hearing from them in due course after I've made my report.' Maisie turned to leave. 'Keep this to yourself, Mr Hodges. London can be a desperate sort of place at the best of times – we don't want to make it more so.'

'Don't worry, I'll keep mum.'

—◦—

'Smelly old gaff, that,' said Billy as they left the dogs' home.

'Well, they do a good job there, and they do their best.'

'I must say, it's something I wonder about, you know, when there's so many people wanting for a good meal in this country and here they are, looking after dogs and cats.'

They walked along the street towards Maisie's motor car, both wearing winter coats, hats and scarves to keep the cold wind at bay. 'It may seem that way, I agree—' Maisie was about to go on, then checked herself. She wanted to say she believed that it was in the act of taking care of animals and showing respect for all life – especially when in need of support ourselves – that a certain dignity is sustained, a self-respect so often compromised in troubled times. But she knew it was not the time to voice such sentiments, especially to a man who walked through the slums of London to get to work each day, and who was himself so deeply troubled. She shrugged. 'Well, I suppose it comes down to a belief that people who care for animals are more likely to be compassionate towards their fellow human beings. Something like that.'

'Yeah, which doesn't say much for whoever killed them dogs, does it?'

'I'm not sure what it says, Billy.'

'I mean, I know you've always said that inside the villain is a victim, but sometimes I find that hard to swallow, y'know?'

Maisie nodded. 'I've only come across the truly evil on two occasions, while working for Dr Blanche. And there's something in the person's eyes, as if they were born with it, as if it were a crippling disease and not something caused as a result of experience.'

'You make me shiver, Miss.'

'It should make us all shiver. I would venture to say that there is no overcoming that sort of ill character.'

'But what about the rest, what about the others who do terrible things, how come they aren't evil? I mean, what caused them to be like that?'

Maisie shrugged and stopped for a moment. 'It's different in each case, but if you go back to the root, I would venture to say it has to do with care. Those people don't feel cared for, don't feel enfranchised. In many cases they are simply invisible. But that's only my opinion, not the last word on the matter.' She stamped her feet. 'Come on, let's get going. It's freezing!'

Maisie dropped Billy at Covent Garden Tube station once more. She instructed him to work on finding Bert Shorter, adding that she would see him at the office later. In the meantime, she planned to return to Fitzroy Square and place a telephone call to Stratton, and if he was not available, she would ask for MacFarlane. And she would telephone Maurice Blanche. Yes, she wanted to speak to Maurice now because she needed a door opened to a very locked establishment. She could think of no other place to discover how a civilian might procure chlorine gas – or, indeed, garner the skills to handle such a substance – than the place she had heard much about but never been near: Mulberry Point, the military testing laboratories for chemical weaponry, close to the village of Little Mulberry in Berkshire.

'Maurice?'

'Maisie – how lovely to hear from you. I am sorry you were not able to remain at Chelstone long enough to come and see me. Your father tells me that you were summoned by our friends at Scotland Yard early yesterday morning.'

'Yes, that's right. Christmas seems weeks ago already. I'll come over to the Dower House next time, I promise.'

'I will hold you to your word. Now then, I have a sense that you have not telephoned to speak of missing me during the festive season – what can I do for you?'

'Maurice, do you have any contacts at Mulberry Point?'

There was a moment's silence on the line.

'Their work is most secret, Maisie. And given the nature of that work, I am now concerned upon hearing of your need to speak to someone at the laboratories.'

'It is urgent, Maurice. I am in pursuit of – and I think it's fair to say this – a most volatile person, and one who has access to some of the more chilling weaponry.'

'Is there a threat to the general population?'

'Yes, in all honesty, I believe there is, though I cannot gauge the level of that threat.'

Maisie knew that, if she were with Maurice, she would see him reaching for his pipe and tapping it on the chimney breast alongside his favourite wingback chair. He would place the pipe in his lap, then with his free hand lean towards the pipe-stand again and lift his tobacco pouch. He continued to speak, even though, as she well knew, he was filling the bowl of his pipe, readying to light it as soon as the telephone call ended.

'Indeed. I see your dilemma. In that case, you should telephone the University of Oxford and speak to Professor John Gale. He's both a chemist and a physicist. He also has a relationship – yes, that's the best word to describe it – with Mulberry Point, and would keep counsel regarding your conversation. He was involved with the Special Brigades during the war.' Maurice cleared his throat. 'Following the first chlorine gas attacks by the

Germans, the military virtually plundered the universities of engineers and physicists, effectively requisitioning brains and research not only to find an antidote, but to develop their own weapons. Britain was woefully behind the enemy in terms of research at the time. John – we are old friends – also has links to Imperial Chemical Industries. As you know, they were founded about five or six years ago, to some extent on the back of our experiences with the use of chemicals on the battlefield.'

'Thank you, Maurice. May I use your name as an introduction to Professor Gale?'

'I will telephone him myself as soon as we are finished, so that he expects your call.'

'Thank you, again.'

'One more thing – do take care. If this man, whoever he is, has enough knowledge to use gas, he may go further. Take every precaution when close to suspects and wherever the man you are pursuing has left his mark. Keep your hands and arms covered, use a mask – as if you were back in the operating theatre, Maisie.'

'Not to worry, Maurice. I remember only too well the precautions we had to take. I'll be careful.'

———

'MacFarlane!' the voice was brusque, and Maisie imagined the Detective Chief Superintendent answering his telephone in haste while barking orders to a subordinate.

'This is Maisie Dobbs.'

'Ah, Miss Dobbs.' His tone softened. 'What have you got for me?'

'I believe it's something important, Detective Chief Superintendent – and I couldn't reach Detective Inspector Stratton.'

'Fire away.'

Maisie described the lead via Billy's contact, and her visit to Battersea Dogs and Cats Home. She recounted the discussion with Dr Hodges, and her own observations when confronted with the carcass of the deceased dog.

'And there's no other explanation for the dogs to have died in this way?'

'Dr Hodges is testing now, but he is convinced it's either chlorine gas or something similar. He was in the Royal Veterinary Corps in France, so he knows what he's seeing. And I've seen it too, when I was a nurse, though obviously I am not au fait with the insides of a dog.'

'Not "au fait", eh?'

Though Maisie shook her head at the hint of sarcasm, she sensed that it was spoken in jest, a gentle teasing, perhaps, to lessen the tension.

'And you've instructed Hodges not to speak of this to anyone.'

'I asked him to think up a dog's disease that has similar symptoms.'

'Good. Right then, I'll get down there straight away. No army of blue, just me and a sergeant in the first instance. Can you come to the Yard at six-ish?'

Maisie looked at the clock on the mantelpiece. 'Yes, though I have to place some telephone calls. I have the name of someone who can advise me further on the procurement of such chemicals. It might also help in identifying the type of person we're after.'

'We're after a wicked bastard, Maisie.'

Maisie was taken aback. Was he testing her with his language and his manner, trying to see whether she could be 'one of the boys', able to work with Special Branch? More to the point, would he have been so blunt with Maurice, who demanded and received the utmost regard from Scotland Yard?

She sighed. If she countered to protect her opinion, she might be seen as thin-skinned – yet she could not let the retort go without comment. 'You know, I am quite aware of the wickedness involved in the murder of innocents, but I think it's best if I reserve judgement on the perpetrator of this crime. If I jump to conclusions too soon, I might well blind myself to the right path when it's in front of me.'

'Well said, but don't forget, we could be dealing with the Irish, the Fascists – I don't trust that Mosley and his band of merry men – or it could be Bolshevik union infiltrators pushing their luck. You name it, and we've got it here, and along with the gangs, there's not one in the clans of malcontents that wouldn't string up his own grandmother for their cause. I'll expect you at six.' He ended the conversation without farewell, leaving Maisie looking at the telephone receiver.

'And good day to you too, Chief Superintendent,' said Maisie to the receiver's continuous dial tone, as she reached forward, depressed the bar on the black telephone for several seconds to disconnect the line, then lifted her hand and began to dial the professor's telephone number at home, given to her by Maurice.

'Professor Gale? My name is Maisie Dobbs . . . Oh, he has? I am so sorry to have to disturb you on a Sunday, but I wondered if I might drive up to Oxford tomorrow to see you – could you spare me an hour of your time, perhaps? . . . Eleven? Yes, perfect. I'll see you then. Thank you, Professor.'

Maisie did not want to discuss any aspect of her work with John Gale on an unsecured telephone line. She knew operators often eavesdropped on calls, flagging one another when a 'good one' came on the line, to which they would all plug in and listen. She was sure Maurice had a secure line, with telephone calls to his number routed via a special government exchange. And the lines to Scotland Yard, especially to MacFarlane's office, would have been subject to the same level of security. But a telephone conversation with a professor at Oxford would not have been safe, and the last thing they needed was the mass confusion brought about by panic. She had already seen, in her career, the terror that can be wrought by an epidemic of fear.

Maisie heard the front door close with a thud, followed by Billy's uneven footfall on the stairs.

'Afternoon, Miss.'

'Did you find Bert Shorter?'

'I found out where to find him, but he wasn't there. I hung around for a while, but he didn't turn up, so I thought I would come back here.'

Maisie looked at Billy as he took off his coat and went to his desk, where he began going through files and his daily list. She chewed the inside of her lip for a moment, wondering whether to broach the subject of Doreen's health, then decided that now was as good a time as any.

'How's Doreen, Billy? Will she be seeing the doctor?'

Billy sighed, shaking his head. 'I've got a confession, Miss.' He leaned forward, rested his elbows on the desk in front of him, and could not meet Maisie's eyes as he spoke. 'She first saw the doctor, you know, about how she was feeling and some of the things she was doing, a couple of months after we lost Lizzie. I saw that she was having trouble and I thought we should do something about it.'

'Oh, Billy, and you've been struggling all this time?'

'Well, it wasn't too bad when we got away to Kent, but as I've told you, as soon as we got back here, it all came rushing back again. And I blame myself, I do.'

'What do you mean?' Maisie pulled a chair across the floor so that she could sit in front of Billy's desk.

'Well, look at what she's had to put up with. First there's me hardly sleeping for years, getting up at night to go for a walk because if I closed my eyes I didn't like what I saw. Then because I was hurting – and you remember this – I took some of that white stuff to help me. I don't know what I was thinking, really I don't.'

'You can't blame yourself. There are so many men, so many families struggling as you have.'

'But then Lizzie died, and it tipped her – as I've told you already. So I broke into the Canada money to take her to the doctor, and now . . .' He pressed his lips together, as if he might himself break down.

'Now what? What's happened now?'

'I didn't want to say anything, because I didn't want to worry you.'

'Billy—'

'They came for her early this morning, with the ambulance.' He supported his head in his hands, and his voice cracked as he continued. 'Things got bad last night. I thought I'd make a cup of hot milk for Doreen, to help her sleep.' Billy breathed as if he had been running, and held his chest. 'I had the saucepan on the stove, the milk was coming to the boil, so I turned around to ask her if she wanted a bit of sugar in the drink – and there she was with the carving knife in her hand, holding it over her wrist. I tell you, Miss, she was just about to slice into her vein, and I nigh on cut myself trying to stop her.' He paused and pressed his lips together for some seconds, as if to stop himself breaking down in tears. 'I banged on the wall to the neighbour, and yelled for them to run for the doctor. I didn't say what it was, mind, but they ain't stupid. They know. Anyway, the doctor came, took one look at what'd been going on and said he had no choice but to commit her, especially as there were children to consider. He gave her an injection of something to knock her out, and said that if she kept on trying to hurt herself, she might go for them too. So, she's been committed. They've taken her to Wychett Hill, out near Epsom. She's been taken to the bleedin' nuthouse.'

'Oh, Billy, it must have been much worse at home than you've let on.'

'It's been bad, Miss. And she's got a temper on her now, I can tell you.'

'What about the children?'

'When we got home yesterday I sent them over to me mum's for the night, you know, to give Doreen a bit of a break. What with all the Christmas goings-on – you know how nippers can get. They're still there. And once she'd gone, the house was so quiet . . . and that's why I came over here to work. I'll go and get the boys from their nan's later.' He sighed, shaking his head. 'Part of me thinks she'll get the help she needs and be back with us in next to no time, and part of me wants to go down there, put my arms around her and bring her home now. But there again . . .'

'There again what?'

His voice cracked. 'There's a bit of me that's just relieved. I won't have to worry about her. Won't have to wonder if the boys've been fed, or if they've been sent to bed with nothing inside them. And there's something else.'

'What's that?'

'She's got to get well, because if she's not all right upstairs' – he tapped the side of his head – 'we won't get into Canada.'

Maisie sat back in her chair. 'Oh dear, of course.'

'You know, there's times I think we've copped more of a bad innings than we deserve, but then I look at what some other people have to look at in life. They've no work, they're still in pain with their war wounds, they haven't got pensions, and their kids are starving – and that's if they haven't lost one or two into the bargain.'

Maisie stood up and paced to the window. 'And they've sent her to Wychett Hill? Why wasn't she sent to the Clifton, where I used to work, or the Princess Victoria? The Clifton's closer, easier for you to visit – and it'd be much better for Doreen.'

'The doctor said it was something to do with who could take her, and the seriousness of her condition.' He shrugged. 'I mean, I don't know the difference. They're all asylums, as far as I'm concerned.'

Maisie began to explain. 'No, not quite. Right at the outset, the Clifton was designed to have a more welcoming aspect than the old asylums. The wards are lighter, there are rooms where people can get together to play games or read. They have an outpatient wing, so I would imagine that, following initial treatment, if she were there, Doreen could be released with regular check-up visits. They are far more modern, nothing like the old-fashioned asylums. And it's also a teaching hospital, so there are many new methods employed, plus it's in Camberwell, so it's not stuck out in the country and hard to get to. The patients don't feel as if they're being isolated away from civilization, from everything they know.'

'But she's in Wychett Hill now. I can't do anything about it.' Billy shook his head. 'I'm stuck, just as if me hands were tied behind me back. I just couldn't think straight. There was all this commotion, what with getting Doreen into the ambulance – I can't believe it's all happened, to tell you the truth.'

'I know someone at the Clifton who might help.' Maisie spoke as she walked over to the card file and pulled out a drawer. She began flicking through the cards. 'In fact, I should see her soon anyway, about this case. Let me make a telephone call and see what I can do.' She crossed the room to the telephone, and picked up the receiver. 'And I'll be in touch with Maurice – perhaps he'll be able to pull a string or two.'

'Miss, I feel awful, I mean, here I am again, in trouble and you're sorting it out.'

'We all have trouble at times.' Maisie held up a finger to indicate that her call was answered, and when Dr Elsbeth Masters was not available, she asked the secretary to let her know that she would call later.

Maisie replaced the receiver and sat down again opposite Billy. 'Look, you go on home now, spend some time with the boys this afternoon. You can see Bert Shorter tomorrow. We'll see if we can get Doreen into the Clifton. And then it won't be long before she's home, right as rain.'

Billy brightened, and thanked Maisie once more. He gathered his coat and hat, and with a wave left the office.

As soon as she heard the front door close, Maisie put her hands to her face and rubbed her eyes, pinching the top of her nose to fight fatigue. The bump on the back of her head still throbbed, yet she had much to accomplish before making her way to Scotland Yard and her next meeting with Special Branch. And more important than anything, now, was getting Doreen Beale out of an asylum with antiquated ways of dealing with its patients. Old ways that, under the guise of kindness, could kill, or drive an almost-sane person mad.

<hr />

Time and tide, time and tide. They wait for no man. Now another letter to Mr Home Secretary. And one to Mr Prime Minister, Mr This and Mr That. Perhaps I'll send one to Mr Robert Lewis MacFarlane, and even one to Miss Maisie Dobbs. Or perhaps not. Another rabbit down the hole, another mouse in the jar, another bird falling down. And will they listen now? Will they hear my voice — our voices? Voices, voices, voices. I am not one man, no, I am legion. And will they remember who we are, and what we are owed?

The man paused and held his head to one side, listening. He looked around to regard the silhouette negotiating the steps down to his door.

Here comes a candle to light you to bed, here comes . . . Croucher.

6

Maisie arrived at Special Branch headquarters at Scotland Yard and was shown directly to Robert MacFarlane's office. He was in the midst of a telephone conversation as she entered, but he waved her in and pointed to a chair. Maisie looked around the room while the call was completed, noticing that it was tidier than she might have imagined, with files and papers stacked in a neat pile, and a clean blotter on the desk. On the walls a series of framed photographs were evidence of a career in the police force, from a young policeman in uniform, to senior officer in an important department. In the middle of the gallery, a single photograph bore testimony to MacFarlane's war service, showing him in the uniform of a Scottish regiment.

'Beaumont Hamel, June the thirtieth, 1916.'

Maisie turned to face MacFarlane. Having finished his call, he had leaned forward in his chair and was making a notation on a piece of paper before placing it in a folder and turning to look at the photograph.

'Just a day before the worst day of my life.'

'Yes, I would imagine it was.'

'And in all my years in the force, the people I would really like to bang to rights are the men who thought taking on the enemy along seventeen miles of the Somme Valley was a good idea.'

Maisie nodded. 'You're talking about men who cannot be touched, Superintendent.'

'Och, aye, lass, I know. But it doesn't stop me thinking about it. I reckon there's more crooks over there in Westminster than there are lurking down the Mile End Road – but let that be between us, eh?'

'I didn't hear a thing.'

'Stratton and Darby should be here in a minute or two. I thought we could have a little chat, a bit of a conversation, about the Battersea deaths. Never thought I'd be interested in dog murder.'

'It could be just the beginning.'

'Aye, of something pretty bloody nasty, if you ask me.' He looked at her without moving for a second or two, then pressed his lips together before continuing. 'Stratton's not sure any more that this has to do with the fellow in Charlotte Street. He thinks it's a bit of a red herring.'

'If you recall—' Having spoken, Maisie wondered if she had chosen her words wisely – after all, the Chief Superintendent gave the impression that there was nothing he would fail to recall. 'The connection to Christmas Eve was drawn because my name was mentioned.'

MacFarlane sighed, signalling a level of exasperation, not with Maisie, but with progress on the case. 'Yes, and that might have thrown us off – have you thought of that?' He did not wait for an answer. 'I'm very familiar with your work, Miss Dobbs, and with some of the more public cases you've been engaged with, and you might just as easily be known – very well known, in fact – to members of the underworld, or, given your social contacts, to the likes of Oswald Mosley's followers.'

'I must point out that I am not at all acquainted with Mosley.'

'Oh, but you know people who are – he was seen at the home of Mr and Mrs Partridge, for example, and was known to be spouting his "come one, come all" rhetoric at a supper there, and I believe you were present on that occasion.'

'I have known Mrs Partridge since I was seventeen years of age. She worked tirelessly as an ambulance driver in the war, and I do not care to have her character besmirched because a certain man was under her roof. To set the record straight, yes, there was a supper. No, he was not invited, but came for drinks – prior to the guests sitting down – with people who wanted the Partridges to meet him. No, he did not stay. No, they didn't really care for him, because he hasn't been invited back. And finally, I was late because I was working, so by the time I arrived, Mosley had left, therefore we did not meet. I know him no better than you, Chief Superintendent.'

'I might know Tom Mosley very well.'

'If you know him as "Tom" and not "Oswald" then you probably do – so why do you suspect me of an alliance where there is none?'

MacFarlane shook his head. 'I've never spoken to him in my puff, but I know where he is, whom he meets, what he does, who works for him. I know about his women. But you're right, I have no reason to suspect you are at all involved with his followers.'

'Then why ask me?'

'Because I have to, because I don't know yet what I'm dealing with. We have a letter, you are mentioned in that letter, and when stated demands are not met – government works at its own pace, and hardly at all over Christmas – six dogs are murdered. And it comes to something when Special Branch gets into the stopping of wickedness to all creatures great and small – I'd rather leave that to the Royal Society for the Prevention of Cruelty to Animals. But the fact that chlorine gas was used to kill the beasts sends shivers up my spine, I can tell you. What, pray, is next?'

As if on cue, there was a sharp double rap at the door.

'Come!'

'Sir, message for you.' The young detective, in civvies, passed a sheet of paper to MacFarlane, who read the note and frowned.

'I'll need my motor car, Bridges, and be quick about it.' He stood up, and as he walked towards the coat-stand he turned to Maisie. 'Hope you've not any plans for going to a ceilidh this evening, Miss Dobbs. We've got work to do.'

'Another letter?'

'Yes, another letter. And with Colm Darby out with his contacts, and Stratton somewhere that doesn't happen to be here, you might as well join me.'

'Where are we going?'

'Number Ten Downing Street.'

'Oh, good lord!'

'No, I would say the Right Honorable Gentleman has never been that good, not with the mess this country's in, what with his shambles of a National Government.'

Maisie took up her document case and wrapped her scarf around her neck, taking her gloves from her coat pocket as MacFarlane opened the door for her. 'I am sure he speaks highly of you, too, Chief Superintendent.'

———

A single lamp illuminated the front door to Number Ten Downing Street as the police vehicle drew to a halt alongside the entrance. The uniformed driver and a plain-clothes man alighted first, opening the passenger doors for MacFarlane and Maisie only after they had checked the street and nodded to the constable at the door, who had replaced the usual night watchman on Christmas Eve. By the time they reached the door, it was open and they were ushered inside.

'Detective Chief Superintendent MacFarlane and . . .' The private secretary looked at Maisie, then at MacFarlane.

'Miss Dobbs, Psychologist and Investigator, is working for me on this case. I asked her to join us.'

'Very well. If you would come this way, the Prime Minister is already in the Cabinet Room with the Lord President of the Council, Mr Baldwin, and the Minister for Pensions, Mr Tryon. Gerald Urquhart from Military Intelligence Section Five is with us, as is the Commissioner of Police.'

'Yes, I know – he summoned me.'

'Good. Now then, here we are.'

Though well used to meetings with important clients, Maisie felt her heart race and her hands begin to shake. But just before they were shown into the Cabinet Room, she closed her eyes for a mere three seconds and imagined her father's garden at Chelstone. Years before, when she was a girl, her mentor, Maurice Blanche, had taken her to his own teacher and friend, Basil Khan, who instructed Maisie in the stilling of the mind. It was with Khan's guidance that she learned that through the art of bringing calm to everyday thought one could delve deeper into levels of knowledge that were available only to those for whom true silence held no fear. And it was Khan who taught her that, in those situations where one became unbalanced in thought due to fear or exhaustion, one only had to bring a picture into the mind's eye of a place where one had known peace. So Maisie saw her father's garden, his embracing smile, and his arms opened wide to hold her. And she was calm.

Having barely noticed her surroundings while being escorted to the Cabinet Room, she was able to look around as introductions were made. Upon first taking office in 1924, Ramsay MacDonald had been appalled at what he deemed a distinct lack of both bookcases and works of art in the Prime Minister's Downing Street residence. Now shelves of books flanked the fireplace, as well as racks of maps, so that when world affairs were under discussion, the relevant map could be pulled out and referred to. On this occasion, all present were quite familiar with the geography of London.

Once again MacFarlane introduced Maisie, who held out her hand to each man present and took theirs in a firm grasp. She thought the Prime Minister quite resembled photographs she had seen in the newspapers and she could see how his physical appearance might inspire all manner of caricatures. His grey hair waved out from a left parting, and it seemed that the dour Scot eschewed hair oil. His small eyes were partially obscured by round spectacles, and there were deep furrows between his brows. His moustache was thick and broad, and he demonstrated an eccentricity in his choice of clothing – a wing collar with a black tie, a long jacket that would have been more appropriate in an Edwardian drawing room, and a pocket watch with a long fob. He clenched a barely lit pipe between his teeth. Despite this, she admired him, for it was no secret that Britain's first Labour Prime Minister was the illegitimate son of a maidservant, who as a young man had taken it upon himself to continue his education after leaving school at the age of twelve.

Ramsay MacDonald turned and took his customary seat at the table, in front of the fireplace. The secretary indicated the company to be seated.

'Now, I have received a letter today – as has Mr Baldwin, as has Mr Tryon, each of us sent identical letters – to the effect that London will know a terror never before unleashed if certain demands are not met.' The secretary placed the letters on the table in front of Urquhart, MacFarlane, Robinson – the Police Commissioner – and Maisie Dobbs. Forgetting protocol, Maisie did not wait and was first to reach for the letter addressed to the Prime Minister. If MacFarlane brought her here, she meant to do her job.

MacFarlane looked at her and, though she could not be sure, she thought he might have winked. 'What do you think, Miss Dobbs?'

Maisie cleared her throat and turned to the Prime Minister. 'A letter-writer reveals much about himself in the manner of his script. That helps us to draw a picture of who he might be, where he might live, what his habits are. It helps us to narrow down the places where we might look. At first glance, the handwriting shows many of the markers noted by myself and Detective Inspector Darby when the first letter was received by the Home Secretary.' Maisie looked at Robinson. 'Sir, seeing as the three letters are identical in content, might it help if I read one aloud?'

He cleared his throat. 'Yes, of course, please continue, Miss Dobbs.' He glared at MacFarlane.

Maisie stood up so her words might carry without anyone straining to hear, and hoped that the shaking in her voice was not too obvious.

'You didn't listen, did you? You sat, fat, by your Christmas Day fires, with your turkey and plum pudding inside you, and you ignored my warning.'

Maisie looked up for a second, to see how the writer's words were being received, then she cleared her throat and went on.

'And while you ate and drank, there were people without. There are people on the streets and among them are men who gave legs, arms and minds for you. And now look at you – you who thought I was nothing, a nobody. Will you do that now? Will you, The Rt Honourable Prime Minister, do something about us all? Or you, Mr Minister of Pensions? And Mr Baldwin, how about you? Or will you scrap among yourselves for your power? I think you know what I can do, the power I wield. Or is the life of mere animals not worth a measure of your time? I will not allow those to suffer who have suffered enough already, but you know what I want and what I can do. I can be hell itself, unless my demands are met. I want every man who served to receive a full pension he can live on – wounded or not. That's where we will begin, Honourable Gentlemen. That is where we will begin. I hope you can come to your senses before another day has passed.'

Maisie placed the letter on the table, and sat down, smoothing her skirt as she took her place once more. She was relieved that she had chosen to wear her smart burgundy costume this morning, and not an older ensemble.

'Thank you, Miss Dobbs,' said MacDonald. He looked at the Commissioner and Urquhart, then MacFarlane. 'Gentlemen, your measure of the seriousness of this threat? Are the people of London at risk? When can I expect word that this man is behind bars, and what precautions will you be taking in the meantime?' He looked at his watch, then at his private secretary.

'Five minutes, Prime Minister.'

The Commissioner cleared his throat. 'I have been briefed by Detective Chief Superintendent MacFarlane that there is a medium risk, that you can expect word within twenty-four hours, and we will be increasing the number of men on the streets.'

Maisie raised her eyebrows.

'Can I have a word?' Baldwin leaned forward. His manner was easier than that of the Prime Minister, with more resonance to his voice. 'Thank you for the summation of your plans, Commissioner, but if I may address the Detective Chief Superintendent' – he looked straight at MacFarlane – 'what is medium risk and is twenty-four hours attainable? We're used to looking over our shoulders, but will I need a neck brace?'

'Sir, "medium risk" means we do not believe all of London will be flattened by midnight. However, we know already that this man has the means to cause some harm if he so chooses. Given what must be an amateur capability, damage – and let us be clear, we are talking about chemical weaponry – would be limited to about a quarter of a mile. And that's if it isn't a windy day when he takes it into his head to unleash his cocktails on a greater area than Battersea Dogs and Cats Home.' MacFarlane coughed and cleared his throat, paused for a second, and looked at Baldwin, then the Prime Minister. 'As to the matter of twenty-four hours, I would say that it is attainable. We are look-ing at the Irish, the Fascists, the possibility of a very disgruntled Bolshevik union man – or men. We're following recently released criminal elements, and of course we might have a lunatic on our hands.'

Feeling a dryness at the back of her tongue, Maisie held her hand to her mouth and coughed. She wondered whether such intimidating circumstances always compromised a speaker's voice, because the visitors to the Prime Minister's residence were either clearing their throats or coughing every time they spoke. 'If I might add a word—' She was aware of the men turning to look at her, and for a heartbeat it seemed as if the hands of time were turning through treacle, for their heads appeared to move so slowly and she could hear her own heartbeat throbbing in her ears. She took another deep breath. 'As we've been speaking, I have had an opportunity to glance at the letters – and they obviously bear greater inspection – however, the manner in which the script has been executed suggests to me that this man is more desperate than he was two days ago. I suspect he is in some pain, and the penmanship suggests he is cold, very cold. Physical deprivation will enhance his emotions, so I would say that we are on something of a knife edge in terms of the threat.'

The men looked at one another as MacDonald thanked Maisie for her summation of the situation, pushed back his chair, and addressed the group. 'I expect a report in twenty-four hours. I want to know that London is safe, that my Cabinet is at no risk of harm. Do what you have to do, Commissioner.'

Along with the other visitors, Maisie stood up as the Prime Minister left the room, followed by Baldwin and Tryon.

'Gentlemen.' The secretary stood by the door, his hand indicating the way, then he turned to lead the visitors from the building.

Maisie reached forward to gather the letters and was about to hand them to MacFarlane when Urquhart leaned over and attempted to grasp the collected papers.

'I'll take those, if you don't mind. Military Intelligence trumps the boys in blue.'

'Oh, but I'm sure—'

'Hang on to those, Miss Dobbs, we don't want the Funnies getting above themselves, do we?' said MacFarlane.

'Now look here, Robbie—'

'I think we'd better catch up with the others. I for one do not want to be locked in here for the night. Now, why don't you take one letter, Mr Urquhart, so that you can conduct your own tests.' Maisie handed Urquhart the top letter, placing two in her document case as she walked at a brisk clip towards the front door, which was being opened by the private secretary. MacFarlane and Urquhart were behind her.

With a dull thump the door closed at their heels and the three stepped on to the pavement at the same time as Robinson, already seated in his motor car, wound down the rear passenger window.

'I'll see you at the Yard, MacFarlane. Soon as you're back.' The window wound up again, and the driver pushed the vehicle into gear and drove away.

'Need a lift, Gerry?'

'Much obliged, Robbie.'

The Superintendent's motor car drew alongside and Urquhart opened the door, holding out his hand to steady Maisie as she stepped on the running board and into the vehicle. MacFarlane sat next to her, and Urquhart pulled down the extra passenger seat in front of them.

'I was surprised to see Miss Dobbs with you, Robbie – reckon that's why the boss wants to see you pronto?'

'I won't be answering that question, my man, especially in the presence of Miss Dobbs, who happens to be a most valuable member of my group.'

'Not on the force though, is she?'

'That's enough, Gerry.'

Maisie leaned forward to speak, thought better of it, and instead rested back on the seat. As MacFarlane had suggested, disagreements between Special Branch and Military Intelligence were sometimes unavoidable as they often tilled the same ground, and the last thing she wanted to do was to get in the middle. She wasn't sure why MacFarlane had taken her to Downing Street for what amounted to a 'heads will roll' meeting. It was clear the government would never bow to a threat. But she had seen the handwriting, the stains on the paper, and she knew she would spend a restless night. There was work to be done, and she would need to be in Oxford in the morning.

Maisie was surprised at having slept so well, given that she had arrived home late following what proved to be a heated meeting with Stratton, Darby and MacFarlane. The four had convened soon after the Chief Superintendent arrived back at Special Branch headquarters. She knew MacFarlane had been brought up short by his superiors, and was doubtless asked to explain why he had asked Maisie to accompany him to the meeting with the Prime Minister. It was a question she hoped to ask him herself, at an appropriate moment. What was clear was that the next twenty-four hours represented a race against the clock.

Twenty past six in the morning. Time to leave London. The air was damp, with a smog so thick she was glad to be travelling by train. Taking the Circle Line to Paddington, she came up from the Underground into the busy station, where a throng of passengers rushed back and forth, or lingered, clapping hands together to keep warm as they waited for departure announcements. Maisie bought her third-class ticket and walked towards the platform, clutching her document case with her left hand as she turned the clasp to secure her shoulder bag.

When she held out her ticket to the station guard, she glanced across and thought she saw Dr Anthony Lawrence on the neighbouring platform. She stopped to look again – after all, one gentleman waiting for a train can look much like another – but a train pulled in alongside the platform where the man was standing.

Maisie approached a guard. 'Excuse me—'

'Hurry up, Miss, can't keep people waiting.'

'I'm sorry – but could you tell me where that train is going?'

'The one just come in on platform six?'

'Yes.'

The guard pulled out his watch. 'That'll be the twenty minutes past to Penzance.'

'Thank you.'

As Maisie walked along the platform, the Oxford train chugged into the station, steam punching out sideways as the locomotive slowed to a stop at the buffers. She took a seat alongside the window, close to the heater, and settled in for her journey, soon so deep in thought that she held no awareness of the carriage filling, or of the guard's whistle and the lumbering side-to-side motion as the train pulled out of the station. She wondered where the doctor might be going on a working day. She knew the Penzance train stopped at stations in Berkshire and Wiltshire and then throughout the west of England on its way to Cornwall, and there were psychiatric hospitals in several places on the way, out in the country where men could be kept away from the noise and struggle of towns, cities and other conurbations. But really, even if it were Lawrence, it was nothing to do with her where he was going, was it?

The porter at St Edmund Hall escorted Maisie along a corridor of the medieval college, knocking on the door to John Gale's rooms and announcing the visitor before allowing her to enter.

'Miss Dobbs. Right on time, that's what I like. Can't bear people who are late, completely befuddles my day, especially as I've a lecture in an hour. Now come along, take a seat by the fire.'

John Gale was almost six feet tall and somewhat thin; his gown seemed to hang on his shoulders. His hair, silver grey and swept back, was longer than was fashionable and, Maisie thought, it might be likely that the business of getting a haircut was something that slipped his mind until the skin around his collar began to itch with chafing.

Maisie reached out to shake Gale's hand, then seated herself as instructed on a low slipper chair of red velvet set alongside a fire-place that could have benefited from a puff or two from the bellows. As if reading her mind, Gale knelt down in front of the fire and proceeded to blow on the smouldering embers to encourage a more active flame, then added more coal from the scuttle. He blew once or twice more, then came to his feet, taking the chair opposite her.

'There, that's better, soon have a roaring fire. I forget myself, you see – working on a paper for a meeting of physicists next week – and then I wonder why I'm cold. In any case, Maurice said you wanted to see me, that it had something to do with my work in the war.'

'Yes, that's right. I'm interested in the gases used in the war. I was a nurse, so I know the effects of various gases – chlorine, chlorine and phosgene, and of course mustard gas – but I want to understand how the government responded to the attacks in the first instance. I understand you worked at Mulberry Point, and wonder if you could enlighten me.'

'Not sure I should be talking about this, to tell you the truth. Mind you, it was a long time ago when I worked there full-time.'

'But there's still research in progress at Mulberry Point, isn't there?'

'Yes, of course. However, there's more organization at the lab-oratories now. In my day it was like a bit of a bun fight, to tell you the truth. We were scrambling to find antidotes, in the first instance, and . . . you know, perhaps I should start at the beginning.'

'Yes, please.'

At that moment there was a knock on the door and the porter entered bearing a tray with tea for two and a plate of biscuits. Gale thanked him, and Maisie offered to pour tea while he con-tinued his story.

'The first attacks – with chlorine gas – were like a cosh on the back of the head to the military, took them completely unawares. They had to scramble, and scramble fast, to provide protection for the soldiers, and to find an antidote. The wounds from the gas were terrible, as you know. Chlorine gas was just the beginning. Before you knew it, the military was crawling over every university in Britain, looking for the best and brightest physicists, chemists, biologists and engineers. They were effectively requisitioning people right, left and centre.'

'And you were one of them.'

'Yes. I was still teaching because I have the most dreadful flat feet, so was passed over for military service. But not this time, not when it came to a different sort of part to play.' Gale looked into the fire as he dipped a biscuit into his tea, biting off the end just as it was about to drop. 'I was drafted to join a special group who were sent straight to France. We were with doctors examining patients, we collected skin samples, cultures and what have you, and some of us returned home to the laboratories as soon as possible. The army took many of the best students, and for those who were left, this was their research. It was all a bit hit and miss, to tell you the truth.'

Maisie watched Gale as he spoke, his eyes now fixed on a coal that had just fallen from the grate and was rolling close to the edge of the fender. He did not reach for the tongs to pick up the still-hot coal, but kept staring at its ashen glow.

'I'd never seen anything like it. They'd taken over the casino in Le Touquet for the gas cases. It was hard to believe that the roulette wheels had been spinning just a year earlier, that men and women were laughing, playing blackjack and poker, placing their bets. Now all bets were off and the only thing you could hear was the wrenching sound of men screaming in pain as they died from their wounds, with gas-filled lungs, frothy and filled with a liquid that looked like the whites of eggs. Funny, I think the place was once called the Pleasure Pavilion, or something like that.'

'What did you do? What was your job?'

Gale shook his head as if the movement would banish the memories, and turned back to Maisie. 'Well, I'm no doctor, but along with other scientists, I was taking samples, as I said, and was questioning those who could speak. We were desperate to know what they saw, what they smelled, what were their first symptoms.' He sighed and placed his cup and saucer on the tray. 'It was the sort of thing that was never meant to happen. The Hague Declaration of 1899 clearly stipulated that poison gas was not to be used in a time of war, and there we were, groping in the dark for a solution, and the best advice we could come up with was to tell the men to hold urine-soaked cloths to the face when attacked by chlorine gas.'

Maisie glanced at the clock, and asked another question. 'Is that how you came to work at the War Department Experimental Ground at Mulberry Point?'

'Yes, that's it. The government bought three thousand or so acres of land, threw a fence around it and set us up in some huts. We had a gas chamber there, laboratories and various other facilities. And – between us – everyone who worked there, from the cleaning staff to the orderlies to the scientists and army personnel, we all became involved in the experiments. If you needed to run a test on a human being, you just called in one of the orderlies, or you tested on yourself. We had to get the job done, you see, there was no time to lose. And it may seem strange, but even with the daily tally of dead and missing in the papers, the press got wind of the fact that we'd used animals in our experiments and they kicked up a fuss. Not that we stopped, but you never knew how an antidote worked on a human being if you'd only ever used it on a dog, for example. Mind you, we wanted to test it on the dog before we moved on to the human, just in case.'

'And you worked on weapons too?'

'Can't have one without the other.'

Maisie was thoughtful. 'Professor Gale, how easy would it be for an amateur to handle gas?'

'Depends on the substance – the risk increases with the effects of the gas and with the level of volatility. However, generally speaking, I would say it would be very, very difficult. And with something such as mustard gas, well, it would be lunacy even to think about it. Simply being close to the body of a man killed by the gas can have you in suppurating blisters from stem to stern before you know it – in fact, I am sure you would have had to take precautions against such secondary wounds in the war.'

'Yes, I remember.' Maisie nodded. 'I understand you still work at the laboratories at Mulberry Point, and though I know your work must be subject to high levels of security, I wonder if you can tell me – and this has just occurred to me – how many people, do you think, took on this kind of work during the war? Tens? Hundreds? And are there many still at Mulberry Point who were there in 1918?'

'I'm still there on and off, for a start, and of course some of the old team are still in situ. But they're like me – it's not my main job, if you know what I mean. This is my work, I am an academic. However, if in the course of my work I can come to the aid of my country, so be it. As to your question, the military scoured the universities, so you are talking about Oxford, Cambridge, Bristol, Durham, Birmingham, London, Edinburgh, Glasgow – every single seat of higher learning and research. Some students didn't even know they were working for the war effort, but they were the best and brightest. Some were literally conscripted right there and then to join the Special Brigades, to spearhead our own chemical attacks over in France and Belgium. But yes, there were a fair number, and, of course, they're all scattered now.'

Maisie glanced at the clock again. 'Professor Gale, I have taken a good deal of your time, and I think you have a lecture in about ten minutes.'

Gale checked his fob-watch. 'Oh dear, thank you for reminding me. Yes, I must be off now. Time and tide wait for no man, eh?'

Maisie smiled and held out her hand. 'Thank you so much for helping me with my enquiries.'

Gale frowned. 'I'm not sure I understand why you are making such enquiries – though I trust my old friend Maurice Blanche.'

'And your trust is well placed. Goodbye, Professor Gale.' Having shaken hands in farewell, Maisie pulled on her gloves, waited as Gale opened the door for her, and said thank you again as she left the room.

<hr/>

Croucher came to see me. Croucher brought apples. He said a bit of fruit would do me good. He brought soup, bread, some cold meat, a packet of Brook Bond, so I can make myself a fresh pot of tea. And matches. He sat and talked for a bit, made me chuckle. Croucher's like that, always was. Makes you have a bit of a laugh to yourself. The sparrow reminded me of Croucher, chirpy little fellow, wiry, quick about his business. Yes, Croucher looks after me. He went out for a sack of coal and made up my fire, kept me warm, for a bit. A bit of this, bit of that, bit of coal, only ever a little bit for a bit of a man. Yes, Croucher's kind. Now he's gone, though, and I've got to get on. Nothing's come from the wireless, so it looks as if I'll have to keep my word.

The man set down his pencil in the middle of his journal, closed the book around it and secured them together with the string. Pushing the book aside, he cleared the table and shuffled across to the cupboard, where he opened the door and with both hands removed a large, empty aquarium. He placed it on the table, went back for the metal lid he'd fashioned to fit like a glove, snug and tight, then made his way towards the back of the flat. Stopping to cough, a phlegmy cough that caused him to thump his chest to clear congestion, he remained still for some seconds before opening a splintered door that led to the postage stamp of a back garden. Once outside he turned to the side and spat out the yellow, blood-threaded debris that had issued from his lungs, then walked in a deliberate manner along the path to a cage-like construction with mesh netting. Inside, birds had been captured, and as the man opened a door and reached in, the sparrows, blue-tits, robins, pigeons and starlings scattered and squawked. He winced at the sound, grabbed a butterfly net leaning against the side of the cage and an old sack, and one by one he removed the birds. Soon there was no furious chirruping, not even aggression between the more dominant birds and those they considered lesser, only their muffled movements as he carried the closed sack into the flat. With care he emptied the birds into the glass aquarium set up on the table, and secured his catch inside with a tight metal lid. He had to be careful, even more careful than last time. He couldn't afford a single mistake.

7

It was mid-afternoon by the time Maisie arrived back at her office in Fitzroy Square. Billy was already there, waiting for her.

'Any news, Billy?' asked Maisie, as she unwound her scarf and hung it over the top of her coat on the hook behind the door. She walked to her desk and took out the narrow wad of index cards she had used to take notes during the return journey from Oxford to London. 'Have you managed to locate Bert Shorter?'

Billy's chair scraped against the wooden floor beyond the carpet as he came to his feet. He approached her desk, his note-book in hand. 'Yes, I have, and it turns out Mr Shorter had seen the man in Charlotte Street before, but usually down in Soho Square. He said the man sat in the park, never with his cap out, but people would usually walk by and press a few coppers in his hand. Shorter told me he stopped to talk to him once, and that he was wounded in the war. He'd lost a leg and the other one wasn't much good. He thought the man might have had a small pension, but not much of a life, as far as Bert could make out.'

'Did he know his name?'

'That's the thing, he said he introduced himself to the man once, but didn't really catch his name in return – reckons it might have been Ian. He said he was in a pretty bad way with his lungs, and that every now and again he wouldn't be in his usual place for a month or so. Bert thought he might have been taken down to the coast, you know, like they do – I was taken once myself, when I got really bunged up in my chest.'

'Then he must be known, must have a connection to a doctor or a hospital – perhaps he's an outpatient somewhere.' Maisie rubbed her forehead. 'I wonder if they would have missed him yet, if he's a regular patient?' She looked up at Billy. 'Did Bert have any idea where he lived?'

'Remember, Bert was only surmising, so this is nothing definite, but he thought the man must've been local, perhaps living down in Soho – there's a lot of boarding houses down there. He probably had a pension, but I bet it didn't amount to much. And it sounds like he couldn't work, even if he could've found a job.'

'So, we've got a man who might be named Ian, who could be living in Soho, crippled by his war wounds. Anything else about him that Bert might have noticed?'

'He said he second-glanced him at first because he always had a book on him. Always reading.'

'Did he see him with anyone, ever?'

Billy nodded, licked his finger and turned over the pages of his notebook. 'Saw him with a man once. Small fellow, well dressed – but not in a toff way, more in a clean way, very correct, everything pressed. Bit like you might see a doorman at one of them hotels up near Hyde Park, when he's off duty and just leaving out the back door. The bloke was talking to him, ordinary, nothing strange, but went on his way when Bert came along with his horse and cart and Ian – or whatever his name is – waved at him.'

'Let's recap again. We're talking about a man who *might* be called Ian, who could live in Soho – or anywhere between, say, Old Compton Street and Soho Square. "Ian" suffered wounds to the legs and the respiratory system, and he liked to read. If he had a pension, it would not have been sufficient to cover the purchase of books, so he must have gone to a library. And if you remember, there was talk of him being on the number thirty-six bus from Lewisham. I think I might take a guess that that little piece of evidence has deflected us from narrowing down the search to find him and his place of domicile.'

Maisie looked around at the clock. 'Billy, I wonder how many lending libraries there are in Soho? Of course, Soho encompasses most of Charing Cross Road, so if we're on the right track, he might have a contact in one of the bookshops.'

'I think I know where there are two lending libraries.'

'Right, you go straight there. Describe "Ian" and see if you come up with anything. I'll go to Charing Cross Road and visit each bookshop. I'll meet you in the caff on Tottenham Court Road – you know the one, where they never say "I beg your pardon" before they pick up your cup and saucer to wipe the table – at about, oh, half past five?'

Billy nodded. 'Right you are, Miss.'

Starting at the top of Charing Cross Road, Maisie began to work her way down the street, going into each bookshop and engaging with the proprietor or assistant in a warm manner, before asking for a book recommended to her by her friend, Ian, who hadn't been well of late. In W. & G. Foyle, Ltd, Maisie consulted the most recent catalogues, and lingered for a few moments to peruse the Solar Radiation and Physical Culture catalogue, which featured a rowing machine for forty-nine shillings and sixpence, a sum that Maisie thought amounted to highway robbery. She shrugged and moved on, enquiring in each department before leaving the shop.

She had continued on her way down Charing Cross Road, and was about to lose faith in her plan – the thought crossed her mind that she was acquiring an almost encyclopedic knowledge of the street's antiquarian book trade – when she opened the door of Tinsley and Sons, Booksellers. The shop was ill lit and somewhat cluttered, with an overflow of books stacked upon every available surface and each step of a cast-iron spiral staircase situated at the back of the shop. A man of about forty-five years of age was at the top of a ladder dusting the shelves.

'Just browsing, or can I help you with something in particular?'

'Browsing, thank you very much. I was advised to come here by a friend.'

The man continued dusting, speaking as he went on with his task. 'Always pleased when people recommend us. What's your friend's name?'

'Ian, he—'

'Ian?' The man stopped dusting and began to climb down from his somewhat precarious perch. 'You know Ian? Wounded in the war – lost a leg and the other one's a bit gammy?'

Maisie nodded and cast her eyes down. 'I'm here, in part, to remember him.'

'Remember him? Is he all right? Haven't seen him since before Christmas, and he was a regular.'

'He's dead, Mr—'

'Tinsley. This is my shop.' He pulled up a chair for Maisie and one for himself, close to the pot-bellied stove that held court in the middle of the floor. 'What happened?'

'He took his own life, I'm afraid.'

'Oh, what a shame, what a terrible thing.' He shook his head. 'Mind you, I can't say the news comes as a surprise – after all, he was in such pain. Not least in his mind, I think. And reading helped, took him away from his everyday life – as it does for so many.'

'Yes, I think you're right.' Maisie took off her gloves as the chill outside left her bones. 'And he certainly loved your shop.'

'Well, I did what I could for him. I knew he couldn't afford much and he was such a voracious reader. I would lend him books, in return for some cataloguing, that sort of thing.' He leaned back to take a ledger from his desk. 'Here, you can see how many books he read in November alone.'

Maisie took the large, leather-bound book from Tinsley's hands and looked at the page indicated: Ian. She could barely read the last name, but thought it looked like Jennings. Flat 15a, Wellington Street, Kennington. A location close to the route of the number thirty-six bus as it made its way along Kennington Park Road.

97

'Was his surname Jennings?'

Tinsley took a pair of spectacles from a pocket in his knitted pullover. 'I must admit, I never really looked at the name – in fact, I trusted him, so I didn't check the books. Let me see – yes, he was up to date. Brought back the last one in early December. And that's why I was a bit surprised at his absence, because I can't imagine him without a book, though I am sure he used libraries. I mean, look at this, he must have been reading one book every two days, something like that.'

She ran her finger across the page. 'Until December, when he only read two books.'

'Yes, I've hardly seen him throughout the month, which is why I've been concerned. I thought I might go to his lodgings, but it seemed rather presumptuous to do so, and then of course December can be so busy.' He took back the ledger and placed it on the desk.

'Can you recall him saying anything after November that might have accounted for the absence?'

Tinsley removed his spectacles and returned them to his pocket. 'I seem to remember him saying he'd met an old colleague again, and they'd sort of struck up a friendship.'

'I've been away from London lately, so I've hardly seen Ian,' said Maisie. 'I wonder who the old colleague was?'

'He never mentioned the man's name, and I can't remember exactly what he said about him. I just thought Ian would come along again when he wanted a book, do some work for me, and we'd carry on as usual. He liked to discuss literature, and I was grateful for the company. It can get quiet sometimes.'

At that moment the doorbell sounded the arrival of a customer, and the man stood up. Maisie thanked him and, before he could say more, left the shop and made her way towards Tottenham Court Road.

'Miss, I reckon I've got it!' Billy was already at the café and waved as Maisie approached the table where he was seated.

She leaned forward and whispered, 'Ian Jennings?'

'Flat 15a, Wellington Street, Kennington,' added Billy. He stood up to go to the counter to buy two cups of tea. 'And I thought I was being dead clever. Got all his particulars from the Boots library – bit of a regular, he was. Took out a book or two a week.'

'And he read a book every two days or so from a shop on Charing Cross Road.'

'Blimey, he must've been a clever one.'

Maisie nodded. 'He was – and I'm gasping for that cuppa, Billy.'

───✦───

So as not to be late, Maisie ran from the Underground station to Special Branch headquarters at Scotland Yard, where she bumped into Stratton as she entered.

'Steady on there, people running in this place end up in the cells if they're not careful.'

'Sorry – I'm a bit late and didn't want to incur MacFarlane's wrath.'

'I doubt you'll do that, Miss Dobbs. Darby thinks that, as far as Robbie MacFarlane is concerned, you can do no wrong.'

Maisie stopped. 'What on earth do you mean?'

Stratton turned his wrist to consult his watch. 'I, however, *can* do wrong – come on, we'll be late.'

Together Maisie and Stratton made their way towards MacFarlane's office, only to find Colm Darby making notes on several sheets of paper.

'Darby.' Stratton nodded as they entered the room.

'Stratton, Miss Dobbs. Any luck today?'

Maisie was about to speak when the door opened with a thud against the wall, and MacFarlane entered the room. His face reminded Maisie of a storm-laden sky, dark and brooding, while

lines around his eyes spoke of the pressure to find a man who had
proved that he could and would kill to be heard.

'Stratton! What have you got for me?'

'Sir, our narks within Mosley's party are coming up with precious little, I'm afraid, though we do have evidence to support
the existence of an inner group who might be up to no good.'

'Can you infiltrate further?'

'I understand money talks. Oh, and apparently there is some
kind of recruiting meeting for those interested in the party, at a
church hall in Kilburn this evening. This inner circle will be in
attendance, and I understand they are a more militant strain.'

'Hmm.' MacFarlane took up a penknife set alongside a collection of pens and pencils on his desk, opened the blade, closed it
again, then opened it once more. He snapped it shut, set it down,
and looked at Darby. 'Colm? Anything?'

'It's quiet, guv, to be sure. I've got my informers, but the IRA
have had trouble regrouping lately. My only lead is a mere hairs-
breadth of information to the effect that there's something of a
move to recruit men who aren't all there upstairs, men who
might have recently been discharged from an institution, for
example. They offer them a sense of belonging, claim their loyalty, then set them off to do their dirty work. Apparently, the
theory is that someone who's not dealing with the whole deck,
if you know what I mean, can be easily directed, and won't have
the same qualms about killing as a sane person.'

Maisie cringed. The suggestion that the insane might be used
to kill had not occurred to her.

'And as to union sympathizers,' Darby continued, turning to
Stratton, 'again, there's a group within the Red Party of Britain,
real Bolsheviks, who could up the ante. Mind you, they've never
been known to keep quiet about who they are. In the meantime,
I've got someone on it.'

MacFarlane opened and closed the penknife again, and looked
to Maisie for an account of her progress.

'And I know the identity of the Christmas Eve suicide. I

discovered his name before coming over here.' Maisie was aware of the attention of all three men as she spoke. 'My assistant is paying a visit to his lodgings before going home this evening. If there is anything to report, he'll make a telephone call to this office. I would imagine we might hear from him soon.'

MacFarlane looked up. 'Name?'

'Ian Jennings. At least, that was the name given to a bookseller he befriended, and at a lending library in Soho – the man was an avid reader. According to the people who had made his acquaintance, he had lost one leg below the knee in the war, and the other leg was crippled with shrapnel wounds. Apparently, he also demonstrated symptoms associated with a gas poisoning.' Maisie scraped back her chair, pulled a selection of coloured wax crayons from her document case, and approached the case map, which was pinned to the wall. MacFarlane leaned back in his chair to watch her make notations, linking various pieces of evidence with red lines and a question mark above a stick figure she named 'the Gas-Man'.

'Ian Jennings began spending time with a friend – he might have been an old colleague – in December. Could this man be our letter-writer? Or could the friend be associated with either Mosley's group, the Irish, or the unions?' She turned to Darby. 'I agree with you – I think we can scale back any surveillance of the latter, though obviously we want to keep in touch with informers.' Looking across at Stratton, she continued, 'Jennings might have been recruited by the Fascists – certainly their rhetoric might resonate with a man living on the edge.'

At that moment the telephone rang.

'MacFarlane!' The Superintendent bellowed, his usually tempered brogue unleashed on the operator. He held out the receiver to Maisie. 'Your man.'

Maisie reached for the telephone. 'Billy?'

'Miss, I'm just leaving Kennington.'

'Right you are. Did you find anything?'

'The landlord lives in the house – old gaff, it is, split into about six rooms that he lets out. Bit grim. You could hold a cup to the walls and have enough water for tea in a minute.' He coughed. 'There's a right old pea-souper tonight, Miss.' He coughed again and she heard him thump his chest. 'Anyway, I talked to the landlord, slipped him a couple o' bob, and he led me upstairs to the room. Says that he was thinking of going in, but the rent's not due for a few days, and even though he hadn't seen Jennings since before Christmas, who was to say he wasn't coming and going? Mind you, I don't know how that poor man managed those stairs, even though he was only up one flight.' Billy coughed once more. 'So, he let me in and we both stood there, just staring, because the place looked like it had never been lived in. Neat as a pin, it was – apart from the mould, of course. But the bed had been stripped and the blankets folded, the furniture had all been wiped. You'd've thought that it was ready to be let out again – in fact, it probably is by now.'

'And you didn't find one thing, one scrap of paper, old photographs, anything?'

'Not until I looked behind a chest of drawers. Found a pamphlet there, about that bloke Mosley. Looked like it had fallen down the back, not hidden there on purpose.'

'Yes, it would appear so, from your description. The tidiness in the room gives me pause, though.'

'Very creepy, if you ask me.'

Maisie sighed. 'Right you are, Billy. You go home – and bring the pamphlet into the office tomorrow morning, please.'

'Miss—'

'Yes?' Maisie looked around at the three men, who were waiting for her to complete the call.

'I telephoned Wychett Hill, before I made the call to you. Turns out Doreen is resting – that's what they said – following a "procedure".'

'What sort of procedure? Did they say?'

'Well, I asked, and of course it don't mean a thing to me. They said something about her being out for the count, and that she'd been on insulin.'

'Insulin?' Maisie was aware of her raised voice, that the men were now all looking at her.

'Is that bad, Miss? I mean, she's never been a diabetic or anything, so I wondered . . .'

'No, don't worry. It was just me, a bit surprised, that's all – nothing for you to worry about. Look, I'll go back to the office – I should have a reply from the doctor I telephoned at the Clifton Hospital. I'll let you know tomorrow morning. Go home to your boys, Billy – is your mother with them?'

'Yes, Miss. Right then, see you tomorrow.'

Maisie passed the telephone receiver to MacFarlane, who placed it back on the cradle.

'Everything all right?' enquired Stratton.

'Um, yes . . . well, no, not with our Mr Jennings. Seems his premeditated suicide – or his departure, anyway – was thoroughly planned. His room looks as if no one ever lived there. I would bet that, if you sent in the boys to check for dabs, he'd have cleaned every surface and they'd come up with nothing. My assistant and the landlord made a thorough investigation of the small room, however, and they found one item of interest, which had slipped behind a chest of drawers – a pamphlet from Mosley's New Party.'

'Hmm – I still think the suicide has been a red herring in this investigation,' said MacFarlane. 'But I don't trust that Mosley. He's been hobnobbing with the likes of the Italian, Mussolini, and there's talk that he's thinking of setting up a Fascist Party here. There's a recipe for terror, if ever I came across it. Look, here's what I want – you and Stratton, go along to this meeting of nutcase Fascists tonight. Dress well, but not too well, look well-to-do without flaunting it, if you know what I mean. Look, listen and find out who's in this inner circle, and what they're doing. And there's something else I'd like you to look into, Miss Dobbs.'

'Yes?'

'There's a little coven of women who seem to have taken it upon themselves to agitate for women's pensions.'

'Yes, I know, sir. I've contributed to the cause. However, I take exception to the idea that they are a coven. Surely prejudice against women hasn't reached the point where we make accusations of witchcraft?'

'You've contributed to their cause?'

Maisie shrugged. 'Why should an unwed woman not receive a pension, when she pays the same contributions as a married man?'

'It's not as if . . .'

'Not as if what?'

'Well, anyway, we've heard word that there are agitators among their number who aren't prepared to wait – just as you'll find in any group. There's always those who splinter off because they think if they show how strong they are, they'll get what they want. There are factory girls in there following their leader, and I'll bet some of them have the know-how to handle those gases.'

'Sir, if I might make a bold statement, I think you're wrong, and we can't afford to have anyone following weak leads.'

'And I think it's one for you, Miss Dobbs, being a woman. Apparently the girls are meeting tomorrow at lunchtime. Please wheedle your way in – here's the address.' He handed a slip of paper to Maisie. 'And in the meantime, Stratton, I want the Mosley group investigated. And the unions, Colm.' He always referred to Colm by his Christian name, with due regard for their years worked together.

'But . . .' Maisie tried not to show her exasperation.

'You need to go to your office?'

'Yes.'

'Stratton, divert to Fitzroy Square, then to her flat. Miss Dobbs, you'll have just enough time to assume some wealthy sort of character while Stratton waits. You'll be brought back to your flat later. All right?'

'All right, sir,' echoed Stratton and Darby.

'Miss Dobbs?'

'Yes, that's all right, however, Superintendent, I—'

At that moment the meeting was interrupted by a single knock on the door. A detective sergeant entered the room, leaned towards MacFarlane and whispered in his ear. The Superintendent nodded and stood up as the messenger left the room. Reaching for his coat he turned to face Maisie, Stratton and Darby.

'I was due to bring the Commissioner up to date, per the Prime Minister's request, but the situation has just become more grave. A policeman in Hyde Park, close to Speakers' Corner, has reported finding some fifty or so birds, dead, on the path. I suspect this might be our man again, and if it is, then he has gone a step further. As you probably all know, chlorine gas did not kill birds in the war. But chlorine mixed with phosgene silenced birds across the Somme Valley. The situation is no longer medium risk, if you didn't know already. This man knows what he's doing. I expect another letter will be received soon. Now, get to work.' He left the room.

◆ ◆

Stratton remained in the Invicta while Maisie ran to her office, retrieving the post on the way. There was a card from Dr Elsbeth Masters. She expressed pleasure at hearing from Maisie and suggested she visit her at the Clifton Hospital the following day, indicating she would be available after one o'clock. Maisie hoped that Doreen could deal with the indignities of Wychett Hill until her release was secured. There was a greater cause for her concern since the telephone conversation with Billy. Many of the old therapies and treatments for depression and mental imbalances in women had been less than humane. Maisie had been appalled observing some of the faradism treatments – electric shock – as doctors tried to encourage traumatized patients to speak again or to lose the stammer that began when a young man saw his fellow soldiers blown up alongside him. But there were other kinds of shock, and insulin therapy had been used on women in mental institutions for many years. The patient was given excessive amounts of insulin so that the body began to break down under the pressure of toxic shock. It was thought that the shock would, in effect, startle the brain and lead to a resumption of normal behaviour. In Maisie's estimation it was barbaric, and the thought of Doreen Beale enduring such terror made her doubly convinced that she must find a way to have her discharged into more tolerable care as soon as possible. She had pinned her hopes on Dr Masters being able to provide a solution.

Until then, though, Maisie knew she had to endure the New Party meeting this evening. Later, while Stratton waited outside her flat in the Invicta, she dressed in a plain black skirt, her burgundy jacket, matching black hat with a burgundy ribbon, and black shoes. Dark clothes seemed to be the order of the day with Mosley's followers. Her hair had grown longer since the summer, and though it was still styled in a bob, it was less boyish, and in that regard followed fashion, though Maisie was not generally interested in such distractions.

Although she was not convinced that this avenue of investigation represented good use of her time, she could not avoid the possibility that the man who committed suicide might have attended one of the meetings. After all, she was the one maintaining that a link between the dead man and the threats could lead them to the door of a man who had already made good on his warnings that he would kill.

Stratton opened the door of the motor car as Maisie emerged from the block of flats. 'You think this is a complete waste of time, don't you, Miss Dobbs?' he said, as she reached the Invicta.

'I confess, I do. Even with the pamphlet found in Jennings' room, I think we're barking up the wrong tree, and we don't have much time to sniff out the right one. And, to be perfectly honest with you, I still wonder why I am involved at all.'

'You are successful in your investigations, and you've been consulted by the Yard, particularly given your association with Maurice Blanche. I would have thought you would be delighted to be taken seriously by MacFarlane. He's a maverick, to be sure, and – if you want my opinion – I believe he's brought you in to shake things up, to challenge the way we do things, to inspire new ways of looking at a given problem.'

'Then why does he appear to dismiss my ideas?'

'Because that's how he goes about his work. He likes us to keep asking questions. And I seem to remember you saying that a question has the most power before we rush to answer it, when it is still making us think, still testing us.'

'Yes, of course, I've said that many a time, and especially when I've been called in to lecture your new detectives. Touché, again, Detective Inspector Stratton.' Maisie wiped condensation from the inside of the window. 'I think we're here.'

The meeting place was a church hall constructed of grey granite. The entrance hall had a pitched roof, with carved eaves just visible through the smog. The front doors, shaped like those of the neighbouring church, were open, and two men flanked the entrance. Another man sat behind a desk situated at the back of the meeting room. Stratton gave their names as Mr and Mrs Hutchinson, and as they walked in, Maisie automatically linked her arm through his. Stratton smiled down at her, and she blushed, hoping he had not seen her reaction to an unfamiliar feeling that touched her. It was not that she harboured feelings for Stratton, but rather that she was reminded of a sense of belonging, one that she had not felt for some time, not since she ended her relationship with Andrew Dene – and even then, there was always a sense of detachment. She wondered if the death, just a few months ago, of her beloved Simon had perhaps released her in some way.

'Let's take these seats before someone else claims them.' Stratton pointed towards two available places at the end of a row of hard, straight-back wooden chairs. 'If we're seated at the back, and on the end of the row, we can make a quick departure before the end, if we so wish.'

'I take it you have other men here, should they be required?'

'Yes. They're ready if I give the signal to move on the leaders.'

Maisie nodded, and began to read the pamphlet handed to her as they entered the room. Following a message of welcome, the pamphlet outlined the New Party's manifesto, much of it based upon a document known as the 'Mosley Memorandum', which supported more power to the government and advocated a strong national policy to overcome the country's economic crisis. Though Mosley's party had not been as successful in the October general election as he might have hoped, the party was regrouping, and the wording of the pamphlet suggested a deeper engagement with the tenets of Fascism. Maisie closed the pamphlet. She had read enough.

As more people came into the church hall, Maisie looked around to survey the scene. Many of those attending the meeting were well turned out, and she thought they would be the target of requests for contributions. There were others, poorly dressed, with hollow cheeks and sunken eyes, people who wanted for a good meal and a warm room. She turned back and was just about to comment to Stratton on the broad spectrum of followers when a scuffle broke out at the back of the room. Raised voices drew attention to the entrance, where several men had grabbed another man and were punching him to the ground.

'I've got as much right to be here as anyone else.' The man's shouts attracted more attention, and Maisie was not the only one to witness two of Mosley's followers pushing him out.

Stratton looked at Maisie, and without words they agreed not to intercede. Instead they would continue to observe. First Maisie would keep an eye on the door, then, without attracting attention, Stratton would look around the room, all the time giving the impression that they were waiting for the meeting to begin.

'I think I know what they're doing,' said Maisie.

Stratton nodded. 'At first I thought they were getting rid of the rougher element, but they're not, are they?'

'No. If I'm not mistaken, they're not letting in any people who look as if they might be Jewish. It's appalling.'

Stratton cleared his throat and nodded towards the front of the room. 'Here we go.'

A man walked up the steps to a small stage, where he talked about the New Party, and about their leader, Sir Oswald Mosley. Encouraging everyone to stand up, he then elevated his voice to introduce the politician Maisie had seen just once before, and whose manner had caused her to shiver. Oswald Mosley's eyes seemed as black as his hair, which was swept back close to his skull, accentuating his high forehead. His moustache was narrow and clipped, and seemed as controlled as his manner of dress. He wore a well-tailored black suit, with a white shirt and black tie. Nothing was out of place.

Maisie closed her eyes as he began to speak and felt again the sense of foreboding as his words rallied those present to his cause. Even though his manifesto reflected what so many wanted to hear, Maisie felt that she was witnessing a man whose ideas for the country might one day, if allowed, become not so much a government, but a regime. She looked at the assembled crowd, watched their eyes seem to catch fire with Mosley's rhetoric.

'We must build up our home markets, we must insulate ourselves from current world conditions and build a better Britain. You cannot build a higher civilization and a standard of life which can absorb the great force of modern production if you are subject to price fluctuations from the rest of the world which dislocate your industry at every turn, and to the sport of competition from virtually slave conditions in other countries.'

His speech continued on apace, as he covered all aspects of life, from defence of the country and using military force only to protect Britain's shores, to the centralization of power, until he began to draw his oration to a close.

'What I fear much more than a sudden crisis is a long, slow, crumbling through the years until we sink to the level of a Spain, a gradual paralysis beneath which all the vigour and energy of this country will succumb . . .'

Another disturbance at the back of the hall claimed Maisie's attention, and as she turned, she saw a man beaten, his wife kneeling to his aid, and then both of them pulled out of the building. In her heart she knew that this was not the place where they would find a clue to the identity of a man who would kill to ensure his message was heard. But it was not a wasted evening, because she had seen evidence that there was indeed another man who would halt at nothing to achieve power. Such a man should be stopped at all costs.

Maisie nudged Stratton. 'I think I've seen enough. Mosley is all but foaming at the mouth.'

Stratton leaned down to whisper, 'You're right. I don't think there's anything for us here. Too obvious. This man, or his followers, would not resort to threats and quiet killing. They're performers and they want to demonstrate power – despite their talk of inclusion.' He looked past Maisie. 'Come on, let's go.'

Maisie stepped out of the row, followed by Stratton, and together they crept to the back of the room and opened the curtain that formed a barrier between the entrance and the main hall.

'Leaving so soon?' A man stepped forward from alongside the door.

'Yes, afraid so,' said Stratton. 'My wife is not feeling very well, so we thought it best to leave. Pity, though, great chap, isn't he?'

The man looked at Maisie, who held her hand to her stomach, then he stepped aside for them to pass.

'Perhaps we'll see you again, Mr and Mrs Hutchinson.'

'Oh, I'm sure you will. Goodnight.'

They left the meeting hall and walked down the road, Maisie's hand resting on Stratton's arm. They did not speak until they were sure Mosley's men on guard outside the church hall were out of earshot.

'Do you think Mosley sanctioned what we just saw?' asked Maisie.

Stratton shook his head. 'I doubt he's given his blessing, but he may be turning a blind eye – you know, "what the eye doesn't see" and all that.'

'But that's approval by default. My guess is that his blind eye will lead to more violence if those men are allowed to continue in such a thuggish vein, then he'll be in trouble.'

'I'm sure you're right.' Stratton looked across the road as the lights on the Invicta came on. 'Ah, here's the motor car.' He whistled and four men emerged from the shadows as he stepped away from Maisie to speak to them. 'You know who to take in, don't you?'

'Yes, sir.'

'Right. Don't wait until the end. Go now, softly-softly. Buckman and Smith are on the other side of the hall, and the van's around the corner. Take those thugs in one at a time and nail them for assault and battery – and that's just the start. Did you get the names of the victims?'

'Yes, sir.'

'Good. I'll see you back at the Yard.'

The first man nodded and opened the door of the motor car. Stratton took Maisie's hand as she stepped aboard, and sat down next to her, looking out of the back window as the Invicta drove away.

'Time to take you home, Miss Dobbs. You'll be seeing your protesting women tomorrow.'

'Another bark up the wrong tree.'

'Oh, I'm sure you're making your way up your own path on this one.'

She smiled, but said nothing.

When they arrived outside the block of flats in Pimlico, Stratton alighted first and held out his hand to steady her as she stepped on to the pavement. She thought Stratton held on to her hand for one second too long, and drew back from him to take her keys from her bag.

'Goodnight, Inspector. I'll be in touch tomorrow.'

'Goodnight, Miss Dobbs.'

Maisie walked towards the glass front door, and when she turned saw that Stratton was still standing by the Invicta, watching until she was inside with the outer door locked once more. She waved one last time, and then stepped towards her flat, key in hand.

Later, as she sat cross-legged in front of the fireplace, a dressing gown covering her loose pyjamas, she closed her eyes to meditate on her day, and to clear her mind for tomorrow. She now knew the identity of the man she had seen blow himself to pieces on Christmas Eve, but she knew nothing about him, except that he loved books and had been wounded and gassed in the war. He had met a friend, a neatly turned-out man, in Soho Square, and he had recently become reacquainted with someone who might have been an old colleague. Could there be two men, and were these men connected? And what of Ian Jennings? Who was he? Where had he come from, who knew him – who might have grieved for him?

Thoughts of grief brought back memories of Simon, of his passing, so recent and still so raw. Simon Lynch was the army doctor for whom she had burned a candle for so long, even though he was no more than a shell of the man who had stolen her heart. It was a strange death: after so many years he had simply slipped away. She felt as if she had been in mourning since the war, but only allowed to grieve for the past few months. Of course, there were the years when she did not see him, when she could not face the memories, or the terror of reflection upon the explosion that had wounded them both. She shook her head, as memories of France in wartime merged with Christmas Eve's tragedy and flooded her mind's eye.

Somewhere, most likely in London, a desperate man was planning another attack – of that she was sure. The dead creatures were just the beginning, until his demands were met or he was found. And as she knew too well, the latter was the only option, because the government would never act upon the petitions of someone considered a madman. She thought of her father, who held strong views on such subjects.

'You know, Maisie, that when you look at one of these politicians, you're looking at a thief, a liar and a murderer, that's the way I see it.'

'Come on, Dad, that's not like you.'

'No, I mean it. Look – they take our money, they lie through their teeth, and then they send our boys off to their deaths, don't they? And all the time, they're in clover, never a day's risk or a day wanting.'

8

Maisie had been to Wychett Hill in the past, and as she turned the MG into the driveway, she looked at Billy in the passenger seat, and saw the tension in his jaw when he, too, looked up at the clock tower. She thought the years had tempered neither her memory of the asylum nor the reality of the building itself. Wychett Hill was a fine example of ornate Victorian construction that seemed both austere and ostentatious at the same time, like so many hospitals opened in the middle of the last century, including the Princess Victoria, the domain of Anthony Lawrence. But there was something even more foreboding about Wychett Hill, situated as it was on the North Downs in Surrey, where clouds congregated all too grey and all too ready to threaten with cold breezes and rain-filled air.

'Spooky sort of place, ain't it, Miss?'

'It gives me the shivers.'

Billy turned to her as she negotiated the final sweep towards an area dedicated to the parking of motor vehicles. 'I appreciate you bringing me here, Miss. It would have taken so long otherwise, what with the trains, then the walk from Tattenham Corner. I would never've been able to do it without leaving at the crack of dawn.'

'I know. But don't worry about it – I'm concerned about Doreen's well-being too, you know.'

'Yes, I know, Miss.' Billy bit his lip and looked out of the window, then down to the base of an adjacent wall. 'You're all right on this side, I reckon that'll do you.'

Maisie braked and turned off the engine. 'Look at that rain, it's really coming down now. Thank heavens for the humble umbrella, eh? Come on, we'd better run for it.'

'You wait there, Miss.' Billy turned up the collar of his rain-coat, pulled his flat cap down deep on his forehead, grabbed the umbrella, and alighted from the vehicle. With the umbrella unfurled, he came to the driver's side and opened the door for Maisie, who was pulling a scarf around her neck, tucking it into the collar of her mackintosh.

'Thank you, Billy.' Clasping her black document case in her left hand, she locked the MG and nodded to Billy. Together they ran to the main entrance, and were assaulted by the anticipated hospital smells of disinfectant and urine.

Maisie ran her hands across her shoulders to flick rain from her mackintosh, and stamped her feet. She looked around her and sighed. What had she ever done to deserve spending so much time in hospitals? But her choice of a professional life steeped in matters of life and death must of course include the place in which humans are tended in a time of sickness, whether that sickness is of the body or the mind, or both.

'That was a big sigh, Miss.'

'Oh, I know, Billy. I was just wondering how many hospitals I will set foot in, in my life. Remember I've an appointment with Dr Elsbeth Masters at the Clifton Hospital this afternoon.' She shrugged. 'Every one has its own mood, its own feel. Yet I could be put into a hospital blindfold and know where I was – there's the smell, the sounds, and if you touch the brick outside, or the plaster inside, there's always that same sensation. It's as if the suf-fering, the hope, the grief expended had seeped into the walls.'

'And don't forget that reek of cabbage boiled until it's nothing but sopping wet shreds.'

Maisie laughed. 'You're right, the smell of overcooked vegeta-bles.' She looked around. 'Now then, where do we go from here?'

'It's this way, Miss.' Billy checked the time on his wristwatch and led the way up a staircase flanked by a cast-iron filigree banister, the top rail rough and cold to the touch.

In the distance Maisie heard a scream, then moaning. She heard footsteps moving back and forth, and echoes from the various wards ricocheting off the brick walls and sliding along the banister, so that it seemed as if the building itself had taken on a certain volatility, and a visitor might believe the staircase would begin to shake at any moment. Billy continued to lead the way to one of the women's wards, then stopped alongside locked double doors with frosted glass at eye level. He pulled a cord to the right of the door and soon a nurse came to let them in.

'Mr Beale. I'm here to see Mrs Doreen Beale.'

The nurse nodded, looking Maisie up and down as she allowed her to pass.

'And this is a very good friend of ours, Miss Maisie Dobbs.' Having introduced Maisie, Billy glanced back and forth along the row of beds. 'Where's my wife?'

'Don't worry, Mr Beale, she's in a recovery ward. She's as well as can be expected, but don't expect her to be able to speak.'

Billy turned on the nurse, his mounting distress revealed by the swollen vein at his left temple. 'What do you mean, "don't expect her to speak"? What's the matter with her?'

Maisie set her hand on Billy's forearm and smiled at the nurse. 'My friend is very concerned about his wife, as you can imagine. Perhaps you could describe her situation as we walk along to see her – has she been taken to a room on her own, by chance?'

The nurse relaxed her shoulders, and pursed her lips, frowning at Billy, but appeared more accommodating as she spoke to Maisie. 'There was a little op, and she was, well, she was making a bit of a fuss afterwards, so we had to put her on her own for a while so she wouldn't start the rest of them off.'

Maisie glanced on either side of her as they walked along the ward. The 'rest of them' seemed to be catatonic, with mouths open or staring into the distance. She suspected that peace and calm were achieved with various pills and medicines. The aroma of sour dairy suggested that some had been put on a milk diet, which Maisie thought had been discontinued a decade earlier. As they approached a third set of double doors, the nurse took a chain from her pocket and selected a key. She slotted the key in the lock, rattled the left door towards her and turned the key back and forth until she was able to unlock the door.

'Always sticks, that one.'

Maisie nodded, but did not look at Billy. She felt his composure breaking again, realizing that his wife was now deeper in the bowels of asylum control, kept behind another set of locked doors.

'I understand that Mrs Beale has undergone some kind of insulin therapy.' Maisie volunteered the statement in a conversational manner.

'Yes, she had the second treatment yesterday.'

'Do you know why?'

'The doctor thought it would get her mind on the rails again, give her the push she needs to overcome her melancholy.'

'And there were difficulties?'

'Nothing out of the ordinary. She became a bit hysterical as she came out of it, so she's been sedated.'

'I see. So, the insulin therapy is having no effect whatsoever, then?'

The nurse did not respond to Maisie's question.

They reached another door, and through the small observation window could see that this was the room where Doreen Beale was recovering. The nurse set the key in the lock and turned to Billy. 'Now, she's not to be excited. She should remain calm – remember she's still not quite conscious.'

She led the way into the room, where Doreen was lying on a cast-iron bed, her eyes wide open, her face contorted as she jerked her head back and forth on the pillow. Her wrists were secured to the bed on either side of her body, and her feet had been strapped to the bottom of the bed. Her slender wrists reminded Maisie of a sparrow's tiny bones, set against the dark leather biting into her skin. Doreen had lost so much weight it seemed as if the sheet and blanket were flush across the bed, with slight protrusions to indicate the position of her feet, knees and hips.

'Oh, my darlin' girl, my darlin' girl.' Billy rushed to his wife's bedside and rested his hand on her damp brow, then leaned down to kiss her cheek.

Doreen stopped struggling and began to weep, tears falling across her face. 'It's bad, Billy. It's bad here. Take me home, please, Billy. I want my boys, I want my Lizzie, take me home.'

'We'll get you out of here, don't you worry. It won't be long now.'

'Don't let them put them needles in me again, don't let them do it.' Her breath came in short, rapid gasps, and her chest rose as she struggled for air.

A staff nurse entered and stepped across to the opposite side of the bed. 'Now then, Mrs Beale, you don't want any more injections, do you? Take a deep breath, come on, Mrs Beale.'

'I can look after my wife while I'm here, Nurse. Please leave us.'

'Now, look here—'

Maisie moved towards the woman. 'I can be of assistance while you are out of the room, Staff Nurse. I am sure Mrs Beale will settle in a minute or two – and I was a nurse in a secure institution, so I understand the importance of summoning you if help is required.'

Doreen calmed as she listened to the exchange, and the rhythm of her breathing slowed as Billy stroked her brow to settle her.

'Ten minutes, that's all you've got.' The staff nurse shook her head and left the room.

'Who does she think she is – ten minutes, my eye!'

'Billy, you're not helping Doreen,' Maisie whispered, as she came to the opposite side of the bed. She took a clean linen handkerchief from her pocket and wiped saliva from the sides of

Doreen's mouth, then turned towards the side-table, where a pitcher and bowl had been placed, along with a square of clean white muslin. Maisie poured cold water into the ewer, then steeped the cloth into the water and squeezed out the excess. Shaking out the fabric, she folded it horizontally and smiled at Doreen. 'Now if Billy will just lift his hand for a minute, let's cool you down a bit.'

Doreen nodded, and looked at Billy, who was trying to release the straps that held her hands in place. And as Maisie wiped her face with soft strokes, then rinsed the cloth and swabbed her neck, she began to weep again.

'I want my boys, I want my little girl.'

'Love, Lizzie's gone now, she's gone. That's why you've come here, so they can help you get over it.'

Doreen began to gasp again, and Maisie shook her head at Billy. 'Let's just keep her calm. If we can get her transferred to the Clifton, Dr Masters will know exactly how to approach her treatment. Let's just settle her so they'll release her from the straps and take her back to the women's ward.'

'I don't want them doing this to her again.'

Maisie continued to draw the cool cloth back and forth across Doreen's forehead, and soon her eyes were heavy, her breathing became more shallow and she began to fall asleep.

'Poor love, look at her, there's nothing of her. She looks barely more than a child herself.' Tears welled in Billy's eyes.

'They'll work through a standard set of treatments, trying to find something that works,' whispered Maisie. 'I am sure she has had some kind of faradism, and as for this insulin treatment—' She said no more, but gave silent thanks for the fact that removal of the ovaries, the fashionable treatment for melancholia in women some thirty years earlier, had long been abandoned.

'What do you think will help her, Miss?' Billy rested his hand on his wife's forehead once again, as Maisie ran the cloth down her arms and into her palms, removing the sticky sweat of fear from the exposed parts of her body.

Maisie did not speak for some seconds, instead stroking the cloth back and forth along the inside of Doreen's left arm, her eyes fixed on the thick leather strap and buckle that secured the sick woman to her bed. 'Time is the great healer. I once knew a doctor who said that his real job was to keep the patient occupied while time and nature did their work. Doreen's grief has run so deep that it now colours every waking and sleeping moment. It has leached down into the fibres of her being, so there are physical as well as mental disturbances and consequences.' She paused. 'I do not want to pre-empt a doctor, however, I would imagine she will need a period of time in hospital, to stabilize her melancholia – the fatigue, anxiety, depression. She has doubtless suffered from the headaches and neuralgia that accompany her condition, so the doctors will want to get her on an even keel, alleviate her physical suffering to the point where they can address the deep-seated grief that has led to her malaise, her instability. She needs good nutrition, she needs to be calmed. And she needs to talk, but not to you or me or someone close to her. She needs to shed her sadness, like a snake sheds its skin, and that can be a troubling process, for a snake is at its most vulnerable at such a time.'

'When you say "talking", do you mean like Dr Blanche did with me, when I went through my bad turn, a couple of years ago? And like you do with the people what come to you?'

'That's more or less what I mean.' Maisie wondered how to express her frustrations without upsetting Billy. 'The trouble is, it's always been those of a higher station in life than either you or I who could afford the sort of therapeutic process that Doreen needs. And progress must be accompanied by direction from a clinician such as Dr Masters.'

'Bleedin' typical, ain't it – about the toffs getting the best treatments, while the likes of us are packed away in nuthouses?'

'You could say that. Frankly, it stems from a belief that the lower classes – and that means both of us – do not think and feel in the same way as our *betters*. Times are changing, though.'

'But not fast enough, eh?'

'No, not fast enough.'

Billy and Maisie remained with Doreen until the staff nurse returned, and as she strode into the room, Maisie lifted a finger to her lips.

'Mrs Beale is resting now,' she whispered. 'May we leave Mr Beale alone with his wife for a moment?' She stood up and moved towards the nurse, taking her by the arm. 'Perhaps you and I can have a word outside, while he says his goodbye.'

The nurse frowned, but acquiesced, allowing Maisie to lead her from the room.

'She's a right nutter, that one,' said the nurse, as Maisie closed the door without a sound.

'I beg to disagree with you, Staff Nurse. She is a woman who is racked with grief, a woman who has buckled under the weight of losing a child. We now have to help her to her feet again, though that loss will always be with her.'

'But thousands have lost, haven't they? They don't all end up inside, though, eh? Made of stronger stuff, that's what they are.' The nurse tensed her jaw, and Maisie noticed the way she rubbed her hand back and forth across her abdomen as she spoke.

'Mrs Beale's husband took her to the doctor, which is why she is here now.'

'I don't know, I think she's had some mollycoddling, that's what it is. I mean, when I lost my—' The staff nurse paused, clutched her hands together, then released them to reach for the door handle. 'It's time for him to go now. If she remains calm like this for the afternoon, then she'll be back on the main ward by evening.'

Maisie looked on as Billy lingered with his wife a moment longer, then she reached forward and set her hand upon his shoulder.

'Better be off now.'

Billy nodded, kissed Doreen on the cheek, and walked from the room without looking back.

'I do hope you can get her out of here, Miss. I'd discharge her, if I could.'

'I know, Billy, I know. She won't be here for long.'

And as they left the building, she thought of her father, and his words echoed once again: this was another desperate sort of place.

~~~

Maisie dropped Billy at Fitzroy Square and made her way directly to Camberwell and the Clifton Hospital. When Maisie was shown into her office, Dr Elsbeth Masters looked up over her tortoiseshell spectacles, smiled broadly, and reached across the desk to shake her hand.

'Maisie Dobbs. I haven't seen you since you worked for dear Maurice – how is he?'

'In his mind, still very busy, but slowing down in his body – he's getting on now.'

Masters held out her hand for Maisie to be seated, then sat down herself, moving a patient file to one side as she spoke. She leaned forward, hands clasped, as they exchanged pleasantries and caught up on Maisie's progression from Blanche's assistant to proprietress of her own business. When Maisie first came to work at the Clifton, it did not surprise her in the least to meet someone who knew Maurice. There always seemed to be someone, somewhere in her life, who was acquainted with her long-time mentor.

'Frankly, Maisie, I always hoped you would move into the clinical arena – we could do with more women doctors in the care of the mentally ill, you know, and things have moved on since my early days at the Royal Free. But I am sure your work is more than satisfying.'

'Yes, it is – very much so.'

'Now then, tell me what I can do for you.'

'There are two reasons for my visit – the first is regarding the wife of my employee. I am close to the family and want to see an end to a difficult situation.'

'Go on.' Masters took off her spectacles and leaned forward as Maisie continued.

'Last year their young daughter died of diphtheria. They have two boys as well, but Lizzie was the apple of her mother's eye, and such a dear, dear child.' Maisie bit her lip and paused. She felt quite ready to weep, an emotion that gripped her with such suddenness that she fought to stem the tears. 'Since their loss the parents have struggled to come to terms with the fact that Lizzie is no longer there, but Doreen, my employee's wife, has taken a downward spiral. She had been under the care of a doctor for some months – the child died last February – when it was decided to admit her for psychiatric care and she was sent to Wychett Hill a couple of days ago with a diagnosis of melancholia and hysteria.'

'Oh, dear . . .' Masters shook her head.

'They have already proceeded with insulin shock and changes of diet, and I can see – we visited her this morning – that she has been sedated with narcotics. When we arrived she had been strapped to a bed and left alone in a room. I think the treatment is rather harsh, and that she would do better closer to home and under your care, if it were possible to effect a transfer.'

'I see.' Masters tapped the desk with her long fingers, the backs of her hands embossed with a mesh of veins and dotted with liver spots. 'Certainly, I believe we could make more progress with such a patient here. Let me make some enquiries – who was the admitting doctor, do you know?'

Maisie reached into her document case, brought out a sheet of paper and handed it to the doctor. 'You'll find all the information you require here.'

'Ah, as efficient as ever, Maisie.' She took the page of notes and slipped it into a fresh file, which she then marked with Doreen Beale's name. 'I take it I could telephone Mr Beale at your office, if I need to reach him as a matter of urgency?'

'Yes, of course. However, we are out of the office a great deal, so if you do not receive an answer, please send a telegram or postcard.'

'Right. Leave it with me. I'll see what I can do.' She scraped back her chair as if to stand.

'Dr Masters, there is one more thing, if you have a moment or two.'

Masters looked at the wall-mounted clock. 'Yes, of course. I've a few minutes.' She smiled and leaned forward again, her hands once more resting on the desk.

'I know you were in France, during the war, and you were involved in the treatment of men with war neuroses of one kind or another.'

'Well, *eventually* I was in France. At first, as you know, they told us women doctors that we should go back to our kitchens, but I joined one of the all-women medical units set up by Dr Elsie Inglis – there was an indomitable woman for you – and was privileged to work with a truly dedicated and professional group of nurses and doctors. Before long my presence was requested by the boys at the top when shell-shock cases began coming through thick and fast, and I was able to work alongside men. And yes, it was my background in neurology and psychiatry that they were interested in.'

'I am familiar with the different levels of war neuroses, Dr Masters, the distinctions between neurasthenia, battle fatigue, soldier's heart and hysteria, but I am involved in a case at the moment that demands – I believe – a deeper understanding of the mind of a man who has seen battle at close quarters and is afflicted mentally and emotionally by that experience.'

Masters tapped the desk again. 'Remember, there were many cases of shell-shock recorded where the patient had been nowhere near a detonated shell, nowhere near the front line of battle. Simply anticipating a move up to the front could turn some men. Unfortunately, despite the best efforts of myself and others with specific training in dealing with injury to the mind of a man, the army doctors – and the brass, I might add – wanted clean-cut delineations between wounded and sick, between shell-shocked and malingering. Wounded and shell-shocked would be granted the "W" armband – and the pension that went with it. Simply being an "S" case – sick – meant you were turned around and sent back up the line at the earliest possible opportunity.'

'I understand. I've also been speaking to Dr Anthony Lawrence – do you remember, he was here for a while, then moved to the Princess Victoria? He has said much the same thing. Anyway, I simply wanted to get some sort of . . .' Maisie looked out of the window as she considered her words with care. 'Some sort of reflection from you, as to what it was like to treat such an affliction.'

Masters ran her hands through her short, bobbed grey-flecked hair. 'That's an interesting question. I don't think anyone's ever put it like that.' She sat back, then forward again, having considered the question. 'I don't know whether you know this, but I was born and grew up in British East Africa. My father had a coffee farm – it's now run by my younger brother – so we had a very different childhood in comparison with our peers here. We were rather wild, if I may admit such a thing. We were both sent to school in England at age eleven, and although I returned briefly prior to commencing my studies at medical school, it is those early years that defined me, defined my sense of what I could do – I wasn't used to anyone telling me that a girl couldn't do this, or that. But here's something that struck me in France. It was the memory of something I'd seen as a child.'

Elsbeth Masters pushed back her chair and walked to the window behind her, where she placed her hands on the bulbous radiator as if to draw from it a warmth she had known at another time. She turned to Maisie and continued, now leaning back against the source of heat. 'I remember going off one day with my friend, a young Masai boy, the son of one of our servants. No one seemed to mind us playing together, out and about for hours until sundown, following the men when they hunted. On this particular jaunt we saw a lion take down a gazelle – and I mean at close quarters. It quite took my breath away. It was as if something happened to the gazelle at the moment of capture, something awe-inspiringly terrible and wonderful at the same time – as if, in knowing the gazelle was to die a dreadful death, ripped apart by the jaws of the lion, the Creator had given the captive a reprieve by taking her soul before she was dead, so that no pain would be felt because the essence had gone already.'

Maisie nodded, able to see the scene in her mind's eye, so charged was the doctor's description.

'And I saw the eyes of the gazelle again in France, and it struck me that perhaps a heartsick God had looked down and taken up a soul, leaving only the shell of a man.' She shook her head as if to extinguish the recollection, and brought her attention back to her visitor. 'I sometimes thought that, in my work, I was really trying to create the conditions whereby a soul might be persuaded to join a man's body once again, thus making him whole.'

Maisie nodded.

'You're probably thinking, "Physician, heal thyself".'

'No, not at all, not at all.' Maisie smiled. 'I was just thinking back to the days when I worked as a nurse with shell-shocked men at this hospital – looking into their eyes and knowing that part of them was lost. Perhaps to return, perhaps not.'

'Now, do you have any more questions for me?'

'Just a couple. Do you know Dr Lawrence well?'

'Curious that you mention him again, because I hadn't heard from him in years, yet I received a letter from him this morning, wondering if we might meet.' She shrugged. 'I suspect he has a paper he'd like me to review before he reveals it to a wider peer group.'

'How were you first acquainted?'

'Funnily enough, it wasn't directly to do with our regular work with the insane, but years ago, in connection with patients who had suffered in gas attacks.'

'I see.'

'Yes. There was a team of boffins – you know, scientists, physicists, that sort of person – working in Berkshire on antidotes to gas. There was some *experimentation,* I think you would call it, and they were interested in having a degree of neurological and psychological assessment as part of their research.'

'Did you work for them?'

'For a very short time. I wasn't sure if it was a command or request, to tell you the truth, but I didn't like what was going on. I looked into it, you see, and realized that they were – if you'll forgive the phrase – playing fast and loose with the health of anyone and everyone who worked there. Anyone or thing who breathed could be dragged in for an experiment or test. I could just imagine it: "Just put down the teapot, Mrs Smith – breathe through this mask and tell us how you feel".'

'And Dr Lawrence? Did he continue?'

'I believe he did, for a while.'

Maisie nodded and looked at the clock. 'Thank you so much for seeing me – and for anything you can do for Mrs Beale. She is in a desperate situation.'

'Yes, I understand. I'll take this along to admissions now – we could have her transferred within the next four or five days if all goes well.'

Maisie stood up to leave, and as she held out her hand to Elsbeth Masters, the doctor stepped from behind her desk. It was only then that Maisie realized the woman was not wearing shoes, and stood before her with bare feet.

'Oh, don't take any notice of me. I just cannot abide wearing shoes to this day. I was barefoot until I was eleven and I try to reclaim that sense of freedom whenever I can. I think I would go quite mad if I couldn't take my shoes off several times a day.'

Maisie said goodbye, and as she moved to leave, noticed a pair of polished brown leather shoes set on the floor just inside the door, each with a stocking folded and tucked inside.

9

'So, what I need to know, for numbers, darling, is are you coming?'

'Coming? Coming where?' Maisie frowned, taken aback when the telephone rang and she picked up the receiver to hear Priscilla's question, without so much as a 'Hello, Maisie' by way of introduction.

'New Year's Eve – party, at our house. Everyone – and I do mean *everyone* – in London will be there. Do not let me down, Maisie, I have a very nice man for you to meet.'

Priscilla was Maisie's dear friend from her early days at Girton College, and though they were as different as two young women could be – Priscilla's devil-may-care attitude towards work and play was intimidating to Maisie at first – they had been drawn to each other in the way that opposites attract. The loss of all three beloved brothers in the war, followed by the death of her parents, who succumbed to the flu epidemic, led Priscilla to escape to Biarritz on the west coast of France soon after the end of the war. It was here that she steeped herself in a raucous social life, and drank to anaesthetize the pain of her losses. Then she met Douglas Partridge, who had been wounded in the war – his arm had been amputated and he required a cane to support his weight as he walked – and fell in love. She credited their marriage and family life with their three sons as having saved her from herself. Since their return to London for the sake of their sons' education, Maisie had noticed that Priscilla was not taking to life back in England.

'Oh, Pris, no – I don't think I could bear another one of your arranged meetings with so-called eligible men, who seem to me to be playing the field for all they're worth.'

'But you will come to the party, won't you? Supper at half past eight, then dancing before we see in the new year – and let's all hope things get better this year. Now then, do not tell me you've had second thoughts. How long have we been friends? And this will be the first turn of the year we've been able to spend together.'

'You're verging on blackmail, Priscilla.'

'I know, look what you've driven me to – do say you'll be coming.'

Maisie smiled and sighed. 'Oh, all right, I'll come – in fact, it will be lovely. I could do with some lightness in my life.'

'You could do with a lot of lightness, if you ask me. So, see you at half past seven for drinks – opening salvo to the evening's festivities. And you never know, you may rub shoulders with the PM himself – not that we expect him to stay, being more of your dour sort.'

Maisie thought she could hear the clink of ice against glass in the background. 'I've already rubbed shoulders with him – and yes, he is a bit uninspiring.'

'You've met the PM?'

Priscilla's voice was louder than was necessary, and now Maisie was sure that she was drinking, but she made no mention of the fact.

'I know what you're thinking, Pris – surprising in my line of work, eh?'

'Well, now that you come to mention it . . . but anyway, see you for the party. Wear something stunning. If you are not suit-ably clad, I will drag you to my dressing room to re-garb you. Remember it's a party, Maisie, not a wake!'

'I'm sure no one will be interested in what I wear—'

'Nonsense. Now, I must dash, so much to do. Bye for now, Maisie dear.'

'Bye, Pris.'

Priscilla's telephone call had come within moments of Maisie's return to her office in Fitzroy Square. Billy was out, and it was already late afternoon. She considered the worrisome possibility of Priscilla drinking so early in the day, before the pre-supper cocktail hour that had become so popular in the past few years, and could imagine her friend pouring a gin and tonic while saying, 'Well, the sun must be over the yardarm somewhere in the Empire!' But she feared that in Priscilla's case the distinction between a pleasant pre-prandial drink and being drunk was beginning to blur once again.

Maisie had intended to catch her breath and bring her notes up to date before going to the meeting in support of women's pensions. She couldn't think why MacFarlane insisted upon her going. She was aware that the interest of Special Branch in groups of women gathering together had started with the suffragettes long ago, based upon the threat they represented to the men who governed the country – yet she could no more imagine such a group involved with poison gas than she could imagine a woman taking over Ramsay MacDonald's job. But if such an investigation brought her ever closer to the real threat, then she had to go.

She set to work, checking the clock on the mantelpiece, for she would have to make her way to Scotland Yard following the meeting of women, but after spending some time making notations on her own case map pinned across the table by the window, Maisie sat back, her thoughts on the conversation with Elsbeth Masters. She had always liked Masters. There seemed to be a wisdom about the woman, a way of carrying herself that suggested knowledge, capability and compassion, without the need to be strident, the latter being an unfortunate trait she had found in other women of a similar professional stature. More than anything, Maisie could not banish the picture of a dying gazelle from her mind, and kept seeing the fine-boned face, the luminous black eyes devoid of a spirit that had ascended as the lion's teeth clutched the animal by the back of the neck and brought it down. And she wondered, *Was that me?* Had her soul abandoned her as shell fire rained down on the casualty clearing station? In her youth, had she been unable to reclaim that essential part of her being? Might it account for her reticence, her lack of emotional mastery when faced with the possibility of a more intimate connection?

She stood up and stepped back from the desk to stand in front of the gas fire, first crouching down to turn up the jets. *Am I healing, now?* She had sensed a newness within her of late, as if spring itself were waiting behind winter's cold cloak. She had felt the need to bring colour into her life, and music, for didn't song lift the spirit and provide a conduit for the soul's voice? And hadn't she read, somewhere, that in dancing we are seeking a connection with the Divine? Had she, simply by engaging in those endeavours that called to her, given her spirit permission to come home? She closed her eyes and thought of Simon, now gone, now nothing more than a memory and ashes wind-strewn across a field. Looking into the past was like looking into a long tunnel, and she knew the tragedy of his wounding and his passing no longer touched her with such an immediate rawness. It was more akin to an ache that came and went, like a breeze that lifts a lace curtain back from the window, then sets it down again. Now, it was as if those jagged and painful memories of him were clothing she no longer needed, that she had laundered, dried and placed in a sealed box in the attic. She might open that box on occasion and look inside, perhaps touch the fabric and hold it to her cheek, but she would never wear those clothes again, because they did not fit. She had changed. It was as if her tentative returning spirit had required nothing less of her.

Maisie looked at the clock once more. Perhaps the unrelenting grief she had worn like a heavy cloak had been akin to madness; after all, it had kept her incarcerated in a cell of wartime memories, and she had been her own jailer, the keys to her past jangling from her waist.

The telephone rang, causing Maisie to jump and put her hand on her heart. She reached for the receiver. 'Fitzroy—'

'Miss Dobbs, MacFarlane here.'

'Good afternoon, Chief Superintendent. I was just about to leave for the women's union meeting.'

'I thought as much. Anyway, change of plan. There's a motor on its way to you now – it should be outside in about five minutes.'

'Have there been developments?'

'Well, if you call finding out who's been messing around with poison gas and building a cache of Mills Bombs a "development" – then we certainly have one.'

'You have the culprit?'

'Culprits. Plural. Stratton is on his way. I'll see you when you get here.' There was a click and then a single unbroken tone as MacFarlane hung up the receiver.

'And goodbye to you, Detective Chief Superintendent MacFarlane!' Maisie set the receiver down and went to the table, where she tidied the coloured pencils and picked up her document case.

The door opened and Billy entered. 'Afternoon, Miss. There's a big old Invicta just pulled up outside – that for you?'

'I'm afraid it is. I'm off to Scotland Yard.'

Billy, placing his coat on the hook, took Maisie's mackintosh down and held it open for her. 'Any progress?'

'Yes, they reckon they've caught the men behind the poison gas attacks.'

'And you don't think they've got the right blokes – I can see it written all over your face.'

'You're right, but I'm going to give them the benefit of the doubt.' Maisie paused. 'Look, come with me. I've managed to involve you, so you should be there. Get your coat on and let's go. I want to talk to you anyway, about my meeting with Elsbeth Masters.'

Billy took down his coat and opened the door for Maisie.

'Miss . . . I'm sorry to bother you, but . . . and I hope you don't mind me asking again, but – do you think we can get Doreen into the Clifton?'

Maisie reached out and placed her hand on his arm. 'No firm "yes" yet, but I believe we'll be in luck. And the sooner the better, after what we saw at Wychett Hill.'

MacFarlane, Stratton and Colm Darby were together in the usual meeting room at Scotland Yard when Maisie arrived with Billy. After introducing her assistant to the policemen, they took their seats for a briefing from Robert MacFarlane.

'Acting on a tip-off, our men interrupted' – he looked at the group over the top of horn-rimmed spectacles, and winked – '*interrupted* a meeting of union troublemakers who had set themselves up in the cellar of a house in Finchley. Caught them red-handed with the wherewithal to make and activate incendiary devices at will. Though the laboratory chaps are still completing their investigation, we are given to believe these villains have constructed gas bombs ready to let loose across the city.'

'How many men?' asked Maisie. She did not look up as she held her pencil ready to make notes on a clutch of index cards.

'Four. And one woman.'

'And you say they are union sympathizers?'

'Yes. We found anti-government literature, along with details of likely targets, et cetera, et cetera.'

'Have you details on the "et ceteras", Detective Chief Superintendent?' She turned to Colm Darby. 'Inspector Darby, have you had the opportunity to view handwriting samples yet? And has there been some sort of psychological analysis?'

Stratton caught Maisie's eye and shook his head, as if to warn her against pressing MacFarlane too far. Maisie looked away, and back at MacFarlane, waiting for an answer.

'Miss Dobbs, I take it you doubt the integrity of our investigation.'

'No, certainly not. You've acted upon credible intelligence and come up with proof of subversive activity that could compromise the well-being of the general public, possibly leading to loss of life on a frightening scale. No, I am not questioning the integrity of the actual investigation that has led to these people being brought in on suspicion of causing terror, but instead I'm wondering whether they are the people involved in the threats received by the Prime Minister, the Home Secretary and the Minister for Pensions, and if they are the ones responsible for the deaths of innocent animals. I am wondering if union sympathizers would not take another course of action – would it occur to them, for example, to show their intent in an initial attack on dogs and then birds? It doesn't seem to me to be the sort of thing a group of union activists might do. What do you think?'

MacFarlane shuffled his papers, set them down, then looked back at Maisie, supported by his knuckles as he leaned across the table. 'I think I would like you to come down to a line-up of our little gang of subversive warriors and tell us if you have seen any of them before.' He turned to Billy, who was following the conversation with an increasing degree of discomfort, and wondering whether his employer was pushing her luck. 'And you too, Mr Beale. You were also walking along Charlotte Street on Christmas Eve – you might recall a face or two.'

Billy nodded. 'Right you are, sir.'

MacFarlane looked at Maisie. 'See, even your man here thinks I'm right.'

She inclined her head and stood up, ready to follow MacFarlane. 'Then let's go down to view the suspects, shall we?'

The group was led by MacFarlane to a damp red-brick room without plaster on the walls, where four men and a solitary woman had been told to stand with their legs apart and their hands behind their backs.

'Let me introduce our motley crew here today,' said MacFarlane. 'First, Graham Tucker, thirty-four, union activist, small-time crook – though his mates here probably don't know about his previous, which includes pickpocketing and receiving stolen goods. Learned a thing or two about explosives in the war, courtesy of His Majesty's army.' He moved along the line. 'Tommy Burgess. Thirty years of age. Mineworkers union and, again, a bit of previous behind him, including assault and robbery.' He shook his head. 'I think we're seeing something of a pattern here. Now to Miss Catherine Jones. Chemist, a university girl no less – and look where it's got her today.'

Maisie suspected Catherine Jones was about to spit on MacFarlane's feet, but had thought better of it and instead looked at the ground. MacFarlane introduced the last two members of the gang, Wilfred Knight and Frederick Ovendale, both union men, both soldiers in the war.

'Right then, we've seen enough, I think we can resume our meeting now,' said MacFarlane.

Maisie spoke in a low voice to MacFarlane: 'I'd like to question Miss Jones, if I may?'

MacFarlane rolled his eyes. 'Be my guest.' He turned to a constable and a woman police auxiliary, and directed them to take Catherine Jones to an interview room, then held out his hand for Maisie to follow.

Maisie turned to her assistant. 'Billy, perhaps you would be so kind as to return to the meeting room and take down my case map. I won't be long – about ten to fifteen minutes.'

Billy nodded and looked at Stratton, who indicated that Billy should follow him.

When they entered the interview room, no more than twelve feet square with eggshell-finished walls and a small window that allowed only a narrow shaft of light in, Maisie held out her hand for the woman to be seated, then turned to the constable. 'Perhaps you'd be so kind as to wait outside. I'll only need your Miss Hawkins here to witness the interview.'

She kept her coat on, for it was cold in the room, and sat down opposite the woman.

'If you think I'm going to be the Judas here, you've got

another think coming.' Catherine Jones spat out the words and did not face Maisie, but sat with her legs to one side, so that she could look at the wall and not her interviewer.

'I'm not going to ask you to be disloyal to your friends, but I do want to establish the extent to which you have already used your skills and knowledge on behalf of the union agitators. You are an intelligent, well-educated woman, Miss Jones, yet you have risked everything by throwing in your lot with these men.' Maisie paused, clasping her hands together on the table in front of her. 'What led you to take such a gamble?'

The woman braced her shoulders as if to fight the urge to respond, then breathed a sigh and slumped towards the table, her head resting on her forearms. The policewoman stepped forward, but Maisie held up her hand. Jones shook her head and looked up. 'This is a bloody nightmare.'

'Yes, it is. But it started somewhere, didn't it?'

The woman sat back. 'I'd give my eye teeth for a ciggie.'

'Sorry, I don't smoke.'

'No, I didn't think so. You're not the type, more's the pity.'

'Tell me how you became mixed up in this, Catherine.'

Jones shrugged. 'I lost my job. Easy as that. Laid off with no money coming in. My parents are dead, my brother was wounded in the war and died in a hospital in Southampton – septicaemia. I'm alone, so I need money to live. I'd joined the union, and became more involved in politics.' She paused. 'You probably have no idea what it's like, do you, not knowing where the next penny's coming from?'

Maisie wanted to respond, but held back, instead letting the vacuum of silence force the woman to continue.

'No, I thought not. You haven't a clue, not a bloody clue.' Jones shook her head again. 'Well, I might as well go on.' Another sigh. 'Looking for a place to go, I walked into the wrong crowd. As I said before – all as easy as that.' She snapped her fingers into the space between her interrogator and herself. 'Soon our band had broken away from the union, and we decided the only way to make our presence felt was . . . was . . . a show of strength.' She sat in silence. 'Not that we'd actually shown anyone anything, to tell you the truth. We were just getting going.'

'So you had your cache of weaponry, but hadn't used it?'

'Not a bloody thing. To tell you the truth, I think we were all a bit scared. It soon became clear to me that Tommy Burgess had more interest in making plans to hold up banks than in making a point by showing the boys in Whitehall that the unions had something to say. I was on the verge of getting out of it, and I was sure that Wilf was an informer – bloody scab!'

'Do you know a man by the name of Ian Jennings?'

'Am I supposed to?'

'Answer the question, please, Catherine.'

'Never met anyone by that name in my life.'

'Could you make a bomb of poison gas?'

'Such as?'

'Chlorine. Chlorine and phosgene, or mustard gas.'

'Old wartime favourites?'

'Yes.'

'No, I couldn't. That takes more of an expert than I can lay claim to being. And I wouldn't. Saw what the gas did to my brother.'

'But you were making bombs.'

'Not like that, though. We might've created a stink, might have caused a few tears, or the police to run away from a march, but no, I'm not in the business of killing like that.'

'But I understand Mills Bombs were found.'

'They might have been found, Miss Dobbs. But I didn't know we had them. I was only involved in developing chemical concoctions to upset the police during our demonstrations. Not killing people.'

Maisie nodded. 'That will be all, thank you.' She pushed back her chair to stand.

'Thought so. I tell you everything I know and I'm still not getting out of here.'

'I'm sorry, Catherine. I have to be honest, I don't think I can get you out. At the very least, you are guilty of conspiring to cause an affray, and the men you were with were in possession of dangerous weapons. But I will record our conversation. It may help when you come up before the judge. And try not to get in with the wrong crowd again – you are far too intelligent a woman to have done such a thing.' She nodded to the police-woman and left the room, passing the constable as she departed. 'You can escort Miss Jones back to her cell now.'

Stratton was waiting for Maisie at the end of the corridor, and moved forward to walk in step with her as she ascended the staircase.

'What do you think?'

Maisie stopped, turning towards Stratton. 'What do you think I think? They might have been planning subversive activity, they might have had a cache of weapons that they surely must answer for in a court of law, but they are not behind the threats we're investigating. I really don't know what's happening here, but—'

'MacFarlane is under pressure to produce suspects.'

'I suppose next he'll round up the women unionists for even daring to ask for pensions.'

'No, not quite, however—'

'Come on, Richard, you know he's wrong. Even he knows he's wrong.' She continued on up the staircase, realizing she had just addressed Stratton by his Christian name. Her cheeks blazed.

'Stop, wait, please, Maisie.'

'Yes?' She turned as he placed a hand on her arm.

'You and I do not have to discontinue the investigation.'

'I know. I have no intention of stopping, even though I am sure my work here on this case has just come to an end, and even though it will be in my own time.' Maisie did not try to hide her exasperation. 'I just know there is someone out there, working alone – or with a close associate – who is on a knife edge. I just feel it. I have been trying to compose a picture in my mind's eye of the type of person we are looking for, and I do not see him reflected in any single member of that group we've just viewed. Catherine Jones may be a trained chemist, may be an intelligent woman, but there's something she does not have, something you would need to be able to kill dogs, birds – and, eventually, a human being. She does not have the *suffering*. Even in the hard nuts who appear beyond any redemption, we see that terrible ache that took root and grew to take over a whole person. She had lost her parents, yes, her brother, yes, but she does not display a level of . . .' Maisie bit her lip, searching for words to describe an emotion she could feel but not give voice to. 'Deep, deep melancholy, a darkness. She is not someone who truly has nothing to live for but to give up her life for others in a similar position.' She turned to continue up the staircase. 'And that makes the man we are looking for very, very dangerous indeed, for he has nothing to lose, not even his conscience. We should be thankful that he is choosing to increase the stakes slowly, but I fear his patience is wearing thin.'

'I think you're right.' Stratton kept pace with Maisie, who was now making her way towards the meeting room at a fair clip.

'Then tell Robbie MacFarlane.'

'Tell Robbie MacFarlane what?' The Detective Chief Superintendent's voice boomed from a room on the left as he walked into the corridor. 'Tell Robbie MacFarlane what, Miss Dobbs?'

Maisie stood tall to answer MacFarlane. 'Sir, I do not believe the people we have just seen are responsible for the threats sent to Downing Street.'

MacFarlane placed a hand on Maisie's shoulder. 'Well, Miss Dobbs, at this moment in time, it does not matter what you believe.' He turned to Stratton. 'I'll talk to you later. I just need a word with Miss Dobbs here.' Bringing his attention back to Maisie, he cupped her elbow in his hand and steered her towards his office. 'Sit down please, Miss Dobbs.'

Maisie took a seat and placed her document case on the floor alongside her chair. She rested her hands in her lap and crossed her ankles, noticing that MacFarlane had followed each move.

'Now then, I know you think we've got the wrong people, and perhaps you are right. I'm not going to dismiss your observations out of hand, but I will save you the time.' He folded his arms and looked at his feet. Maisie noticed that the fabric of his jacket was taut across his shoulders, and thought he might have bought the jacket when he was a younger man and the intervening years were not accommodated easily by his clothing.

'Miss Dobbs, your services are no longer required by Special Branch. Your contributions have not been without merit, but now that we have suspects in custody, there would be unwanted speculation if we retained you for any longer than necessary, especially in these times of tight budgetary oversight. In short, the bean counters are watching me, so you had better be on your way.'

'And you no longer have to keep an eye on me because my name was mentioned in a threatening letter sent to the Prime Minister's office?'

'We believe that to have been a shot in the dark, perhaps a device to throw us off the scent, so to speak. Plus, you have been mentioned in the newspapers before in one or two cases involving former soldiers.' He laughed. 'And I doubt you could make a bomb, Miss Dobbs.'

'Yes, you're right – bombs and poison gas are hardly in my line.' Maisie reached for her case and rose from the chair, holding out her hand. 'Thank you for the opportunity to work with you, Detective Chief Superintendent MacFarlane. I am glad to have been of service.' She cleared her throat. 'I take it my account will be settled promptly.'

'I will personally ensure you are not out of pocket.'

'Thank you.' She turned to leave, but MacFarlane reached out and placed his hand on her shoulder.

'I hope we meet again, Miss Dobbs.'

'Yes, of course. I am sure our paths will cross.' She pulled on her gloves. 'Now then, I should be off.'

Maisie made her way to the meeting room where Billy was in conversation with Stratton and Darby.

'Ready, Billy?'

'Yes, Miss.' He held up a rolled-up length of paper. 'I've taken the case map.'

She turned to Stratton and Darby, holding out her hand to each in turn. 'Gentlemen, it was a pleasure working with you. I wish you the best of luck.'

As soon as they were outside, Maisie raised her hand to summon a taxi-cab.

'Pushing the boat out, aren't we, Miss?'

'I need to get back to the office, Billy, so we can get on with some real work.'

A cab drew alongside and Billy opened the door for Maisie to take a seat before he instructed the driver and then clambered aboard. 'I thought we were working, if you don't mind me saying so.'

'As the Chief Superintendent said, Billy, I do not have the knowledge to make a bomb or some other sort of terrible weapon. But someone out there does and he's been letting us know that he has every intention of using that knowledge if his demands are not met – and we must assume they definitely will not be met.' She looked out of the window at the already darkened skies of a winter's mid-afternoon, then turned back to Billy. 'So, our job is to find the person who has that knowledge.'

'There's a lot of people like that about. I mean, I could knock together an incendiary device if I had to.'

Maisie shook her head. 'But you are guided by goodness, Billy. Our man doesn't know what it is to feel that goodness any more.'

I feel as if I have been shouting at someone who is walking away from me, and who cannot hear. It has been like that since the war. And so, because I don't want to shout louder, I turn back, I don't bother. But now I have to bother. I can hear myself screaming inside my head. I can hear my voices, telling them how wrong they are, how wrong they have been. I can no longer plead in my prayers.

Listen to me. Listen to me. Please, please, listen to me. But no one listens, because the man with his hand held out, the man who cannot walk as he once walked, or think as he once thought, has nothing that anyone wants to hear, not any more. So now I have to shout. Only I no longer shout with words. There is no point. They only listen to me when I take action. Then they have to listen. So I shout with the doing, and it always comes back to what I do well.

IO

The taxi-cab dropped Maisie and Billy at the junction of Warren Street and Fitzroy Street. As they walked around the corner into the square, a black motor car parked on the flagstones in front of the mansion that housed their office caught their attention. They both stopped walking and stood for a moment to observe the vehicle.

'It's not a police motor, but it is official,' offered Maisie.

'Could be for someone else.'

'It could.' She paused. 'But it isn't. Come on, let's see who it is.'

They did not look into the motor car as they passed and made their way up the steps to the front door, but as Maisie took out her key, they heard a door open behind them and a voice call out.

'Miss Dobbs? And this must be Mr Beale. Jolly good to have caught you.'

They turned around, and Maisie slipped the key into her pocket.

'Gerald Urquhart. Remember me? Well, I just dropped by to have a little conversation, a little chinwag, as they say.' With a lightness of foot, he came up the steps towards Maisie and held out his hand. His voice was now low. His coppery brown hair was slicked back by oil that made it seem darker, and he wore a grey suit with white collar and black tie. His shoes were polished to a deep shine. 'Military Intelligence, Section Five. It's a business matter. Let's go up to your office, shall we?' He nodded towards the door for Maisie and Billy to lead the way. 'Just a few points to discuss. I'm sure you want to keep the Funnies up to date, eh? MacFarlane and his boys can be so cloak and dagger, can't they?'

Opening the door to her office, Maisie approached her desk, and set her document case on the floor and her shoulder bag in a drawer. 'Billy, pull up chairs for yourself and Mr Urquhart, please.' She sat down behind her desk and waited for the men to be seated. Behind Urquhart's back Billy caught Maisie's eye and raised his hand to his mouth as if holding a cup. Maisie shook her head. There would be no offer of tea for the man from Section Five.

'Miss Dobbs.' Urquhart pulled at the trouser fabric close to his knees as he sat down. 'I understand that our friend Robbie MacFarlane has dismissed you from the investigation regarding the source of those letters sent to the Prime Minister et al.'

'Detective Chief Superintendent MacFarlane has a group in custody and believes them to be behind the threats. They are union activists, and one of the group studied chemistry at university, so has an understanding of combustible substances.'

'I see. And you think he's wrong.'

'I think it's worth continuing the search. I think it's worth leaving no stone unturned.'

'Do you know why you've been dismissed?'

'I would have thought it's clear.'

'Not at all.' He crossed his legs, leaning back in a manner that Maisie interpreted as proprietorial. 'No, you were dismissed because of Robbie's tendency towards maverick acts. Taking you to Number Ten was not one of his better strategic moves.'

'I understood I was asked to accompany the Chief Superintendent because I was available and was working on the case. I believe he wanted to bring some immediacy to the meeting, to show that he was not thinking in the usual way, so to speak – that he was willing to consider intelligence beyond Special Branch.'

'Or in other words, that he could do what he liked in his personal bailiwick.'

Maisie did not respond. She wasn't about to agree with Urquhart, or disagree, though she could see his point.

'Moving to a more fruitful dialogue, I hope, I understand you have a – now, what would your old teacher Dr Blanche say?' Urquhart put his finger to his chin in mock thought. Maisie said nothing, though she felt a welter of dislike for the man. She waited for him to continue.

'Oh, yes, he'd say that you had a *sense* of the author of the letters, wouldn't he? Good old Maurice.'

Fighting the urge to stand – she didn't want to give the impression of needing height to have a voice with power behind it – Maisie responded with a certain coolness. 'Dr Blanche has been decorated for service to this country and, as you know, much of that service has been in intelligence, so I would prefer it if you referred to him with the respect his contribution to our nation's security deserves.'

'I beg your pardon, however—'

'However,' Maisie continued, aware that she might have sounded overprotective, 'I do indeed have a sense of our letter-writer.'

'And would you care to let me have a glimpse of your *sense*?'

Maisie rested her forearms on the desk. 'Mr Urquhart, your manner has done nothing to endear you to me, though I realize you did not come here in search of my friendship. If it weren't for the fact that I believe we have little time to find the letter-writer – who has proved already that he has the wherewithal to do the sort of damage to life that brings a chill to the bone – I would not be continuing this little *chinwag*. But we have no time to lose. I will make no secret of the fact that I do not intend to wash my hands of this case, even though I really do need to concentrate on work that brings in an income.'

'We'll pay for information.'

'Yes, you will.'

Urquhart took a deep breath and exhaled. 'Miss Dobbs, tell me what you know of this man we're all after. We have our own specialists working on this case, but we . . . we feel that you may have a greater knowledge.'

Maisie leaned back and looked across at Billy, who seemed to be on the edge of his seat as he followed the back-and-forth volley of words. She stood up and walked from the desk to the middle of the room, then walked back again. She continued pacing as she spoke. 'The man we are looking for has most probably been released from a secure institution during the past two years, though there should be a margin for error – remember, this speculation is not an exact science.' She paused to look out of the window, then began walking back and forth again. 'In general, such a man would most probably have remained close to the institution in question, not making any significant moves to another region, unless there were family there to receive him, so I think we can expect him to have been previously in care in one of the London hospitals for the mentally ill, or a home specifically for soldiers with a psychiatric or emotional affliction. He is, I would say, poorly nourished, and has few, if any, friends. He has some difficulty with physical adroitness and most probably suffers from night tremors and hallucinatory dreams. He is a haunted man.'

'How can he handle chemicals with volatile properties if he has tremors and such like?' Urquhart was writing in a notebook, but paused and looked up at Maisie as he asked the question.

'Training. I would say that this man has some sort of training, perhaps as a chemist, an engineer, a physicist. He might have been a doctor. He is an educated man – though I suspect he might come from lowly beginnings, and that there were other losses in his life. In my experience – and I am sure you are fully apprised of my professional experience – the men who suffered the most from the various war neuroses were those who had some difficulties in childhood, though that is by no means prescriptive.'

She took her seat again, folding her arms as she faced Urquhart and looked into his eyes. 'He's lonely, but at the same time is weary of company, has barely the will to communicate with others. He might have one friend, one person he trusts, but I am not sure. He feels disenfranchised. He may have tried to get work, but was turned away – we might even assume he has obvious wounds that are not attractive, scars and the like. He may be unable to control spittle when he talks. There are many manifestations of psychological wounds that are not pleasing to the eye, and those tics and so on are not something that people want to see, or want their customers to be exposed to. If you watch a man thus afflicted walk down the street, you will see the people coming towards him part as a river divides when it reaches an island. It becomes easier for him to go out after dark.'

Urquhart was silent for several moments. 'This means going through a lot of records. And what if he's moved in from somewhere else?'

Maisie sighed. 'I didn't say this was a certain bet. It's a template, an idea rooted in my own understanding of the gamut of war neuroses, and also in the conversations I've had with experts at two hospitals.'

'And they don't recognize the description you've given us?' Urquhart leaned back in his chair, resting his arm along the back of a vacant chair next to him.

'The description I've given you could probably match hundreds of men still held in asylums, but, to answer your question – no, they don't, not specifically, otherwise I am sure we would have the person in a cell by now.'

'Do you think he might be part of one of these trouble-making organizations – the unions, the Fascists? Sounds like he would be drawn to them.'

'I believe he is a solitary person, one who would not be welcomed into such company. But he might have tried to join, perhaps while looking for a suitable vehicle for his discomfort, his anger.'

'So he might be in with one of these mobs of anarchists?'

'He might. Perhaps.' She drew back from the desk and leaned

into her chair. 'His body might also be disfigured. A curvature of the spine, lameness, and it might come and go, so he may well be listed as having physical disability.'

'Blimey, we'll be going through records from now to kingdom come!'

'Yes, you're right, it may take a while.' Maisie picked up a pencil on the table and tapped it on her palm.

'And you've nothing else to add? Names?'

'No, no names for you. I am sure you have contacts at the psychiatric hospitals and you can have your men in there faster than I can visit all of them.'

Billy cleared his throat. 'I'll see you downstairs, then, Mr Urquhart.'

Urquhart stood up and extended his hand towards Maisie, who remained seated.

'I trust you'll contact me should you acquire knowledge that will help us.'

'I have made the same promise to MacFarlane, so *I* must trust that he will inform you of all useful information that comes his way.'

Urquhart walked to the door, where Billy was standing ready to escort him to his motor car. He turned to Maisie as he set his hat on his head. 'You'll hear from Robbie MacFarlane again, I shouldn't wonder.'

Before Maisie could respond, he left the room and was gone. Billy looked at Maisie and raised his eyebrows, then followed Urquhart down the stairs and returned as the motor pulled away.

'The cheek of it!' Maisie came to her feet.

'Bet you're glad he's gone, Miss.'

'If he'd remained one second longer, I would have boxed his ears.'

'He was a bit familiar, wasn't he? It's not on to talk about the Chief Superintendent like that.'

'There's probably no love lost between Special Branch and Section Five.'

'You gave him a lot of information, I thought.'

Maisie reached for the telephone. 'I can't, ethically, withhold information. We're under the gun, simply as people who live in London.'

'You think it's that bad?'

Holding the telephone receiver in one hand, Maisie flicked through a series of index cards. 'Yes, I do. We have to keep looking, even if we aren't being paid.'

'Oh, I think there will be something for us.'

Maisie rested the receiver back in its cradle. 'What do you mean?'

'Well, I think Urquhart had a point. If you don't mind me saying so, I think the Chief Superintendent has taken a bit of a shine to you – I could see it myself. He won't see you go short.'

'That's enough of that sort of speculation, Billy. Now then, where was I? Oh, yes . . .' She reached for the telephone once again, but it rang as her fingers touched the receiver.

'Fitzroy five—'

'Miss Dobbs?'

Maisie turned away from Billy. 'Chief Superintendent. What can I do for you?'

'Our little Catherine the chemist says she wants to see you again. Could you come back to the Yard? I can have a motor car pick you up.'

'No, that won't be necessary. I'll come straight away by taxi-cab.' She replaced the receiver and turned back to Billy, and spoke to him while keeping her head down as she leafed through papers on her desk.

'I have to go to Scotland Yard immediately, and I am not sure how long I'll be.'

'What do you want me to do, Miss?'

She looked up, now with less of a blush to her complexion. 'First job – review all current client work in progress, see where we are, and make sure we have something to report to our clients. We can't afford to lose business. Next – compile a list of every single psychiatric hospital or convalescent home in London. I'd like to know how we can get a roster of patients who've been discharged over the course of the past two years.' She took a key from her shoulder bag and opened the bottom drawer of her desk. Taking out an envelope, she removed several pound notes and held them out to Billy. 'You may need this to ease the flow of information.'

'Right you are, Miss. Meet back here at the usual time?' He held out Maisie's blue woollen coat for her.

'Of course. See you later.' She smiled as she left the room, but called back as she ran downstairs, 'And, Billy, don't wait if I seem to be taking a long time. You should go home.'

Billy walked to the window to watch Maisie run down the steps and towards Warren Street Station, then he turned to the bank of wooden drawers that held the collection of index cards. There was much to be accomplished before he saw his employer again.

— ⁓ —

As Maisie approached Scotland Yard, she counted four police vehicles screeching away from the kerb, bells ringing as both motor and horse-drawn traffic pulled aside to let them pass.

'Oh, no . . .' she spoke the words aloud as she ran towards the main entrance, only to almost collide with MacFarlane, Stratton and Darby as they left the building.

'Excellent timing, Miss Dobbs.' He pointed to an idling black motor car. 'There's been another attack. We'll brief you on the way.'

Maisie took a seat alongside the passenger window, while MacFarlane sat next to her and Stratton and Darby took the pull-down seats to face them.

'Has anyone been killed?' Maisie knew that this time the stakes would be ratcheted up a notch, that human life would be at risk.

'Yes. A junior minister with the Home Office, at his flat on Gower Street. They're cordoning off the street now and my instructions are not to touch the body. Sir Bernard Spilsbury and his cohorts have been called.'

'Do we know the cause of death?'

'He was found by a housekeeper, and from the description – oh, merciful God help us . . .' MacFarlane closed his eyes and pressed his lips together as if in prayer. Both Stratton and Darby looked away, mirroring each other's unease.

'What has he used this time, Chief Superintendent?' Maisie thought she knew the answer, even before it was spoken.

'I can't fathom how he's done it, but from the description we've received, it has all the hallmarks of mustard gas.'

Maisie felt the colour drain from her cheeks, her hands become cold and damp, but she recovered quickly given the urgent circumstances. 'Not only must we not touch the body, but people should be evacuated until we know the extent of possible exposure. And no one else should go into that building without protective clothing – gowns, gloves and masks.'

'Don't worry – I'll get on to it as soon as we're there,' said Stratton. 'I'll have someone procure gowns and whatever else we need from the hospital.'

MacFarlane was still deep in thought, talking as much to himself as to the group. 'Could someone, an ordinary person, not only develop such a substance, but bring it to a private address and then kill another person with it?'

Maisie responded. 'It would be a difficult task, but not insurmountable, especially for someone trained in the handling of volatile matter. Until we have a laboratory analysis we don't even know if it is mustard gas – it might be something completely new, or certain compounds might have been used to leave clues to tempt the olfactory system into thinking it is something known.'

'But now he isn't even giving us the time he stated in his last letter – you've got forty-eight hours here, a day there, and it feels as if every day he's throwing out more proof that he can run rings around us. How does he do it? There must be a gang, a crew.

One man could not pull off this sort of murder – that's what it is, murder.'

'He may have no concept of time. The deadlines quoted in the threats are just what comes into his head.' She turned to face MacFarlane. 'You see, this man is just existing in his everyday life. He may not be aware of passing time except in the vacuum that is his world. There is only one point of control, and that is in this ability to work with chemicals.'

'And it's not little Catherine Jones, is it, Miss Dobbs?'

'Not unless she can creep out of your cells in the middle of the morning.'

'I apologize if . . .'

Maisie was aware of Stratton and Darby exchanging glances and directed her next question to ensure they were included. 'Inspector Darby, do you agree with my speculation regarding our man?'

Darby looked at his hands. 'Like you, I think he is at the edge. We may have only hours before he strikes again. However . . . however, he may now be exhausted. This outing may have worn him out, so he may lie low, may sleep fitfully for some hours, especially if – as you have suggested – he is poorly nourished. We may not hear from him for some time, but again, we may hear tomorrow.'

The brakes screeched as the vehicle came to a halt outside the Georgian terraced house on Gower Street, close to Bedford Square, and MacFarlane barely waited for the motor car to stop before he swung the door open and stepped on to the street and towards the front door. 'Get these people off the street, Constable.'

Stratton remained aboard, ready to go straight to University College Hospital. Maisie spoke to him before joining MacFarlane. 'Inspector Stratton, it's most important you ensure the housekeeper is kept in isolation at the hospital, and that everyone who has had contact with her is also quarantined. Talk to the doctors – they must know that they are probably dealing with a very dangerous substance. There may be no cause for concern but, though I don't want to cause panic, my instinct tells me to be careful.'

'I'll send the driver back with the gowns and gloves, and ensure the registrar is notified.'

Maisie and Darby stepped from the motor car, which sped off along Gower Street with the bell ringing. They joined MacFarlane, who was speaking to a constable. He pointed to a gathering on the other side of the road.

'I want this road completely closed from Great Russell Street all the way up to the Euston Road, and I want all streets blocked from Tottenham Court Road across to Woburn Place. The only people on this thoroughfare should be in uniform.'

'Not quite, Robbie.' Gerald Urquhart slipped past another police constable and stood beside Maisie. 'Nice to see you back in the fold, Miss Dobbs.'

'Never mind the pleasantries, Gerry.' MacFarlane turned to walk into the house.

'Wait!' Maisie reached for MacFarlane's sleeve. 'Chief Superintendent, I cannot impress upon you the importance of delaying your investigation of the premises until suitable covering has been procured.' She turned to the constable. 'Is anyone in there?'

'The photographer went in some time ago, and another constable. Should have been out by now, I would have thought.'

'Blast!' Maisie opened her document case and removed two linen masks. She handed one to Darby. 'Come on, we'd better go in.' She reached into her bag for a pair of rubber gloves, which she pulled on to her hands, then turned to MacFarlane and Urquhart. 'I'm sorry, I don't carry supplies for an army, just myself. I think it would be best if you waited – I am sure the driver will be back soon. Is it all right if we continue, Chief Superintendent? I thought it best to give the mask to Inspector Darby, given his forensic knowledge.'

In truth, Maisie did not want to enter the property without a witness and, given Urquhart's earlier veiled insinuation that MacFarlane might have designs on her, she did not want him to see her and the Chief Superintendent crossing the threshold together.

'Go ahead – I'll join you as soon as I can.'

Maisie and Darby stepped inside the house, closing the door behind them. The hallway was typical of those found in terraced houses built from Georgian times onward. It was long and narrow, with a staircase ahead leading to the upper floors. A dado rail ran along the wall several feet up from the skirting board, with dark green paint below the wooden rail, and cream above. To the right, doors led to reception rooms, and if one continued along the passage past the staircase, there would be stairs down to the kitchen, and there would also be a means to enter a small walled garden, possibly through French doors at the back of the property.

Maisie's eyes began to water, and as she looked at Darby, he was pulling a handkerchief from his pocket to wipe his eyes.

'Nasty stuff, whatever it is.'

Maisie nodded. 'Hello! Anyone there?'

A groaning came from a room to the right of the hallway.

Maisie and Darby ran towards the room, where they found the photographer and the police constable slumped on the floor, and the body of the junior minister partially covered by a white sheet.

'We need to get them out of here, now – look, the back door. There's a small garden at the back.' She looked around the room. 'Cover your hands with something before you touch them.' Darby opened doors until he found a lavatory, and grabbed a cloth towel hanging next to a hand basin. Together they dragged the two collapsed men out into the cold, diminishing daylight of a winter afternoon, now silent, given the lack of traffic noise from Gower Street.

'Close the door into the parlour, and if you can find a bowl or bucket, bring me cold water to bathe their skin – and bathe your hands and face too, anything exposed to air in the house.'

Though she was in the garden, Maisie heard the front door slam in the distance.

'What the bloody hell's going on?' MacFarlane shouted as he entered the house with Urquhart at his heels, both wearing doctors' gowns, surgical masks and rubber gloves.

'Exposure to the substance the visitor employed to kill the junior minister,' said Maisie as the men came out into the garden. 'They'll be all right, but we have to get them down to the hospital – and quarantined, like the housekeeper.'

'The PM should be informed,' said Urquhart, his tone dictatorial.

'Sod the PM for just a minute, will you, Gerry? I swear, I will knock your block off one of these days, so I will.'

'Now then, Robbie, I don't know who you think you are, but—'

'Don't you come the old "I don't know who you think you are" with me, Mister Cambridge University. This is my murder, my case, and I'm in charge until the Commissioner decides otherwise. Right then, now we've got our matching frocks on, if you want to stay and observe, shut up and follow me.'

Urquhart did not look at Maisie, who had exchanged glances with Darby and both had raised their eyebrows. She came to her feet and reached out for one of the white hospital gowns held by MacFarlane.

'Thank you, Chief Superintendent. I'll show you where the body is.' Maisie led the way into the parlour, cautioning the men first. 'Keep your masks on at all times, gentlemen, and do not under any circumstances touch the body with your bare hands.'

'I think I've seen it all by now, lass, no need to warn me, though Gerry here might faint.'

'Careful, Robbie.' Urquhart's retort was bitter, his face still flushed with embarrassment.

The junior minister had been a man of approximately forty years of age, and was wearing a shirt, tie and woollen trousers when the attacker had struck. His jacket had been placed on the back of a chair and there was an open box with papers strewn across the table. The flesh of his face appeared to be melting across his cheekbones, and the skin at his neck was sunken, as if pulled in by the fight to breathe through what was left of his nose, and the frothing mass that had once been his mouth. With her gloves on, Maisie pressed against the back of the dead man's hands, only to see the skin concertina like the top of a custard when pulled away by a serving spoon. The veins broke open, and blood oozed in small clotted lumps.

'I would say that he invited the attacker into the house, brought him into the parlour.' Maisie pointed to the table. 'The victim reached for some papers – it's possible he was looking for something to write on – and when he turned around a substance was unleashed upon him with some sort of pneumatic spray, perhaps, to have accomplished such coverage. Pain was immediate, and he was blinded, falling backward. His tongue is doubtless little more than liquid where he opened his mouth to scream, and you will see his lungs have belched up froth as they have also liquefied. His hands took the brunt when a second dose was administered.'

Urquhart began to cough, and left the room. He could be heard retching in the garden as policemen in white overalls, masks and gloves helped the photographer and constable to a waiting ambulance.

'Was it a gas, do you think?' MacFarlane spoke softly, then began to rub his forehead.

'We should all leave this room now,' said Maisie. At that point, the police pathologist and two assistants arrived, each of them dressed as if to paint a room, rather than remove a body from the premises.

Within half an hour the house was evacuated of both the living and the dead, and with the hospital gowns removed for incineration, Maisie was on her way back to Scotland Yard with MacFarlane, Stratton and Darby.

'So, what do you think, Miss Dobbs?' Once again, MacFarlane singled out Maisie to answer a question.

'I think that, somewhere in London, there is a very clever man who has been marginalized by society. He may just have invented a new and very dangerous substance. At first blush, it could be taken for mustard gas, but I'm convinced it's something different – for a start, I don't like the look of this white powdery residue, but the laboratory people will no doubt get to the bottom of its chemical structure.' She shook her head and looked around the room. 'What we have to assume is that a man who has the ability to kill one person can use this same substance to kill many.'

'And the way he's escalating his attacks, he could kill and maim a whole street – or the whole of London – tomorrow,' added Stratton.

'Urquhart will have alerted the PM by now.' MacFarlane looked out the window as he spoke.

'What does that mean for the investigation, sir?' asked Stratton.

'It means it becomes a three-ring circus. The Funnies, Special Branch, those boys at Mulberry Point, and not forgetting the mad professors. That's all I bloody well need – a cartload of boffins to deal with.'

Maisie said nothing as she reflected upon that morning – was it just yesterday? – when she was about to board a train for Oxford, and saw Anthony Lawrence at Paddington Station, waiting for the Penzance train. A train that just happened to stop in Berkshire, close to the village of Little Mulberry.

I I

30th December 1931

*Sometimes it seems there is only sleep. There is nothing to do,
nowhere to go, and unless Croucher comes, there is no one to speak
to, no human sound other than the voice in my head. Ian was
another voice, but now he is gone. If only he had waited. If only he
could have fought through Christmas, we might have brought them
to their knees, these men who sit with their full bellies, by their
warm fires, and wonder why we cannot work.*

The man moved to the iron-framed bed and drew back a
mildewed blanket, damp to the touch, the wool like wire to his
fingertips. He curled under the threadbare cover and continued
to write with a pencil.

*I have taken a life. One more life. They should have believed me,
after the dogs, after the birds. I told them. And now they know. I was
discarded, not wanted, thrown aside. And soon someone, somewhere,
will remember. They will remember me and they will know, when
little men with their little microscopes discover that what is in their
little dish of flesh is something they haven't seen before. Then they
will know what I have. Then our situation will change. There will be
something more for us, men who are still waiting for their armistice.*

As fatigue dragged on the man's eyelids and cold seeped
through his skin, layer by layer, it seemed as if the very blood in

his veins were slowing to bring him to the edge of death, a place where he would linger, in neither this world nor the next, until his eyes opened once more, still encrusted with sleep.

— ～ —

Maisie had allowed Billy time off to visit Doreen at Wychett Hill, and was waiting for the clock on the mantelpiece to strike nine so that she could telephone Dr Anthony Lawrence. She was now officially part of MacFarlane's team again for the duration of the case, and there was much work to be done.

Continuing with her notes, she was startled when a bell sounded, indicating that someone was at the front door. She walked to the window and looked down towards the door, but could see only the back of the visitor's coat as she waited for the door to open. Maisie glanced around the square, and was about to turn away when she saw a flash of blue in the distance – and the distinctive nose of a Bugatti parked on the far side of the square where it met Conway Street.

'Priscilla?' Maisie whispered to herself as she ran to the stairs and then downstairs.

'I thought you'd never get here!' Priscilla used her thumbnail to eject a cigarette on to the flagstones before stepping across the threshold when Maisie opened the door. She stopped briefly to kiss her on each cheek, then held out her hand. 'You'd better lead the way, Maisie – show me up to your hive of industry.'

'What are you doing here, Pris?' asked Maisie as they ascended the stairs. She drew Priscilla into her office, and pulled two chairs in front of the gas fire, turning up the jets for more warmth.

'So, this is where you beaver away day after day in the quest for justice, or whatever it is that you do here – you know, chasing criminals and the like.'

'Would you like a cup of tea?'

'Do you have coffee, by any chance?'

'Sorry, Pris.'

Priscilla waved a begloved hand. Always elegant, she was dressed in a pale grey costume, the jacket falling at thigh length with a narrow belt at the waist, and the straight, almost fitted skirt brushing her mid-calf. A black fur cape was draped around her shoulders, a match for black shoes and handbag, from which she took a packet of cigarettes.

'Do you mind?'

'Well, actually, I would rather you didn't. I'll be coughing all day.' Maisie rubbed her arms, feeling cold despite heat from the fire. 'Is everything all right, Priscilla?'

Priscilla's eyes welled with tears. 'Oh, nothing, really. I just thought . . . look, perhaps we can nip out, somewhere where I can light up.'

'You can wait for a bit. Come on, what's wrong?' Maisie looked at her friend of old, who even in her darkest hours had never been one to slouch, now slipping down in the chair and clutching her cape around her as if she yearned for comfort.

'Oh, Pris . . .' Maisie knelt at Priscilla's feet and enveloped her with her arms. 'Tell me what's wrong.'

'I – I just don't know what's got into me. Look at me – I have a lovely home, three simply smashing boys, a husband I adore, who adores me in return – and I am just flailing around like a woman drowning.' Priscilla did not draw back, but allowed herself to be held, and seemed to be curling up like a child against her mother's chest, so that she was surrounded by her friend's warmth and strength. 'I feel such a goose. I have felt this knot inside me getting tighter and tighter for days – and I am supposed to be looking forward to a party.'

Maisie allowed silence to encroach upon Priscilla's weeping, and did not try to prevent the tears. Soon Priscilla sat back, but kept a firm grip on Maisie's hand.

'I don't know what I would do if you weren't here. All the time I was in Biarritz, I missed your company very much, you know.' She pressed her lips together, then continued. 'But I have felt so at sea here.'

'You've had a huge change, Priscilla. Don't underestimate it. Life is very different here in London.'

Priscilla nodded. 'I just don't feel . . . I don't feel . . . as if I'm home.'

Maisie nodded and, while allowing Priscilla to continue holding her hand, pulled a cushion from her chair and sat down at her feet.

Priscilla sniffed, drew a handkerchief from her bag and dabbed her eyes, then her nose. 'I want to go back to Biarritz, only now, after that rather shaky start, the boys are thoroughly enjoying being in London, and Douglas is doing incredibly well indeed, so he's in no hurry to rush back.' She sighed. 'Oh, I don't know, I just can't seem to settle.'

'You settled in Biarritz.'

Priscilla nodded, and her eyes welled with tears once more. 'What's wrong with me, Maisie? You know all about this sort of thing. What's wrong with me?'

'I can only tell you what I believe ails you, Pris, though I may be wide of the mark.'

'No, please, tell me. Tell me what you think is wrong with me. I mean, I am weeping from the time I say goodbye to my boys in the morning to the time they come home. And I bite my lip to maintain a cheerful face at social engagements.' She dabbed her eyes again. 'I feel so bloody selfish, Maisie. I mean, there are people starving in this country, men who can't work, people who dream of the advantages I have. And I'm a wilting mess.'

'Priscilla, when I came to Biarritz last year, you talked to me about your life there. You were brutally honest with me, and you helped me to see how I hadn't stared down the dragon of my past – the dragon of all our pasts, men and women like us, who saw the war at first hand. I remember you telling me how you had come back from the brink, how you had built your life again, about your family and what they mean to you. You found a place where you could heal, a place that became your home. And that's what we are all looking for, isn't it? A home. We're looking for where we belong.'

'But I belong with my family, and they're here.'

'Yes, of course, but don't underestimate the wrench of leaving the place where you found life again, Priscilla.'

'And I came back to the place where death stalked me.' She looked down at her hand entwined in Maisie's. 'I couldn't wait to get away from here, you know. England *was* my home. I didn't know it before the war, but my family was my cocoon. I was so happy, Maisie, so happy. I had my brothers, my mother and father, and life was just one big party, or so it seemed – then it was gone. Just like that.' She snapped her fingers. 'And I am so scared of losing it all again.'

'You won't lose it, Priscilla.'

'But I'm losing it already. My boys are growing, like little men. And I worry so.' She paused. 'Remember that summer before the war? None of us saw it coming, not really. I think of that summer all the time, think of my brothers, think of the past. And I am so scared it's all going to come crashing down again and I will lose them.'

Maisie reached forward and clasped both Priscilla's hands in her own. 'You know, none of us can guarantee the future. Your boys will be growing up wherever you are. They are as much at risk here as they were swimming in the Atlantic in Biarritz – you know that. You are torturing yourself with imaginings, Priscilla.'

'What can I do? I sometimes think my head will explode with all these thoughts.'

'Then counter them with action. Do something, get yourself out of that head of yours. It is no good lingering in the future, you have to drag yourself back to the present.'

'How on earth . . . ?'

'Take your motor car into the country and find a place to ride – you used to love being out on a horse. Or do some voluntary work. I know you can't stand all that committee lark, but you never know, you might find a way to do some good. Worry about someone else's worries – there are plenty of them about, you know.'

'You're right, it's terribly indulgent.' Priscilla's smile was tight, a curve of red lips drawn up to show resolve.

'No, it's not indulgent. It's genuine, and what you feel comes from your love of your family – just don't let this emotion rob you of your time with them. I know your boys are growing fast, but remember that each day you are weaving a memory. Make sure you don't look back at these times through a veil of tears.'

Priscilla nodded and reached for her handbag. 'Look at the time. I've to be at Fortnum's this morning to meet Duncan's dowager aunt.' She pulled on her black leather gloves. 'She's a bit of an old misery, to tell you the truth, so I will take it as fair warning – be not like Gertrude!'

━━✦━━

Maisie saw Priscilla to the door, waving to her until she reached the Bugatti, then returned to her first-floor office. She sat back in her chair alongside the fire, turning down the jets to save money, and thought about her dear friend Priscilla, who had countless advantages, or so it seemed. Yet with money, position, a happy family and a magnificent roof over her head, she still searched for some sort of anchor, some part of her soul that seemed to be missing. Even with such abundance, Priscilla did not feel safe.

With these thoughts on her mind, Maisie picked up her notebook and ran her finger down a list of names. She picked up the telephone receiver to place the call that had been interrupted by Priscilla's arrival.

'May I speak to Dr Anthony Lawrence, please?' She waited for a moment until a second voice responded to her request. 'Not in, but you *expect* him tomorrow. I see. Yes. Do tell him that Miss Dobbs telephoned and would like an appointment at his earliest convenience.' She paused again. 'Yes, would you ask if he would be so kind as to telephone me at my office? Thank you.' She gave the telephone number and set the receiver in the cradle once more.

It was not unusual for Dr Lawrence to be unavailable, given his responsibility to the patients of more than one hospital, but the clerk who answered the telephone could not judge when he might return, which was unusual. Maisie was about to reach for the receiver again when the telephone rang.

'Fitzroy—'

'Miss Dobbs.' MacFarlane's voice was low, as if he feared being overheard. 'I'd like you to come to the Yard. Expect a motor car to be outside your office in the next ten minutes – a chariot to bear you here as usual.'

'Have there been developments?'

'We can discuss the reasons when you get here – and not on this line.'

'Right you are, Chief Superintendent.'

Maisie replaced the receiver, consulted the clock on the mantelpiece once again, and lifted the receiver to dial an Oxford number. She cleared her throat, ready to speak.

'Yes, may I leave a message for Professor Gale?' She wove the telephone cord through her fingers. 'Thank you. Tell him that Miss Dobbs telephoned, and I would like to speak to him at his earliest convenience.' Once more she spelled her name and gave the office telephone number. Doubtless both calls would be returned while she was out of the office, and there would be more telephone calls on her part until she effected conversation with the men. That is, if she chose to wait that long.

As the police vehicle made its way through the streets of London, Maisie wondered, not for the first time, why a man she did not know had mentioned her name in a letter. Had he known her after all? Could he have been a patient in the wards where she had nursed the casualties of war who were wounded in the mind? There were so many of them, men who had lingered, forgotten as time faded memory in the way that the sun took colour from the back of an armchair set in front of a window. Had she known the man when she worked for Maurice? To each question she drew a blank. She had been familiar with the records of every man in her care, and there was no one with the knowledge to build a deadly weapon. For the most part these men had been bank clerks or carpenters; they had worked on the docks and in post offices; they had worked the land, the factories and the canals. And though the war might have rendered them a danger to themselves and others, there was not one who was as calculating as the man who had murdered the junior minister.

'What do you make of that, Miss Dobbs?' MacFarlane skimmed a manila file across his desk towards Maisie.

She leaned forward and took the file; then flipping open the cover, she began to read. The senior pathologist was Bernard Spilsbury, the famed forensic scientist. His notes were precise. The victim's death had taken place within three minutes of exposure to a substance with which the department was not familiar. Three minutes. She had only been sitting on the visiting side of MacFarlane's desk for about three minutes, and it felt like half an hour already. Three minutes in which one of the government's rising stars could feel himself dying, could feel his flesh being eaten by – what? The report concluded that the poison had been administered in a powder form, probably thrown into the man's face when he turned towards the murderer. A powder that had never been seen before.

'I see a sample of the powder has been sent for additional testing.'

'Yes, to University College, the Department of Chemistry.'

'Is a carbon copy of this available?'

MacFarlane held Maisie's gaze before pursing his lips and responding to her question. 'You want to take the report to someone?'

She nodded. 'Yes. And a sample of the powder.'

MacFarlane shook his head. 'You can sit here and take notes

165

from the file, but you cannot have a sample. This stuff might be in powder form, rather than a gas, but we're not taking chances with even one speck of it in the air in London.'

'I assure you I will take every care. I just want a small sample, a few grains.'

'Who is he?'

'Professor John Gale. He's a professor at Oxford – a scientist – and he also works at Mulberry Point. He might be able to tell us if it has been used before, even in a laboratory setting.'

'This will cost me my job if it gets out.'

'It won't.'

He stood up, pushing his chair back against the wall. 'I'll think about it. In the meantime, remember Catherine the chemist wanted a word with you. She's being transferred to Holloway to await trial.'

Maisie nodded. 'I'd better get on with it then.'

Catherine Jones was sitting at the same table as before. She had made it clear that she would speak only if Maisie were left alone with her, though it was pointed out that a woman police auxiliary would remain in the room throughout the interview.

'You wanted to see me, Catherine?'

The woman nodded. She seemed frail, and betrayed her nervousness in the way she shook her head at the end of a sentence, as if this experience of incarceration could be dismissed as never having happened. She rubbed her upper arms in a self-embrace, and tapped the floor with one foot and then the other.

'What is it you have to tell me?'

She shrugged. 'Don't know if you'll be interested.'

'You've made it clear that you wanted to see me, so I am interested already.'

The woman nodded, and rubbed her hands back and forth along her thighs. 'I remembered someone. Someone who came to one of our meetings.'

'A man?'

'Yes. Said he wanted to take action, that there were too many without work, that it was all very well the politicians wanting you for their armies when there's a war to win, but they didn't want to know about you and your problems once you were back.'

'I'm sure there are many men and women who share those feelings.'

She looked at Maisie – who did not flinch from her gaze. 'You have no idea what it is like to be without work, what it's like for the men and women who walk from place to place each day in search of a job. Some haven't worked for years. *Years*. Year after year of walking and begging for a job every single day. Except the days when they don't have the will to walk any more, when their insides are growling so much for want of food, it's as if the body is eating itself. Then there is only sleep. That's all you can do. Sleep until you wake and then walk again.'

'I know, Catherine.'

Catherine rubbed her arms again, and moved to sit sideways on her chair.

'Is there more you can tell me about the man? Do you remember his name?'

'I didn't think you were interested.'

'Of course I am.'

She sighed before continuing her story. 'I remember him because he seemed, you know, a bit off.'

'A bit off?'

'Not that he was soft in the head, not like some of them who come to the meetings.' She paused. 'He was bright. Very sharp. He talked about being over in France, in the war, about what he'd seen. It seemed as if every bone in his body shook when he talked about it. And he said he hadn't been able to get work, not since he'd lost his last job.'

'Did he say where he worked?'

'He said he couldn't tell me, that it was a secret.'

'What else did he say – and what else gave you cause to doubt him?'

'Oh, I didn't doubt him, Miss Dobbs. No, I didn't doubt him, because we talked a few times about work, the sort of work I used to do but don't now because I don't have a job. This man knew what he was talking about. I would say he knew a lot more than me.'

'Then what is it that you question?'

'Miss Dobbs, I do not know if you are aware of the leaps one has to take to become a university student, especially if one is a woman, and all the more so if one does not come from wealth.'

Maisie allowed no emotion to show on her face, or in her manner. 'I am aware of what is required to gain entrance, especially if one's field of study is in the sciences.'

'And you know the cost?'

'Yes.'

'Well, this man said, one day, that he was a foundling. "I might have had a better chance in life, had I not been a foundling." I thought it was a bit archaic, using the word "foundling". I thought he was gilding the lily, telling a lie about himself to spark interest. I mean, he could have been a boy from one of the Barnardo homes, couldn't he? But how many of them go to a university to study?'

'Did you believe him, when you reflected on the conversation afterwards?'

'I didn't know what to believe, to tell you the truth. He might have been a man with a gift for a tall story, and he certainly didn't seem all there.'

'Did he have obvious wounds?'

'Sometimes he limped, then at other times he didn't, as if it came and went. And on those days when he was lame, there was no doubt that it was genuine. I had the feeling that he only came along for the company, and as I said, he only turned up to a few meetings.'

'Were you afraid of the man?'

Catherine was silent for a moment, considering the question before she replied. 'Funny you should ask that, because I *was* afraid of him. When you were talking to him it was as if you were in one of those rooms where the floors aren't level, you know, the sort you get in an old house, where the ground has settled and you could put a marble on the floor and it would start to move because there's a slope. You never felt as if you were on firm ground.'

'Is that enough to point the finger at a man?'

'Probably not, Miss Dobbs. But he did tell me, the last time I saw him, that he could bring the city to its knees before the year was out.'

'His name?'

'Oliver. Just Oliver. As in Twist, I would imagine.'

12

Maisie checked her watch upon leaving Scotland Yard. It was now past noon. She had briefed MacFarlane on her conversation with Catherine Jones and thought he seemed sceptical at best.

'Oliver bloody Twist? A right joker, that one. If she thinks she can get out of—'

'I'm going to follow the lead anyway, Chief Superintendent. We have precious little to go on, so this may be just the breakthrough we need.'

'Stratton's working on another tip-off, so I can't spare anyone to help you.'

'That's all right, it's best that I work alone, or with my assistant.'

'Telephone if you need anything.'

'I will.'

'And you can have that sample by tomorrow morning. I could be shot for this, Miss Dobbs.'

'You won't be, Chief Superintendent. And thank you for your trust in me. I doubt if anything but a specialist laboratory will be able to shed light on the constituent properties of this particular compound – and I think I know just the person in just the right place to do the job.'

Maisie asked the driver to take her directly to her flat in Pimlico. From there, she collected her MG, went to a petrol station to fill the tank, then drove to the asylum, where she hoped to find Anthony Lawrence. On the way, once again she tried to negotiate the web of clues left in the wake of a man who would kill to be heard.

Following the Embankment, she wove her way towards the City, then away from the river, and as she drove along the Gray's Inn Road, she remembered walking this very route just a couple of years before, on her way to Mecklenburgh Square. And she remembered wondering about the rubble left behind following the demolition of a hospital built some two hundred years earlier, a place of great innovation in its day. It was not an institution where medicine was practised, though it could be argued that it was a place where lives were saved. It was a place where unwanted children, some just hours old, were left to be cared for. Now it was closed, and with only part of the original building left standing, the site was languishing in the midst of the country's economic depression. Maisie felt a sensation across the back of her neck, as if the gossamer wings of a butterfly had touched her skin. She remembered the name: the Foundling Hospital. When first built, it provided respite for children who might otherwise have died on the streets, situated as it was amid fields and gardens. Now it was part of a growling metropolis where horses were giving way to motor cars, where trains belched their way across and underneath London, and trams clattered back and forth. If she remembered correctly, the Foundling Hospital had not closed entirely, but had moved out of London so the children would be where they were originally intended to be – in the country.

Foundling. It was a word used only by those of a certain generation, a word that spoke of the time in which the hospital was first built, when the life of the poor was all but worthless, and new life was cast aside to die in the gutter. *Foundling.* An infant deserted at birth, a child abandoned, unwanted. Maisie turned the word around in her mind. Could the man who had the power to kill thousands have been an orphan? And if he were, how would he have gained an education? How might someone of that order— Maisie checked herself. Though there was no witness to her thoughts, her cheeks burned with shame. She had been considered of a lower order herself, and but for good fortune and a serendip-itous discovery by her employer, she herself might never have had the advantage of an education, or a profession. Other gifted children of working-class origins had been sponsored by her mentor, Maurice Blanche, but it was an unusual opportunity – and one for which she was eternally grateful. But to begin life as a foundling represented a more arduous ascent. And if a boy was able to make such a climb, he would be known and remembered. Unless, of course, he was something of a chameleon. Like herself.

Maisie slipped into a lower gear as she approached the Princess Victoria Hospital. She parked the MG outside and ran up the steps to the main entrance, where she pulled open the oak doors and stated her business with the porter.

'I'm afraid the doctor has only just arrived for his rounds. He was at the Queen Elizabeth all morning, and is very busy.' The porter checked a list of staff, then verified the information again on a timetable of rounds that was hanging up on the wall behind the counter.

'Yes, I am sure he is. However, I wonder if you could tell me when I might see him.'

The porter pulled a fob-watch from his waistcoat pocket and frowned, then ran his finger along a row on the timetable with Lawrence's name at one end. 'Well, I doubt it will be before two.'

'May I wait?'

'Suit yourself, madam, but as I said, you could be here for an hour or so.'

'Right, Mr . . .'

'Croucher.'

'Right, Mr Croucher, I'll just wait over there, if you don't mind. Perhaps you'd be so kind as to let me know when the doctor is available.'

The man straightened his spine and looked at his watch again, then at the clock on the wall above the bench where Maisie was now seated. He pursed his lips and shrugged his shoulders. 'Well, don't blame me if you're sitting there for a long time today.'

Maisie took a notebook from her bag and smiled at the man. 'Don't worry, I won't.'

It struck her that the porter was as short in his manner as he was in stature. He was a stocky man, yet his movements were exact, and she observed – as she watched him across the counter – that he checked and rechecked every task, whether placing mail in departmental pigeonholes, or giving instructions to his fellow workers. He would say everything twice, verify an action twice, and then he would sweep his hands through his hair and back across his head. It was a lifetime habit, thought Maisie, looking at his receding hairline. And how old was this man? Probably about forty years of age, she thought.

She continued making notes, noticing that, as the turn of the hour approached, Croucher lifted the telephone and called to see if Dr Lawrence had returned to his office. Half an hour later, a shrill single ring issued from the telephone and, after responding to the call, Croucher summoned Maisie to the counter, his finger crooked as he beckoned her to him.

'Dr Lawrence is in his office now and can see you.' He pulled a chain from his pocket at the end of which was a large ring and several keys of varying sizes. 'I will have to accompany you, of course.'

'Of course, I understand. I once worked with Dr Lawrence, you know. Many years ago now, when I was a nurse.'

The man's eyes opened wider at the news, though his only comment was, 'You'll know how busy he is, then.'

⁓

'Thank you, Croucher,' said Anthony Lawrence, when Maisie arrived at his office. 'I'll summon you when Miss Dobbs and I have finished talking.' He turned to Maisie, holding his hand out towards the visitor's chair, and took a seat behind his desk. 'I didn't expect to see you again so soon, Miss Dobbs.'

'It's good of you to spare me some time, Dr Lawrence.'

'What can I do for you?'

'I understand that you once worked at Mulberry Point, the government's weapons testing laboratory, in Berkshire.'

He shrugged, much in the way that Croucher had shrugged earlier. 'It was quite some time ago now – just after the war. Not there long, short-term business.'

'I understand that you were there to monitor the psychological effects of testing, and the effect of such work on the men who were employed at the laboratories.'

'How do you know?'

'I met with Elsbeth Masters this week – on quite another matter, I might add – and she happened to mention that you had worked together there.'

'I see. Yes, as I said, it was a long time ago.'

'Dr Lawrence, may I ask about your work at Mulberry Point?'

Lawrence slid his hands on either side of a pile of papers, aligning them on the desk. He pushed them to one side, then pulled them to him, before pushing them away again.

'It was work to be held in the strictest confidence. I do not know what Dr Masters thinks she's doing, telling all and sundry.'

'I believe she felt confident in divulging the information.'

Lawrence lined up a collection of pens and pencils and graduated them by size next to the files. Then he changed the order, and placed writing instruments of like colour alongside one another. Maisie, now accustomed to this habit, watched each movement, waiting for his response.

'It's clear you know about the work that goes on at Mulberry Point, so I see little harm in allowing the following. The nature of experimentation at the laboratory is such that both physical and psychological responses to various substances had to be monitored. There is only so much testing that can be done on dogs, cats, birds and mice – and it seems the public are far more worried about the well-being of animals than they are about human life – so various workers volunteered themselves for experimentation, in the interests of serving their country.'

'That sounds rather dangerous.'

'To a point, yes, it was.'

'Were people always aware of the consequences?'

Lawrence began moving the items on his desk again. 'Miss Dobbs, remind me why you are asking these questions?' He gave a half laugh. 'I am finding it hard to reconcile the memory of an adept nursing sister with the woman who is questioning me now.'

Maisie let the comment settle, and continued with her line of enquiry. 'Was the testing with regard to weapons that might be used against our countrymen, or weapons that our scientists were developing?'

'Can't have one without the other.' Maisie noticed that Lawrence's response was candid. He continued as if speaking to a child unable to grasp simple concepts. 'You have to be one step ahead of the enemy, you know. As I said, my job concerned the mind's response to weapons that cannot be seen, the onslaught that can only be felt, experienced.'

'I see.'

'Is that all?' Lawrence shifted his chair, as if ready to leave the room.

'Yes, I think that's all – oh, no, one last thing.' Maisie gathered her document case and stood up to face the doctor. 'Did you ever get to know the men – or women, I suppose – who worked at Mulberry Point?'

He shook his head, and looked at his watch. 'No, not my job to make acquaintances of my patients.' He indicated the door. 'Shall we? I expect Croucher is in the corridor somewhere – he'll show you out.'

'So, you wouldn't have known a man called "Oliver", then?'

'Good heavens, no. No names, no pack drill, just numbers. In fact, I have never known an Oliver in my life – except Twist, that is!' He opened the door and shouted along the corridor for Croucher, who came at once when summoned.

It was clear to Maisie that both Anthony Lawrence and the porter, Mr Croucher, had been glad to see the back of her. The former did not care for her questioning, and the latter appeared to object to anyone taking up space in the entrance hall, over which he seemed to reign supreme. She felt sure that Lawrence was holding something back. Or could his manner be put down to being a doctor, one who was not familiar with having his word questioned in any way, especially by a former ward sister? He would object to her enquiry as it suggested she doubted him, and in Maisie's experience, doctors saw their diagnosis as the last word, and their last word as law. One did not question the doctor's decision.

She glanced at the clock on the way out and walked to the MG at a brisk pace, then drove back to Fitzroy Square. She parked in Warren Street and walked across the square, in time to see Billy Beale opening the front door to enter.

'Hold the door, Billy!' Maisie ran the last few yards.

'Afternoon, Miss. Sorry I'm a bit late, but the train was delayed. According to the guard, there was a fair bit of ice on the line up from Epsom this morning, and it's slowed everything up all day.'

'Not to worry. Come on, let's get a quick cup of tea and then get to work.'

'Something come up?'

At the top of the stairs, Maisie unlocked the door to the office and, well used to their ritual, both she and Billy took off their coats and hung them behind the door before Maisie ignited the fire, and Billy put the kettle on. Having not stopped to eat, Maisie was hungry, but food would have to wait now as there was work to be done. Soon they were sitting at the table by the window with the case map spread out in front of them.

'Do you remember the Foundling Hospital?'

'Over towards Mecklenburgh Square?'

'Yes. It closed – oh, I think in 1926 or '27, something like that. Can you remember where they placed the children? I don't think it was closed as in never to open again, but I seem to recall it was moved, out of London, to the country.'

'I remember reading about that, Miss. I remember talking about it with Doreen, saying it was sad, you know, that little children aren't wanted, and have to live in them orphanages, growing up with—'

'But where did they go?'

'I could have sworn it was down Surrey way. Somewhere like that – Dorking? Reigate? Redhill? Come to think of it, I think it was Redhill.'

'Find out for me – as soon as you can. I want the address, and I want the name of the principal, the headmaster, whatever they call the person in charge. Then I have to pay them a visit.' She looked at her watch. 'You have to get back to your boys soon, Billy, so I'll go alone.'

'You'll never get down there at a decent hour today, Miss. Don't mind me saying so, but no one will see you.'

Maisie gave a half laugh. 'This is where I need a black motor with bells and a blue uniform. Or the words "Detective Superintendent" in front of my name.' She paused. 'In fact . . .' She drew her chair back and stepped quickly to her desk, where she lifted the telephone receiver and placed a call to Scotland Yard.

'May I speak to Detective Chief Superintendent Robert MacFarlane, please?' She paused. 'Well, is Detective Inspector Stratton there?' Another pause. 'Detective Inspector Darby? All out. I see. In that case, as soon as Superintendent MacFarlane returns, please ask him to return my telephone call.' Maisie gave her name and telephone number and replaced the receiver.

'Now what?'

'As soon as you have the information about the Foundling Hospital, Billy, I'll make an appointment and go tomorrow morning.'

'What will you tell them?'

'Anything – whatever I have to say to gain an audience with someone who in turn has access to the records.'

177

Billy nodded as he stood up and went to the wooden card file set against the wall alongside his desk. Maisie noticed his matt-grey skin and the lines around his eyes, which seemed even more pronounced than yesterday.

'Oh, Billy, I am sorry. I was so anxious to get to my desk that I forgot to ask about Doreen – and she has been on my mind so much. How is she?'

Billy bit his lip. 'I want her out of there, Miss. I wish I could have just brought her home, but – I don't know what's right any more. I don't know whether taking her out is worse than leaving her there, but at the same time, you should see her – I don't know what they're doing half the time. It seems to me they're keeping on with this business of trying to shock her mind into going back to what it was, as if they're trying to get a big enough jolt in her to come to terms with what happened to our Lizzie. She's holding on to it – with all her mind she won't let our little girl go. But she's gone, and I miss her just as much. There's the boys to think of, and our future, and the way things are going . . .'

'Come on, sit down, Billy.' Maisie took Billy by the arm. 'I'll telephone Dr Masters again right now, to see if there's been any progress. I'll ask if she can bring any more urgency to getting Doreen transferred.'

'I feel as if I'm giving up, Miss. Nothing seems to be going right for us, does it? Just when we think we might be on our way up the river, so help me a bleeding great wave comes and knocks the stuffing out of all of us. And the boys know it, it's taking its toll there, make no mistake.' He sighed, taking in such a deep breath that it sounded as if it might be punctuated by a bronchial cough, but was not, for he continued talking. 'Time was, I would look at all them poor sods walking for work, lining up for subsistence, and think, "At least we ain't got that to put up with." But now I don't. I don't feel better off any more, because we've been playing with a rotten deck of cards, me and Doreen.'

'It'll be all right, Billy, I promise. Look, you go and put the kettle on for a fresh cuppa, and I'll telephone Dr Masters.'

Billy nodded and set about collecting the tea tray, and when he left the room, Maisie picked up the telephone receiver. She had not wanted to place the call while he was in earshot, in case the news was other than they had hoped for.

'Dr Masters?'

'Yes – oh dear, it's you, Maisie. I have been meaning to get in touch since yesterday, but I am clinging on to sanity myself. We always have more admissions at this time of year. Christmas and New Year, I am sure, sends everyone around the bend. Now then, you've called about Mrs Doreen Beale – that's it, isn't it?'

'Yes. Do you have news for me?'

'Good news. We can admit her in the new year, but we have to wait for the seasonal influx to be whittled down.' Maisie could hear a shuffling of papers. 'Right, here we are: we'll admit her on Monday, January the fourth. An ambulance has been arranged to bring her up from Wychett Hill – I have to complete some documents and then admissions will expedite matters.'

'Oh, Dr Masters, thank you.'

'Not at all, not at all. Sounds like the poor woman was in a dreadful state, doesn't it?'

'Yes, and she has since suffered through more procedures.'

'I'll assess her as soon as she arrives. We'll look after her, not to worry.'

'Thank you, again, Dr Masters.'

'Yes, as soon as I heard your voice, I knew you were ringing to ask about either Mrs Beale's transfer or the business of Anthony Lawrence.'

'Is there something else you can tell me about Dr Lawrence?'

Dr Masters sounded distracted, as if other matters to hand were claiming her attention.

'Oh, yes, I'd just heard from him for the first time in years when you came to see me, hadn't I?'

'That's right.'

'It wasn't about much, really. He is writing a book, about the effects of nerve agents and other such weaponry on the human psyche. Naturally, he wants to draw upon some of the work we did together years ago, so he sought permission to reuse material from several papers we co-authored at the time.'

'I see. Was he worried that you might publish first?'

Masters laughed. 'If he was, his mind is at rest now. I do not feel the need to leave any legacy other than my work with my patients. When I have given papers at meetings of my peers, it is to advance the work of us all. Oh dear, I really must rush in a minute or two. What was I saying? Oh yes, this field is changing all the time. In years to come, we will be laughed at and, though I hate to say this, I believe that any book hitherto written on this subject – and on the issue of what the public refers to as "shell-shock" – is tainted by political interests.'

'Even with someone as eminent as Dr Lawrence? When I worked with him I thought he was one of the best at his job.'

'And so he was – and still is. But when you have dedicated your life to your work, when you have more of that life behind you than in front of you, you start to think of ways in which your reputation can live on after you've gone.'

'Yes, yes, I understand.'

'Frankly, as soon as I'm gone, I'm gone, and that's all there is to it. In the meantime, I must now bring this conversation to an end, but if Mr Beale is with you, may I have a quick word?'

Billy had just walked into the room, so Maisie held out the telephone receiver to him and mouthed the words *Doctor Masters*.

Setting down the tea tray, Billy took the receiver and listened to the news regarding his wife, and Maisie moved away towards the case map, which was now pinned to the table by the window. She looked at her assistant and believed she could see the lines diminishing from around his eyes. 'I don't know how to thank you, Dr Masters, really I don't.' He rubbed his forehead to hide his tears as he spoke, then said goodbye and ended the telephone call.

'Almost there, Billy,' said Maisie, as she heard the receiver returned to its cradle.

'Miss Dobbs, I thought she was going to be in that Wychett Hill place for ever, I really did.' He brought Maisie a cup of tea. 'I don't know how to thank—'

'You don't have to thank me, Billy. But I do need the number for the Foundling Hospital, wherever it is in Surrey.'

Ten minutes later, Maisie was calling a Dr Rigby at the Foundling Hospital at its new location in Redhill. She would see him tomorrow morning, at nine.

———

At Maisie's insistence, Billy left early to return home. Even though Doreen would be moved to a hospital according to her recommendation, where she believed the care to be more humane, it was still an asylum. She hoped her instinct had served her well, and that Doreen would make progress and begin her slow ascent from the depths of her instability to make a good recovery.

Maisie placed two manila folders, each containing a collection of papers, in her battered old leather document case; put on her navy-blue woollen coat, her cloche and her gloves; and then pulled a pale-blue cashmere wrap – a gift from Priscilla when she was in France – around her shoulders for additional warmth. She looked around the office, turned off the lights, locked the office behind her, and left the building.

A dirty ochre smog clung to her in the cold winter darkness as she walked to the MG, and the thick air seemed to lift up the click-clack of her shoes on flagstones, only to bring the echo back to her as if she were being followed. Once she would have been disconcerted by such a sound, would stop to listen, might even have called out, 'Who's there?' Now she was more confident in her surroundings, she knew the streets, the shopkeepers, and if she were worried, she could run into the Prince of Wales public house – someone would help her if help were needed.

Reaching the MG, Maisie unlocked the door and placed her bags on the passenger seat before starting the motor. As she was about to take her seat, she saw a lame man come out of the swirling pea-souper smog, and with a shuffle and clump he moved past her. He did not wear a cap, and Maisie could not see the detail of him, but he moved with a deliberate slowness, as if his balance might fail him. There was a sour odour as he passed, a dank blight that the homeless carried with them, and she thought she might go after him and press a coin or two into his hand, for he was indubitably a man who had been to war, and it was the least she could do. But he had passed, the hard metal tip of his cane clattering against the pavement as he vanished into the noxious blend of smoke and fog.

I don't think I can stand another year of invisibility, another year of being one of the unseen. We make our way along the streets and are passed by as if we have no place, no value and worth. Ian could not bear such an existence any more. He had only two friends, me and the man at the bookshop, who he thought did not even know his surname, even though he wrote it in a ledger each time he borrowed a book. Of course, he knew Croucher, and Croucher did what he could. And I know, now, that Ian was right. No one wants to see the broken, in body or in mind. We are better off kept out of sight in cold, sterile wards of efficient nurses, and doctors who only know you by the notes at the end of your bed. Or we are better off dead.

I thought some sign that I had been heard might follow my letters. I did not want to take life. I have seen too much death. But now it seems I have only one more opportunity to raise my voice. To be heard. The end of the year is almost upon me. There's only one thing left to do. St Paul's, on New Year's Eve. For Auld Lang Syne, my dears. For old times' sake.

13

It was almost eight when Maisie arrived home. And even as she was looking forward to preparing a light supper, with perhaps a small glass of sherry to warm her from the inside out, she had a feeling that she would not be alone this evening.

'Miss Dobbs?' Robbie MacFarlane's voice reached her before his large frame emerged from the smog as she stepped from her motor car.

'Chief Superintendent?'

'I hope you don't mind me coming to see you at your home.'

'Not at all – has something happened?' She squinted beyond him in the darkness, to see if a police vehicle awaited the detective. He was alone.

'No, no, not yet.' He seemed unsure of his words, almost stuttering his response to her question. 'You telephoned the Yard today and I wanted to make sure everything was in order.'

'Yes. Look, would you care to come in? It's no good standing out here to talk, is it?'

'Thank you. I don't want to impose, but . . .'

'Come on.' Maisie walked towards the main door of the building and opened the outer glass door leading to a foyer that on a clear summer's day would be bathed in light streaming through the windows, illuminating the centre staircase. Once inside, she turned left towards the door to her ground-floor flat. 'It's nothing grand, but it's home.'

MacFarlane closed the door behind him and followed her along the hallway as she turned on the lights and walked into the drawing room. She ignited the fire, drew the blinds, and placed her document case and shoulder bag on the dining table before offering to take MacFarlane's overcoat and hat.

'I'll put them in the box room at the end of the passage – the main pipe for the heating runs up the wall there, so the room is always warm, whether I've turned up the radiator or not.'

'Very nice flat, if I may say so, Miss Dobbs.'

'Thank you. I'm happy here. Do take a seat.'

MacFarlane sat down on one of the chairs close to the fire, and looked around the room. Above the mantelpiece was a water-colour painting of a woman on a beach, looking out to sea – a woman who resembled Maisie – and on the far wall behind the dining table was a simple woven tapestry. It was a blend of vibrant reds, golds, mauves, blues, yellows and greens and brought together wave after wave of colour to depict a sunset across summer countryside.

'Interesting taste in art, Miss Dobbs.'

'The watercolour was a gift, and the tapestry is one of my own – it's very simple, I'm not an expert at all.'

'But you're an artist.'

'Oh, no. Not me.' Maisie paused. 'Look, Detective Chief Superintendent, I must confess I have barely eaten a thing all day and I am famished. I have a hearty soup already prepared, some bread and cheese – would you care to join me?'

MacFarlane turned to face her, and the colour rose in his cheeks. 'Thank you, yes, I'm a bit peckish myself.'

'Right then. There's a bottle of sherry in the sideboard, and some glasses, so do pour us both a glass – just a small one for me. And before you ask, there's nothing stronger – in fact, there's nothing else – so you won't find a single malt lurking away in the back.'

'Sherry will be quite welcome.'

Maisie stepped into the kitchen and leaned against the stove. What on earth was she thinking? Inviting the detective to stay for supper? What would he think? What would anyone think?

A stockpot of soup, made the day before, sat on the top of the stove. She pulled it towards the larger burner and lit the gas-ring, then held the match close to the gas jets in the oven. She brought a wedge of cheese from the larder, along with a cottage loaf, placing the cheese on a wooden board and the bread in the oven. The bread was not in the first flush of youth, so she hoped a warming would soften it up. She brought knives and spoons from a drawer in the dresser, a tablecloth and cloth napkins from another drawer, and set the dining table for two.

'There you are, Miss Dobbs.' MacFarlane held out a glass of sherry.

'Thank you, Chief Superintendent.' She took the glass and held it up in a toast. 'To the new year.'

'Aye, it's not long now. To 1932.'

'Do take a seat in front of the fire. The soup will be ready soon – it's oxtail with carrots, potato and onion.' Maisie returned to the kitchen, brought out two large soup plates, took a quick taste of the broth, and ladled the soup on to the plates. She set the hot bread on the wooden board alongside the cheese and took the board to the table. After she'd brought in the soup, she returned to the kitchen, opened the back door and lifted a porcelain butter dish from a covered pail, which also contained a half bottle of milk.

When he was summoned to the table, MacFarlane smiled and thanked Maisie again. 'Miss Dobbs, this is kind of you.'

Maisie nodded. 'Dig in, Chief Superintendent, or it will get cold.'

They had been eating in silence for some minutes when the detective set down his spoon. 'It's been a long time since I had a home-cooked meal.'

'Too busy?'

'For the most part.'

Having sated her initial hunger, Maisie spoke again. 'You wanted to know why I telephoned you today.'

'Yes, indeed, that's why I came here.' MacFarlane lifted his spoon and dipped it into his soup once more.

Maisie thought back to Billy's comments and wondered if there was more to the visit. Surely anxiety to see the case closed had led him to wonder why she had placed a call to him, which inspired him to wait for her at her flat – though he could have come to her office, instead. But the flat was more convenient to Scotland Yard, so it made sense that he would wait for her here.

'I don't know yet if my enquiry will carry weight, but I was not ready to dismiss Catherine's story today, about the man who had come to their meeting.'

'I am sure there are dozens of nutters out there looking to join the agitators, Miss Dobbs. It's the need to belong to a group, isn't it? I've come across it before, and you've heard Colm Darby talk about it. Boys and men who'd never been in trouble, but they've been out on the edge somewhere, and they find family of sorts among men who would exploit them. One minute they are tired, lonely, misunderstood – some of them are misfits, in their way – and then they discover they are among people who give them a feeling of attachment. The next thing you know, they are up to their eyes in crime of some sort or another. The man described by Catherine Jones sounds the same – someone not quite right, someone who is shunned, so he tries to join this lot, only they don't take to him and he's on his own again. I'll concede there's a chance that he's our man, but it's also more than likely that the inventive Catherine is trying to ingratiate herself with us and thereby hoping to receive due consideration when it comes to sentencing. Seen it many times, I'm afraid.'

'I'm looking into it anyway.'

'Good.' MacFarlane reached for the bread knife and sawed two thick wedges of crusty loaf, sliding one on to Maisie's plate with the knife.

'Thank you.' She began to butter the bread, placed a sliver of cheese on top, and continued. 'Apparently he referred to himself as a "foundling". The term is a bit old-fashioned, and was enough to pique my interest. I remembered the Foundling Hospital, the one built by Thomas Coram in the 1700s. It only moved out of London about four or five years ago, and now it's in Redhill. I'm going there tomorrow, to see if I can look at their records. There are a couple of members of staff who have been with the hospital for over thirty years.' She paused. 'And yes, I know it's a bit of a leap of faith, but if I assume that our man is, say, in his mid-thirties, I can perhaps isolate the years when he might have been there. And if his name really is Oliver, that gives me more to go on.'

'And if you come up with nothing?' MacFarlane did not look up as he swept a scrap of crust around the edge of the bowl to soak up the last of the broth.

'I've asked Mr Beale to compile a list of other orphanages – the Barnardo homes, for example.' She watched as MacFarlane finished eating. 'Would you like some more?'

He smiled. 'That was a lovely bit of broth – and if there's more in the pot, I'll take it.'

Maisie reached for his bowl and went to the kitchen, returning with a second helping, which she set in front of him. She continued outlining her plan. 'I have been back to see one of the doctors I worked alongside years ago, when I was a nurse – I told you about him. He's an expert in the care of men who have suffered war neurosis, and he also has experience in working with men and women who have been exposed to weapons such as gas, nerve agents and so on – in wartime and in the laboratory.'

'And what does he say?'

'Surprisingly little. He is writing a book at the moment, which might account for his reticence to speak. But he was most helpful at first, giving me vital information with which to outline a template of the kind of person we're looking for.'

'Ah, yes, the template.'

'I know you think I've wasted time.'

'We've all wasted time, Miss Dobbs. When you don't know where you're going you run around in circles at first, whacking the bushes to see what vermin come out. Rather than a specific template, it's the scatter method of acquiring clues. Shake out every nasty piece of work you ever came across and see what sticks to the bugger.'

The words echoed into the room, and then there was silence. Maisie looked at MacFarlane as he lifted his spoon again, and gauged the degree to which she should take him into her confidence, whether to share her belief that she would find a thread of possibility at the hospital tomorrow. There was a sense she had, an excitement that welled in her chest when she was close to the trickle of information that would lead to a stream, and the stream to a river. That sensation was with her now. She set down her spoon and leaned forward.

'Chief Superintendent.'

MacFarlane had just lifted a spoonful of broth to his mouth and stopped when she spoke. 'Yes, Miss Dobbs?'

'I think tomorrow's appointment will bear fruit.'

'I know you do.'

She nodded. 'I believe I am close, very close.'

'Aye, lass, you may be. But we all have to go on with the search, which is why Stratton is keeping an eye on the Fascists, and Colm Darby is still sniffing away at his Irish leads. We've seconded two of Dorothy Peto's women detectives to shadow our latter-day suffragettes, and we have infiltrated the unions. Our friend Urquhart tells me that there are German agents who have been trying to test their own nerve gases on our Underground railway for months now – it's a wonder he told me anything, but this is no time for us all to take to our corners, much as we have to fight the urge to get into a huddle. And you have your orphans, and your doctors and your professors. We're all hoping for that little tap on the shoulder, aren't we? The wee bit of excitement when we know we've got something.'

Maisie nodded.

MacFarlane's voice had taken on a softness she had not heard before. 'So, you go on down your path, and you keep me well informed. And if you get that fish on the line, don't think you can land him yourself. I've seen your resolve, seen what you've accomplished – remember, it was my job to investigate *you* – but bringing in this man may take more than even you think.' He finished the second bowl of soup, wiped his mouth with the table napkin, and leaned back. 'Now, I don't want to outstay my welcome, Miss Dobbs. You've done me proud.'

'I'm glad to have had the company, Chief Superintendent.' Maisie stood up. 'I'll get your coat and hat.'

Having closed the main door behind Robbie MacFarlane and watched as he walked into the night, Maisie returned to the flat and locked the door. While attending to washing the plates, cutlery and utensils, she realized that she really was glad to have had the company. Though there was the occasional supper engagement, so often her evenings were spent alone, her staple diet being the large pan of soup she made at the beginning of the week. And later, as she donned her flannel pyjamas and pulled a pillow from her bed to the floor, where she sat cross-legged to meditate before sleeping, she acknowledged that the Chief Superintendent gave no more weight to her enquiry than he had to the other leads being investigated by Special Branch and Military Intelligence. But he had made her feel as if she were accepted, part of his group. He let her know that she was not alone, that, in a way, she belonged.

31st December 1931

Maisie began her journey before seven in the morning. Although she was close to the river, and the mist that wafted in swirls around motor cars, horses and riverboats, the morning was crisp, and the ribbon of grass alongside the flats dusted with frost. The roads would doubtless be icy, so she expected the journey to take longer than usual.

Setting off, Maisie crossed the Albert Bridge and made her

way towards the Brighton road, which would take her out of London, through Streatham and Coulsden, then down to Redhill. As was her habit, she used the journey to reflect upon the case in hand, and thought back again to the meeting with Anthony Lawrence. There was something changed about him, she thought. Was it a certain disillusionment with his work? At one time he had demonstrated the mark of an innovative thinker, but now, though he seemed no less dedicated to his role, there was something jaded about his demeanour. Perhaps writing the book was part of an endeavour to rekindle his former energy. She also remembered that, despite promises, he had never managed to effect access to the hospital's records so that she might peruse the lists of men discharged from care during the past several years. And she hadn't pressed him because they had discovered the name of the Christmas Eve suicide. She reminded herself that, though Christmas seemed as if it were months ago now, it was only a few days past, with the new year almost at hand – not the best time to try to overcome the machinations of a hospital's administrative departments. And besides, she knew Urquhart's men were supposed to be doing just that, and hoped they would alert her if they found something of note.

She checked the hour on a church clock as she drove through Purley, and wondered if she might have time to go on to Oxford following the meeting with Dr Rigby. She wanted to question John Gale further, but reminded herself that she would need to collect the substance sample from MacFarlane before setting off again.

The sun was poking through as she approached Merstham, where she stopped to check the address of the Foundling Hospital, before proceeding on to Redhill, the next town. Already busy by half past eight in the morning, the High Street was flanked by two lines of shops and a large red-brick town hall, another testament to Victorian ostentation. Soon she was approaching the Foundling Hospital, now housed in a former convent, a building almost as dark and gothic as the Wychett Hill asylum.

Dr Rigby greeted Maisie with the efficiency she had observed before in those responsible for the institutionalized. He checked his watch upon greeting her and repositioned the monocle that made him seem older than his years, though he must have been past sixty. With his furrowed brow emphasizing his importance, she thought he resembled photographs she had seen of Rudyard Kipling, when the newspapers published photographs of the author and his wife visiting the battlefields of northern France in search of their only son's final resting place.

'Dr Rigby, thank you for agreeing to see me.'

'Quite, Miss Dobbs. I understand this is a police matter.'

'Yes. I am currently seconded to Scotland Yard – I have a letter of introduction, if you would like to see it.'

'If you don't mind, yes.' He held out his hand to a chair, then waited until she was settled before taking his seat on the opposite side, next to a window overlooking the playground.

Maisie took an envelope from her document case and handed it to Rigby, who adjusted his monocle several times as he read.

'Detective Chief Superintendent . . . Special Branch.' He raised his eyebrows, a move requiring another repositioning of the monocle, then handed the letter back to Maisie. 'What can I do for you?'

'Sir, I'm looking for a man who might have been one of your children, perhaps some thirty-five years ago. I have little to go on, except that I suspect he would be in his mid-thirties at the present time.'

'Do you have a name?'

'Oliver.'

'May I ask what the man has done, why he is wanted by the police?'

'I am sorry, Dr Rigby, I cannot divulge that information. However, the man I am looking for is – I think – an intelligent and academically accomplished man.'

Rigby shook his head. 'Then you won't find him among our boys.' He leaned back, then forward, and clasped his hands together, circling his thumbs around each other as if part of his body had to continue moving at all times. 'Right from the start, our boys here are groomed for military service, a fine place for a young man who has none of the advantages of a higher-born life.' He pointed to photographs on the wall, of young boys in military-style trousers and jackets, and girls in the uniform of domestic service. 'Our girls are steered towards service, where they will have a roof over their heads and, with a strong moral compass instilled in them, will not repeat the folly of their mothers.'

'And what if a child shows a particular academic inclination?'

Rigby pulled a collection of school exercise books towards him. 'This is my marking for this morning. Have a look through the children's work.'

Maisie took several of the books from the top and began to leaf through. The children's penmanship was perfect, the lines sharp, the curves exact. And though the number work did not demonstrate academic excellence, there was a level of workaday proficiency that would stand each child in good stead.

'When our children leave us, they leave with the ability to care for themselves. They can read and write, they understand the importance of personal hygiene and a strong individual discipline. In addition, they are exposed to the arts, to music and to a healthy level of recreation. But there are no academic miracles, no pauper-to-university stories to tell you.'

'Thank you, Dr Rigby.' Maisie replaced the books on the top of the pile. 'However, I wonder, might it be possible to look at your records for the years 1892 to the century's turn? Just in case I find something?'

Rigby shrugged. 'As you wish. Of course, the records are packed away – we expect to move again in a few years, into new premises in Hertfordshire. The old convent here is but a stopgap. However, our records are catalogued. I'll have them brought to my office here.'

Less than an hour later, Maisie closed the last ledger and placed it back into the box from which it came. She checked that she had replaced every folder, every book and piece of paper as it was found, and stood up, rubbing the small of her back. She had discovered nothing. Nothing among the Thomases, Fredericks, Arthurs, Alberts and Williams. Many of them had joined the army, and most of them were probably now dead. As instructed when Dr Rigby left her to work in his office, she pulled a cord on the wall, and one of the school's secretaries came into the room.

'I'm finished now. Could you inform Dr Rigby that I am ready to leave?'

Rigby returned, and began walking her to the front entrance. Maisie stopped to watch children playing a team game on an adjacent field.

'They are happy enough, Miss Dobbs.'

'Yes, I can see that.'

'They have fresh air, they have food, an education, and our staff here are as dedicated today as Sir Thomas Coram was when he founded the hospital.' He walked down the steps, and turned to Maisie. 'I must confess, I am not sorry that you are leaving empty-handed. It would be a sad day when the actions of one of our boys or girls attracted the attention of Scotland Yard in such a way. Of course, there are the wayward ones, but the fact that you are involved with Special Branch in a police investigation is gravely ominous.'

Maisie nodded and smiled. 'Thank you. I am grateful for your time and assistance.'

She drove slowly along the gravelled driveway, careful in case a child should run across chasing a ball. Pulling out through the gates and on to the road, she shook her head. She had been sure, absolutely convinced, that she would find the thread she was looking for today. And now she had nothing, and that nothing tugged at her all the way through Merstham, through Purley, Coulsden, Streatham, across London towards Lambeth and Scotland Yard. She would report to MacFarlane and watch his face as he observed her disappointment. Robbie MacFarlane would know how she felt. She would telephone Billy to gather the list of orphanages, and in all likelihood MacFarlane would ask if another line of enquiry might be more fruitful. She parked the MG, entered Scotland Yard, and was taken to Special Branch headquarters by a police constable.

'There you are!' MacFarlane's voice echoed down the corridor when he heard Maisie talking to Colm Darby, who had also just arrived back at the Yard. 'There's been a man on the telephone asking for a Miss Maisie Dobbs.'

'Me?'

'Yes. Name of Rigby. Didn't want to talk to me, or to anyone else, but wanted Miss Dobbs, "if you would be so kind" – *be so kind,* if you don't mind – as to place a telephone call to him.' MacFarlane pointed to his office. 'So you'd better get to it. And when you're done with that, I have something for you to take to Oxford.'

Maisie stepped into MacFarlane's office and reached for the telephone while taking an index card from her document case. 'Could you put me through to a number in Redhill? Yes. Thank you.' She gave the number and waited.

'Rigby.'

'Dr Rigby.'

'Ah, Miss Dobbs. I had a thought after you left. Strange – didn't put two and two together before. I tried to catch up with you, even sent a boy running after your motor car, but you'd gone.'

'What is it? Do you recall a boy who fits the bill?'

'In a way, yes, I do, though he was not one of ours, strictly speaking.'

'Go on.'

'Sydney Oliver will probably go down as one of our most dedicated teachers. He spent every moment at the school, put his life into his work.'

'How old is he?'

'Oh, Sydney and his wife – Amelia – are gone now. Amelia passed away some time ago now, and Sydney died a couple of years past.' The line crackled.

'Hello!'

'Yes, still here. Anyway, to continue – no, it's not Sydney I thought you would be interested in, though he was an interesting study. Brilliant mathematician, but he devoted himself to our children rather than to life as an academic. Amelia was a house-mother of sorts and taught our girls the domestic arts. But it's their son I wanted to tell you about. Sydney and Amelia came to us before Stephen was born, having made a pact to dedicate their lives to helping unwanted children. So, he was, in fact, a late child, born while they worked at the Foundling Hospital.'

'And how old would Stephen Oliver be now?'

'If I am right, he would be thirty-six years old. However, there's more I must tell you.'

'Yes?'

'He was considered to be something of a genius, always excelling at school.'

'Where was he educated?'

'That's the thing – Sydney and Amelia saw fit to send him to boarding school as soon as he was old enough. At six he went away to a prep school, in Eastbourne, I think. Then off to King's, Canterbury, at eleven.'

'You sound as if you found that odd.'

'I confess, I did find it odd – and I am sorry, I was so busy thinking about the children here today that it didn't occur to me that you might be interested in Stephen.' He paused and the line wheezed again. 'You see, they had wanted a child very much – so I was always surprised that they sent him away at such a young age. There were perfectly good schools in London, and though I could see sending him at eleven or twelve, six seemed a bit much, and he was awfully upset. Here at the Foundling Hospital, we try to ensure our children are not unduly wounded by life in an institution, and Sydney was one of those who was almost soft on the children, and had a great deal of empathy for them. So you can imagine how it seemed, when they sent their own son away.'

'I get the impression that, in your estimation, Sydney Oliver did not have that same empathy for Stephen.'

'He held him to very high standards of accomplishment and behaviour. They even had a tutor for him in the holidays, so he hardly saw the light of day. He went up to Oxford at seventeen, if I remember correctly. I confess, I lost track of him after that – it seems that when children reach a certain age, suddenly they're adults, and before you know it you find out that their parents are off to see the grandchildren. Only that wasn't the case with Stephen.'

'He wasn't married?'

'No, it's not that. He was killed, in the war.'

Maisie felt the excitement drain from her body. 'Oh. I see.'

'But he was quite brilliant, at the time considered to be on his way to greatness in his field. He was a scientist.'

'You have been most helpful, Dr Rigby. Is there anything more you can tell me?'

'No, I don't think so, but if you like, I'll look through his father's record of employment here, and if I come across any details that might be of interest, I will be in touch again.'

'Thank you. And I'm sorry to have to remind you, but I must ask for your confidence in this matter.'

'Of course. I am responsible for the lives of many children who come to me as foundlings. I am well used to secrets.'

Maisie bid the man goodbye and replaced the telephone receiver.

'First you look excited, now you look as if a bomb has dropped,' said MacFarlane as he re-entered his office.

Maisie sighed and, without thinking, slumped into his chair. 'I had my man, then he slipped through my fingers.' She ran her hands through her hair. 'And to make matters worse, I could barely hear Rigby when he was speaking.'

'And how did he slip through your fingers?'

'He was killed, in the war.'

'Are you sure?'

'I was just told as much.' Maisie bit her lip and ran the telephone cord through her fingers.

MacFarlane smiled and narrowed his eyes. 'But you don't quite believe it, do you?'

She shook her head. 'You're right. I don't. I've worked on enough cases to doubt the official line regarding the dead and missing.'

MacFarlane leaned across the desk towards Maisie, resting his weight on his knuckles. 'Then keep chewing on that bone, Maisie Dobbs. My gut tells me you might be on to something. Now then, if you don't mind, you're sitting in the chair of the Detective Chief Superintendent.'

Maisie apologized and stood up. She thanked MacFarlane and moved towards the door.

'And thank you, again, for that lovely drop of soup yesterday.'

Stratton was passing the open door, so walked alongside as she left the office. 'What soup?' he asked.

14

Before leaving Scotland Yard, Maisie was given a vial of the powder extracted from the clothing of the junior minister who had been killed by a suspicious substance. The pathologists had corked the vial and sealed it with wax, then wrapped it in cotton wool before placing it in a small tin resembling one that might have been used for tobacco, the lid also being sealed with wax. Maisie placed the tin in a plain brown paper bag and pushed it down into her document case. MacFarlane warned her to take care, though they had agreed that it was better she travel alone and without a police escort, in case her movements were being observed.

'It's completely against all protocol for handling this sort of thing,' said Stratton, as he opened a door for Maisie on the way to her motor car. 'This stuff should be under armed guard.'

'And attract the attention of newspapermen, anarchists and – perhaps – the man who killed a junior minister of His Majesty's government?'

'I should come with you.' Stratton seemed almost terse when he spoke.

Maisie stopped and faced him. 'Look, don't worry. I shall drive straight to Oxford and go immediately to see Professor Gale. I know he will be in his rooms because I checked his teaching and tutorial hours last time I saw him, and doubtless Billy has contacted him by now, telling him to expect me.'

'I wish you'd change your mind and let me come with you,' offered Stratton.

Maisie shook her head, and they continued talking as they walked.

'We've got everyone out on this one,' said Stratton, 'but if I can see my way clear to looking into the Oliver lead, I'll get to it – if only to help put your mind at rest. Nothing like nosing after a suspect only to find he's dead.'

They reached Maisie's MG, whereupon Maisie set her document case behind the passenger seat, and settled into the motor. She started the engine as Stratton added, 'Do be careful, won't you?'

'I'll be all right. Now then, MacFarlane will be bellowing along the highways and byways of Scotland Yard for you, so you'd better get a move on back up to his lair.'

The greyness of noontime held all the promise of a bitter, frost-bitten night, one that she would rather spend at home in front of the fire with a book, and not at a party. Though her wrap was wound around her shoulders and up to her neck, and she wore gloves, she was still cold as she followed the A40 route out of London and on towards Oxford. The going was slow at first, but just as she was able to pick up speed on the outskirts of London, she became aware of a black motor car maintaining a certain distance behind the MG. It was close enough to keep her within sight, but not so close as to encourage a second look. At first she decided to pay little attention, but it became apparent – when she passed another vehicle, sped up or slowed down – that the motor car was following her. She took care to keep up with other traffic on the road, and accelerated when one vehicle pulled on to another road, or peeled off towards a shop. She began planning her exit from the MG when she reached Oxford – she wanted to be able to reach Professor Gale's office before she was approached by the occupants of the motor car, which she thought might be a Wolseley Straight Eight, a vehicle much faster than her own.

To her chagrin, the pack ahead soon dissipated, and now with no other cars immediately in front or behind, the Wolseley gained speed, pulled around her and braked, leaving just enough room for her to brake in turn without crashing into the rear. She locked the MG's doors and waited as a man emerged from the back of the jet-black vehicle. It was Urquhart. He strolled towards her without urgency and came alongside the MG, whereupon he leaned over so that his face seemed to fill the side window, and smiled. Maisie opened the door and turned sideways to look him in the eye.

'I'm in a bit of a hurry, Mr Urquhart. Is there anything I can do for you?'

Urquhart smiled. 'I am sure you can do better than that, Miss Dobbs. Indeed, I'm surprised you can be so calm, seeing as you're in possession of a volatile substance that could probably do us all a mischief.' He brought his hand to his mouth and cleared his throat. 'Now then, where do you think you're going with your precious cargo?'

'I am on my way to meet an eminent scientist who I am sure will be able to identify the constituent properties of the substance. It will not tell us who the junior minister's killer is, but it might point us in a given direction.'

'Yes, I know all that.'

Maisie gave no evidence of surprise, and simply looked ahead. 'May I continue now?'

'No. Well, not in the direction you were going, Miss Dobbs.' Urquhart looked up as a vehicle slowed down and pulled around them, the driver shaking his fist at the inconvenience. 'First of all, if you would be so kind as to open the passenger door, I'll be accompanying you.' Maisie leaned across and unlocked the door. Urquhart continued talking as soon as he was settled. 'Bit cramped in here, isn't it?'

'It suits me, thank you very much.'

'No need to be like that. Now then, follow the Wolseley, if you will. He'll pull over as soon as we find a suitable place for you to park, then we'll continue on in a bit more comfort.'

'And may I ask where we're going?'

'Mulberry Point. And do not be unduly concerned about your appointment – Professor John Gale will be meeting us there.'

Maisie said nothing as the journey continued, and as Urquhart promised, they stopped only once, to leave the MG safely parked next to a post office. After Maisie was settled in the saloon's back seat, they sat in silence as the Wolseley's driver took the motor car to top speed on its way past Reading to Little Mulberry. Maisie was tired. The days since Christmas had been long and the visit to the Foundling Hospital in Redhill already seemed more than just a few hours ago. She listed back and forth, in and out of wakefulness, and only when Urquhart spoke did she realize that she had given in to sleep.

'We're here, Miss Dobbs.'

'Yes, yes, good.'

Urquhart looked around and smiled. 'Look, Miss Dobbs, I really don't know why you're worried about us. We're all on the same side, you know – we just work in different ways. Big Robbie does things his way and we do things our way. And no one gets anywhere when they're keeping secrets.'

'Detective Chief Superintendent MacFarlane has said the same thing.'

'Hmm, which is why you were on your way to Oxford with a valuable sample of heaven knows what and I wasn't kept in the picture.'

Maisie bit her tongue, even though she thought of several suitable retorts.

A soldier emerged from a guardroom as the Wolseley drew alongside a barrier. He looked inside the vehicle as Urquhart pulled a wallet from his inside pocket and opened it to reveal his identification.

'Meeting Professor John Gale.'

The soldier checked Urquhart's credentials, and read the letter provided by Urquhart, which was from Military Intelligence, Section Five.

'And is this Miss Dobbs, sir?'

'Yes.'

The soldier peered across to the back seat. Maisie smiled, and though it was overcast, she thought the soldier blushed.

'Right you are, sir. Know your way?'

'Yes, Corporal. Thank you.'

The motor continued on, and with the window still open, Maisie could smell the sharp freshness of countryside, of cold air across barren fields, and in the distance she heard the bleating of sheep.

'Here we are.'

As soon as the Wolseley rumbled to a standstill, the driver came around and helped Maisie out of the vehicle.

'Follow me,' instructed Urquhart, as he walked towards a series of low hut-like buildings that Maisie could see were well lit – and well guarded.

Urquhart led the way to the first building, where a soldier asked to see identification. When the uniformed man was satisfied that they were who they claimed to be, with a salute he allowed them to pass. A man in a pair of white overalls and a mask pulled down around his neck met them in the makeshift reception area. In the distance, coming from another low hut, Maisie could hear dogs barking.

'John's this way,' said the man. 'He's waiting for you in the lab, along with Christopher Anton and Walter Mason, both scientists under his guidance.'

'Very good,' said Urquhart.

They were shown into an anteroom adjacent to the laboratory, where they were joined by Professor John Gale.

'Miss Dobbs.' He extended his hand to Maisie and smiled. 'All very cloak and dagger, isn't it? Sorry about that.' He turned to Urquhart, said the man's surname and nodded his head in acknowledgement, and then brought his attention back to Maisie. 'Now then, Miss Dobbs, I understand you have something for me. My colleagues and I are anxious to start work.'

Maisie reached into her document case and retrieved the brown paper bag. She held it out to Gale. 'The vial is inside.'

'Very good.' He moved to leave, then turned back again. 'Would you like to observe? You've worked in laboratories as a student, so you are well used to the environment. We have protective clothing available for you.'

Anxious not to spend time in conversation with Urquhart, and anticipating that he would decline such an invitation – she was always surprised at how many men in his sort of position could not bear to be in a laboratory – Maisie nodded. 'Yes, I would be most interested.'

Urquhart shook his head. 'I'll go for a cup of tea and a bite to eat until you've got something for me – and don't worry, I know the way to the canteen.'

Maisie followed Gale along a corridor, which she realized was a connecting route between two huts. All the buildings were linked in this way, she suspected.

'Here you are. Put this pair of overalls on – there's a dressing room over there. Make sure the sleeves come right down to your wrists. You'll find masks, et cetera, in there.' He pointed to a cupboard, then nodded towards another door. 'We'll be in that laboratory.'

Having taken the necessary precautions, Maisie joined the three scientists, and was introduced to the other two men in turn. She stood to one side and watched as the vial was removed and placed inside a glass tank that looked as if it had been designed to house goldfish. There were holes for the scientists to reach through, and soon all but a small amount of the powder was divided on to a series of glass slides, and secured with a clear substance. Maisie did not interrupt to ask questions; instead, she continued to watch as each man took two slides and went to work, first placing the slides under his microscope.

Gale called her to his side. 'What we are looking for at the outset is the nature of the substance. Can we identify the constituent particles? How does it behave, and is there movement?

Then, when we've each compiled a series of notes, we take samples into the experimentation room.'

'Experimentation room?'

'Yes, my dear. Might not be something you want to watch – we expose animals to the substance and we see what happens. There's enough here, and remaining in the tank, to replicate something of the effect it had on the man who died – even though he was exposed to a greater dose.'

Maisie nodded, but said nothing.

'You can talk to me while I'm working if you like, Miss Dobbs. In fact, I sometimes find that if I am having a conversation I discover more in what I am seeing. I think it has to do with letting the trained side of my brain do the work while the judgemental side of my brain is occupied with fielding questions.' Looking into his microscope, he frowned. 'Hmm, this is a sophisticated little stash of something, isn't it?'

Maisie cleared her throat. 'Professor Gale, I wonder, did you ever know of a young man called Stephen Oliver?'

In the laboratory's bright lights, Maisie saw colour drain from Gale's face. She wondered if he would tell the truth.

'Stephen Oliver?' He moved the slide he was handling to one side, and Maisie noticed his hands were shaking. 'Well, yes, I certainly remember him. Very, very bright young man. One of those who came out to France – I told you about it, after the gas attacks and help was needed in identifying the substances and in developing antidotes. His work was invaluable.'

'I have heard that he was killed.'

Gale nodded, and set the slides in an enamel kidney-shaped bowl, along with the remaining powder, still in the vial.

'If I remember rightly, he was one of the first to take the work into the field. We'd asked for volunteers to go out and examine men who were gassed, so we could find out more about their symptoms closer to the time of the event, so to speak. In effect, we asked him to go into battle, because he was even issued a gun.'

'And that's when he was killed?'

Gale pointed to the small bowl. 'Sorry, Miss Dobbs, but I must move on – the sooner we know what we are dealing with, the sooner we can be prepared if it's used again, and on a greater number of people.' He summoned his fellow scientists, who noted where the substance was moved to and from; then they left the laboratory and made their way in the direction of the barking. Maisie followed until they reached a series of huts where, from the sounds and smells that issued from them, animals were kept. They went into an adjacent laboratory. When a dog was brought in, Maisie decided that, strong as she was, Gale was right – it was probably better she did not watch. She left the room and waited in the corridor outside.

She could hear the men speaking to one another, and one of them speaking softly to the dog in a soothing manner. Then there was silence for some seconds, followed by a loud initial screech, then yelping. Maisie placed her hands over her ears and walked away, but soon the noise subsided. A bell rang outside, and as Maisie looked out of the window, into the gritty winter afternoon, she saw two men in overalls come to a side door and be given entry to the laboratory. They left moments later carrying the deceased animal between them, wrapped in sacking and a heavy rubber sheet.

Maisie was joined by John Gale, who led her along the corridor. 'We expect to have more to report tomorrow morning. At this stage we have, we believe, identified the constituent properties of the powder, and we will replicate it and test it again here. Then we will work on an antidote. But it all takes time – frankly, it usually takes months. But we are used to responding to government requests with some speed, so we have to make assumptions that, as scientists, we might not usually leap to until we are much further along in our work. Sometimes we get a lucky hit. It's a bit like a game of darts. You'd like to be on firm footing, you'd like to stand and consider your shot, but if the other team is baying for you to go on, you just throw the dart and hope it hits the bull's-eye.'

'Do you know anyone who has the knowledge to develop an agent such as this?'

Gale stopped in front of a sink, turned on the tap, and began to wash his hands, taking up a brush and scrubbing every crevice of skin. He looked up at Maisie. 'We were just talking in the laboratory, and from what we have deduced thus far, the characteristics of this particular weapon – it is a weapon, no other word for it – required an innovator of some advanced ability. In fact, I would call him a genius.'

'And there's a thin line between genius and insanity, isn't there?'

Gale nodded and dried his hands on a towel, which he threw into a laundry bin alongside the sink.

'Is that how you would have described Stephen Oliver?'

'He was brilliant, but—'

'Is that how you would have described him?'

He put his hands to his face and pulled them down towards his chin, then rubbed the skin along his jawline. Instead of resembling an absent-minded academic, John Gale bore the look of a man shouldering a great weight. He folded his arms and looked down at the ground before speaking to Maisie again.

'Come along to my office, if you would, Miss Dobbs. We will have to go through a proper cleansing process first, though. When you go into the ladies' changing room you'll see a receptacle for your overalls, cap, gloves and mask, and there are instructions on the wall for you to follow. I will join you outside in the corridor. Hopefully that man Urquhart will still be occupied in the canteen.'

Maisie followed the instructions to the letter, and when she emerged, Gale was waiting for her. He led the way to an office close to the first laboratory. Whereas his office at Oxford was colourful and cluttered, this office was spare, with few papers on the desk. A series of filing cabinets were each padlocked at the top, and Gale had taken out two keys to unlock the door to the office to gain entrance. He pulled up a chair for Maisie and flicked on an electric fire before taking his seat on the other side of his desk. He wasted no time in continuing the conversation.

'Stephen Oliver was an interesting study, even before the war. He was seventeen when he came up to Oxford. His academic record was about as unbeatable as I have ever seen in my days as a teacher and scientist. On the other hand, he lacked what one might term "social skills", though he was a compassionate person, I would say.'

'In what way did he lack social skills?'

Gale shrugged. 'There was this absolute finesse when working in the laboratory, and a fluency when delivering a paper or addressing a group of students, or even when engaged in defending a position regarding his research. But if you asked him down to the pub for a drink, you would have thought he had never been out. He was uncomfortable around women. I would imagine that, as a boy, his teacher might have observed, "This boy does not know how to play".'

'So you had known him for some time?'

'Yes, he was one of my students. Later, he became involved in laboratory research and was already an accomplished scientist when the government effectively drafted us all in to deal with the crisis brought about by the enemy's use of chemical weaponry.'

'Tell me about his death.'

'That's where it gets . . . difficult.'

'In what way?'

'Stephen lost his mind in the trenches. Even before he went up the line, he was probably not dealing with the situation as well as most.'

'What do you mean?'

'The percussion affected a lot of people – even the noise in the distance, the constant ba-boom, the shells sounding as if they were coming ever closer. I tried to overrule his offer to go to the front, but – it was chaos, Miss Dobbs.'

'Yes, I know.' Maisie paused. 'So, he came back from the trenches changed.'

'War neurosis. Immediate repatriation to England, where he was placed in an asylum.'

'Not a hospital for men with neurasthenia?'

'Strictly speaking, he wasn't in the army. As I said, it was chaos. He went into an asylum.'

'What about his family?'

'Ah, yes. The family.'

'What do you mean?'

'The family – his mother and father – were shocked when they saw him. There he was, a young man, constantly drooling from the mouth, not able to control many of the basic human functions. He was shaking, and was so very sensitive to sound.'

Maisie nodded. 'Yes, I understand. And did the parents try to have him moved? Was there a point at which he returned home?'

'No. In fact, his parents said that it was more than they could take on. By all accounts, they were committed to their work with orphaned children. Overcommitted, I would say.'

Maisie leaned back in her chair, as the truth dawned upon her. 'They told people their son had died – didn't they? It was the embarrassment, the possible humiliation of having their once brilliant son diminished.'

'Yes.' Gale looked up. 'But he did get better, for a while.'

'To what degree?'

'To the degree that he could take lodgings in Oxford, and continue with research at the university. In fact, the regimen seemed to help him – the order, the necessary discipline of the scientist, seemed to bring an element of control to every aspect of his demeanour. And communication with his parents remained severed, as far as I know.'

'What happened to him?'

'A relapse. We brought him to work here.' He held up his hand. 'I know, I know, you may ask about the integrity of such a decision, but you have to realize, he was a brilliant man, a genius. We needed him. We were testing antidotes to every gas used by the Germans, and we were also involved in analysing those we knew they'd developed but hadn't used. And we were working on our own weapons, everything from a biological agent to kill crops in Germany – the government thought we could starve the country to its knees – to gases and other nerve agents.'

'And it was too much for him – he had a breakdown.' Maisie offered the statement as speculation.

'Yes. In hindsight, it was to be expected. He was testing on dogs at the time, and the next thing we knew he had completely lost his mind again. Fortunately, one of our psychiatrists was here, and he took charge of the situation.'

'And he took him into care, didn't he?'

Gale frowned. 'How do you . . . you know, don't you?'

Maisie sighed, and stood up to pace back and forth. 'Dr Anthony Lawrence, wasn't it? He took charge of the situation by removing Stephen Oliver and taking him to one of the hospitals where he worked.'

'Yes, that's it.'

Maisie paced again, then stopped in front of the desk. 'And if I am not mistaken, Stephen Oliver recovered again, didn't he?'

'Yes.'

'And you needed him, so back he came once more. Until the next breakdown.'

Gale nodded. 'He's still locked away, poor man.'

Maisie shook her head. 'On the contrary, I suspect he was released between six months to two years ago.'

Gale rested his head in his hands. 'So it was Stephen, then. That dreadful substance we've just watched kill a dog is Stephen's work.'

'I can't say for certain, but I believe it could be.'

Without warning, and with no attempt at a knock, the door to Gale's office was flung open.

'Sorry to interrupt this little meeting of scientific minds, but I need *you*.' Urquhart pointed at Maisie.

She held out her hand to Gale. 'Thank you, Professor Gale,'

she said, and turned to follow Urquhart, but looked back as she reached the door. 'You knew it might be him, even before we brought the vial to you today. Why didn't you say anything?'

'I – I didn't want to believe it. I knew he was unsettled, but I – you see so many people in my line of work, and so many of them are . . . are *eccentric*, and – he is a very brilliant man.'

'And very dangerous.' Maisie stepped into the corridor, as Urquhart, who had not heard the conversation between Maisie and Gale, stepped back into the office and informed the scientist that he would be in touch the following morning to check on 'progress'. The staff at Mulberry Point would be working around the clock.

'What's happened?' Maisie enquired as she was hurried towards the waiting Wolseley.

'To his credit – because he's never been one for playing the game with our department – Robbie has just been on the blower. His informers must have told him we were here, Miss Dobbs. Anyway, it transpires another letter has been received at the PM's office. And this time the trouble could be big.'

'What did the man say?'

'That it will be a happier new year for some, or something like that. Your boss man didn't elaborate.'

'He's not my boss.' Maisie climbed in the back of the motor car.

'Well, whatever he is, we're on our way to see him now. You can pick up your little roller skate of a motor and follow us to Scotland Yard.'

The Wolseley set off again, and as they were cleared to leave the guard post, Maisie wondered if she should tell Urquhart that she thought she knew the identity of the letter-writer. She was about to tap him on the shoulder, but drew back. Something was stopping her from making such a claim. Even though it seemed most likely that Stephen Oliver was their man, it was as if a small voice within was urging her to wait, not to show her hand. She leaned back as the motor car accelerated once more, and wondered if the feeling was simply one of loyalty, that having worked with MacFarlane, she thought he should be the first to know of her discovery.

⸺❦⸺

I always knew, always, that I would die alone. That there would be no caring relative, no wife, no mother, no love to say goodbye. So I will have to take some companions with me. For old times' sake. Tonight, I will go to my death as if to a party. I wonder whether that woman who tried to save Ian, that Maisie Dobbs, is going to a party? I'd seen her before, seen her walking along to the station, or crossing the square. I know what she does. I thought she would have found me by now. Not so clever, that clever woman. She always gives something to the people who hold out their hands. Pennies for the children, pennies for the beggars, pennies for madmen. Yes, I'd like to take her with me. She would be good company, perhaps. But not Croucher, even though he feels sorry for me. Even though I am pitied. Pity. 'It's such a pity,' said a woman passing me on the street. I never saw her again. Never saw my mother again, not after she thought she had a madman for a son. Not that it would have made much difference. She barely even knew me.

The pencil began to scratch, so the man took up his knife and whittled away slivers of wood until more lead was revealed. Then he licked the lead, and began to note a series of numbers and letters. John Gale, or another scientist, might have understood the notations. The man stuck out his tongue as he wrote, and on to the paper, alongside the numbers and letters, drops of spittle punctuated a new formula, one that he had been twisting and turning around in his mind for days.

15

Maisie held the letter by the corner of the page, and brought it closer to the light to read.

'Written in pencil, again – and see here, there's the same evidence of moisture.'

Colm Darby nodded, adding, 'It's definitely the same man.'

'Yes . . .' Maisie was thoughtful as she read.

I have no further use of this life, of this body, or of this mind. But before I go, before I decline the opportunity to step forward into another year of sidelong glances and piteous abuse, I will make my mark. You will be sorry, so sorry not to have listened to me. I wanted only to be heard, only to be heard on behalf of those who cannot speak, the men whom war has crippled and poverty has silenced. There will be no parties, no gathering of joyous anticipation for us, the forgotten. So I will stop the big party. For Auld Lang Syne.

'What are we supposed to do – police every drunken party in London on New Year's Eve?' MacFarlane paced in front of the gathering – Stratton, Darby, Urquhart and Maisie.

'We can stop the public affairs – the steps of St Paul's Cathedral will be packed tonight, and I wouldn't mind betting that's our man's bull's-eye.' Urquhart made his suggestion with a shrug.

'You could be right,' said Stratton. 'Public gathering at St Paul's was supposed to be banned, and still hundreds come – but we can have mounted police on duty and turn people away.' Stratton looked towards MacFarlane, as if putting a question to him.

'Turning away the inebriated on the eve of the new year has never been a wholly successful venture.' MacFarlane paused. 'But it's a start.' He clapped his hands together. 'Right, then, I want all known venues of public gathering on December the thirty-first to be closed down. Turn the punters away and tell them to get on home.'

'Guv, you'll have a riot or two on your hands,' said Darby.

'Better that than have tomorrow morning's papers telling the world that a crowd of London revellers has been killed by a mystery substance – a nerve gas, if that's what he's going to use. At least we can explain a riot without causing wider public chaos.'

'Robbie, I'm off back to HQ now,' said Urquhart. 'I've had men all over London for the past few days, and I want to know what I've got at my end. I'll be in touch.'

'We'll be on each other's toes again, Gerry.'

'I know – I'd rather it that way and not risk leaving a stone unturned.'

'Aye, you're right. Be in touch.'

Urquhart left the room, and as she heard the door click behind her, Maisie cleared her throat.

'I may have a lead on the letter-writer. I'm not one hundred per cent sure, but I would be remiss if I did not bring this information to your attention for want of more corroboration.'

'Go on, Miss Dobbs.' MacFarlane turned towards Maisie, his attention followed by that of Stratton and Darby.

Describing the visit to Mulberry Point, Maisie recounted her conversation with John Gale. MacFarlane, who was standing in front of his desk, folded his arms and leaned back, causing a pile of papers to fall to one side. He made no move to set them straight, but attended to Maisie's words with a nod or a raised eyebrow. He waited until she had finished before he spoke.

'I would have warned you that Urquhart was on your tail, if I could have – but even though he gets under my skin, he has resources at his fingertips that I don't, and whether we like it or not, we do have the same goals at times, so we've got to try to work in tandem – and that means we pedal in different directions, most of the time. Now then . . .' He looked at the floor for a moment and rubbed his chin. 'Miss Dobbs, I want you to go to your Anthony Lawrence and see what you can find out.' He looked around at the clock. 'Bloody hell, time flies. Not even six hours to go before Big Ben strikes twelve – and half of London gone home.'

'I'll leave now.' Maisie stood up ready to leave.

'Your man should be here. Beale. Where is he?'

Maisie shook her head. 'I hope he's on his way home. I would prefer it if he were with his family on New Year's Eve.'

'Going soft on the help?'

Maisie collected her hat and gloves, ignoring the comment. 'I'll be in touch as soon as I have something to report – I want to catch Dr Lawrence before he leaves for the evening.'

She left Scotland Yard with haste, making her way with as much speed as she could in the direction of the hospital known as 'the Bin'.

* * *

Maisie was pleased to find Mr Croucher in the porters' office. Even though the man had never been particularly cordial to her, he was a familiar face.

'Oh, Mr Croucher – is Dr Lawrence here?'

'No, madam. Dr Lawrence has taken leave, won't be back for another two days.'

'Oh dear. Look, I need to see the record of one of his former patients. It's a matter of some urgency.'

Croucher shook his head. 'Can't do that without Dr Lawrence.'

'May I see Matron?'

He shook his head again. 'Sorry, madam, you'll have to come back after the new year now.'

'This is a matter of life and death, Mr Croucher – may I please see Mrs Kennedy?'

'Madam, I've told you—' Croucher seemed to soften, as if reconsidering his obstructive stance. 'Look, I'm sorry, it's New Year's Eve and Mrs Kennedy isn't here anyway – it's late you know. Normally she'd be here all hours, but—'

Maisie could feel her stomach become tense. Time was ticking away towards midnight. 'Mr Croucher, I appeal to you to help me – do you know if there was a man here by the name of Oliver? Stephen Oliver? A former patient.'

Croucher sighed, looked down at his ledger and shook his head. 'Don't mean a thing to me – never heard the name, and I see everyone in and everyone out, so I would know.'

Maisie looked at him, his balding head, his sagging jowls. It seemed as if his job represented his only opportunity to assert himself.

'Thank you, Mr Croucher. You have been most helpful.'

Maisie turned to leave, but as she opened the main doors, she turned back to look through the glass at the porters' office. Across the counter, she could clearly see Croucher putting on his overcoat and hat. He seemed rushed, and it appeared he was giving another porter instructions for his absence – she could see him pointing to a timetable of sorts on the wall, stabbing it with his forefinger to make a point. She knew from the way he moved that his departure was the result of a sudden decision: he seemed flustered and was still calling out instructions as he opened the door that led from the office into the entrance hall. He walked quickly towards the door. Maisie stepped to one side, partially hidden by a bush so that she could not be seen in the shadows. Croucher was in a hurry. He came out into the cold air and pulled up his collar before making his way down the steps. Then he was gone, all but vanished into the thickening smog.

Maisie ran to the MG, started the engine, and drove along the road until she caught sight of Croucher again, lumbering towards a bus. He leaped on board just as it was about to pull away from the stop.

Keeping her distance, she followed the bus for some time, then waited when Croucher stepped off and caught another, which rumbled along the Marylebone Road. She was certain that Croucher would lead her to the man who had written the letters – the man who had taken innocent life, both animal and human. What kind of man was he? Someone who was abandoned, and had in turn abandoned life, to the extent that life was easy to take? She remembered conversations with Maurice, when they had talked about the nature of the killer, how some kept their secret close to them, like a seed planted deep in the soil, waiting for the perfect time to bloom – for the perfect time to be revealed. Some secrets could be hidden for years, while there were those who yearned for their secret, their crime – whether of passion or pre-meditation – to be discovered. Waiting for truth to come out. She had known case after case where the perpetrator instigated his own discovery – the stupid mistake, the blatant error, or the con-fession made to someone who might tell. Slipping through the MG's gears as the bus stopped again, she wondered if this killer wanted to be discovered, wanted to be noticed, to be acknow-ledged. He might want to be stopped before he killed again.

Once more Croucher stepped off the bus, walking a quarter of a mile to another stop. This was not an unusual journey – she knew that if Billy did not walk a good way to work to save money, he would be taking three buses instead of one. Now, watching Croucher from her parked motor car, the engine idling, Maisie wondered whether his pacing back and forth in front of the bus stop, his constant glancing up at the clock on a nearby church, was borne of nerves or the cold. She studied his move-ments with careful attention and noticed the nervousness to his gait. She recognized the fear. *He's on his way to warn him. To let him know we're on to him. He's going to see – Stephen Oliver?* She looked around for a telephone kiosk, and saw one illuminated just yards away from the MG. Leaving the motor running, she left the MG and stepped towards the kiosk. She opened the door, lifted the receiver, and dialled Scotland Yard, all the time keeping her eyes on Croucher as she asked to speak to MacFarlane.

'Yes!'

'It's Maisie Dobbs.'

'Have you made any progress?'

'I'm calling from a telephone kiosk, on the Marylebone Road, going towards Euston Road. I've followed a man called Croucher – hospital porter. I think he's on his way to see our man.'

'And what makes you think that?'

Maisie paused, wondering whether brutal honesty would stand her in good stead. 'I can just feel it – is that good enough for you?'

'Makes a lot more bloody sense to me than all that scribbling across the walls. We'll find you. Don't take any chances.' The telephone clicked.

Maisie returned to the MG in time to see another bus come along, and Croucher jump on board. She pulled in behind the bus and followed it along Marylebone Road. She began going through the events of the past hour, since she first spoke to Croucher. Could his hasty departure from the hospital have simply been due to her detaining him with questions? Did he then have to run for a bus that he normally caught with some ease, given the time his working day ended? She wondered if she could be wrong in her conjecture, but shook her head. No, she knew where he was going.

Now she could barely see ahead of her in the thick pea-souper, and if it weren't for the bus and street lights casting their smudged shadows around and ahead of her, she might not have seen him jump off the rear platform of the bus and make his way along the Euston Road, then turn into Warren Street. At that moment, she felt an icy sensation at her neck, a feeling she knew came as a warning, tingling to attract her attention when all was not well, when something was not quite as it should be. It had alerted her on many an occasion, and now as it turned to a radiating pain, she wondered if the writer of the letters, if the madman himself, had been under her nose all the time.

She followed Croucher along Warren Street, and because the

street was busy with people going in and out of the pubs – perhaps a little more raucous than usual on the last night of the year – she parked the MG where it could be seen by the police and then continued on foot, keeping Croucher in view. Where was MacFarlane? Was she being observed without her knowledge? Croucher continued on, and she wondered why he had not stepped off the bus earlier, when he'd had the opportunity, opposite Great Portland Street Underground station. He could have simply walked across the road from there. Maisie allowed a distance to grow between Croucher and herself. It occurred to her that he might know he was being followed and was testing his theory by taking a circuitous route to his destination. With each step as she drew further away from the more populated area around Warren Street, she knew she was on her own.

Turning again, this time into the top end of Cleveland Street, Croucher snaked back and forth across neighbouring streets until he stopped at the top of a flight of steps leading down into a basement flat. She stepped back into the shadows when he stopped and looked behind him. Though she could only see him as a grey shape in the darkness, she was aware that it was only after he had scanned back and forth several times that he began his descent. She approached the house with care and took stock of the neighbourhood.

It was said of the environs of Fitzroy Square – and they were not far from the square – that a peer could sit next to a plumber at supper, and neither would feel the worse for it. There were well-appointed houses adjacent to tenements, and clean properties neighbouring slums. There were mansions where two people lived in comfort, and bed-sitting rooms where the landlord asked no questions, as long as the rent was paid. Some had only the soot-covered walls to look out upon, and others had compact walled gardens, where a riot of colour fought against the greyness of buildings assaulted by smoke and damp. She could see that Croucher had come to visit someone who lived in a cold-water flat, cheap accommodation for a person on the breadline – an ugly place to live for someone who could not afford anything more, where the occupants vanished into the night, and were all but invisible during the day. It was a place where a sense of disenfranchisement could grow unchecked, where disappointment and despair were bedfellows, where a clammy damp kept the blood cold, and where warmth was sucked out, along with hope.

Peering over the iron railing, Maisie saw the pale light from an oil lamp grow, as if the occupant lived in the dark, but now, with a visitor, turned up the wick to illuminate the room. She moderated her breathing, placing the fingers of her right hand against her coat, just three fingers width below her waist, balancing herself so that she would breathe with ease, and move with dexterity. She looked around, just in case MacFarlane's men had discovered her whereabouts and help was on its way, but could wait no longer. She made her way down the steps and stood against the wall alongside the window.

The men's voices were low, almost indistinct. A few seconds passed, then there was movement towards the window, and she heard the voice of the man she knew to be the one for whom she searched. His words were thick, as if the man's gullet itself were mucus-filled. He cleared his throat and wheezed, coughing before he spoke again.

'I don't need you to protect me, Croucher. I am able to look after myself. You have shown kindness, in bringing me food.'

'You've got to look after yourself, sir. You need better food, and I can't always get it.'

'Don't worry. It will soon be all over, anyway.'

'What do you mean, sir, what do you mean?' Croucher's voice escalated in tone, edged with a whine, as if he were a man facing the inevitable. Maisie frowned. The tone of the porter's response suggested he was trying to control the man in the flat, and was without power against his will.

'I mean, it's almost over. Midnight. Then they'll see.'

'But you can't, please don't do it. I can't cover for you any more. The Dobbs woman came back to see Lawrence this evening – didn't make an appointment first, just came to the hospital. I know she's after you, I know she'll find you. I've seen her type – she's a terrier.'

Keep your mouth shut and leave. Leave now . . . Maisie whispered into the cold night, knowing Croucher was playing with fire. *Don't say another word, just leave.*

'I think you should just lie down, sir. Let me make you a nice broth, or a cup of tea – look, I've brought you some bits and pieces of food. Slim pickings today, but enough to keep you going.'

Maisie flinched upon hearing something crash to the ground – a jar, perhaps, or a can and two or three items. Had the man swept Croucher's offerings from the table? She held her breath again as he raised his voice.

'I don't want your pity, and I don't want you telling me what to do.'

The man slurped as he spoke.

It's him, I know – it is him! thought Maisie.

'But I'm only trying to help—'

A dull thud made Maisie flinch again. Had the man been pushed too far? Had he assaulted Croucher, perhaps with a sturdy walking stick, one with a steel tip, perhaps, or a brass handle? She closed her eyes and imagined a cane brought against a head at a certain angle with weight behind it, and she knew that Croucher was down, and probably unconscious. He might even be dead.

She closed her eyes and in that moment asked for guidance, asked a God she had doubted on many an occasion to aid her, for she knew – knew in the gut – that when the man left the flat, it would be with the intent to kill and he would not kill just one person. In the distance she heard a clock chime. It was past eight o'clock. Crowds would be congregating on the steps of St Paul's. People were already in the pubs – one only had to walk along to Charlotte Street to see that both rich and poor alike were merry-making. With barely a sound she stepped up into the street and looked both ways. Nothing. No sign of the men from Special

Branch. She had hoped the police would find her distinctive MG and then conduct a sweep-search of the neighbouring streets. If the man left his flat, she couldn't wait for them to arrive – she would have to stop him before he set foot on the street. At risk to her own life, she had to prevent him leaving.

———

The man pulled back his chair and watched blood ooze from Croucher's broken skull into a shallow puddle on the floor. He felt a coldness take over his body. It was not a chill that was the opposite of heat – he had, in any case, become used to the cold and damp, though sometimes it brought him down, took away his strength so that he could not emerge from his bed. No, this was another biting numbness. It was the thread of unfeeling that ran through his body as mercury runs in a line through a thermometer, the weight of the matter channelled along the tunnels of life, taking from him all sensitivity, all sense of horror, so that even when he regarded Croucher as his skin grew cold and his bones stiff, the man felt nothing. No shame, no sadness, no fear, no . . . nothing. If he had a soul, he could feel it no longer.

He looked down at Croucher as if observing an experiment, watched the blood coagulate and stop in a pool, then thicken, so that, if he pushed a finger against it, it would wrinkle. He had never struck a man before. It was not his way. But it did not matter. *What does anyone matter, after all?* He pulled the leather-bound notebook towards him, unfurled the string that bound the pages, and took out the pencil. He ran his thumb across the lead, and winced when he felt a sliver of wood against his skin. Limping to a drawer, he brought out a knife and a sharpening steel, and took his seat again in a way that suggested he was losing his balance. Sweeping the poker-like sharpening steel back and forth across the blade, his brow furrowed as he brought every ounce of his attention to the task at hand. Once more he tested the blade, and, satisfied that it was now up to the job, he set down the steel and whittled the pencil again until the lead was sharp, with a good eighth of an inch free of the wood. He placed the knife on the table and began to write.

> *This is my last entry. I will write no more, for I will be gone. And no one will miss me. But I will not go alone, and perhaps, perhaps, perhaps, someone will take notice. I know my limitations, know the extent of what I can do, and if I could take the Prime Minister, or his self-serving cohorts, then I would. But I can't, so I must take who I can, and then those fools in Westminster will know what it is to be invisible. One of the forgotten, one of the lost.*

The pencil dragged across the page in a jagged line. The man closed the leather book, bound it with string, and placed it in a pocket inside his threadbare greatcoat.

Through the window, with barely any light to cast a shadow, Maisie Dobbs watched him turn up the wick and move to a cupboard. He removed a jar, and though she squinted, she could not tell whether it contained a viscous liquid or a thick powder. He collected matches and a vial. And as she watched, she knew she could not let him leave, could not let him go on his way. She could not let him kill again. She turned away from the window, took one step to the side, and knocked on the door.

16

'Who's there? Who's there at this time of night?'
'Mr Oliver?'
'No one of that name here.'
Maisie bit her lip and tried again. 'Sir, I think you know who I am. My name is Maisie Dobbs. I believe you mentioned my name in a letter, delivered on Christmas Day.'
Silence.
'Sir?'
'What do you want?'
Maisie cleared her throat. 'I'd like to talk to you, if I may.'
'What about?'
'Well . . .' She paused. 'We could start with Ian Jennings. I believe you knew him, and so did Mr Croucher. They were both friends of yours, weren't they?'
'*Weren't* they?' The man's eyes narrowed.
She realized her error – she had referred to Croucher in the past tense. *They were both friends of yours.* Now he knew; now the man knew she had heard him strike Croucher. She heard the rattle of a chain, then a key unlocking the door, and a bolt drawn back. The door opened.
Maisie showed no emotion when she saw the scarred face, the livid line that ran down from the man's forehead and across his eye until it reached his jaw. His back was curved as if he were a hunchback, and one foot was splayed to the side. His right shoulder was held higher than the other, and his hands were like fists in front of him as he stood before her. She imagined that he

might once have been a tall man, perhaps six feet or more. Now, though, he was diminished by circumstance, and she could only speculate as to what might have happened to him. But she knew she had seen him before.

'I've seen you before, on Charlotte Street, I—'

Without warning, the man reached forward with one clawed hand and dragged Maisie into the room by the collar on her jacket. He slammed the door behind him.

'I have come to help you, sir. I—'

'Well, you're too bloody late!'

In the flickering shafts of light and dark caused by the oil lamp's wick burning down, Maisie fought the urge to steal a glance at the floor and the body of the man she had only seen as a taciturn hospital porter. Looking into the killer's dark, expressionless eyes, she knew an empathetic approach would gain her nothing. She had been surprised by his strength, and knew that there was no connection, now, between rational thought and his actions.

'Sir, I believe I understand why you've taken the lives of both men and animals, and I understand the . . . the great weight—'

'Oh, do me a favour, please!'

They stood facing each other, and Maisie wondered what words, what actions might placate a man for whom all accepted modes of human communication seemed to mean nothing. Even as he was facing her, his eyes rolled back in his head and saliva issued from his mouth.

'You have committed murder, and I believe you intend to murder again, only this time you plan to take the lives of many more innocent victims.'

'Innocent? Innocent? Innocent of what? Innocent of being blind towards the plight of other people, when you can see with your own eyes what they have to put up with? That's a terrible thing, Miss Maisie Dobbs. I don't see innocence. I don't see innocence at all.'

Maisie collected her thoughts again, hoping to play for time, hoping that soon the police would be searching street to street, door to door, for surely they would have found her motor car by now.

'I saw you. I saw you on the street and gave you what I could.'

The man nodded. 'Yes, and you tried to give something to Ian.'

'It was you, then, the man who was watching me.'

'Yes. It was me, I remembered you. Only I didn't know your name until I heard that bloke yelling at the top of his voice. "Maisie Dobbs! Miss Maisie Dobbs!" But now you're working for them, aren't you? You're part of the merry-go-round. You don't know – none of your type know – what it is to be like us, to be alone, what it is to know that . . . no one knows you.'

'Then how did you know Jennings? And Croucher?'

He looked at the floor. 'Oh, yes, poor sparrow Croucher.'

Maisie frowned, wondering what the man meant. She felt as if she were walking on ice that might crack at any moment. She felt as if her world could upturn in the time it took to take a breath. Still she did not look down at Croucher, though she could smell the death on him, could smell time sucking the warmth from his body, leaving it hardened and cold.

'I met Ian somewhere. I don't know where now. I can't remember, though it might have had something to do with Croucher, or . . .' The man seemed distracted, as if he had suffered a sudden fatigue. 'I might have known him years ago. And he tried to help me, even though he needed the help.' The man stared at the lamp, which was growing ever dimmer, and sighed. 'They let him down, you know, the army pensions people. Called him up in front of three know-alls who said that he could do a job, what with his mind and the fact that he could get about.' He drew his attention back to Maisie, his eyes rolling back as he tried to focus. He shook his head and spoke again. 'But of course, poor Ian couldn't get a job – it's all a man with the parts still intact can do to get on, isn't it, Miss Dobbs?'

She nodded, anxious to appease him. 'These are hard times.'

'And Croucher, bless him.'

'What do you mean?'

'He's one of those eternal helpers. Don't know what made him do it, but he saw me – I can't remember where he saw me, to tell you the truth – but he saw me, and he might have seen Ian, both of us holding out our hands in different places. And he tried to help.' He shook his head from side to side, like a man trying to correct blurred vision. 'Oh, yes, that's where I met Ian. I think Croucher brought him to me, to be my friend. I think he thought we had known each other, years ago.'

'And were you friends, you and Ian Jennings?'

He shrugged. 'He should have waited.' He pointed to his head. 'Not right up here, Jennings. I told him I had a plan, that I'd had enough of waiting, that I could bring this country to its knees. But he got lost in his mind, silly boy.' He shrugged again. 'Don't know why I always called him a boy. I don't even know if he was younger than me.'

'And how old are you, sir?'

The man winced and clutched either side of his head. 'I must be nigh on forty now, or thirty-eight, or—' He brought his attention back to Maisie. 'I don't want to talk any more. I've got to get on. In fact, I should do something about you. After all, I don't want you stopping me, don't want you—'

In the distance the ringing of a bell on a police vehicle could be heard, coming closer. Then another from the opposite direction. The man cocked his head this way and that, as if to try to ascertain where the sounds were coming from. Maisie took the opportunity to step back, but the man was quick, and lunged towards her, pulling the flank of his left arm around her throat as he held her from behind. Despite his disability, his strength overpowered her.

'Oh, no you don't. You've seen too much as it is.'

'You can't leave here, sir. I know what you plan to do, I know where you're going with that jar.' She wondered whether to play her trump card, and knew there was no time to take chances. She choked out her words, with the crook of his arm resting against her gullet. 'The police know and so do the Secret Service. So you see, you don't stand a chance. Don't leave. I am sure—'

Maisie gagged and coughed, and with her hands tried to drag his arm away from her throat. She began to feel light-headed, with coloured threads of light pulsating across her peripheral vision as she fought for air. With as much strength as she could muster, she pushed back, jabbing the man hard in the ribs with her elbow. She felt him lose his balance. His arm came free of her neck, and he fell against the table. The bells travelled closer; she could hear muffled voices in the distance, as if men were running to and fro, coming closer, then away again.

Gasping, Maisie turned to face the man she knew to be mad, a man whose thoughts were not tempered by the constraints that would bring his behaviour within limits considered 'normal'. As he used his strength to regain some semblance of balance, the jar rocked and fell to one side on the table, where it rolled back and forth. The man followed the jar with his eyes as if dazed, as if what he could see had no relation to the visions in his mind. Maisie lurched for the jar, and felt its weight in her hands, but when she looked back, it was into the eyes of a killer. He held out a knife towards her.

'Give that to me.'

'Sir, this is a dangerous substance. The police will be here soon, and if you give yourself up, there will be leniency, you will be cared for, you will be—'

'Put away where I belong, eh? Put away where no one can see me and where I can't be a danger to myself. They always want you put away, until they need you again, until *your country needs you*.' He mimicked the tone of wartime recruitment posters, and waved the knife in front of her, but she kept the jar clutched close to her body. 'And they'll want what's up in here, won't they?' For the second time he pointed to the side of his head. 'But I—'

The voices came closer, and when the man looked around to follow the sound, Maisie kicked out at him, as hard as she could.

He fell backwards again, and braced his fall against the wall. Maisie staggered, feeling her feet slide in blood that had seeped from Croucher's broken skull. Still clutching the jar with one hand, she reached for the table to keep herself steady. Sweat poured from her brow as the man began to lumber forward again. Then he stopped and looked out the window, his face tilted upward to view the street. Footsteps running back and forth echoed on wet flagstones, but Maisie knew that even if she called out she would not be heard from inside the basement flat.

The man brought his attention back to her, as if he had just been woken from a deep sleep, his eyes moving slowly, reminding her of a patient after an operation, when the effects of ether were still evident, before full consciousness had been regained.

'It's over, isn't it?'

'Yes, it is,' said Maisie, her voice soft. 'It's over now.'

'They won't take me, you know.'

Maisie felt tears prickle against the corners of her eyes. She remembered Ian Jennings. She could see him in front of her, could see her hand held out to try to stop what she knew was about to happen, and she could feel, again, the knowing that came to her, that the man would take his own life.

She nodded. 'Yes, I know.'

'Do you think there's a heaven, Miss Dobbs?'

Maisie cleared her throat. 'I think there's a better place than this.'

The man lifted the knife to his left wrist and then, with a second's hesitation, the right. Without a sound he sliced deeply into the flesh. And as he fell to the ground, the lifeblood pumping from his body, she began to weep. With one last ounce of energy, he held the knife steady with blade pointed upward, and rolled on to it so that his heart was pierced.

Maisie cried out and, still clutching the jar to her chest, moved around the body, opened the door and ran up into the street.

'MacFarlane! Are you there? MacFarlane!'

Two policemen came out of the layers of smog towards her,

whistles blowing. Soon a black Invicta swung around the corner, and even before the driver had manoeuvred to a halt, the back door opened and Robert MacFarlane was running to her side. He put his arms around her, and spoke with a softness, she realized later, that she had never heard before.

'It's all right, it's all right. We're here, we're all here, it's over now. It's all over.'

Maisie allowed herself to be soothed, allowed herself to weep into MacFarlane's shoulder. Police cars swooped down the street, and soon MacFarlane had taken Maisie to the Invicta, and was barking orders to the men. Stratton and Darby arrived in minutes, and while Maisie leaned back into the firm leather upholstery, the scene of a murder and a suicide were secured, and the pathologist summoned.

The passenger door of the Invicta opened, and Maisie looked up, expecting it to be MacFarlane or Stratton. It was Urquhart.

'Nice work, Miss Dobbs. Two dead bodies and no one to question, and – oh, I think that's for me.' He reached out towards the jar, but Maisie held firm.

'Mr Urquhart. Two dead bodies, not two hundred. One murder – and I can recount the whole event to you now, if you like, or you can await my statement via Scotland Yard. I can also tell you about the suicide, which was going to happen anyway, because that's what the man had planned. Only he didn't take anyone with him – except Mr Croucher.'

Urquhart shook his head. 'I'm sorry – you look like hell.'

'That's how people look, when they have seen hell through another's eyes.'

'May I?' He held out his hand towards the jar.

Maisie waited a moment, then handed it to him. 'Be careful, Mr Urquhart. I believe that within that jar is one half of another destructive agent – and if you go into the flat you'll find a vial which I think is some sort of catalyst to render whatever you have there into a veritable killing machine.'

'It will be going directly to Mulberry Point.'

'I don't care where you take it, Mr Urquhart, as long as it goes as far away from innocent human beings as possible.'

'Thank you, Miss Dobbs. I know we haven't enjoyed the best working relationship, given that you're a civilian attached to Special Branch, but you've done a good job.'

Maisie nodded and closed her eyes. 'Shut the door as quietly as you can, if you don't mind.'

～●～

Maisie made her statement and was questioned for over an hour at Scotland Yard, after which she joined MacFarlane, Stratton and Darby in MacFarlane's office. It was a quarter to twelve at night and it had been a long day for all concerned.

'We're going to have to be back here first thing in the morning – early.'

'But—' Before he could say more, Stratton stopped speaking.

'Problem with that, Stratton?' MacFarlane looked up from notes taken during a search of the basement flat.

'No, sir. It was nothing.' He stole a glance at Maisie, who knew Stratton had a son with whom he had doubtless promised to spend the first day of the new year.

'Right then,' MacFarlane continued. 'Here's where we are.' He looked at Maisie, then at the men. 'Obviously our investigation will continue. For now, I can tell you all that there was nothing in the flat to identify the man who killed Mr Edwin Croucher, a hospital porter residing in Catford. There were no letters, no bills, nothing.'

'What about the landlord?' Maisie sat forward on her chair.

'According to the landlord, the man paid his rent in advance, from one week to the next, and was never late. He gave no name when he rented the flat, about eighteen months ago, and the landlord was happy to have the money, so no questions asked. The rent was always paid with coins – pennies, threepenny bits, halfpennies, florins. He paid his rent with the fruits of his labours, sitting with his hand out on the streets of London.'

'You mean there was not one single item in that flat that we could use to put a name to this man?' Darby frowned as he faced MacFarlane.

MacFarlane picked up a package wrapped in muslin and folded back flaps of cloth. 'Nothing but this, the man's diary. The ramblings of a barely-there-at-all man.'

'Have you read it, Chief Superintendent?' asked Maisie.

'I've had a quick gander.'

'May I?' She reached out towards MacFarlane, and he placed the cloth-covered diary in her hands.

'Be careful, Miss Dobbs, that's got to go down to the lab boys.'

'I understand. May I read it?'

'Well, you can, but before you do that, I thought you might all like to join me in a toast.'

'Toast?' asked Darby.

'Colm, my old boy, we've been forgetting ourselves.' MacFarlane stood up, opened a filing cabinet, and from the bottom drawer removed a bottle of malt whisky and four tot glasses. He lined up the glasses on his desk and poured a full measure of the amber liquid into each glass. Keeping the bottle in his hand, he took a glass and clinked it hard enough against each glass in turn so that the members of his staff, including Maisie, had to be quick to grab their whisky as it tilted towards them.

'A happy new year to one and all. Slainte!' MacFarlane gulped his whisky, then slammed the glass on the table to pour another, just as Big Ben began to chime the hour and the passing of the old year.

The men emulated their boss, drinking the toast back in one, while Maisie closed her eyes, tilted her head, and took but a single mouthful while trying not to cough.

'That's it, lass, get it down you, it cleans out the tubes – and it'll help you sleep tonight. Anyone for another?' He waved the bottle, then poured a second measure each for Stratton and Darby.

Maisie cleared her throat, which was burning. 'I wonder, Chief Superintendent, may I use your telephone?'

'Stratton, show Miss Dobbs to the next office – give her a bit of privacy. If someone wants to place a telephone call when the new year is still in swaddling clothes, you can bet it's personal.'

'I can find my way next door. I won't be long.'

Closing the door of the empty office behind her, Maisie went to the desk, lifted the telephone receiver, and placed a call to Priscilla's house. The telephone at the Holland Park mansion was answered by a housekeeper, and Maisie was asked to wait while Mrs Partridge was summoned.

'I do hope you have an excellent excuse.' Priscilla sounded terse, and – as Maisie expected – upset.

'Actually, Priscilla, I have an excellent excuse, only I can't tell you about it, not yet, not now.'

Priscilla's tone softened. 'You sound exhausted, Maisie.'

'I am a bit. How are you? How's the party?'

'Lovely, as parties go. We're still at the champers, still dancing, still weaving our way into the new year with all the glee we can muster.'

Whether it was the whisky or the events of the day, Maisie felt emotion well in her voice. 'I've missed seeing you, Priscilla.'

'Oh, darling, I've missed you too, my friend. Are you sure you can't come tonight? We're still going strong, and breakfast won't be served until half past four to finish off the celebrations, then everyone can go home.'

Hearing the eagerness in Priscilla's voice, Maisie was loath to upset her once more. 'Pris, I – I'll see how I feel when I get back to the flat. But don't bank on it.'

Maisie thought she heard Priscilla weep, and there was a pause before her friend spoke again.

'I suppose I'm being terribly selfish, aren't I? I just find the New Year so trying. All that looking forward and saying 'happy new year' and I'm standing here wondering what might happen before December the thirty-first rolls around again. I feel as if I'm under siege.'

'Hush, Pris, hush. Go back to your party, shine that smile of yours at your guests, and though I can't promise, perhaps I'll get a second wind by the time I get home.'

'Happy new year, Maisie.'

'You, too, Pris. You too.'

Maisie returned to MacFarlane's office, where the men continued to discuss the case. With one ear to the conversation, Maisie picked up the diary and began to read.

My name's not important any more. I am not a person, not the person I was, and I can't remember who that person was anyway. I did what my country asked of me, I stepped forward to do my bit, and then, when I came home, they didn't want me any more – well, except for my mind. No one wanted me, no one wanted to see me, or speak to me. They wanted me tucked away in a place where they wouldn't have to see me ever again. I am the man they sent to war, I am the man who went forward at their battle cry. And there are thousands of me, so many hundreds and thousands of me, all of us back here, but never to return home. Home doesn't even exist for us . . .

'Well, you can't sit there and read all night.' MacFarlane held out his hand for the dead man's diary, and instructed Stratton to escort Maisie to her MG, which had been brought to the Yard by a detective constable.

'Will you need me here tomorrow, Chief Superintendent?'

MacFarlane shook his head. 'No, shouldn't think so.' He looked at Maisie and smiled. 'You've done a bloody good job, Miss Dobbs. We might not know that man's name, but we do know he was our letter-writer, and we do know he was our murderer. You brought him down before he killed in a way that doesn't even bear thinking of, ever. You should go home and rest.'

Maisie shook hands with Colm Darby and with MacFarlane,

who might have held her hand for a second longer than was necessary.

'It's been a long day, hasn't it?' said Stratton, as they made their way to Maisie's motor car.

'Yes, but we have our man.'

'You were right to follow that lead, Miss Dobbs.'

'And you were right to follow every other lead – MacFarlane could not limit his resources to just one possibility. He couldn't put all his eggs in one basket – and who knows when one of those groups might decide to up the ante and choose a more violent method of making a point, though I doubt whether the women fighting for equal pensions will resort to dynamite or chemical weaponry.'

They reached the MG. 'Well, happy new year, Miss Dobbs – and a safe one. I daresay we will be in touch in due course. There's still much to do on this case. For a start, we'll be bringing in your Dr Anthony Lawrence to identify the body tomorrow.'

'Of course.' She paused. 'I'm sorry you'll be missing a day with your son though.'

Stratton shrugged. 'Name of the game, Miss Dobbs. I'll make it up to him.'

Maisie smiled and as she took the driver's seat of her motor car, she looked up at Stratton. 'Happy new year, Inspector.'

Stratton stood back as Maisie eased the MG out on to the road. She drove home on all but empty streets, as the bells of London continued to peal, and those who could afford such levity raised another glass to 1932.

~

Settling back into a soothing hot bath, Maisie considered Priscilla's party and how much her friend had wanted her to be there. For her part, the last thing Maisie wanted was to see Priscilla with another drink in her hand to dull the fear in her heart. Even so, Priscilla was her dearest friend, and to Maisie, close associations always mattered. She sighed, closed her eyes, and thought about her day from beginning to end, and again saw Croucher running for his bus, and the final meeting with the man he had befriended, perhaps when he recognized his solitary condition. Men like Jennings and Oliver – she had assumed it was Oliver, though they had yet to find any letters or documents to confirm the killer's identity – were both incarcerated by their wounds, the latter being a man who had lost all semblance of rational thought, and in whose head the battle continued to rage, day after day. He had been an intelligent man, a man thought 'brilliant' by his peers, and yet had taken up weapons to fight on behalf of those passed on the street and forgotten when war was done.

As the bathwater began to cool, Maisie's thoughts moved to Billy's wife, and it occurred to her that Doreen and Priscilla suffered from variations of the same affliction. But whereas Doreen was caught in the past's quicksand, trapped in a world where she ached for a daughter who was dead, Priscilla feared the future. She had fought the onslaught of grief in Biarritz, a place removed from the connections of her girlhood, where the only early memories were happy recollections of family holidays. Unlike England, Biarritz held no reminder of her parents' terror upon hearing of the loss of their sons, of her own sorrow when she received news that her brothers were dead. But now she had returned to the country from which her siblings left for war. Now she feared for her own sons, for the eldest, who would be on the cusp of manhood before the decade's end. And her fears were taking her back in time – a time when drink dulled the ache in her soul.

Priscilla had been safe in the world she controlled in Biarritz, as safe as a patient in a hospital. But now she was back in the thick of London society, and it was clear she was floundering. And she needed a friend.

Maisie stepped from the bath, towelled herself dry, then put on the black day dress that also served as suitable garb for a cocktail party. She had no gown to wear, but she was sure Priscilla wouldn't mind. Either that or Priscilla would drag her off to her dressing room to find something she considered more suitable. But that was all right: Maisie would allow her friend the indulgence of having all her guests in evening dress. After styling her hair, applying some kohl to her eyes, just the faintest dash of rouge to her cheeks, and red lipstick, she put on her black leather shoes with straps that buckled at the side, followed by her coat and hat. She pushed a handkerchief, some money and the lipstick into a black clutch bag, picked up her keys, and left the flat. It was a quarter to two in the morning when she set off for Holland Park.

'Maisie, darling, I knew, just knew you would come!' Priscilla's eyes filled with tears as Maisie was led through the throng of guests who had spilled out into the entrance hall, and shown into the drawing room. Waving her cigarette-holder in the air, Priscilla called out to her husband. 'Douglas, Douglas, look who's here. It's Maisie.'

As Douglas Partridge waded through the crowd towards them, taking a glass of champagne from a maid as he went, Priscilla turned to Maisie once again, linking her arm through Maisie's and looking into her eyes. 'I know you must be terribly worn out, I can see it in your eyes, but . . . but . . .' She began to cry, pulling her arm away from Maisie so that she could squeeze the bridge of her nose to prevent the tears.

'Oh, Priscilla, don't weep. This is your party, your time to celebrate being here in London with your family. Come on, Pris, come on, look, here comes Douglas.'

Douglas Partridge stood alongside his wife, rested his cane against his thigh, and put his arm around her. 'Tears of happiness, aren't they, darling?' Keeping his arm around Priscilla's shoulder, he winked at Maisie and leaned forward to kiss her on each cheek. 'We're so glad you could come. Priscilla's been looking forward to this evening for weeks. And it's a thumping good party, isn't it, love?' He looked into his wife's eyes, then kissed her on the nose. 'Now, I am going to leave you with your dearest friend and see if I can find Raymond Grasslyn for a chat.'

Priscilla took a deep breath to temper her emotions, and looked Maisie up and down, feigning bossiness. 'Come on, five minutes in my dressing room. I want to see you in a gown. You're not in one of those Scotland Yard morgues now – it's a party!'

If it had been anyone but Priscilla, Maisie would have been offended, but on this occasion, she nodded and laughed. 'Oh, all right, let's get it over with.'

Fifteen minutes later, after Priscilla had pulled out four gowns for her to choose from, Maisie came downstairs to renew her entrance to the party wearing a gown of deep-purple silk that reflected the colour of her eyes. The boat neckline and hem were embellished with bands of sequins, as were the cuffs, which came to a point across the back of each hand. The dress was narrow to the hip, where a sequinned seam sat above a fuller skirt that fell in soft folds to the floor. Maisie wore a pair of Priscilla's diamond teardrop earrings, and was relieved that she took the same size shoes as her friend, because she was now wearing a pair of black satin pumps with a low heel.

'Now then,' said Priscilla. 'Let's introduce you.'

For the next hour, Maisie was introduced to guest after guest, always with Priscilla at her side, and always presented as 'My dear friend Maisie', or 'This is my bestest ever chum, Maisie Dobbs.'

The dancing continued on, and though Maisie was weary, she took to the dance floor several times and found that as the music played, so her fatigue was beaten back. After thanking the gentleman who had asked for what she hoped might be her last dance, she went again in search of Priscilla, moving through the waves of people before reaching the bar. She always knew she would find Priscilla close to the bar.

'May I have a large glass of water, please? And some ice, if you have any left.'

The waiter poured water from a crystal jug into a glass, which he passed to Maisie. She drank half the liquid and then turned to her left, where Priscilla had her back to her and was regaling one of the guests with stories of Biarritz. She tapped Priscilla on the shoulder.

'Oh, Maisie, are you having a lovely time?'

'Yes, I am – and I seem to be holding up against the onslaught of sleep.'

'Good girl, not long now until breakfast is served. The spread is being set up in the morning room even as we speak.'

'Pris, what's your new year's resolution?' Maisie asked the question, drank the remaining water, and set her glass on the bar.

'That came out of the blue,' said Priscilla.

'And what is it?'

Priscilla nodded to the waiter, who brought her another glass of champagne. 'I don't know. I'll think about it tomorrow.' She took a sip from her glass. 'You look as if you are about to tell me what it should be.'

'Come with me, Pris.' Maisie took her friend's glass and placed it on another waiter's tray as he passed.

'Where are we going?'

'Upstairs.'

'Upstairs?'

Maisie had stayed at the house before, so knew the geography of the Partridge home. She walked towards the large bedroom where Priscilla's three sons were sleeping and opened the door with care. A night-light was glowing on a table to one side of the room, and the two women looked in at the boys, asleep. The youngest, Tarquin, had thrown off his bedcovers and slept at the bottom of his bed, with one leg over the side. The eldest, Timothy, lay on his back, with one arm bent across his eyes. The middle son, Thomas, slept under the covers, the bump under the eiderdown making it seem as if an animal were in the midst of hibernation.

Priscilla began to weep again.

'They're all here,' said Maisie. 'And they're all safe. You can't keep them so for ever, because one day they will be men, and I know they will be very fine men. But now they are safe, and they are well, and they are loved. You need do no more, or less, for them.'

'But, I—'

Maisie closed the door without a sound. 'But what you can do is not try to dull your fears with drink. You know, more than anyone, that it doesn't take away the pain of grief or fear, it only robs you of today.'

Priscilla nodded. 'I suppose I know what my resolution should be.'

'Darling? Are you up there?' The voice of Douglas Partridge echoed on the stairs. 'Ah, I might have known I'd find you here with "Tante Maisie". Come on, breakfast is about to be served and – believe it or not – even after that never-ending supper, everyone's famished.'

'Just coming!' Priscilla turned to Maisie and took her hand. 'Thank you, Maisie. Thank you for coming tonight. I know you were exhausted, but your being here means so much to me.'

'I'm glad I came too,' said Maisie. Then, louder, 'You know, I am very, very hungry. Douglas is right – let's go down to breakfast.'

17

After a late start on New Year's Day, Maisie arrived just in time to join Frankie for a midday meal of rabbit stew and mashed potato. Father and daughter sat together at the kitchen table with the door of the cast-iron stove wide open, so the warmth of the blaze could be felt even as the sky outside was wreathed in the shimmering grey clouds that were known to herald a dusting of snow.

'I'll have to get Jook out soon, just in case that weather closes in.'

Maisie pushed some potato on to her fork and looked out of the window. 'I'll take her if you like, Dad. You stay here in the warm.' She turned back to her father and continued eating.

'We'll go together, down to the meadow, across the field beyond, then double-back around through the woods to the front of the manor. I want to check on the horses, too. Drop in temperature like this can bring on a colic.'

'And you'd better wrap up warm, Dad. You don't want to catch anything yourself.'

As soon as they'd finished the meal, Maisie dressed in thick corduroy trousers more suited to a farm labourer, with a flannel shirt and a heavy pullover to keep the cold at bay. Woollen socks and heavy wellington boots would keep the moisture and, hope-fully, the cold from her feet, and she wore her old cloche to hold the warmth in her body – otherwise Frankie would remind her that heat escaped from the top of the head. Soon father and daughter were making their way across the field, with the lurcher at heel but ready to run in pursuit of a rabbit if given leave to do so. Maisie walked at a slower pace than she might if alone, for her father could not move as smartly as a younger man, and when they reached the bottom of the meadow, he stopped to catch his breath. Barely a sound dented the silence; on such a cold day not even birds sang. In the distance, they watched a fox steal across the top of a snow-dusted field, and all the while, the dog remained still, her head tilted up as she watched Frankie's eyes, her skin attuned to his every move.

Frankie turned his head at another sound, one that did not come from nature. 'There's a motor car coming, just pulled up along by the Dower House.'

'Is Lady Rowan expecting anyone today? Or Maurice, perhaps?'

'No plans for guests, as far as I know – and I always know who's coming and going.'

Maisie looked back at the Groom's Cottage, and turned to her father. 'We'll see who it is soon enough, when we come around the front. Ready then?'

'Right you are, love.'

They began walking again, though Maisie wondered about the crunching of tyres on gravel, a sound that echoed in winter's stillness as the vehicle pulled into the estate. Motor cars were rare in the village still, and never seen on a Sunday or bank holiday. And because the Comptons did not entertain quite so much now, the arrival of guests was always known and expected, and the unexpected was unwelcome by the Comptons and their servants alike.

Leaves still crisp from an overnight frost crackled underfoot, disturbing the silence of a winter woodland. They crossed the stream where it narrowed, and Maisie held out her hand to help her father up the bank to join the path again. Now Jook was walking on in front, her head low, her nose to the ground as she loped along with such a light step that her paws left barely a print underfoot. Father and daughter climbed over a stile to begin the last lap of their walk, which would bring them out to the front of the estate, where they would continue along past the lawns until reaching the turning off to the Groom's Cottage, Frankie's home.

As they approached the narrow turning to the right, they could see smoke from the cottage's two chimneys lazily snaking upward, and the thought of easing back in armchairs on either side of a crackling fire caused them to walk a bit faster.

'I think I might sit down in that chair and go right off like a top, what with that lovely drop of stew inside me and a bit of fresh air. I can have a look at the horses later.'

'You should, Dad. It'll do you good.' Maisie was tired, and thought the idea of an afternoon's forty winks sounded like just the prescription she needed after the events of the past week and a late night behind her.

'Well, who's this then?' Frankie Dobbs stopped at the top of the lane leading to the cottage, and looked straight in front of him. His lurcher stood at his side and began to growl.

'Oh no, now what?' Maisie linked her arm through her father's. 'They've no right to come here.'

'That your Scotland Yard blokes then?'

Maisie nodded. 'I could tell that black Invicta anywhere, Dad. Yes, it's them.'

As Maisie and her father approached the cottage, Stratton and MacFarlane emerged from the motor car.

'Sorry to disturb you on New Year's Day, Miss Dobbs.'

Maisie thought MacFarlane seemed less than contrite. 'I trust you wouldn't have come to my father's home unless it were urgent.'

'Yes, it is important,' said Stratton, who held out his hand towards Maisie's father. 'Mr Dobbs, a pleasure. And I'm sorry we've had to come to your house today.'

Frankie shook hands with both Stratton and MacFarlane, and stepped up to the front door. 'You'd better come on in, instead of standing out here in the perishing cold.'

Maisie made a pot of tea, which she served in front of the fire in the small sitting room. Frankie said he wanted to read the racing pages anyway and took his seat alongside the kitchen stove.

Maisie passed a cup of tea to MacFarlane. 'What's happened?'

'Bit of a problem, I'm afraid. We brought in your man, Anthony Lawrence, to identify the body.' MacFarlane took a gulp of the hot tea and winced as it went down. Then he set the cup on a small table next to his chair and folded his hands in his lap. 'Anthony Lawrence says he's never seen this man in his life, and it's not Stephen Oliver, because Stephen Oliver is in a secure wing at the Princess Victoria Hospital, or should I say the loony bin?'

'It's not Oliver?'

'No.'

Maisie was silent. 'But we know our man was the one who wrote the letters, and was the same man who killed the dogs, birds and a junior minister – and who planned to kill again, most likely at St Paul's.'

'Yes, that's right,' said Stratton. 'Our guest in the morgue is definitely the man we've been after. But we don't know who he is.'

MacFarlane spoke again. 'A couple of things came to light during the post-mortem.' He handed Maisie an envelope. 'You will see he had areas of deep scarring to the legs, and upon closer examination there was a significant amount of shrapnel still embedded in his flesh. There was also that scar on his face and jaw. All of this indicates a man who served in the war – and given his age, it wasn't the Boer War. He was definitely British, we know that. Mind you, he might have gone overseas before the war, when thousands of boys went off to find their fortune, so he could have served with any army from the Canadians to the South Africans, the Anzacs or the Doughboys. He could have been an airman, which I doubt, or on board ship, though evidence of his wounds would suggest a battlefield. But we should remember that men from the navy were pressed into the artillery and infantry, because that's where they were needed.'

Maisie had been reading the contents of the envelope as

MacFarlane spoke. Now she replaced the pages and pulled out the dead man's diary, which had also been placed in the envelope. She leafed through it, stopping at a page here and there, then closed the diary and returned it to the envelope, which she passed back to MacFarlane.

'You're very quiet about this, Miss Dobbs. What do you think? Who do you think this man might be?'

'I don't know, Chief Superintendent MacFarlane. My search led me to think it was Stephen Oliver, but there was an element of doubt – in fact, I think there's always an element of doubt. We know we have our man, and we're as sure as we can be that he acted alone, even though he had a friend, Ian Jennings – oh, and I wouldn't be too sure that Ian Jennings was the man's real name. Of course we were given to understand he received a pension, but we never saw any official forms with his name, did we?'

MacFarlane and Stratton looked at each other. Stratton cleared his throat. 'What are you saying, Miss Dobbs?'

Maisie wondered how to couch her response, how to best present her sense of the situation. 'I am saying it's a possibility you'll never discover the man's true identity. He might as well be John Smith. He destroyed or did not retain any identification and did not reveal his name in either his diary or to me when I was in his flat. If Croucher knew, it's too late, he took that information with him when he died, as did Ian Jennings.'

'We've searched Croucher's rooms and there's nothing there, though it seems he was in the habit of trying to help out men who are homeless and who were soldiers in the war. We'll have more on him by tomorrow, in any case.' MacFarlane sighed. 'Well, at least we know there's a killer off the street and we're all safe, don't we?' He placed his hands on the arms of the chair, as if he was about to stand.

'I don't think we can be that complacent.'

'What do you mean?' MacFarlane sat back again and looked at Maisie, then Stratton, and back at Maisie.

'Chief Superintendent, in our man we saw the symptoms of a

disease. He was wounded in body and mind in the war – indeed, he was wounded in his soul. He came home to endure a great deal of pain and felt as if he had become invisible, as if he didn't exist – read that diary, it says as much. Now, according to Dr Lawrence, there were about sixty, seventy, eighty thousand men who suffered some sort of war neurosis – shell-shock – to a greater or lesser degree. And if you listen to Lawrence for long enough, he'll tell you how that number has been massaged since 1915 – first, to put the lid on a syndrome that few understood, and secondly to limit damage to the Exchequer from a never-ending pensions liability. Lawrence says that some two hundred thousand men are alive today who were shell-shocked, and if you agree that anyone who served has sustained a psychological wound of some description, then you are looking at more than just a few time bombs.'

'Are you saying that all these men are likely to go off and cook up nerve agents or get up to some other mischief?'

Maisie shook her head. 'Of course not. Our man was clearly someone who knew his way around a laboratory, and who was capable and inventive enough to create those conditions in a small cold-water flat. He might be someone you can find on the basis of that skill alone, but don't count on it.' Maisie considered her words with care. 'Many of those men came back to loving families. When I was a nurse at the Clifton Hospital, you would see mothers and fathers who treated their sons with such care, such gentleness, as if they were children again. There were others who could not bring themselves to see a son so maimed, or you'd see a sweetheart, a young wife, perhaps, who could not bear to go unrecognized by her husband, who could not envisage sharing a home with a mate who was not the man she had taken into her heart. Many of those men were discharged from hospital care at the earliest opportunity, allowed to leave, told to find a job and settle down and live a normal life. But life will never be normal again, not when you've gazed into the jaws of death, not even when you have only heard the cannonade in the distance. The screech of tyres on the street or a motor car backfiring can send a man running for cover, can lead him to lose control of his physical movements, of his speech. And the people look away, don't they? We all know when someone isn't quite right, and for the most part it's an element of our nature to want to be out of the way of people who aren't what we consider to be "normal".'

'So what are you saying, Miss Dobbs?'

'That there are others like our man. Most of them will never do what he has done, but others will be moved to do something. They might cut themselves off from those who love them, they might be cast out by relatives to live on the streets, or they could be alone, as alone as they have always been. They might take their own lives, because what is in their minds cannot be borne a second longer, or they could make their families' lives a misery, with jagged moods keeping everyone on tenterhooks as they try to placate the demon inside the man. They might have a short temper, followed by a time of regret, of extreme affection. They could be drinkers, or resort to narcotics to ease mental and physical anguish. Or they might just exist, until they die.'

'But somewhere', said MacFarlane, 'there's a man who is a time bomb, who wants to be seen and heard.'

'Yes.'

'And that man may sooner or later cause damage on a bigger scale.'

'It's a possibility.'

'And we'll never know who he is until it happens.'

The three were silent for some moments, each alone with their thoughts.

MacFarlane slapped his knees and stood up. 'Well, this will never get the eggs cooked. Come on, Stratton, we'd better get back to the Yard.'

Maisie came to her feet. 'You travelled all this way for such a short meeting?'

'We thought it best to come to see you personally with the news,' said MacFarlane. 'And we wanted to discuss the outcome with you – and not on the telephone.'

246

Stratton shrugged. 'And I think we've got a lot more to chew on now.'

Maisie nodded. 'I do have one more thought.'

'And what might that be?' MacFarlane raised his eyebrows.

'Bring in Catherine Jones to identify the body, just to make sure. I know you've already heard from a very credible source, but I'd be interested to know whether the man in the morgue is the same man she saw and spoke to at one of the meetings, the one she told me about.'

'I suppose it wouldn't hurt. I'll see what can be done. Thank you, Miss Dobbs.'

'Thank you for coming, Chief Superintendent, Inspector Stratton. Let me see you out.'

Frankie came to the sitting room upon hearing the door open and the company bid their farewells. Both Stratton and MacFarlane shook his hand again, and as they left, MacFarlane informed Maisie that they would be in contact if she was to be consulted again, though her presence at the inquest would be required.

As the black Invicta made its way towards Chelstone's main gate, Maisie watched the rear lights become smaller and smaller.

'Come on, love, let's sit by the fire now, eh?' Frankie was solicitous in his tone, setting his hand on Maisie's shoulder with a gentle touch, as if to apply greater pressure would hurt her.

'It's all right, Dad. Don't worry – I'm all right.'

But Frankie remembered the early days of Maisie's recovery, after she came home from France in 1917. And still fresh in his mind was her breakdown during a return journey to France just fifteen months earlier. Even though she seemed more at peace now than at other times in recent years, he often found it best to move with care around his daughter, as a person might negotiate an unknown path in the dark.

18

As sometimes happened following a visit to Kent, the city had a chill to it that went beyond a sense of the air outside. Though Maisie loved her flat in Pimlico, there was a warmth to her father's cottage, to being at Chelstone, that made her feel cocooned and safe. And she felt wanted. The flat was hers to do with as she wished, and to do exactly as she pleased within those walls, but sometimes she felt it still held within it the stark just-moved-in feeling that signalled the difference between a house and a home. Of course, it still was not fully furnished, and there were no ornaments displayed — a vase, perhaps, that a visitor might comment upon and the hostess would say, 'Oh, that was a gift, let me tell you about it . . .' There were no stories attached to the flat — but how could there be, when she was always alone in her home. There were no family photographs, no small framed portraits on the mantelpiece over the fire in the sitting room as there were at her father's house. She thought the flat would be all the better for some photographs, not only to serve as reminders of those who were loved, or reflections of happy times spent in company, but to act as mirrors, where she might see the affection with which she was held by those dear to her. A mirror in which she could see her connections.

Maisie went to the kitchen to put the kettle on. She rarely kept much in the way of food in the flat, for fear that it might spoil during the long days of her work. The pot of soup made on a

Sunday night would set her up for a few suppers at least, and sometimes she would bring home fish and chips, which she would eat from the newspaper, not seeing the point in setting the table just for one. And except for the times she joined Priscilla and her family for the evening meal, she was alone. Most of the time, though, she was not lonely, just on her own, an unmarried woman of independent means, even when the extent of the means – or lack thereof – sometimes gave her cause to remain awake at night. She knew the worries that came to the fore at night were the ones you had to pay attention to, for they blurred reasoned thought, sucked clarity from any consideration of one's situation, and could lead a mind around in circles, leaving one drained and ill-tempered. And if there was no one close with whom to discuss those concerns, they grew in importance in the imagination, whether they were rooted in good sense or not.

Having taken her cup of tea while sitting on the floor in front of the fire with a copy of *The Times* spread out in front of her, Maisie recognized that she was restless. Yet again, the case concerning the man who was not Stephen Oliver began invading her thoughts. To a point, she had accepted that he might never be identified. In fact, as it stood, chance favoured such an incomplete conclusion. But she wasn't so sure, and could not draw back from a curiosity about the man's state of mind, and how he might have felt in the months leading up to the attack on the dogs. And more than anything, she wondered if one could take leave of one's senses, even if one had no previous occasions of mental incapacity, simply by being isolated from others. Is that what pushed the man over the edge of all measured thought? Were his thoughts so distilled, without the calibrating effect of a normal life led among others, that he ceased to recognize the distinction between right and wrong, between good and evil, or between having a voice and losing it? And if that were so, might an ordinary woman living alone with her memories, with her work, with the walls of her flat drawing in upon her, be at some risk of not seeing the world as it is?

She shook her head and stood up, pacing in front of the fire-place. Then, with barely a moment's thought, Maisie ran to the hallway, took her coat and hat from the stand, picked up her keys, and left the flat to walk to the telephone kiosk close to her home. She stepped inside, lifted the receiver, slipped coins into the slot and dialled a number. As she waited for the connection, she wiped condensation from the panes of glass with the back of her begloved hand. She did not care to be in such a small space without being able to see outside, even if she could see only darkness.

'The Partridge residence.'

'May I speak with Mrs Partridge?'

'One moment, please. May I say who's calling?'

Maisie gave her name, suspecting the housekeeper had almost added, 'At this time of night.'

'Maisie, darling, to what do I owe the pleasure?'

'Priscilla, I've just arrived back at the flat and was thinking about your party, and how little we've seen each other lately – and we didn't get *that* much time for a good talk at the party, did we? I wonder, are you at home tomorrow? Perhaps I could drop in for elevenses – will you be there?'

'Are you all right?'

'Yes, yes, fine . . . no, nothing wrong with me. Elevenses, then?'

Maisie thought she could hear Priscilla smiling. Priscilla was given to dramatic pauses in conversation, pauses that extended to her use of the telephone. Maisie had always maintained that a caller could hear the expression on her friend's face.

'Of course, that's splendid news – do come. I feel as if I've caught some of the crumbs falling off the table when you come to visit. You won't change your mind, will you?'

'Am I really that bad?'

'Well, you do get a bit carried away with that work of yours. But I'm glad you'll come – we might even pop out to the shops. January sales. Time for that?'

'Yes, I think I might have time. See you tomorrow, Priscilla.'

Maisie set the receiver back on its cradle, pulled up her collar and set off into the night again, this time with a warmth in her heart as she thought about seeing Priscilla the next day.

'All right, Billy, so as I said, you should leave by eleven to go to the Clifton – didn't they say Doreen would be arriving there at twelve?'

'That's what they thought, yes.' Billy paused, a frown creasing his forehead. 'Look, Miss, are you sure? I mean, I've had a lot of time off lately, so I expect to see it docked from my wage packet.'

Maisie shook her head. 'We've had a good month, and the Scotland Yard bill will stand us in good stead. It was a nice start to the year – financially, that is. And Doreen being at the Clifton will make it easy for evening visiting, won't it, though I am sure Dr Masters has some advice about not overtaxing her.'

'I'm going to be talking to her about that today, Miss.'

'Good, now—'

Maisie was interrupted by the telephone ringing.

'Fitzroy—'

'Miss Dobbs.'

'Detective Chief Superintendent MacFarlane.'

'We're having a bit of a tête-à-tête here today, what you might call a post-mortem on the investigation in which your assistance proved to be invaluable. Would you care to join us at, oh, eleven o'clock?'

'I'm sorry, Chief Superintendent, but I have a previous engagement. Would two o'clock do?'

Billy looked across at his employer.

'We'll do it this afternoon, then. See you at two.'

'Right you are, see you then.'

Maisie rolled her eyes as she replaced the receiver. 'That man was definitely being sarcastic. *"In which your assistance proved to be invaluable."'* She recounted the conversation to Billy.

'Sounds like you put him in his place, Miss.'

Maisie shrugged. 'I've an important engagement this morning, and did not want to cancel it for MacFarlane or any other client. Not this time.'

<hr>

Maisie sat at one end of the sofa in Priscilla's sitting room. Her friend had taken the other, so they resembled bookends, both with shoes kicked off and their legs folded to the side.

'. . . and before you arrived, the funny bit was when Tinker Osborne – do you know him? Bit of a lark, I must say, though if you read him in *Punch,* you would wonder why the government hasn't had him done away with – anyway, as I was saying, the funny thing was when he thought he could balance a bottle of champers on his nose. Normally that sort of thing just bores me rigid, but you should have seen him, tottering all over the place, especially as he came with that crashing bore Judith Burton, you know, the daughter of, oh, what is his name – yes, the architect, Otto Burton.'

Maisie smiled, though she could not imagine finding Tinker Osborne in the slightest bit amusing.

'It was a good New Year, Priscilla.'

'All in all, not a bad one. Of course, predictably, I glanced up at the staircase as the hour approached, only to see my three toads – in pyjamas, mind – sitting on the stairs and watching everything through the banister. I nudged Douglas and he waved them down, so they joined us for the celebrations and even had a little tipple each – won't hurt them, a little drop of champers. No wonder they were asleep by the time you arrived.'

Maisie nodded, watching Priscilla as she sipped the last of her coffee and set her cup and saucer on the side-table before glancing over towards the drinks cabinet.

'How are you feeling now? I've been worried about you since you came to my office.'

'It comes and goes,' said Priscilla, 'but mostly it comes. I am not happy here, not as I was in Biarritz, and it's troubling, especially as I'm the only one in the family not to have settled, in one way or another.'

'You were very busy in Biarritz, though, weren't you? You took the boys to the beach, you drove down into the town, saw friends, and even when you went to Paris a few times a year, you were among people you knew, and who knew you. You'd all, for the most part, gone down to Biarritz after the war to lick your wounds.'

Priscilla was silent for a moment, running her hand up and down the arm of the sofa, as if she were stroking the back of a frightened animal. 'Well, I'm a bit of a slug here, I must say. It's so . . . so . . . restricting. Or do I mean constricting? Perhaps a bit of both. And it's a bloody depressing place, if you ask me.'

'I had a thought. Remember you had that grand plan of opening up the family house, where you grew up? Why don't you do it? Why don't you put your mind to setting up your home there, get out into the country and start enjoying yourselves and perhaps claim some of that freedom you had in Biarritz.'

'But, Maisie, the boys are at school here and they love London, and Douglas . . .'

'It's not that far – what, an hour or two's drive out of London? You could go down on a Friday as soon as the boys are home from school, then come back on either a Sunday night or Monday morning. They can bring their friends and you can have the best of both worlds. And I bet you'll have all sorts of guests coming to see you.' Maisie reached over and placed her hand on Priscilla's arm. 'Do you remember what you said to me, when I was in France? *Face your dragons.* That house holds your memories, but think of the new memories you can build there.'

Priscilla bit her lip and walked to the drinks cabinet. 'I think you're right. I had all sorts of plans for the place when we first came back to England.' She turned around and faced Maisie, changing the subject. 'By the way, did I ever show you the photographs I took while you were with us last year? I found them the other day, as I was unpacking some boxes' – she picked up an envelope – 'and I put them out to show you.'

Priscilla passed each photo in turn to Maisie, reminding her of what had happened and when. 'And this is you with Tarquin – look at that smile. Just like my brother, you know. He's definitely an Evernden through and through, no doubt about it.'

'May I have this one?'

'Well, yes, of course. Would you like this photograph too? It's you and I in the garden, and here's one of you with all three toads. Tante Maisie is quite a hit with the boys!'

Maisie left Priscilla's Holland Park house after lunch, knowing that she had sown a seed of possibility in the mind of her dearest friend. And as she settled in the driver's seat of the MG, she sat for a while before setting off for Scotland Yard. She wanted to look through those photographs once again, photographs for which she would buy frames as soon as she could.

'Right, gentlemen – and lady.' MacFarlane shuffled papers in a folder on his desk and took out the document he was searching for. Darby, Stratton and Maisie sat on the opposite side of the desk. He looked up at Maisie and smiled as he said *lady*. 'Time for our little post-mortem here.' He cleared his throat. 'You all know that our man has not been identified. Anthony Lawrence didn't know him, and – thanks to you, Miss Dobbs – we brought in Catherine the chemist. The poor lass began listing to starboard as soon as she saw the body, and though she wasn't sure at first, she said it wasn't him because the man who came to their meeting did not have a scar on his face.'

Maisie shook her head.

'Anything to say, Miss Dobbs?'

'No, not really. It's a strange thing, though. Had I not spoken to Catherine, and had the word *foundling* not come up, I might not have found the killer.'

'Oh, but you would have.' MacFarlane tapped a pencil on the file in front of him. 'You found our man because you were suspicious about Edwin Croucher. There was something about his manner that made you think twice, so you followed him. And that's good police work – listening to the gut while wearing out a bit of shoe leather.'

'But I might not have been at the hospital had I not wanted to speak to Anthony Lawrence before he went home – and he'd gone already.'

'Then it was luck. And I know your Dr Maurice Blanche has a lot of time for a little bit of luck.'

'Anything new from the pathologist?' asked Stratton.

MacFarlane flicked through more pages in front of him. 'Interesting thing. Our man was lame, carried one hip higher than the other, and one shoulder similarly out of symmetry, giving the impression that he had suffered some serious wounds to the spine. Yes, there was scarring and shrapnel fragments still embedded in his legs, but the pathologist says that there was no physical reason why this man could not have walked upright, with perhaps the slightest limp.'

'Shell-shock,' said Maisie.

'Shell-shock?' Stratton turned to Maisie.

'Yes. Shell-shock. What you're describing is another sign of a deep wounding of the psyche, the outer manifestation of the scars in the mind.' She paused, sighing before she continued. 'When I was at the Clifton, I observed similarly afflicted men who, under the influence of hypnosis, shed their crippling disability and walked tall as if they were ready for the parade ground, only to shrivel again when taken out of the trance.' She looked at each of the men in turn. 'And before you say or think otherwise, these were men who were good soldiers, who had exemplary military records, men who had been repatriated after demonstrating some level of neurosis or hysteria that led to an inability to function as a soldier. They were not shirkers, but broken men.'

MacFarlane, Stratton and Darby were silent for a moment, then Darby spoke. 'What happens now, guv? Do we go on trying to identify him? What's going to happen to the body?'

'We're pretty sure he was working alone, so there's no urgency now to identify the body. However . . .' He looked at Maisie, then back at Darby and Stratton. 'I've been thinking about what Miss Dobbs has said about this sort of person, and it's clear he may not be the last. So we will be doing a wee bit of what Miss Dobbs does very well – building a template of a type. In the meantime, the body will be released to Dr Anthony Lawrence as soon as we've tied up our loose ends.'

'Dr Lawrence?' Maisie leaned forward.

'He made a special request, said the cadaver could be used for research purposes in the fields of' – he looked at a sheet of paper, then back at Maisie – 'neurosurgery and psychiatry. They want to see what's in his brain. I would have thought you'd've understood that, Miss Dobbs. I'm sure you've cut up the odd cadaver yourself.'

'Yes, of course, but—' Maisie did not continue, realizing that, of course, there was no family to receive the body. But she was still unsettled by the news.

'Anything else, Miss Dobbs?'

'What about Croucher?'

'Ah, yes, Croucher.' MacFarlane shuffled the notes once again. 'Another one living alone and with nothing in his rooms to indicate who our killer might have been, though he did not live as much a spartan life as his two friends. There were other papers, other items that would identify him.'

'But might there have been anything else there that would connect him to our man in some way? Something to indicate that he has known him for some time, perhaps?' asked Maisie.

'The only thing amiss with Edwin Croucher – aside from the fact that he was associating with a man bent on killing half of

London on the steps of St Paul's — was that he had a memory problem. Turns out he wrote down such things as when he had to be here or there, lists of what he needed for this or that. At work he tended to check, double-check, and then go back again for another look to make sure that something had been done. But there's nothing to be found in the rooms with either Ian Jennings' name or our Mister No-name.'

'That's strange.'

'The pathologist says the nature of the man's forgetfulness was probably limited to certain tasks, the jobs that were before him each day. It would not affect his functioning as a member of society, though I can see why he lived alone. Imagine being married to someone who kept asking where they put something, or what was for dinner for the tenth time. There was a place for everything in his rooms, and those places were labelled.'

'He was lucky to have a job, I suppose,' said Stratton, as if to remind MacFarlane that he and Darby were in the room.

'But he's certainly not lucky now, eh?' quipped MacFarlane.

The men's laughter was nipped in the bud by Maisie, who had more questions. 'Chief Superintendent, I wonder, would it be possible for me to speak to Catherine Jones? I'm still curious about the man she claims came along to the meeting of union activists — I'd like to ask her a question or two more, if that's all right.'

MacFarlane shook his head. 'Bit too late, I'm afraid, Miss Dobbs. Miss Jones has been released. The prosecutor went through everything we gave him and concluded that there wasn't enough evidence there to bring her to trial.'

'Not enough evidence? I thought—'

MacFarlane shrugged, but did not look at Maisie directly, closing the folders as he answered her. 'We always do our best, Miss Dobbs. We pull together as much as we can, then we send the whole case to the prosecutor. Her fellow anarchists will be sent down, but not Miss Jones. He's concluded that she was a person in the wrong place at the wrong time.'

Maisie nodded her head as she replied, 'I see. In the wrong place at the wrong time. Lucky Catherine.'

'We can't win them all, Miss Dobbs.'

Maisie began collecting her document case and shoulder bag. 'Well, if that's all, Detective Chief Superintendent MacFarlane, I had better be off. As they say, time and tide wait for no man – or woman, come to that.'

'Oh, but before you go, Miss Dobbs.' MacFarlane stood up, as did Darby and Stratton. 'I've decided to celebrate Burns' Night in London with my immediate colleagues here at the Branch. I've bought tickets for a show at the Palladium for everyone, and there will be supper afterwards upstairs at the Cuillins of Skye – it's a pub, just off Covent Garden. January the twenty-fifth – I hope you will join us.'

Maisie looked at MacFarlane, then at Stratton and Darby, as if to ask if they were going.

'You'll not be the only lassie there, Miss Dobbs,' added MacFarlane.

'Perhaps I can let you know in a week or so, Chief Superintendent. And thank you for the invitation. Now, I should be on my way.'

MacFarlane thanked Maisie again for her part in bringing the case to a close, and handed her an envelope with a cheque inside. She shook his hand and hoped she had made it clear by her demeanour that his occasional flirtatious manner had not borne fruit.

'I'm glad that's all over,' said Stratton.

'Are you?' said Maisie.

'Of course I am. Can you imagine what it would be like if our man were still at large?'

Maisie opened her mouth to say more, but paused and instead commented on the invitation. 'What's all this about Burns' Night? It's a bit unusual, isn't it, being treated to a night out by the Chief Superintendent?'

'I know. Darby says he's done it before, taking a whole gang out for the evening. Apparently he thinks it's good for morale, brings everyone together.'

Maisie took out her keys as they reached the MG. 'I think there's more to it than that, Inspector Stratton. I think he's a bit lonely. Didn't you say his wife left him?'

Stratton nodded. 'A few years ago. It's a hard life, being married to a man who's married to his job. She was alone a lot, and as far as I know, took up with someone else and just upped and left.'

'And now he's the one who's alone. That's why everyone's invited to go out with him on Burns' Night.' She inclined her head. 'I really do have to rush now.'

'Going anywhere interesting?'

'The Princess Victoria Hospital – only don't tell MacFarlane, will you?'

'Mum's the word,' said Stratton as he brought a forefinger to his lips. 'Do you think—'

'I'll let you know.'

A porter informed Maisie that she would have to wait to see Dr Lawrence, and that he might not even be able to see her at all, given that he had been with his students for a good two hours this afternoon already and was late getting to his rounds.

'I'll wait,' said Maisie, taking the same place as before on the bench seat facing the porters' office.

Over an hour passed before the porter came out of the office. 'He's still on his rounds, Miss. Would you like a cup of tea while you're waiting?'

Maisie opened her mouth to answer, but was interrupted by Lawrence, who approached from the corridor behind her.

'Miss Dobbs! I wasn't expecting you today, so this is something of a surprise. What can I do for you?'

'May we go to your office, Dr Lawrence? I would like our conversation to be in private.'

'Yes, of course. One moment while I just use the telephone in the porters' office.'

Lawrence stepped into the office, placed his telephone call, and joined her once again, leading her up the staircases and through locked doors that led to other locked doors before opening out into the floor that housed the staff offices.

'Here we are.' Lawrence looked at his watch. 'I'm a bit short on time, Miss Dobbs, so—'

'Oh, this won't take long, Dr Lawrence. I just wondered if I might visit Stephen Oliver. I learned so much about him, you see, as part of my investigation, and feel rather sorry that he's here without visitors.'

Lawrence began running his fingers back and forth along the files on his desk, setting them two inches from the right side and two inches from the top, so they were positioned much in the same way that a stamp would be attached to an envelope. 'Miss Dobbs, I cannot allow such a thing. After all, you are not a relative, and you must appreciate that Dr Oliver is in a very delicate state.'

'Yes, I suppose if one's seen as nothing more than a cadaver available for experimentation, he would be in a delicate state, wouldn't he?'

'Now you look here, Miss Dobbs—'

'The man who wrote the letters, who killed dogs, birds, a junior minister, and who planned to kill a legion of revellers on New Year's Eve was Stephen Oliver, wasn't he?'

'I categorically assure you—'

'Tell me what happened.'

'Nothing happened, Stephen was a brilliant scientist—'

'I know how brilliant he was. I've heard it from two people already. And I know you do not have Stephen Oliver here at the hospital.'

'And I assure you that we do, now if you don't mind—'

Maisie reached for the telephone receiver. 'If *you* don't mind, I think I'd like to hear that from Sheila Kennedy. By the way, do you know how I am acquainted with Mrs Kennedy? She was the Sister-in-Charge of the casualty clearing station where I was stationed in the war. I don't know if she'll remember me, but you never know.' She dialled the operator.

Lawrence leaned forward and pressed down on the bar, cutting off the call. 'No, don't.'

Maisie replaced the receiver. 'Are you going to tell me what's going on?'

Lawrence scraped back his chair, stood up and began to pace, then sat down again. 'You should cease wondering about this case, Miss Dobbs, because you are out of your depth.'

'I don't seem to be floundering, Dr Lawrence, but if you are having trouble with the truth, then let me tell you what I think has happened here, and you can correct me if I'm wrong.'

Lawrence clasped his hands together on the desk. 'I have little time to indulge you, Miss Dobbs.'

Maisie pressed her point. 'Stephen Oliver was admitted to the Princess Victoria on at least two occasions since his initial release from an asylum where he was committed during the war. I know that you witnessed at least one breakdown at Mulberry Point, and I know he was a very valuable person with regard to work undertaken at the government laboratories. And he was also a very interesting specimen, wasn't he? A man who had not only suffered shell-shock, but was so intent upon finding answers to the questions that dogged him in his work that he even became his own guinea pig.'

'They all experimented on themselves, all of them. They don't call them mad professors for nothing.'

'But the madness didn't stop there, did it? You increasingly saw Oliver as your own experiment. After all, time was marching on and you had a legacy to leave – a book about the psychological effects of chemical and biological testing on those exposed to contaminants. And every time he regained some semblance of normal functioning, you willingly went along with requests to send him back to Mulberry Point, because Stephen Oliver still had a razor-sharp mind when it came to his work – it was unfortunate that he just didn't have the emotional foundation for sustained experimentation, did he?'

Lawrence nodded, but was silent as he listened, his only movement being to pick up an item on his desk, look at it, then put it down again.

'Now, I haven't worked out the details yet, but at some juncture he was discharged. Was it an oversight at the pensions office? A young clerk perhaps, who added a name to the list of someone who should never have been added? Or was it that you had to release a certain number of patients to make economies, and because he could take care of himself, he was released? On the other hand, perhaps his release was part of your experiment – and then he managed to give you the slip.'

Maisie bit her lip. Lawrence's manner was unsettling and she wondered if her speculation had been wide of the mark.

'Either way, you lost him, lost a valuable man who could only control himself physically and mentally for short periods of time while engaged in the same sort of work he was undertaking when he was first wounded – again, in his mind as much as his body – on the battlefield. That work was in the development of weapons that should never be given the light of day. And he could only immerse himself in such an endeavour for so long before the cannonade went off in his mind, when he collapsed in a state of nervous exhaustion.'

Maisie sat back and looked out the window, the view of falling snow obscured by iron bars. Iron bars, even in the offices of a doctor for whom she once had the utmost regard. She was about to speak when there was a knock at the door, and without being summoned the visitor walked into the office.

'Sorry, Lawrence, it took me a bit of a while to get here.' Gerald Urquhart took off his hat and looked at Maisie. 'A delight to see you again, Miss Dobbs. Now, I wonder what might bring you back to see Dr Lawrence – after all, you're not on Special Branch time now, are you?'

Maisie looked at Urquhart, then Lawrence. 'Is this what you meant by out of my depth?'

'Yes, it is.'

'Oh, so Stephen Oliver was more than an experiment for you. He was an experiment for the Secret Service as well. Even though there was a risk to the general public, you knew he would continue with his work in whatever way he could.' Maisie shook her head, her mind racing. 'Or was he released deliberately, just to see who might come out of the woodwork and claim him, who might try to squeeze him dry before tossing him aside?' She looked at Urquhart again. 'No wonder you were panicking when you lost him. You knew who you were looking for the moment that first letter was received, but you just couldn't find him, even with an array of intelligence resources at your fingertips.' Drumming her fingertips on the desk, Maisie paused for thought before speaking again. 'And I'll bet you didn't show your hand to MacFarlane until Catherine Jones was brought in – or perhaps you got to Jones first, and only later did the Commissioner step in and put an end to speculation by announcing the case closed.'

'The case *is* closed, Miss Dobbs. It is only you who are showing continued interest in the man who tried to kill a significant number of innocent people.'

'I think it's time for me to leave.' Maisie stood up, collected her bags, and stepped towards the door, but before leaving she spoke directly to Anthony Lawrence. 'I am sure you will write a very good book, but there will probably be something missing.'

'What on earth do you mean?'

'Speak to Dr Elsbeth Masters. Ask her what happens when a gazelle becomes a lion's prey.'

Maisie left the office, but when she reached the first set of double doors she realized she was trapped without keys.

'Damn!'

'Rather a hasty exit, Miss Dobbs.' Urquhart waved a set of keys as he approached. 'I'll escort you out.'

'I won't ask why you have a set of keys.'

'No, better not.'

They walked in silence down the stairs and through several more sets of locked doors before reaching the empty entrance hall.

'I'm sorry I can't tell you more, Miss Dobbs.'

'Oh, I think I've got the gist of the matter.' She looked over at the porters' office, then back at Urquhart. 'I have a feeling that Edwin Croucher was once a porter or employed in a similar caretaker job at Mulberry Point, where as we know almost every member of staff became a subject in an experiment at some point or another. I suspect that's how he lost his short-term memory – possibly through overexposure to a nerve agent of some sort. But he never forgot Stephen Oliver. Perhaps Oliver had shown him a kindness, so that when he found out the scientist had been brought to the Princess Victoria, he applied for a job as a porter. Or it might have been just one of those serendipitous events in life. Am I getting warmer here, Mr Urquhart?' Maisie raised a hand. 'No, don't answer, but let me see if I can work this out. Lawrence didn't know about Croucher's previous employer, because people like him never see people they consider to be minions. He interviewed the scientists and those of a certain level working at the laboratories, but not the tea ladies or the other ancillary staff.'

'An admirable imagination, Miss Dobbs.'

'And I haven't finished yet. Croucher was a kind man, a man who gave the impression of being brusque, but really he was trying to keep his life in order, so that he could keep a job. But he always tried to help the men on the streets who had fought in the war – he had doubtless been a soldier himself. And then he met Jennings, saw that he was an educated man, and thought he and Stephen Oliver would be company for each other. Croucher must have wondered what he had done, when Oliver began planning his revenge on those he saw as perpetrators of want.'

Urquhart nodded his head in a knowing way, so that even this movement smacked of sarcasm. 'Considering you haven't had any formal training in intelligence-gathering, Miss Dobbs, you do very well, don't you.'

'But that's where you are wrong, Mr Urquhart. I have had training from an expert in such matters. I just don't work for you.'

'Well, you never know.'

Maisie turned to leave, but Urquhart caught her arm.

'Miss Dobbs – before you go, please don't think of telling that wonderful story to anyone else, will you?'

Maisie shook off his hand and walked away.

Maisie drove towards Pimlico amid snow flurries and sleet. More than anything, she wanted to shut the door and wrap the walls of her flat around her. Outside, the world could do as it wished. She parked the MG and walked towards the main door, only to see MacFarlane's motor car waiting outside.

'Oh, not again!' Maisie uttered the words under her breath.

MacFarlane emerged from the vehicle. 'Miss Dobbs, glad to have caught you.'

'I don't have any soup, Chief Superintendent.'

'And I'm going out to supper, so I'll pass on your kind invitation.'

Maisie looked aside. 'I'm sorry. That was unkind of me.'

MacFarlane regarded her for a moment, then set his hand on her shoulder. 'It's hard, but there are walls you can't hammer your way through.'

'I know, I know. But aren't you angry, aren't you furious at what they've done, what they're doing, and how this *experiment* got out of hand? That a man . . .'

'I've learned over time to pick my battles, and to know when not to crush my knuckles pounding at doors that won't open. Urquhart had his job to do, Lawrence was doing his, and if you speak to your John Gale, he too knew about all or part of what was going on. When you get into the realms of the country's security, you find the right arm never ever knows what the left arm is doing. We both have to get on with our work now, Miss Dobbs, and allow this case to be closed. All right?'

Maisie nodded. 'All right. I know, I know. This is not the first time I've hit my own fist against that wall. And as they say, it's best to let it slip away, because time and tide wait for no man.'

'I'm sorry, lass, you'll have to be a bit more explicit.'

'They all said that, you know. It's one of those sayings that people pick up. I heard John Gale say it, then Stephen Oliver wrote it in his diary – and don't worry, I won't mention his name again. Anthony Lawrence repeated it too. It's a common phrase, but you find people tend to repeat that sort of thing when they live or work together. It only takes one to start the ball rolling.'

MacFarlane laughed and shook his head. 'That's something Blanche would have noticed. Anyway, talking of starting the ball rolling, I'll see you on the twenty-fifth, I hope.'

'What's on at the Palladium?' Maisie called after him.

'Oh, you'll enjoy it. The show's been on the bill several times over the past few months now with that grand gang of funny men – you know, Flanagan and Allen, Jimmy Nervo, Teddy Knox, Charlie Naughton and Jimmy Gold. They call it *Crazy Week*.'

19

Maisie wished it were closer to the week's end, so that she could pack her bags and drive down to Kent. She was fed up with London and was feeling a blend of frustration, anger and deep sadness every time she thought of Stephen Oliver and those like him, men who would only ever see life through a lens of instability. The war had been at the root of their distress, and for so many of those who came home – including Priscilla and herself – war dogged them still. And there was little or nothing she could do to help – unless she went back to nursing, but those times were behind her now. She had always felt that in her role as a psychologist and investigator, she had a part to play in the healing of those touched by crime and injustice. Maurice Blanche had instructed her in what he termed the 'forensic science of the whole person', an enquiry that went beyond a dissection of the body and demanded engagement in a deeper investigation into the life of a person, who might be either the victim or the perpetrator of a crime. Every time she thought of Stephen Oliver, she could not help but wonder how much of his distress could have been avoided, and how much was caused by men who were hungry for his knowledge, who would sap him until there was nothing left, until he was all but invisible.

But the fact remained that it was Tuesday and not the end of the week, so after sitting with Billy to go through other current cases, and to look at one or two enquiries regarding her services that had been received since the turn of the year, she knew it was time to begin the process she referred to as her 'final accounting'. This accounting did not require her to add or subtract rows of numbers, but rather to look back at a case and consider what had happened, person by person, event by event, and then to close the book so that work on new cases might begin with renewed energy. Indeed, it bore a resemblance to the passing of the old year, when one took stock of what had passed and started anew on New Year's Day, filled with determination and looking forward to what might come next.

Having given Anthony Lawrence due consideration, she realized that she could not let her previous regard for his work slide into the quicksand of recent experience. She had no knowledge of what had passed between Lawrence, Gale and the men of Military Intelligence, Section Five, but she knew that she could not burn her bridges. His actions had surely been directed by ambition and a professional curiosity, for even though he was a doctor, he was also a scientist, his area of expertise the geography of the human mind.

She took up her pen and began to write a letter to Lawrence. It was not a long communiqué, but spoke of her regard for his work, her appreciation for what he tried to accomplish with the men under his care, and how much she hoped his book would bring him the acclaim he deserved. She did not say that she thought he must have learned much from Stephen Oliver, and would continue to owe him a debt. Nor did she say that she thought his association with Urquhart ill-considered, as she suspected he might have had little choice. As her pen wavered towards the end of the letter, she wondered how she might refer to the previous day's heated exchanges without apology. She regretted neither her words nor her accusations, so puzzled over how she might phrase a sentence that would reflect her sadness that there had been such a level of discord, while also expressing that she felt betrayed by a level of subterfuge that undermined the words 'first, do no harm'. Tapping her pen on the desk, she wrote:

I am sure we will both reflect on the events of the past weeks with regret, and with concern that there might have been a more positive outcome. For my part, I believe there is much I can learn from what has come to pass. I remember you to be a man who cared deeply for his patients, and who always looked at what might have been done in this situation or that, and I believe the case of Stephen Oliver has given us both pause to reconsider how we could have conducted ourselves in our work in a different way, a way that might have been better for all concerned . . .

Maisie tapped her pen once again, then finished the letter with a note to the effect that she hoped that, when the body of Stephen Oliver had served its purpose, there could be a respectful disposal of the remains, and that she would like to pay her respects at that time. She asked Lawrence if he would be so kind as to inform her when a service of cremation or burial would take place.

With the envelope sealed, Maisie decided to walk to the post office to mail the letter herself. Having struggled to find the appropriate words, she thought it best to send the letter before she tore it open, ripped up the pages and started again. Halfway along Warren Street, she was drawn by the three golden spheres above the pawn shop and decided to drop in to see if there were any inexpensive frames for sale. Pawn shops had been doing brisk trade in recent months, with all manner of goods going up for sale at knockdown prices. She peered though the window, then opened the door and went in, the bell ringing to summon the proprietor.

'Miss Dobbs, keeping well?'

'Very well, Mr Lombard, though it is a bit nippy out, isn't it?' She removed her gloves and unwound her scarf.

'Not going to get any better, if my rheumatism is anything to go by.' He took out a handkerchief and rubbed his half-moonglasses. 'Looking for anything in particular, or just looking?'

Maisie laughed. 'I'm not your best customer, am I? All I ever do is poke around and never buy anything.'

'No charge for looking.'

'I'm actually after some smallish frames, for photographs.'

The man shuffled around the counter to the front of the shop, and began moving an assortment of items displayed on a bookcase – a pair of binoculars, a geometry set, a collection of gentleman's brushes, a glove stretcher, a camera – before reaching for a trio of matching silver frames.

'Wait a minute.' Maisie came to his side and pointed to the camera. 'Is that easy to use?'

'Nearly new, that. Owner bought it in New York, then came back to London and went bankrupt, if you can believe it.'

'Oh, I believe it.' She reached for the camera and began studying it, turning it around with care.

'There's a handy little book that came with it, and rolls of film too. They're all up there in a box. It's called the Number Two C Autographic Camera, and it's got this thing that goes with it. They call it a rangefinder, helps you out when people are standing a bit of a way off.' He looked up towards the top shelf and squinted over his half-moon glasses, then reached for a box. 'See, it's made by the Eastman Company. Lovely piece of work, that.'

'But do you think I could operate it?'

'Have a look at this book – looks simple enough to me.'

Maisie studied the book, then opened the camera and pulled out the bellows. 'How much?'

'Well, reckon that cost a pretty penny when it was first bought, you know. Let me have a look in the ledger.'

Mr Lombard stepped behind the counter and opened a thick ledger, running his finger down a list of entries. 'What was the number on the ticket, Miss Dobbs?'

'Seven hundred and fifty-three.'

'Here it is. Now let me see. Yes, I can let you have that for thirty bob.'

'One pound ten?' She reached out to return the camera to its place. 'I don't think I can run to that.'

'What about a guinea?'

'Fifteen bob?'

'Phew, that's a bit of a difference, eh? A pound?'

'Seventeen and six if you add the frames.'

'You'll see me poor, Miss Dobbs.'

She smiled and looked around at the contents of the shop. 'Oh no I won't, Mr Lombard. Not with this little earner you've got here.'

The pawnbroker laughed as Maisie pulled a one-pound note from her purse and set it on the counter. He packed up the camera along with six rolls of red and yellow film, and the small instruction book, then balanced the frames on top and gave Maisie her change. 'You might be back for more frames then?'

'I'm sure I will. Goodbye, Mr Lombard.'

———

As soon as she arrived back at the office, Maisie penned another letter, this time to John Gale. She did not need to see the professor again, but he was a friend of Maurice's and he had been as fair as he could in his dealings with her, so recognition of his time and expertise were warranted. She found his work unsettling, but she thanked him for his time, and his willingness to help her.

When she had finished with her letter-writing and other tasks, she gathered her document case and shoulder bag and the box containing her new camera. Balancing the frames on top, she left the office and collected her MG, which was parked in Fitzroy Street. But she wasn't going back to her flat. Despite the fact she had drawn back from visiting Lawrence and Gale, there was one place she wanted to see again, to consider from afar, before returning home. She started the motor and began driving out of London on the Reading road.

She parked the MG on a hill overlooking Mulberry Point in the distance, close to a sign that informed anyone passing that entry beyond the barbed wire was forbidden, that the land was government property and that trespassers would not only be taken to court, but could be shot. The wind whipped around her as she stepped from the MG. Maisie counted ten or more huts clustered together in the shallow valley, and she noticed that, to the left of the compound, construction work was in progress. More building, more laboratories in which to invent and test the weapons of war. She remained for a while, considering Mulberry Point and wondering if spring itself might pause in such a locale. Did birds fly overhead as the grass grew tall? And could flowers bloom around a place where people's minds were on the business of killing? Where they worked towards the invention of a means of death less visible to the naked eye, with no sound, unless one counted the screams of the poor souls who were struck down.

<hr />

6th January 1932

'How's Doreen settling in at the Clifton, Billy?' Maisie found that, increasingly, her first question of the morning was regarding Billy's family.

Billy set an enamel mug filled with hot tea on Maisie's desk, and picked up another for himself. He stood with his back to the fire as he replied. 'Not so bad, Miss. They drugged her up a bit for the ambulance, so she's been a bit wobbly on her pins. I only saw her the once, but I'm going in on Saturday.'

'With the boys?'

'No, Dr Masters says it's best not to bring them yet, though Doreen might be up for it the following weekend.'

'Has she spoken about treatment?'

'First of all she said they needed to stabilize her diet. None of this milk-only lark, and no procedures – well, at least until she's been there for a bit, then we'll have to see.'

Maisie nodded. 'I'm going in to see Dr Masters today. Nothing to do with Doreen, though. I have to complete my final accounting, and wanted to see her so that I can get on with drawing my work on this case to a close.'

'Wonder if she'll say anything about Doreen?' Billy turned to face Maisie.

'She won't tell me anything that she wouldn't tell you, Billy. Don't worry, your Doreen is in very good hands now.'

'I know, I know, but . . . it was seeing her in that other place, the way they strapped her down, the things they did to her when she hadn't even been there for five minutes.'

'But she's away from Wychett Hill now, so you have to get that particular institution out of your mind.' Maisie sipped her tea. 'How are the boys?'

'On the one hand they're missing their mother, but on the other, I think they're scared of her coming home. My old mum has been a diamond, coming in to help out, so they've been used to things being calmer, if you know what I mean. But I worry about her, because even though it's not far for her to walk to ours, she's not getting any younger.'

'Is Bobby still having trouble?'

'Not so much, not really. I did what you said, tried not to draw attention to it, just kept him nice and dry. Bit of a job, in this weather.'

Maisie looked out of the window and saw snow falling again. 'It doesn't help matters, does it?' She turned her attention back to Billy. 'Don't worry, you're doing everything you can. It will be all right.'

Elsbeth Masters was sitting sideways next to her desk, with her stockinged feet resting against the side of the radiator, when Maisie arrived at her office.

'Oh, come in, come in. Do excuse me, but I cannot stand this cold weather. It goes straight to my bones.'

'I've felt like that since I was in France, in the war. A friend once asked me how I could be that cold and not be dead.'

Masters laughed. 'What can I do for you? Is this about Mrs Beale?'

'No, I wanted to see you to thank you again for your time, not only in helping out the Beales, but in answering my questions when we last met.'

Masters swivelled her chair to face Maisie, setting her feet on the floor. 'And was it a case of all's well that ends well?'

Maisie nodded. 'To the extent that it could be, in the circumstances.'

The doctor pressed her lips together as if gauging whether to make further comment. 'Lawrence was sailing close to the wind, wasn't he?'

The women looked at each other for a few seconds before Maisie replied. 'You could say he was taking some chances with his research.'

'Was anyone harmed?'

'Not as many as might have been.'

'You managed to control damage, then.'

'By the skin of my teeth, but that's between us.'

Masters picked up a pencil and tapped it on the desk. 'Not in my interests to tell tales out of school. As I told you before, I am in no hurry to create a legacy based upon publication to impress my peers. The sheer fact that I was accepted for medical training speaks as many volumes as I need to have to my name.'

Maisie smiled. 'I know. But your counsel helped enormously.'

'Good.' She sighed, 'I still wish you'd chosen to move into clinical practice.'

'I love my job.'

'Your country needs you, you know.'

'Oh, I doubt that very much.'

'Anyway, it won't compromise my patient's health or compromise confidentiality to tell you that I believe Mrs Beale will make a full recovery. It won't happen overnight, but it will come to pass. Our first steps will be towards getting her on an even keel, then we'll see what needs to be done to help her leave the past behind. In a month I expect she will be able to go home on Saturdays and Sundays, then we'll build it up from there. In about two weeks her boys can visit – only for a short time at first, mind. But all of that can change if she has a poor response to treatment.'

'Have you told Mr Beale all this?'

'Not yet.'

'Please tell him soon. It will give him something to look forward to, something to imagine. He's rather lonely, I believe. His world revolves around his work and then his family, and he has such plans for the future.'

'Canada?'

Maisie nodded.

'Not before a year has passed, I shouldn't think.'

'I thought as much.' Maisie stood up. 'Anyway, I should be getting along now. I've appreciated making your acquaintance again, Dr Masters.'

'And you too, Sis— Miss Dobbs.' Masters shook her head and smiled. 'Old habits. Almost called you Sister Dobbs then. Time and tide, eh, they wait for no woman.'

The visit to Battersea was brief. Mr Hodges was not on the premises, so Maisie penned a brief note, and then set off again, back to her flat, where she once again took out her camera and the instruction book. She had never used a camera before, let alone owned such a thing. Two copies of a magazine called *Kodakery* came with the camera, more evidence that the previous owner had serious intentions regarding photography as a hobby when bankruptcy changed his plans. And on the following weekend, Priscilla gave Maisie an opportunity to test her new purchase, when she issued an invitation to her family's country home – she was about to embark upon redecoration.

'The boys are coming and Douglas will join us on Saturday afternoon. I have made arrangements for various people to come in to look at what needs to be done – painting, some carpentry, brickwork repairs, that sort of thing – so that I can gather estimates. Elinor is coming too, so she'll keep the toads under control, and we can have some fun – do say you'll come.'

'Yes, of course I'll come. I'll bring my new camera – I can't wait to use it.'

Priscilla laughed and warned Maisie to keep the camera well away from the boys. 'They break things, you know.'

Maisie was still smiling when the telephone rang. It was Robbie MacFarlane.

'You said you'd let me know if you were coming to the Burns' Night bash. What's the verdict?'

'Oh, I'm sorry. I've been very busy, so I—'

'It had better be a "yes", Miss Dobbs. Can't have this lot together without you, not after you worked with us on the letters case.'

'Yes, yes, of course I'll come. The Palladium first, for *Crazy Week*.'

'Aye, that's it. Then we'll all go on to the Cuillins of Skye from there.'

❦

6th January – 24th January 1932

With her final accounting complete and her notes up to date and filed away, Maisie was glad to turn her attention to challenges of helping several new clients who had come to her with problems requiring enquiry services. There was sufficient new work in hand to inspire what amounted to a rosy outlook regarding the fiscal health of her business.

Doreen Beale remained at the Clifton Hospital. Though her progress was slow, Billy reported that she was looking a bit better each time he saw her, which he took as a sign that life was looking up for the family.

At the same time, Maisie was spending more time with Priscilla, in particular a memorable sojourn at their country estate that was punctuated by deep conversation and much laughter. Indeed, despite the cloak of depression enveloping much of the country, for the first time in a long time, Maisie felt an optimism, a freedom that had been diminished by her wartime service, and that she had struggled to rediscover ever since.

❦

25th January 1932

Stratton, Darby and Maisie were still laughing by the time they reached the upper dining rooms of the Cuillins of Skye, while Robbie MacFarlane was regaling one of the women detectives with the history of his family tartan.

'I think he's a bit crazy himself, only he doesn't restrict himself to a week of it,' said Stratton.

Maisie shook her head. 'No, he's all there. Doesn't miss a trick. But I've never heard of a night like this, not from the Yard.'

'And I certainly haven't.' Stratton reached for his glass of whisky, which appeared to be the only beverage on offer.

MacFarlane cleared his throat as the hot cock-a-leekie soup was served. 'I'll now say the traditional grace, and for you Sassenachs, this is known as the Selkirk Grace.' He cleared his throat again. 'Some hae meat and canna eat, and some wad eat that want it. But we hae meat, and we can eat, sae let the Lord be thankit.'

Courses followed speeches, and speeches followed more drinking. Maisie eventually bid farewell to MacFarlane, Stratton and Darby, and by the time she stepped into a taxi-cab it was the early hours of the morning. She arrived back at her flat, glad that she had made one glass of the amber liquid last several hours. As she opened the door into the hallway and switched on the light, she saw a plain brown envelope waiting for her – it had been pushed under her door. She picked it up, recognized the handwriting and ran to the dining table, flicking on lights as she went. As luck would have it, she had discovered that one of the residents at the block of flats was a photographer, and to make extra money, he would develop film for friends and other associates. Maisie had taken a roll of film up to him as soon as she returned home from her weekend in the country with Priscilla and her family.

She spread out the photographs and began picking up each one in turn. The early prints revealed a lack of familiarity with the equipment, but later photographs demonstrated that she had become more adept at focusing the lens, at using the rangefinder. As she studied each successive image again, she smiled, and though the flat was chilly, she felt the residue of the evening's warmth rekindled. Unwilling to wait until she could buy more frames, she brought a small box of drawing pins from the kitchen and began to pin photographs to the wall, and soon they flanked the painting of a woman alone on a windswept beach. Then she looked at each photograph once more. There were the Partridge boys sitting on the MG's bonnet, and Priscilla and Maisie bearing the brunt of a snowball fight – she had passed the camera to Douglas and he was clearly a better photographer. There were photographs taken during walks, photographs taken of the boys in the garden. And as she looked at the prints, she felt as if the eyes that had looked into the lens were looking straight at her, and she knew she belonged.

Soon she would add more photographs. There would be Frankie and Jook, and Maurice. There would be photograph after photograph of the people she loved. But as was her way, Maisie could not help but think of Stephen Oliver again, and of Ian Jennings and those like them. She thought of the dispossessed who saw nothing but people moving to one side as they shuffled along the street, people who looked down as they passed so that they need not catch a glimpse of desperation lest it be a disease – something they might catch if they weren't careful. Maisie grieved for the two men, despite their crimes. She grieved for the men they could have been, men who were complete in body and soul. And she grieved for their innocent victims.

Again her attention came back to the prints, this time to a single photograph of herself. She leaned closer to the image and concentrated on her own eyes. And she smiled, for at last she knew she had reclaimed her soul.

Acknowledgements

I would like to thank the following friends and colleagues who became, in effect, my 'pit crew' as I wrote *Among the Mad*. Holly Rose – thank you for being my first and number one writing buddy and reader. To my cannot-be-named 'Cheef Resurcher' (yes, the spelling is a joke between us), who has given me so much valuable information on the inner workings and history of Special Branch – thank you. To my parents, Joyce and Albert Winspear – as always, thanks for fielding those questions about the London you knew and loved in the best of times and the worst of times.

Once again, deepest thanks to the terrific team at Henry Holt, especially John Sterling, Maggie Richards, and Kelly Lignos.

I can never extend enough gratitude to Amy Rennert, agent extraordinaire, friend and mentor.

And to the Bluesman – my husband, John Morell – thanks for your unfailing support. It means the world to me.